He Who Sleeps

DAGMAR AVERY & AURORA MARIS

He Who Sleeps
9798289384140

Dedication:

To the girls that want it all... but know no one can be everything.

And to the girls that know that having it all means they are all just a little bit psycho.

We see you. And we agree.

Prologue

Black night, Halloween eve

The city was alive with wonder, spooks and monsters. One more night 'til Halloween, and the excitement was everywhere. Petra stood waiting for the light to change, the lone person not in a costume in the crowd. Having just gotten off from her second job at the animal shelter, she was in scrubs and reeked of bleach from cleaning the cats' cages, and was on her way home, whereas those around her were clearly off to do something much more interesting. Parties, parades, clubs... So many amazing things to do.

Sadly it wasn't in the cards for her. New to the city, she still hadn't found a full friends group, and the ones she did have were not the Halloween type. It was something she missed from her life back home, but she was patient, and she knew that it was very possible next year would yield her in costume with others of a like mind tearing it up.

The light changed and she crossed, slowing to let the throng of people pass her. Just two blocks from the university, she could hear the music from the outlying frat and sorority houses on both sides of the street. She turned down the side street, and then another left, taking her away from the main drag, the streets getting quieter.

Turning once again, she stepped onto a darker street and smiled, knowing she was only a few blocks from home, when she saw something quite out of character.

Seven men, dressed in black with masks on, were carrying a clearly struggling woman behind a row house.

The fuck?

She stopped, just outside the cone illuminated by the street's lone light, and watched as the girl writhed and bucked, straining at the bonds they had on her. She heard her panicked moan as they turned the corner behind the house. Whatever was going on, she should keep walking. It was Halloween after all and she didn't wanna ruin anyone's fun, but this felt different. The terror coming off that girl...

No, this was a bad thing and she needed do something. Calling the cops was going to be a waste of time, considering they rarely came through to University City in general. If anyone was going to do anything to help the girl, it was going to have to be her. There wouldn't be a calvary.

Creeping closer, she slipped into the darkness that surrounded the house, entering what ended up being a large courtyard, the backs of buildings that were not homes blocking it in. Murmurings came from beyond the foliage and bushes she was now crouched in, and she stayed low, coming closer, stopping just at the edge of a cobblestone circle lit by torches.

The girl was on what looked like an altar in the center, two of the masked men, one in a devil mask and one in a goblin mask, were tying her down, and it wasn't the kinky kinda tie down, either. The ropes looked thick and scratchy, and the rope in her mouth keeping her from speaking looked the same in the firelight.

"Time?" someone asked, she wasn't sure who, as all their faces were covered.

"Fifteen minutes," one of the others replied.

Their voices were modulated, slightly thick but with reverb, almost mechanical. She was reminded of that movie of the man in the mask with the voice modulator, and then almost screamed as the mask from the movie looked in the direction she was hiding. What the fuck was going on here?

Now finished, the two tying the girl down walked over to where the others were standing and then they walked single-file into the building. It was now or never.

Stepping from the shadows, she rushed over to the girl who saw her, and squeaked, pleading with her eyes.

"It's cool... I'ma get you out," Petra tried to reassure her as she started to work on the ties, making quick work of the knots. Clearly the guys that had taken her weren't super into knots, or they were half-assing it. Either way it worked for her. One arm, then another, and she was at her ankles as the girl was helping with the other. Eventually they managed to free her completely from the altar.

"Thank you..."

"Are you okay?" Petra asked in a whisper. "What happened?"

"I don't know. I was walking out of my building and..." They both looked up as the door opened at the house.

"Go. I'm right behind you," she whispered to the girl, who nodded her thanks again, and they were into the foliage in seconds.

They kept low, just under bush height, the girl quick. They made it around the side and heard the shout before the girl balked and ran, out into the street, away into the night. Petra went to follow her, when she was stopped by a pair of boots just in front of her. She bolted left, saw another pair and went right, seeing another.

Shit. They were herding her. She rushed the only way she could, back toward the house, hoping to god the girl she'd rescued realized Petra wasn't with her and sent the cops. As she broke through the foliage in the courtyard, she saw four of the men standing there and skidded to a stop. Shit.

"Well, well...what have we here?" The guy in the mask that looked like the devil stepped toward her as she shrank back, aware that the others were coming up behind her.

"Uh...that's not the girl we had before," one of the others said, his horrifying mask tilted slightly as he studied her. He looked like something from a horror flick—pieces of skin rudely stitched together into a warped facsimile of a face.

"No, it is not," the one in the goblin mask offered.

She swallowed, looking around her.

"You will find there is no leaving," the one in the neon mask said. "Though clearly you don't want to...why else would you trade places with our plaything?" He reached her first.

Shit. Shit. Shit. Shit. Not willing to go down without a fight, she moved closer and kicked him in the balls, watching as he crumpled to his knees with an oof.

"One step closer and I will do the same to the lot of you," she warned.

"Oh, I like her!" the man in the snake mask breathed, amusement ringing in his tone. "It's almost a shame we have to kill her."

"There is another option," the devil said thoughtfully, moving toward her. She kicked out, but he moved almost faster than she could register, dodging to the side as he grabbed her foot and yanked. She went sprawling to the ground on her back and he moved over her, swiftly pinning down her limbs under his implacable weight. "What do you think, guys? You want to play with this little bunny? Perhaps we could get our sacrifice in pleasure rather than death."

They were all quiet for long moments, Petra looking into the blacked out eyes of the devil's mask, his weight not uncomfortable, but also there and pressing. Sacrifice? What were they playing at? And why were they even there at all?

"Touch me with a single appendage and I'll cut it the fuck off," she gritted through her teeth.

"Let her up. Give her the deal," she heard, the modulated voice coming from one of the others that hadn't spoken before. "If she takes it..." The rest of the statement hung in the air.

"I'll let her up if she gives me her word she'll listen and won't try to fuck us up," the devil said softly, the black eyes fixed on hers. "Give us five minutes to explain the deal, during which you have my word that none of us will hurt you. Understood?"

Anything was better than being under this guy. She nodded, swallowing again, her fight or flight instincts raging inside her.

"Don't run. You do, and Ghosty here will just slice your throat. Crude, but it gets the job done," the goblin said as she stood, looking at the guy with the Ghostface mask messing with a bowie knife.

"And that," murmured the devil as he eased back onto his knees, "would be a crying shame."

She looked at the Ghostface guy once more and then at the crew of them that were all standing together. Seven masks, all different, the malevolence wafting off the group palpable. "Talk. I wanna go."

"That all depends on your answer," Goblin said.

"Who are you kidding?" The guy with the stitched skin mask snorted. "She either dies or she accepts the deal. She isn't going anywhere soon."

"Stitches!" the devil snapped and she could hear the snarl in his voice. "Shut the fuck up."

"Sorry." Stitches dipped his head in acknowledgment and the devil turned back to her. "So here it is...we have to make a sacrifice on this night, every year. Since you've deprived us of our intended victim, you either take her place, or you let us harvest the life force we need in other, less mortal ways."

"Less mortal ways?" She frowned. "Great. So, I'm dead or I'm raped...and then dead." She rolled her eyes, the possibility of dying ensuring she wouldn't go a meek and delicate thing. "You try either, I'm taking at least one of you with me."

"And that just won't do," Neon said. "Why did you save the girl?"

"Why? Because you assholes tied her down and she did not look like she consented to that."

"No...she didn't," he said to her. "And if you could stop that...random women dying for something they don't understand?"

She arched a brow. "I don't want people to die." Didn't want to die herself, either.

"You take the deal, no one dies," Neon said. "Not even you...unless you cross us." She could hear the smirk in his modulated voice.

She looked to them, the malice still there but tempered. She didn't feel completely safe, she just felt...interest. "What's the deal?"

"Fucking." The devil shrugged. "Orgasms generate life force. All seven of us and you over two nights should do it."

She blinked. "What?"

"Two nights a year, you belong to us," Goblin clarified.

"Any two random nights?"

"Black Night and Samhain," Neon said. "Two nights. All seven of us. No death, except the little death. And no faces."

"No...no faces? I don't get to know who you are?"

"It's safer," Neon offered.

10

"Besides, we're not idiots and we're not going back on our word," Stitches said. "Do as we ask and you get to walk out of here in two days' time. We're not going to let you see our faces so you can go running off to the cops."

"You aren't going to hurt me?" she asked, the scene in *American Psycho* with the medical instruments playing in her head.

"We guarantee nothing... But you will walk out of here on your own, and you won't be any worse for wear," Neon said.

"Well, you're not going to require hospitalization," Stitches amended. "Some of us are kinky fuckers, but we know what we're doing. There won't be any scarring or lasting damage."

Jesus fucking Christ. "And I don't have a choice, do I?" she asked, weighing the pros and cons...or attempting to in the space of a few heartbeats.

"There is always a choice," a voice she hadn't heard yet, which she assumed was Ghostface, spoke up. "Make it."

Fuck it. Whatever they had in store for her was probably more interesting than ice cream and late-night television. "Yes."

Chapter One

Three years Later.

Petra looked in the mirror and smoothed down the lapel of the long wool coat she was wearing, the black material sumptuous, her fingers catching on the small devil pin on the edge. A gift from the man himself, his choice for her this year. After three years, things had not changed, not with the seven, though they were getting more involved.

She had walked out of that arrangement on All Souls that first year and, true to their word, she had been intact. A little roughed up from what she had experienced at their hands, but only a little. The seven had pushed limits, and introduced her to things she never thought possible, or ever thought she would like. Seven orgasms each night, at least, and to her surprise some of them played with each other.

They never asked her name, never asked anything about her, and she had left the situation, and that house, altered and owned. She knew that now. The seven owned her body, her mind and everything else she was. Two days of attention. And then it was over. For months afterwards, her body felt the effects of their attentions, and she had tried to find them, but the building she had been with them in was gone, torn down soon after All Souls. No record of what happened.

And the next year, she was treated to a packet in her mailbox, no return address. Directions to get her affairs in order, and to ensure she was theirs from sundown on Black Night to dawn of All Souls. The gifts started arriving on the twenty-ninth that year—a long dress, shoes, a coat—and the same again the year after. It was no surprise when the packages started arriving this year.

A dress. Shoes. A coat.

Directions to be ready at sundown, when a car would be waiting.

Travel out of the city into the mountains, where she would meet her seven at a mansion bright with light.

Each year she would indulge their desires, and some of her own, learning things about herself. And each year she would walk out of the mansion alone, the place void of life, and drive back to the city to sleep off forty-eight hours of debauchery.

They knew who she was, where she was, things about her others did not. And she was at a loss, because the seven were ever elusive to her. They fucked her with their masks on. They welcomed her with their masks on. Their voices were always modulated, and after it all, the details of themselves were largely fuzzy. She was sure they drugged her to keep that happening.

She wasn't sure why they had chosen her, past the opportunity. Wasn't sure why they kept to the pact. But they had. Fall disappearances from the city were down. She knew; she'd checked. The mystery of her seven had led her to be sure that they were keeping to the pact. And so far they had.

She looked to the clock. The town car would be there shortly, to whisk her to the mansion, and she needed to be perfect.

Her black hair had grown, as she wanted to please her seven...which was a truth she had only recently started to explore. They liked her hair long, and she was endeavoring to keep them happy. She wasn't sure when that actually happened, but this year...it felt different because she had decided things would be different.

This year she was getting answers.

She glossed her lips just as her phone buzzed. The car was there. Grabbing her keys, she walked out and down her fifth-story walk up to the street below. The driver was there, standing by the door, which he opened as she approached. He held his hand out, and she placed her keys and phone in his, a condition of their arrangement, and smiled at him. He was wearing a half mask, black with a spider across the side, but he didn't acknowledge her. He never did.

She slipped into the back seat and moments later they were crawling through the streets and onto the interstate toward her destination. She looked down, seeing the note, and the glass of champagne.

Drink. Relax. We will be in the dining room.

She did what they asked and settled in, knowing that whatever she was ingesting would relax her enough to not care where she was going, or how she got there, as with previous years.

The trip was quick, though it could be that she was used to it, and it wasn't long before the car was stopping, and she was being helped out by Spider. She nodded to him and walked up to the house.

A sprawling affair, it was all black, with columns holding the façade up and the double doors flanked by stone gryphons, the knockers black and sooty. The place, always interesting to her, set her mind reeling with hazy memories from prior years. But she couldn't focus on that. Beyond the doors *they* waited.

Each year it was something else. The first year at the mansion, they met her in the foyer. The second they had been in the sitting room. Now, they waited in the dining room. As she stepped up the steps to the doors, they opened and she passed through, feeling the whoosh as they closed behind her. Intimately acquainted with the house, she walked to the left and down the hall to the door where she knew they would be waiting.

Unbuttoning her coat, she looked down to the glittery, high-end heels she was wearing, and attempted to get her nerves and excitement under control. Whatever was beyond the doors waiting for her, whatever they were planning, she was both terrified and intrigued.

She never knew why they did this...didn't have one fucking idea why she was even following through with it. Aside from the fact that the seven made her...feel. Two nights a year she was a person she wasn't sure she liked, but craved to be. Because of them. Because of what they put her through.

She opened the doors to see them all sitting, sprawling, masks in place, dressed in dark suits, black on black on black.

They were like a renaissance work of art, flame-lit and tenebrous, and it was clear they were going for effect. Which seemed kind of crazy. Were they trying to impress her with their display? It wasn't like they needed to. She'd made the agreement—two nights a year to stop them killing anyone. They didn't need her approval in any way, and yet here they were, laid out in a feast of masked flesh.

"Like what you see?" It was no surprise that Stitches broke first. She'd learned he was the most impulsive of them all, even though his kinks took a...delicate touch.

"Of what I can see, yes," she said boldly.

"Take the coat off," Neon commanded, sitting forward. She suspected he was the one that had chosen the dress this time. Shedding the coat, she placed it on the chair just in front of her, and looked back to them. The dress was black, as it always was, tailored perfectly to her curves and generous ass, satin but for the large swaths of mesh and lace that tore through the center like razor strikes.

The top was a sweetheart, the satin just covering her nipples, the rest of her flesh peeking through, and the bottom was tight to her hips and then flared well above her knees to give her movement. Squaring her shoulders, she stood there for their perusal.

"Do a spin, princess," Snake commanded her.

She did, slowly like she knew they liked, allowing the firelight to glint off the material and the jet beads that were sewn into the lace. She heard a low growl, still not sure who had the ass fetish when she turned.

"Remind me to blindfold you and sink my teeth into that juicy ass," Devil murmured. "Fucking beautiful."

She turned all the way around, a smirk on her face. If she had her way, she *would* watch him sink those teeth into her ass. She stood still, her body alight with sensation at the eyes she knew were on her. Her nipples pearled under the material, her core clenched, and she welcomed the feeling. At first it had freaked her out how much this pageantry turned her on, but now...

"The perfect dark bride," Neon said softly.

"Who wants to go first?" Devil asked, his voice still soft behind the mask so she had to strain to hear it over the crackling fire. "No, not you, Stitches. You went first last year."

"And she needed extra recovery time," Goblin said. "Ghosty neither."

Ghost turned toward him and flipped him off, his glove-covered hand glinting in the light as much as the knife he had sticking in the table.

"I'll go first," Snake said, rising to his feet with graceful poise.

She shivered, trying not to react. Snake's brand of attention was both the most and least invasive and, since that first time, he had her fiending for what he did with her. She had hoped it would be him or Devil to start. The rest were...a lot.

"A request for my room?" she asked and looked to Devil, who seemed to be their defacto leader. Once dawn hit for the day ahead, they left her 'til the evening to recover, replenish and nourish her body.

"What do you want?" His eyes were dark and impenetrable behind the mask, but they didn't seem unkind.

"Arnica Epsom salts," she said, knowing after at least three of them that night, she would need to soak.

"Way ahead of you," Stitches assured her. "You mentioned it last year. I made a note."

"Anything else?" Devil sounded amused, although whether it was at her or Stitches was anyone's guess.

"No..." she said softly. She wasn't there for her demands...they gave, she received.

"Then step into my parlor," Snake said, gesturing for her to walk ahead of him into the hallway beyond.

Turning with a smirk, she walked out, hearing a quiet curse from one of them, although it was so quiet she wasn't sure who. The audible intake of breath at the sight of her ass in the dress only made her put more sway in her hips as she walked.

"Tease." Snake smacked her ass and then laughed when she jumped at the impact. "Still so twitchy after all this time... What say we get you good and hazed on orgasms, hmm?"

He was chattier than he had been before. Their first time he barely said anything to her, just tied her over a bench and shoved a vibe inside her, forcing orgasms from her as he watched. The following two years he'd barely said twenty words to her the whole two nights. Now it seemed he was more invested.

"Is it a crime that I enjoy winding you all up?" she asked as they turned a corner. She was jumpy but only because her body was primed, needing and close to going off. She hadn't had a voyeur kink before meeting these men, but now, the fact that they liked to watch, and the anticipation of each man's desires for her, made her crave being seen.

All because she took the place of a sacrifice. One she was enjoying.

"No, but you are playing with fire," he told her, less teasing in his tone. "We're not the kind of guys you want to see snap."

She wasn't sure about that. "No, I don't suppose I do. It would mean play time would be over." She looked over her shoulder. "Though you did promise I wouldn't be hurt...so why not tempt you a bit?"

"We didn't say we wouldn't hurt you," he corrected her. "We said we wouldn't maim you or leave you requiring hospitalization. I could make you delirious with pain and not break either of those rules. We all could. Besides, are you sure you want to trust the word of seven killers?"

"I have trusted you for three years," she said honestly. "You could kill me, but you won't. I serve several purposes..." She turned just before the door they were walking toward. "I don't pretend to expect you wouldn't end me if pushed, but I don't push." She smiled. "It feels good to know I affect you." Words she wouldn't have said before this night.

Snake didn't say anything in response, but he wasn't gentle as he guided her into a room and shut the door behind them. "Strip," he told her, his tone cold. "Since you think you hold some power here, perhaps I should make you feel powerless."

She shrugged and reached behind her, unzipping the dress, letting it fall to the floor. She was naked but for the shoes, and she raised her leg, gripping the heel of the stiletto. She had practiced how to stand and walk in them, ever since the first year where she was a bit wobbly. She looked at him, a question to keep them, or take them off.

"Take them off. I don't want you hurting yourself while you're helplessly squirming on this." He'd opened a wooden chest and retrieved a piece of equipment she hadn't seen before. Flat on the base, it was curved at the top with something sticking up out of it. "You ever ridden a Sybian before?" he asked.

She stepped out of the shoes, making her almost five inches shorter, and shook her head, interest apparent on her face. Snake loved to watch her, but he never really touched her. All the others had fucked her with their own dicks, but Snake...he never did. "I ride it like a saddle?"

"Essentially, yes, but I will strap you down on it so you can't move and can't escape, and you will go crazy from endless forced pleasure." There was a flash of teeth behind the mask, a savage grin.

She didn't see the problem, not really. The idea of being pleasured by something, not having to pleasure...no matter how forced... It wasn't a deterrent. Especially because she enjoyed everything he had done to her in the past. Instead of telling him she was interested, she swallowed audibly and then nodded. "I'm here for you," she said softly.

"You're here for all of us." He set the device over a sawhorse and moved her over it. "You can take that dildo at your own pace," he said magnanimously, walking away to fetch straps.

Looking down at the piece she was hovering over, she shrugged and slid down it. She was already wet and she had taken way bigger without any easing; Ghost had seen to that. Full, she slid to the base, noticing the grind pad that would rub her clit if she was strapped forward.

"I meant the collective you," she said, settling better so she was comfortable, full but comfortable. "Though technically I'm here for all the women you'd kill otherwise."

"All the women we'd kill over Samhain if you weren't spreading your legs for us every year?" He snorted a laugh. "If that's what you have to tell yourself, you do you, but I've heard you moaning like a fucking slut on every dick you ride here. I know you come here because we give you what no one else can. You're a filthy little cock-sucking whore and you love it."

He shoved her forward so she was in contact with the grind pad and proceeded to strap her in place, body and limbs, so that she couldn't move an inch if she wanted to. He'd been right—she couldn't lift off the pad even a fraction of a millimeter. She was in for the ride until he took mercy on her and let her come down. He sprawled in an armchair where he had a good view of her, the unbuttoned collar of his shirt stretching to show some of the tattooed skin she knew was underneath, and grinned, his teeth flashing in feral delight behind the snake. "Enjoy," he growled and flicked the switch in his hand.

She gasped and closed her eyes, hands grasping at nothing. The vibrations and the cock moving inside her, it was fucking heaven. Gods... "Oh fuck..." she hissed and looked at him, just out of reach, and could feel his eyes on her. So far as she could figure, Snake's kink was being a voyeur, and he didn't touch her more than he had to. She bit her bottom lip as some particularly strong vibrations rolled through her, and cried out as her first orgasm came barreling through her.

His words rolled through her head, since she could do nothing but think and feel, and thinking was going to stop in short order once she had another orgasm or two. He was right, of course, she did love it, but not for the reasons he thought. True, they did give her what no one else could, allowing her to let go and explore things no decent man would consider on the to do list they gave her...but it also allowed her to have no regrets for what she wanted.

And she wanted them. Three years was more than enough time to know. Fuck, she knew on All Souls last year, the black rose left in the car for her sealing it. Something within each of them was hungry for what she gave them as well...

He watched, unmoving and merciless, as a second orgasm rolled into a third and then she was coming helplessly, unable to make it stop, overstimulated right to the edge of pain as every muscle in her body contracted again and again in waves. For a second he lifted the controls, but then he shook his head slightly and let his hand rest on the chair again, just watching her come completely undone.

"Ah..." she moaned and closed her eyes, determined to endure. If this was going to work she needed to. Snake, he was so much more removed from it all. And her plan... She wasn't sure it would work with him.

"Snake..." she moaned his name, well, the name she had for him, and looked up to him. "Fuck, this is so good..." she hedged. Truth was, it sucked bad. She was going to be raw, but it was his turn and she had to sell it, though in the beginning it had been bliss.

"Don't lie to me," he snarled, flicking a button to turn the strength of the machine up. "You're starting to cramp. Your clit is overstimulated. Your abdominal muscles are aching like fuck. You're on that machine because I want you to know. Your. Place. You have no power here. And you'll keep fucking coming until I say otherwise. Understood?"

"Ah! Fuck yes, of course..." she moaned and licked her lips. "But it is fucking good..." she hissed and shuddered as she came again, goosebumps breaking out on her skin. "Coming isn't a hardship, it's the denied orgasms that Devil does; that's fucking hard. Ah!" she arched as she came again, her body seriously close to giving up. But she would endure. She needed to, and she needed to goad him to her to get her hands free.

"Not a fucking hardship..." he muttered, shaking his head. "If you're enjoying it that much, maybe I'll just leave you there the whole time I have with you. Won't be a hardship for me, either." He pressed the button to increase the power again.

"You didn't plan to?" She moaned and shook. "That's what I expected. Snake leaves me with something inhuman chugging away in my pussy...no attention from that glorious cock I see outlined in your slacks." She licked her lips.

"That's off limits," he snapped. "To you, anyway..." For a moment it looked as though he was debating what to do and then he set down the controls and reached for the button of his pants. "Watch and weep that you'll never get to taste this." He pulled his cock out and fisted it, running his hand up and down the ridiculous girth of it in idle motions as she writhed and squirmed before him.

With a cry she came, watching him touch himself, her body past anything she had ever experienced. Still she endured, needing to get through it all. "Oh fuck, that's so fucking hot, Snake." She moaned again. "Fuck, you're so beautiful..."

"Tell me how much you want to touch it," he goaded her. "Tell me you want to taste it. Tell me you want to feel it deep in your sloppy wet cunt."

23

This she could do. "Fuck yes. All those things. I want to run my tongue over it, feel it in the back of my throat as you fuck my face, ah!" She swallowed as another orgasm ripped through her, this one slightly more painful. She gasped and panted. "Oh fuck, I would die to feel you finally fucking me with that monster..." She looked at his face, tearing her eyes away from his hand pumping his thick shaft. "But I know you won't..." she moaned. "Please let me help you...let me stroke you... Please?" she gasped again.

As her begging became more and more incoherent and frantic, his hand sped up until he came, thick pearly strings spurting up his stomach and over his hand. "No." He reached for a cloth and wiped himself off, cleaning everything except the palm of his hand, and then he came to stand in front of her shuddering body. "I'll fuck you with many things, but not that. Deal with it." With the palm still coated in his cum, he grasped her face and tilted it up toward him. "You can take every filthy thing we do to you, and you'll still never earn the privilege of touching my dick. What do you say to that?"

Her tongue snaked out and licked his cum from his hand, and she shuddered. Fuck but he tasted good. Sweet like pineapple, slightly salty. She shuddered and looked up to him. "Crying fucking shame I can't have more of that." She licked her lips again. "Haven't you figured it out yet?" Another cry and she slumped forward.

"Figured out what?" He slapped her twitching ass with his still wet palm. "Still so fucking cheeky and entitled. I should have gagged you."

She gasped and shivered. "All I want is this..." she moaned, attempting to lift her head. "Being your toy...being used by you." By all of them, but she would have to work on them individually. "Being yours..." she choked out softly. Her ass burned where he touched her, the most perfect tingle. The spank was good, but the fact that he had touched her...

"It's not about what you want." He walked away again, somewhere behind her, and then she heard running water. "You're a fuck toy to us. A means to an end. Less clean up than a killing." The water shut off and he came back into her field of vision, drying his hands on a towel. "You're nothing, Petra. Your wants are nothing. You're a pretty power bank with tits and ass."

"Maybe..." she said with a gasp, tears starting to run down her cheeks. "But you just used my name." They never used her name. Ever. Not once in the three times she had been with them. She knew they knew it, but he was right, this was about her being a toy. One that enjoyed being played with. And he had used her name. Dead tell. He was trying to hurt her, and maybe yeah it hurt a bit, but...as with everything else with these lunatics, there was hope.

"You think we haven't done our research?" He sounded amused, but there was a slight tone to it that betrayed his annoyance, although whether it was at her or himself was anyone's guess. "Of course I know your name. I know everything about you. It means nothing other than that I care about what happens to my brothers."

"A name means you know me...know I'm more than your little fuck doll...that you think of me as more," she said confidently, though it was through gritted teeth and tears. The machine was putting her into a state, and one that she wouldn't be handling well later. Thank God she asked for those Epsom salts. "Let me be more, Snake..." she gasped again. "Please."

"No." He sat back in his chair, tossing the towel aside. "Poor deluded little girl, thinking your name means anything." He shook his head with a mocking tilt. "You were a security risk. That's all. But now we know how much you want it...how you crave it...how you'll break that body of yours any way we ask you to, you're not even that to us any more."

"I was never a security risk. I accepted this from the beginning," she hissed. "I don't want it. I want you. All of this is a means to an end." She moaned and bit her lip as she cried out in pain, slumping, her body all but giving out.

"Well now I know you're fuck drunk," he snorted, all amusement this time. "You're not even making sense anymore."

She didn't move, couldn't, the vibrations making her twitch, but she needed to save her strength.

"Well, I guess we're done." He finally, blessedly, turned the damn machine off and the relief set her trembling all over again. He started on the leg straps first, laughing as her limbs tumbled uselessly out of the restraints like over-cooked noodles. The back strap was next and then, finally, he reached for the arm straps.

She waited, knowing he would take her off the machine instead of letting her move at her own pace, because he was nothing if not careful with his own implements and he had to know that she wasn't in control of her limbs. As soon as he lifted her...

He took his time, rubbing the circulation back into her hands, his tenderness belying the cruel words he'd used. She hadn't even realized she'd been fighting the restraints so hard, but her body felt jelly-like and soft, so the pain barely registered. "You're going to have to go up vertically," he warned her, lifting her at the shoulders so she was sitting upright, and then moving in close so he could lift her off the machine that was filling her still rippling pussy.

She whimpered, letting him lift her, and clumsily wrapped her thighs around his hips, clinging to him as much as possible. He moved her toward the bed, and she hummed, the afterglow setting in regardless of the fact that she was largely in agony. Away from the toy, surrounded in him, her arms lying on his, hands behind his head, she took the chance, and removed his mask.

He reeled back, letting her slip from his arms into an ungainly sprawl on the floor. "What the fuck do you think you're doing?" he roared, snatching the mask back from her and turning away to put it back on.

"I saw you...Easton," she said softly, looking up at him. Easton James, the hot as fuck artist that had shown in the gallery she worked at four times. Easton, the one that never talked to her, only gave her dirty ass glances a few times.

Easton was...Snake?

"Don't say that name!" Mask back in place, he turned on her, fury blazing in his eyes. "What the fuck were you thinking? Now we have to kill you!"

"No, you don't," she countered. "You think that because I know who you are I won't keep this secret?" she asked and licked her lips. Shit, she needed water. "I told you: I'm not here because of the pact." She looked up to him. "I'm here for you." *All of you.*

"You don't get to decide that!" He was pacing now, clearly anxious. "Devil is going to skin us both alive for this."

"Who is going to tell him? You?" she asked, struggling to her feet, as sensation started to come back into them. "I'm certainly not going to."

"Fuck!" He slammed a fist into the bedpost. "Fuck you for trying to make me choose! He's been my brother for years and you're what? Some fuck bunny we've had for six fucking nights!"

"I'm not trying to make you choose anything," she said as she stood straighter. "And that's on you assholes for this six night thing. Ever think I might want more?" She leaned back against the bed post. "I wanted to know; I wanted more. Seeing your face doesn't change anything. You can keep wearing that mask when you have me; it won't change a thing. I'll still be yours, still submit to you, and them, and nothing changes."

"What the fuck are you saying?" Snake shook his head, backing away from her. "It's not up to you to give me fucking permission to wear my mask. No faces was the deal. What you agreed to. That's all we need or want from you. Two nights a year to feed the Dark God. And you think you can just waltz in here and just change the terms when you feel like it? That's not how this works!"

She shrugged. "This changes nothing between us, Snake. You wanna keep playing these games? I'm in. You want to take it further? I'm in." She looked at him pointedly. "Kill me if you want, if that's what you really want. I won't fight it."

"What do you mean by 'take it further?'" he demanded. "There are rules! Rules that we don't get a choice about following!"

"Then if you are all about the rules, Snake, kill me and have done so you don't mess with whatever you think you're messing with."

"I can't do that on my own!" he reminded her, sounding agonized. "The others have to be here for a sacrifice. Fuck! Devil is going to lose his shit!" He sat down on his chair and put his head in his hands. "I should have fucking known something was up with the way you walked in here all ballsy and shit. How am I supposed to trust you when you go pulling crazy shit like this??"

She sighed. "How am I supposed to trust the seven of you to keep your word each time we meet?" she countered. "You just do. And all hot girls are crazy. I kept coming back and you honestly didn't think I would want to know more about you?" She went to him and got on her knees in front of him, sitting back on her heels, "Do you have any idea how hot you make me? You think any of this is a hardship? Snake..." She put her hands on the arms of the chair, steadying herself to lean into his warmth. "Let me ask you something. Me knowing, does that change whatever it is that Dark God of yours gets?"

"I don't fucking know if it changes the energy," he replied frankly. "And we didn't ever expect you to trust us, because we knew we could just kill you if it looked like you were about to blab."

"Why would I fucking say a word?" she asked. She didn't think he got it. He, they, had changed her, shown her parts of herself, parts she couldn't show to anyone else. She wasn't lying when she said she was crazy, because she was, and she reveled in that knowledge. "Regardless, I do trust all of you, which is fucked up I know..."

"That's an understatement," he snorted. "What's your end game here, Petra? What did you think you'd achieve by taking off my mask?"

She shrugged. Telling him the full truth wouldn't be smart; he wasn't as invested as she felt some of the others were. Treading carefully was important with Snake. "Knowing you. Knowing who I stroke off to when I'm alone all year." That was part of it. She wanted more than that, but would take things slowly with his volatile ass. "Seeing the guy that won't let me touch him." Even this close, a hair's breadth from each other, she wasn't touching him.

"Then you're not as smart as I gave you credit for," he said bitterly. "And what about the others? You going to try and pull this same shit with them?"

She had never claimed to be smart when it came to them. In fact she was pretty sure she was the stupidest woman alive, but she wanted what she wanted, and if that meant the seven...she was going to get them or die trying. But she couldn't tell him that. Instead, she shrugged. "Maybe. And maybe they will be more receptive to it. Or they will just haul me into your study and you can kill me as a group. Either way, it's a win for you if you keep it to yourself."

He was quiet for a long moment and then sighed. "Fine. Make it someone else's problem. This is above my paygrade." He shoved her out of the way and rose to his feet. "Clean yourself up. I'll send the next guy in."

She nodded. Snake was not going to be easy. "Okay. Thanks for the orgasms. And finally showing me that stunner." She winked at him.

He paused on his way to the door and looked back at her with a serious gaze. "You wanna watch that smart mouth around the others," he warned her. "They're even less tolerant of sass than I am."

She shrugged. "Well then your problem will take care of itself." She watched him walk out the door and stood, walking shakily to the ensuite to clean up a bit. She wasn't sure who was going to find her next, but she needed to freshen up.

Chapter 2

"Something is different."

Neon looked up from his tablet to see Ghosty leaning against the door frame, fiddling with his knife as usual. Goblin, Plague, Devil and Stitches all looked to him. Ghost rarely talked, but when he did, they all took notice.

Snake was engaged with their girl, and Neon knew why he wanted to go first. He wanted to get it out of the way. Out of all of them, he was the most reluctant for the arrangement, but the rest of them were all in, to the point where they had made her their yearlong obsession.

They had inserted themselves into her life in several ways, to make sure she wasn't a snitch, but she wasn't. Never once did she utter a word about them, or the situation. Oh, she was researching them—they'd have been surprised if she hadn't tried to find the house or some idea of their identities—but she wouldn't find anything they didn't want her to. They made sure of that.

They didn't know exactly what she believed, because she didn't get to spend a lot of time talking while they were together, but it was clear she thought her two nights was the bare minimum contribution to stop them from killing other women. It couldn't be further from the truth. The energy they were harvesting from her, and pooling between them, was more potent and varied than anything they'd sent below to the Dark God before. Not that she needed to know that. She was a tool...one they were all obsessed with, for better or worse.

When they were presented with her as an option, it was an easy choice between getting covered in blood or coated in cum. She shined like the sun, the brilliance of her spirit almost too much to bear. They had thought corrupting her soul would be easy, but the light in her hadn't changed. And while sliding a knife through flesh was satisfying, nothing beat getting a nut with a willing woman. And she was willing, past their pact.

She craved what they did to her, that was obvious, and in that she was special as well. What single woman would be that perfect as to enjoy all their varied attentions, their various interests in pleasure? She did. And while her pleasure was important, it was more her submission to the acts, the acceptance was more potent than the fear. The orgasm was always a bonus they all enjoyed.

Regardless of who they were, they were still men, and Petra was insanely hot. And even with their various tastes in women, she ticked all the boxes for them.

For him, her tears were sweet fucking bliss.

"Yep, hair is longer, and that ass is as perky as those perfect tits," Goblin said to them. "Our girl has been working out."

"Yeah, but you knew that," Neon said, knowing Goblin was in a yoga class with her. He looked to Ghost. "I agree, something is different. She's more confident, and I think she's hiding something."

"Maybe she wants to be here as much as we want her to be here," Stitches said. "I fucking missed her. Maybe she's started to miss us. You know she ain't getting dick like this from anywhere else."

She wasn't getting it from *anyone* else. They had made sure of that. Any guy that seemed interested had been discreetly warned off, either collectively or individually. That vibrator she had was almost out of warranty with the amount she used it through the year, and Neon knew she was only thinking about them.

"I got that impression," Goblin mused aloud, "that she wants to be here. Her bearing..." he trailed off. "She has the countenance of a woman knowing her worth in this situation."

"And one that needs the attention," Neon added.

"This is when it kind of sucks that we only need to sacrifice once a year," Plague said thoughtfully. "If we had more Sabbaths, we could tell her to come more often."

"This is the only time of year the veil between worlds is thin enough for the Dark One to receive all of the energy from the sacrifices," Devil reminded him. "Trying to repeat the ritual at other times of the year would only give him a trickle of energy at best."

"Better some than none," Stitches smirked. "His hunger knows no bounds."

"And he gets a lot from Petra," Neon said. They all got a lot from the woman. Given their own proclivities, women were, for most of their lives, a non-entity. Oh, they all had needs and handled them, but getting close to anyone was verboten, until her. She served so many purposes, but none as important as soothing the monsters that lived inside each of them.

Seven lunatics, psychos, mad dog killers... She had challenged them three years before and had been rewarded since. And it seemed she didn't want that to stop.

"You know she's keeping that body tight for us."

"Unless she's got better endurance, I'm going to say it's for *you*," Ghost said. They all knew his brand of play with her. He liked a runner and, so far, she had delivered, but they knew it wasn't that much of a challenge. He had planned something more elaborate for this year.

"And if she does want to stay?" Goblin asked.

"What? You just wanna ask her? She doesn't even know what we fucking look like," Neon offered.

"Besides, we'd have to discuss something of that nature with the Elders," Devil reminded them. Any outsider coming in posed a threat to the organization. Even though she had been thoroughly vetted after that first year, when they knew she was coming back, she was still a risk. They'd have to be damn certain of what she wanted before even thinking of doing anything about it.

"Maybe we should put a request in," Goblin said. "She's young enough that we could potentially get her in as a brood mare. Even Snake would..."

Neon shook his head. "We would have to be sure she was into it. Otherwise they'll kill her."

"Yes. No requests until we know for sure," Devil said. "They've already approved this little experiment of ours, but they're watching us closely. Let's not push it for now."

Neon nodded. "She's worth more serving as a sacrifice right now."

"So who is going next?" Goblin asked as Snake walked in.

"I'll go." Stitches jumped to his feet. "I'm not gonna take long. My big scene with her is set up for tomorrow." He headed out, bumping Snake's knuckles on the way, and Snake closed the door behind him.

"How did it go?" Plague asked and Snake shrugged, even though they could all see him smiling behind the mask.

"She's fire. You know that." None of them missed the jab at Plague's kink and a couple of them chuckled.

"You didn't wear her out, did you?" Neon asked, as it would be between himself and Goblin after Stitches. Both Ghost and Devil had ideas for their main night, and Neon, well...he just needed her on her knees.

"Of course not!" Snake actually sounded affronted. "I'm not that much of an asshole." There was a muffled comment from somewhere near the fire that *nah, he just likes to take it up the asshole* and everyone burst out laughing this time.

"You notice anything different about her?" Goblin asked, circling back to their original conversation. "Ghosty thinks something is different."

Snake stiffened almost imperceptibly, just for a second, but then he shrugged. "You mean like how she's been working out? You could bounce coins off that ass, it's so perky."

"That it is." Neon grinned. "You really going to bite it?" he asked Devil.

"I'm sure I'm not the only one with plans of that nature," Devil snorted. "I'd be surprised if Stitches hasn't done it already."

"He's never been one for impulse control," Plague agreed, chuckling.

"And unless he's in a scene, he's never been much for drawing things out," Goblin said. "So, who is going after him?"

"Whoever it is must not mind being clean up crew," Ghost grunted.

Neon looked to Goblin. "You decide."

"You," Goblin said. "And if you tie her up and leave her where you finish with her, I'll take it from there."

Neon nodded with a smirk. "Can do."

Goblin looked to Devil. "She's going to be blindfolded...you wanna tag in with me?"

"Sounds good." Devil nodded. "Just let me know when you're ready to go."

Neon grinned and looked at the clock. "One. I should be done and she should be sufficiently ready for the two of you by then."

Goblin laughed. "Understood."

35

Chapter 3

Cleaned up, Petra smoothed her dress down her body and then zipped it up and stepped back into her heels. She wasn't sure who was coming up to her next, but she wanted to be presentable at least.

Her body was still tingling, and her clit, her poor clit was going to be throbbing and not in a good way for the rest of the night. But this was all a means to an end. She had succeeded already once, though it didn't have the desired effect she wanted, but it was Snake, the most reluctant of her seven. He wasn't really interested, normally, so her actions were met with his normal amount of anger. Though his words, they hurt. She knew she'd started out as nothing but a fuck toy for them, but now...surely she wasn't the only one feeling this?

Brushing her hair, she shook it out and then left the bathroom, walking through to the room beyond to see Stitches standing in the doorway.

"Hey, gorgeous." It was impossible to see his mouth behind the mask, but somehow she just knew he was smirking.

"Hi," she said with a smile. Stitch, for all his quirks, had never hidden his want of her. "So I get to play with you now?" His tastes ran toward some pretty hardcore stuff, but he didn't look like he was in the mood for his normal fare.

"Uh, no. *I* get to play with *you*," he corrected, his teeth flashing a grin in the shadows of his mask. "Come." He grabbed her wrist and tugged her toward the door, no doubt heading for his own room, and they stepped out into the hallway. They'd barely taken three steps before he groaned and muttered something that sounded like 'fuck this,' and before she even knew what was happening, she was crushed up face front to the wall, her dress dragged up above her hips and his cock shoving between her thighs.

"Gonna fuck you right here where anyone can see you," he whispered, a rough hand covering her mouth as she whimpered. "Spread your legs so that anyone who walks by can see what a little slut you are."

Now this...this was what she expected. And, wonder of wonders, with the heels on she was the perfect height for him to just take her. She did as he asked, and popped her ass up, giving him even more room to work with. Stitch's cock was a work of art, and she couldn't wait for a reintroduction.

She was swollen, and sore, but she needed something real, she needed the feel of this man.

"So fucking wet," he groaned. "I love fucking you after Snake, because I know it's all you. You're just this fucking filthy and desperate for us." His cock drove home inside her, the ridges and bumps of all the piercings making it a sensory experience impossible to recreate. And gods help her, she'd tried.

Even those monster dildos with all the ridges and suckers didn't come close to the sensation of cold, hard metal ramming into her in one velvety slide. "Tomorrow I'm going to play with you, but tonight I just need this," he told her. "So just fucking take it like a good girl."

She nodded. Moaning into his hand, she nipped his finger, licking it with her tongue after. Fuck, that was perfect, just fucking perfect. No one, not one of them felt like her Stitches did, and she craved it constantly. She whimpered, the slide and glide of his perfect cock inside her as he took her hard, causing her to clench around him. Orgasms were never in short order with him.

"You're a little exhibitionist, aren't you?" he growled, the hand holding her hips in place tightening to the point of pain. "You fucking love the idea of one of the others walking up the stairs and seeing you spread open and taking it up against a wall like a common whore." He shifted his hand so his fingers were in her mouth, making her gasp as she fought to suck them, desperate for the sensation anywhere other than in her cunt and the flat press of the wall against her front.

"You were so good with the needles last year," he whispered. "I've planned something extra-special for you this year. I'm going to get you naked and make you a skin corset. It's going to be fucking stunning. And then I'm going to fuck you while you're too scared to move."

"Ah... Please..." she moaned as she came for him, her sheath flooding, soaking him. The needles were...different, but the man knew what he was doing and while she had been scared the first couple of times, this time she was intrigued, having done her research on his kink to understand it better.

"That's it, come on my cock," he growled, his hand sliding down to her throat and squeezing. "You can do better than that. Give me another one."

"Oh..." Her gasp was punctuated with her sheath clamping down again, one of his piercings hitting the exact right spot. "Stitches!" she cried out, shuddering with the force of the orgasm. With this, she was undone, and past needing with this insane man, but he played her so well. They all did.

She reached back, gripped his side through his shirt, and squeezed, pulling as if to tell him to go harder, though she knew if he was going to go super hard, he would have to turn her to face him. If he did, she was going to take that mask off and set eyes on the face of the man that had opened her eyes to some things about herself she never thought to explore.

"That's it," he crooned, satisfaction in every tone. "You've earned a rest." Pulling out in a way that made her feel suddenly and shockingly empty, he spun her on her wobbly legs and pressed the cold, dead skin of his mask to her mouth in a horrifying facsimile of a kiss. She was still reeling from that when he bent down and scooped her up, startling a squeak from her as she left the floor altogether, her knees hooked over his elbows as his muscles bunched and flexed. He pressed his hands against the wall, spreading her wide open and helpless in front of him, like a butterfly pinned to a specimen board, and then pushed back into her, devastatingly slowly.

"Oh god..." she moaned and arched as much as was possible in their position. "Stitch..."

"That's right...such a hungry little cunt," he chuckled. "You take it so well. All that fucking hardware and you don't even flinch."

"I love it," she moaned, her head tilting back against the wall. "So fucking good. Harder. Please, Stitch..."

"So demanding," he teased, stopping his forward slide. "More, Stitch. Harder, Stitch," he mocked her in a high-pitched tone. "You think you have another orgasm in you?"

"For you I can fly," she moaned as her eyes rolled back in her head. "Fuuuck..." Her body tensed as she felt him pound into her harder, his attention on what he was doing. She wrapped her arms around his shoulders and arched to give him more room, and to hold on. He seemed intent on the sight of his cock driving into her, watching the wet slide between them, so she gripped the side of his mask and pulled as she came, screaming his name as his face was revealed to her.

He came too with a heavy grunt, pounding it into her as their skin slapped together. It was almost like he hadn't noticed that the mask was gone, but then he kissed her, soft-hard lips demanding and plundering.

She took it, kissing him back, moaning into their fused mouths, her sheath fluttering for him as he pumped into her, his motions now lazy and perfect. Her brain put two and two together. She had seen his beautiful face before...daily actually. Stitches ran in the same park she did each morning, always smiling and nodding hello. Fuck. The hot runner. Stitches was in her life, too. She ran her fingers through the hair at the nape of his neck, her body satisfied and replete.

"You play a dangerous game," he murmured eventually when his movements had stilled and the kiss had been broken. "I mean, I'm not going to say I didn't enjoy the fuck out of being able to take your mouth and pussy at the same time, but if the others catch us, you're dead." As though the reminder disturbed him, he looked up and down the hallway and then bundled her quickly through the door into his room.

"You can't go pulling this kind of shit with the others," he told her seriously. "I mean, I don't care. I know you won't tell anyone who I am, but the rules are the rules and I don't want you getting yourself killed because you're an impulsive little bitch. You hear me?"

"It wasn't impulsive," she said and smiled at him. "You think I didn't plan this, Stitches?" she asked and pulled him closer, running her mouth over his. "I needed to know who you were. After last year, I needed to know." She nuzzled him. "But I understand," she said softly. "I knew it would be perfect..." she smiled again, dopey, seriously fuck drunk on the man. "I won't fuck up." She looked into his bright hazel eyes, and bit her bottom lip. "I love the way you kiss."

"Well, you might have known I'd let you get away with it because, let's face it, I'm not as fucking serious as the others, but don't go planning this kind of shit with anyone else, okay?" He kissed her again. "I like to hurt you, but I don't want to have to kill you. It'd be a waste of this perfect fucking ass."

And fuck, she liked when he hurt her. She nodded. "That's not my end game, Stitches," she said softly. "This just makes what you are going to do better." She chuckled. "And now I don't feel so bad about fantasizing about the hot runner I see every morning. I mean, he wasn't one of my seven, but he did push my buttons. Now I know why."

His eyes clouded over. "You can't change the way we interact when we see each other outside of here," he told her. "The others can't know that you know who I am. It's too dangerous."

"I wouldn't give the game away, Stitches. Ever. You guys might not understand it, but I like this. I like my life with you seven in it. I don't want that to change." And she meant it. "Nothing changes."

"Okay then." His eyes were still troubled, but he forced a smile. "Be careful, okay?" He kissed her again and then moved away, tucking himself back into his pants. "You can use the bathroom in here to clean up. I'll go send up whoever is next."

"Stitches?" she asked as he went to walk away.

"Yeah?" He paused and turned back to her.

She got up and went to him, pulling him into another kiss. "See you tomorrow." She grinned. "Sleep well."

"You, too." With a last grin, he pulled his mask back on and left the room.

***

Neon found her slumped against the wall, a silly smile on her face. She watched him squat down and run his fingers down her arm.

"Stitches fuck you good?"

She nodded.

"So good." She had loved it, the man taking her hard and fast against the wall. She didn't think she'd had any more orgasms in her after Snake's Sybian, but her Stitches had dragged them out of her anyway. Seeing his face had been the icing on the cake.

First Snake, then Stitches, though Stitches was more amenable to what she did. Neon was going to make number three. She hoped.

"You going to fuck me good as well?"

"I think you know I always deliver."

She smiled at his neon mask, catching his finger when he ran it over her bottom lip, sucking it into her mouth. "And you know just what I want."

Neon was easy. He was obsessed with her mouth and having his cock in it. Tonight would be a quick play for them, which meant tomorrow... She nipped his finger and he hissed.

"On your knees," he ordered and she went to the floor immediately, hands going to his slacks to unbutton and unzip. She had him in her hand in moments, the thick tattooed length heavy in her palm.

"Open." She did and closed her eyes as he gripped her head, shoving his length into her mouth, choking her. She gagged and shivered, trying like hell to relax her throat. Neon was brutal in his attention, fucking her mouth as he gripped her hair, going for long, deep strokes, all but cutting her air off.

Before him, she never thought breath play would be her thing, but with Neon it was a craving. She was soaked, feeling herself dripping down her thighs, both

Stitches' cum and her own. And her nipples ached with how tight they were, reveling in the rough treatment.

"That's a good girl, taking it so well," he grated from behind the mask. She moaned, the vibration on his cock making him hiss. "Ah fuck, this throat is too fucking good..."

She moaned again, her hand squeezing the base like she knew he liked, readying herself. He came with a growl, shooting down her throat and filling her mouth with cum, which she greedily drank down.

"Ah, don't waste a drop," he said as she moaned. When he started to pull back, she licked his shaft, sucking all the fluid off it, pulling back with a pop.

"Present," he ordered and she leaned back, opening her mouth to show him she had swallowed it all, and then darted her tongue out and licked what was at the corner of her mouth. He groaned and had her on her feet in seconds, her knees like jello, weak and barely holding her up, as he pushed her against the wall. Apparently that was going to be the theme of the night with these men.

His fingers found her wet, and she arched as he slipped two of them inside her without resistance. "Such a dirty girl, so wet, cum sliding out of you... So fucking hot. You like being full of cum? Like knowing you sucked me fucking dry?"

She moaned and nodded, her core clenching his fingers. "Good girls get rewards, and you are being so good." He fucked her with his fingers. "Tell me you love it."

"I... oh, I love... Please... Neon!" she screamed as she came, her sheath clamping down on his fingers, and he groaned.

"Oh, that's nice...that's it, flutter...fuck, let's have another."

In her haze she closed her eyes and she felt his hand on her face. "Open. Look at me. Always look."

She opened her eyes as he gripped her throat, and she surrendered to him, her body softening, and she could feel his triumph.

And she reached up and pulled his mask off.

Surprise hit his beautiful face...a face she actually knew, if just in passing. She had seen him before, at the coffee shop, and the shelter fundraiser. Her brain remembered seeing him, thinking he was beautiful, but not one of her seven.

"Em... Emerson?" she breathed. She thought that was his name.

"Fuck." He cursed, but he didn't pull his hand from her body. His eyes looked down at her, startling blue with silver flecks, and she arched into him. Emerson Grant was Neon and he was fucking perfect. "Why did you do that, Pet?" he asked, squeezing her throat. She gasped and licked her lips, the constriction setting her off. She flooded his hand, moaning, and he smirked. "Little cumslut...fuck, you're perfect." He leaned in, his forehead to hers like he normally did with the mask on, and let up on the squeeze.

"*Your* little cumslut," she whispered, her throat raw. "All of yours."

There was a look of regret in his eyes. "I'm going to have to kill you, Pet..."

"If you must, but seeing you changes nothing between us," she said softly.

"Then why do it?" His eyes narrowed. "If it didn't matter..."

"So I know who I'm fantasizing about when I fuck myself?" She arched again. "I needed to know."

He was quiet for long moments, his face giving nothing he was thinking away. "You...you're playing with fire."

"No, I'm playing with you and your glorious cock." She reached between them to squeeze his shaft and he grunted. "Plague likes fire," she offered. "Do what you must, Neon." She used his mask name, letting him know nothing had changed. "I'll go with a smile on my face."

"Well we can't have that," he murmured. "The point of a sacrifice is fear and pain. You need to forget this, Pet." His whisper was light as air. "You can't tell any of them."

"It's between us, Neon," she said softly. "Our secret."

He scoffed. "What's another secret, right?"

Pulling away from her, he stuck his fingers in his mouth and closed his eyes. "Fuck, you taste like peaches. Do you always taste like peaches?" he asked absently and then shook himself and looked to the clock hanging on the wall above her head. "We only have a few moments." He pushed off her. "You need to be blindfolded."

"Kinky," she giggled.

"It will be."

He set her up but didn't say another word, and her mind was reeling, thinking about the fact that she had been successful with three of them, and she knew all three of them from a distance in her daily life. Did she know *all* of them? Arching as he tied her arms behind her back, she looked at him, a question in her eyes.

"So you don't try that again. They aren't like me; they might fuck this up." He leaned in and kissed her lips. "Have fun." He winked as he settled the blindfold over her face and slipped his mask on. Then he was gone and she was alone, void of sight and waiting for what was to come next, a smile gracing her lips.

Chapter 4

"Look at her." She heard Goblin's modulated voice and licked her lips. "And doesn't she look ready?" She was on her knees now, blindfolded, her arms corset-tied behind her back. Neon was good with his ropes. "You ready for us?"

Us? She nodded without hesitation, but a frisson ran through her. Was it all four of them that were left? Or was it just Goblin and someone else?

Gentle fingers touched the crease between her shoulder blades, making her shiver as they traversed her spine and tested the blindfold. She opened her mouth to say something, but a sharp slap made her close it again. Okay, so that's how they wanted to play it.

"I will have to thank Neon for presenting you so perfectly," Goblin said. "We both will."

A sharp intake of breath came from her as she felt fingers pinch her nipples. Rough, they rolled them, and she arched slightly, the pinch sending zings to her core.

"And look how wet her thighs are," she heard Goblin say. "How much of that is you, and how much of that is Stitches?" A hand grabbed her hair and pulled. "Answer."

"Me," she gasped, as her head was wrenched back. "Maybe some is Stitches." She moaned.

"Neon make you come so hard it's all you?" Goblin chuckled. "Well, it's not all you're getting tonight. Heads or tails?" She heard him ask the question, but no one answered. Who was with him? Not knowing was driving her crazy in the best kind of way with anticipation. "Get her in a finger trap? Excellent."

Whoever was behind her moved with precision, binding her fingers in a trap she knew from experience wasn't worth fighting. The more she pulled, the tighter it would get.

She felt herself fall forward, stopped by something with just enough give. Pillows? A bolster?

Something nudged her entrance, thick and hot, now that she wasn't sitting on it. She whimpered as it rubbed against her clit and then slipped into her. She sighed, feeling the invasion, the fullness of whomever was there. It was clear they wouldn't tell, and that was part of the fun. She felt fingers on her jaw as they gently prodded it to open. She did, and closed her eyes behind the blindfold as a cock was slipped into her mouth gently and slowly. She licked, giving over to them both.

There was no warning before a sharp smack stung her ass and she squealed, choking on the cock in her mouth as she automatically jerked away from the sting.

So a fucking and a spanking...okay. She felt hands in her hair again. Whoever was in her mouth gripped her head as they steadied her. She was spanked again and again, at intervals, as she sucked and pushed back on the cock inside her. It was maddening, going so slow, so careful, the careful swats on her ass. Her body was building to an orgasm, working her to a fever pitch.

The moment her skin would start to burn with unbearable stinging, the man behind her would switch to the other side. Who was it? Couldn't be Snake again...he didn't fuck her with his own dick. Couldn't be Stitches...he'd never be able to keep his mouth shut. Was it Plague, maybe? Had he ever played with others? The constant assault on her senses made it hard to think.

Moaning, she heard a groan from in front of her, but with the modulation, it could have been any of them. Not knowing was both hot and frightening. She did trust all seven of them, but this was maddening. She knew Goblin was there because this was his kink.

Sensory deprivation play was quickly becoming one of hers as well, as Goblin always had such care with her. And the orgasms had always been deep and thrumming and sublime.

But now, with the second in the mix, with no indication, the unknown lover kink was high in her mind. Who? Fuck, did it even matter? She moaned again and pushed back on the cock inside her, her control teetering on the edge of orgasm.

Her lower body began to coil and tighten and whoever was behind her clearly felt it because they reached around underneath her to play with her clit.

She shattered with the extra attention, sobbing as she came, the cock in her mouth getting deeper and almost cutting off her air. The asphyxiation set her orgasm rolling again, fluttering over her as she moaned and swallowed on the cock in her mouth. The hands in her hair gripped tighter as she felt them move, tunneling deep into her mouth and throat as the same was being done to her already tender pussy.

Seeing stars in her mind she cried out as she came again, this one hard and heavy, her sheath clamping down hard on whoever was behind her. She was rewarded by the rhythm behind her faltering and then a rumbling groan that she felt rather than heard as whoever it was came hard, filling her up with hot jets of cum.

Whoever was in front of her followed their compatriot, filling her throat full with thick salty cum. She swallowed it down as both cocks were withdrawn from her body and then slumped down and over, panting. The binds on her hands and arms were suddenly gone and she blinked as the blindfold was pulled from her eyes, to see Goblin, just Goblin, in the room.

"You did so well." He ran his fingers up between her breasts. "Rest." She closed her eyes, a smile on her lips. Tomorrow. Tomorrow she would unmask her sweet Goblin, and whoever decided to help him.

Chapter 5

Devil sat by the fire, watching as the others talked quietly in pairs around the room. Something was off, but he couldn't quite put his finger on it. At first, he'd thought Neon was right—the shift in energy was because Petra was acting differently. He'd felt it in her when he'd fucked her with Goblin. The energy stream had felt different as he'd channeled it away from her, and her submission had been...softer...more willing.

But watching his brothers now, he thought there was more to it than that. Stitches was laughing too loud, and if Devil didn't know better, he'd think the guy was avoiding him. Snake seemed uncomfortable. He wasn't a fidgeter, but he was shifting in his seat and playing with a flick knife. Even Neon was off. Something had happened, but he didn't know what and no one was talking.

Clearing his throat, he waited until all eyes were on him and then said, "Does someone want to tell me what the fuck is going on?"

Ghost looked to him. "Plague and I have figured out how we will deal with her before dawn. He will go up shortly and lead her down to the gardens, where I will finish the game."

"That's not what I was asking." Devil shook his head. "You're all twitchy as fuck. Did something happen?"

"Oh. Then I don't know," Ghost said. He was always the first one to speak up, especially if a question was asked, but he wasn't acting off like the others.

Neon sighed, his modulator off. "She's different, and it's got me off balance," he offered. "She wants it, begged for it. Called my name when she came." They all knew how unusual that was. When they'd had her before, she had never acknowledged them by name.

"It's just throwing me off. Got me thinking that she does actually want this in a different way."

"What about you guys?" Devil turned to Stitches and Snake.

"She was more mouthy than usual." Snake shrugged. "Maybe a bit more clingy than usual, too, but then you know I don't get that close to her."

Devil frowned, certain that Snake wasn't telling him everything, but he didn't want to push. Not tonight, not when their harmony as a team was important. "Stitches?" He turned to the other man and wished for once that they didn't have their masks on. Stitches' face was an open book, but behind that dead, stitched skin, it was impossible to tell.

"What Neon said." Stitches shrugged. "She begged for it. Wanted it. Said some nonsense about fantasizing about it all year round."

"That is interesting," Goblin mused. "But not out of the realm of possibility. I mean, we have made it our business to keep her isolated from other men, hell women, if her day to day is any indication. She only talks to friends online. Doesn't have a life outside of work or the volunteering at that shelter. It's plausible that she sees us as more than tormentors or a pact. She is a twisted little thing."

"What are you saying?" Devil frowned. "What's not out of the realm of possibility?"

"That she wants more," Goblin said, turning completely to him. "Surely you felt the difference tonight? I mean, she didn't struggle, didn't fight it and, fuck, that release from her was so fucking potent... He will be pleased, more so than he has been before."

"Yeah, but 'wants more'? What the fuck is that supposed to look like?" Devil shrugged. "There's no point her being here the rest of the year. The veil is only thin enough to feed the Dark God tonight and tomorrow night. If we wanted a more permanent or frequent arrangement, or if we wanted to think about bringing in a woman to start having kids, we'd have to petition the Elders. It's a risk. I'm not sure they'd take it."

Goblin shrugged. "I don't know what that looks like. I do know that she's different, and I know she's lonely. Seeing her at yoga weekly, it's just the feeling I get. She's isolated herself because of us."

Neon sighed once more. "I don't know, either, but I said it before—I feel like we have only been given part of the story. How the fuck is He Who Sleeps supposed to subsist on two nights a year, especially on singular blood sacrifices? Our fathers had our mothers full-time for a few years, and you cannot tell me that they didn't have approval from the Dark God for it. You can't tell me they didn't hold rites in that time, either. If they were fucking, He was feeding."

Their fathers were all gone except Ghost's, who was an Elder. The others had all been sacrificed to the Dark God when the seven came of age to take over their sect. It was the natural progression, according to the Elders, and Neon had long talked about how things didn't add up. It seemed he was thinking about it again and, to a certain extent, he had a point. None of them knew the full details of what had happened to their mothers, or how their fathers' sect worked. By the time any of them were old enough to observe the rites, their mothers were long gone.

"We do have rules," Goblin broke his train of thought, "but who is to say Neon isn't right? There is so much we have been told but they've never backed it up with a scripture or a ritual."

Devil couldn't believe he was about to say this. "Do you...we, collectively, want to go to the Elders then? Demand answers? Ask to keep her? Are you prepared for what the fall-out from that might be? Excommunication from The Order? Even death. Do you all want her enough that you would risk all of that?"

"I would." Stitches was the first to answer, surprising no one. "She's not the only one that's lonely and fantasizing."

"Yes," Neon agreed with a nod. "We have leverage right now. By all accounts, we're raising more power with her than any other group is with the regular sacrifices, and it's getting more potent every year." Their own coffers were filled, the Dark God rewarding them with both power and influence.

"He is right, Devil," Ghosty said. "Stephan confirmed it to me personally. He asked me how we were doing it and I couldn't say because I didn't know. The only difference is her." Stephan, Ghost's father, for all his Elder status, kept up with his progeny and kept them in the know.

"I will...consider it." Troubled, Devil waved a hand to let them all go back to speaking amongst themselves. Even now, the atmosphere was expectant and hopeful, as though they'd all taken fire from the conversation and were burning brightly with it. He needed to think on how he was going to present this to the Elders. One wrong move and even their power and popularity wouldn't save them from the Dark God's wrath.

Chapter 6

Sunlight filtered through the steel grey sheer drapery, rolling across her body as she lay on the massive bed. Checking the clock, she noticed it was almost eleven, and that meant she had only slept about five hours, as Ghost had carried her back to the house from the garden as the sun hit the horizon.

Five hours was nowhere near enough sleep, but she had time for a couple more naps before she would be summoned to dinner, and maybe another nap as she waited for sundown, when she would see her seven once more. Spending the day alone and eating alone weren't her favorite parts of the process, though she was thankful for the reprieve to relax and heal.

Sitting up, she noticed a teapot and covered plate on the small table, just off the cold fireplace, which was a staple of her time there. She was normally a coffee drinker, but the tea was apparently something that helped with healing and her peace of mind, or so the note had said the year before. She didn't knock it, as she had felt better for her second night after consuming it. Slipping from the bed, she gingerly ambled to the table and uncovered the plate. Croissants, a bowl of oatmeal with pineapple, and a cut up peach were there, along with a note from them reminding her to take a long soak. As if she could forget.

Pouring herself a small cup of the herbal tea, she slowly walked into the bathroom and started the tub, dumping the entire bag of the arnica Epsom salts into the massive garden tub, along with some lavender oil to help with her relaxation. The aroma of blueberries and lavender hit her nose and she smiled, sipping from the cup. She prepared towels and a razor and other things she knew she needed for the soak, and then left the tub to fill, to have her breakfast.

She ate quietly, looking out the window to the forest beyond. She knew that night she would be hunted through the forest by Ghosty, his favorite, and she knew she would end that scene with the man himself naked but for the mask and her bent over something hard as he railed her. Ghost was a lot of fun, and she was excited to show him her new speed. Oh, the fun in the garden was more hide and seek with him, but tonight she would be his prey and that knife he constantly carried was going to be front and center. The idea made her shiver.

Was it wrong that she liked his version of foreplay? That the idea that he could slip with that knife was not a deterrent?

"Jesus, I'm turning into a fucking sicko..." she muttered to herself as she stood, popping the last of her peach into her mouth. Feeling more relaxed and alive, she padded into the bathroom and took off her robe, then slid into the hot salty water, sighing as she lay her head back. The water was just to her nipples, the lap of it kissing them as she got herself comfortable. Her body was sore, but enjoyed the water, even with the sting between her thighs. Closing her eyes, she sighed.

"You are stunning when wet," she heard from by her ear, and smiled.

"Neon..." she said softly and turned her head.

"Not right now. Right now I'm just Emerson." He smiled at her. "Want company?"

She nodded. "You sure you're not going to get in trouble?"

He laughed. "The guys are either sleeping or out somewhere."

"And you're not sleeping why?"

"Couldn't. Not when I knew you were here, and you knew who I was."

"Bold of you to come see me."

"How could I not?" He stood and started to take his clothes off, which consisted of sleep pants and a t-shirt. He stepped in and motioned for her to scoot up, then settled behind her, pulling her against his chest, hands on her torso under the water. His knee came up and she ran her fingers over it, softly, enjoying the warmth and silence cocooned in him.

"You doing okay?"

She nodded.

"Good. Tonight is going to be...extra. Originally the plan was to ease you in, see if that changed the potency, but you walking in looking like a fucking gift changed that. None of us were ready for how amazing you looked in that dress."

She smiled to herself, thankful for her yearlong mission to make herself a goddamn snack. "Who picked it out?"

"Goblin," he said. "Plague picked the shoes this year."

"Generous."

"Nothing is too good for our little sacrifice." He leaned forward, running his lips along the shell of her ear. "Honestly, though, who else are we going to spend money on?"

"I don't know. I don't know if you guys have wives or girlfriends or anything..."

"No and no," he chuckled and kissed her shoulder, fingers stroking her belly. "Our lives aren't conducive to relationships. I mean, how do you hide the fact that you murder people, right?"

"You are dudes. I'm sure you are getting your needs met."

"Possibly? Some of us are a bit too...volatile in that respect to be set loose on the public. I can tell you that since you swallowed my cock that first time? It's only been you."

"Romantic." She giggled and leaned back more. "Is that like part of the pact? Do you guys have to follow rules, too?"

"You mean when we're with you, or the rest of the time?"

"I don't even know where to start," she admitted. "I want to know everything."

"I can't tell you much. The seven of us were raised in a cult, and in exchange for keeping a dark god fed, we are gifted lives others would kill for." She heard the smirk in his voice. "Pun intended."

"I see. And the fact that you're fucking insanely hot doesn't throw women at you at all times?"

"No, actually. I'm good natured in my day to day, but I don't get close. I don't date and I don't get attached to anyone. Except the others. Except you," he offered. "You are a constant obsession. To all of us."

"Even Snake?"

"Even Snake," he said carefully. "Why do you think he doesn't like you?"

"He's never touched me unless he's treating me as a tool to be checked for flaws before putting me back in a drawer until next year," she said softly. "Everything is apparatus, nothing is him."

"Ah. Well..." He kissed her again. "He has his needs."

"And they aren't me."

"Does that upset you?"

She nodded but didn't say more. How could she say wanted them all and not seem like she was totally delusional? Though Emerson wouldn't judge her, she was still on the cusp of judging herself.

"You know, it's kinda awesome that I mention the whys of our arrangement, and you don't bat an eye at the idea of a dark god offering favors in exchange for life force."

"Obviously I'm skeptical, but I'm not ruling it out. There's more in this world than we can see, or touch. So, you say you're killing people, and now rearranging my guts for two nights a year, to feed him and it makes a twisted kind of sense. Fucking and dying are two ends of the same spectrum. Whether pageantry, truth or psychosis, I'm all in."

"Which is also baffling to me." He shook his head. "Don't get me wrong; the fact that we get a goddamn smoke show to play with that's down for anything is kinda amazing, but why embrace it?"

"The choice between enjoying what seven talented men do to me, introducing me to things I never would have thought I liked, or being afraid of what my body feels isn't a choice." She turned her head to look up at him. "I don't think you guys understand, but you awoke something in me, something sleeping and needy, and it responds only to you. To them."

Turning completely she went to her knees, hands on his beautiful face. "I miss you all when you're not here. The year alone sucks, and I live for these two nights. I get to feel alive. I get to experience the truth of who I am."

His smile, the look in his eyes, she shivered. "Damn it, Pet..."

Then his lips were on hers and they were kissing, him pulling her into his lap, sitting her on his hips. She moaned, her hips rolling on his lap as she whimpered. Gods, being able to have this, this stolen moment with him.

"Fuck, Pet, you are so fucking sexy." He slid fingers down and into her and she winced, which stopped him cold. "No. You need to heal more."

"But I want..."

"Oh, I didn't say you weren't getting anything. There's something I very much want from you. Something I haven't ever been able to do."

"What? Cuz I have never..." she squealed as he lifted her off him and onto the ledge around the far side of the tub, sitting her on the towel there. They kissed and then he was sliding down while lifting her hips to his mouth.

"Holy shit..." she moaned and arched hard into what his tongue was doing to her clit. It was like a balm, long sure strokes to her poor abused clit calmed through his onslaught. "Em... Fuck, Emerson, that's sooo good..." Her body shook as a lazy orgasm rolled up her spine and she sobbed, the softness, the deep thrum sending her into outer space.

"Peaches everywhere," she heard him say, realizing she was back in his arms, in the water, snuggled close.

"Did I...how did I get back in the water?"

"I pulled you down after watching you sigh and twitch with that lovely orgasm. Do you know how long I have wanted to get my face between these thighs?" He nipped her shoulder. "Fucking peaches. You are fucking addictive."

She giggled. "That why you left me the peach?"

"Obviously." He pulled her closer. "You need a nap, yeah?"

"Will you stay with me 'til I fall asleep?" He nodded. "Good. You are comfy, Emerson."

Moments later she was under blankets, yawning and cuddling with him. "If I sleep..."

"You are halfway there, love. Sleep, trust. I will see you later."

"No, Neon will see me later."

He chuckled. "Yes he will, and you will enjoy it."

She nodded, well aware he was right, and slipped off into dreams.

Chapter 7

Dinner was happening. When she woke from her hours long nap, Neon was gone, and there had been a dress laid out for her, as well as shoes. She knew from the year before that dinner would be alone in the sitting room attached to her bedroom, and then she would have a few hours to rest, digest and relax before the main night would begin.

She had showered, dried her hair, and put on small amounts of makeup, then donned the slinky silk slip dress in emerald green, the slit over her leg rising all the way to her groin. She felt sexy, and the silk against her body was sensual in a way she didn't often feel. She had slipped her feet into the shoes, open-toe wedges in green velvet, and shook out her hair before walking into the study, famished for dinner.

She smiled to see Stitches sitting on the table, a glass of something in his hand. "Hi." She couldn't seem to stop grinning. "This is a pleasant surprise. Did you pick this out?" She motioned to her body.

"Nah, I'd have put you in red," he admitted. "You look good enough to eat, though."

"You like red? I'll have to remember that." She grinned and walked toward him, taking the glass he offered her. "Thank you." Taking a sip, she closed her eyes at the crisp flavor of the sweet wine. "How was your day? Get any sleep?"

"I slept like the dead." With an easy grin, he slid off the table and kissed her cheek before moving to one of the seats. "How about you? Did you sleep?"

She nodded. "I always sleep well here. I don't know if it's the bed, or whatever is in the tea, or the fact that the seven of you wear me the fuck out," she gave him a cheeky grin as she settled into her own chair, "but I slept about five hours, then woke, had breakfast, a long soak in the tub," where Neon had seen her through some wonderful time together, "and then took another nap. Woke up about an hour ago." She lifted the lid on the meal in front of her and smiled.

A salad with pears and cheese to start, followed by grilled baby vegetables, quinoa, and mushrooms in a wonderful smelling broth greeted her. She was a vegetarian, and they clearly took that seriously. "Wow..." she offered and looked to him. "This smells amazing. Have you eaten already?"

"No, we all eat together in a bit. I just thought I'd sneak in and say hi...spend some time with you, now that I don't have to wear my mask." He paused, frowning temporarily. "I hope it goes without saying that you can't tell the others anything about this."

"Well, I could be coerced into not saying something," she said cheekily, clearly teasing him. "Provided you tell me something."

"What do you want to know?" he asked, sipping his drink. "I'm an open book."

"So many things...but we can start with your name?" She cut a piece of carrot and bit into it, closing her eyes at the incredible flavor. Whoever cooked this was a genius.

"Leo," he said, easily enough. "But you can call me whatever you want."

"You're Stitches when you have the mask on," she said to him as she took another dainty bite. "But you, you are Leo." She nodded and accepted it. "You run with me in the morning. Are you all in my life in some way?"

"I can't tell you that," he hedged carefully. "In truth, I don't know all of it. But I can't tell you what I do know. It's not safe. It's one thing to know me and quite something else to unmask the others."

"That's not what I'm asking. I was just thinking that if you were close then odds are the others are, too." She knew at least two of them were in her life, if not directly. Neither had spoken to her before in real life, but they had been there. "But it's okay, you don't have to tell me. I would say I could answer questions, but I'm pretty sure you know everything about me," she said wryly. "So tell me about why we are in this in the first place. Some god?"

"The Dark God," he confirmed. "He Who Sleeps. We're part of a small but global organization that benefits from his powers, but in return, we must feed him the life force he needs to be sustained. Until we met you, that was with human sacrifices. Now, through our contract, we can harness the life force from your and our orgasms and feed him that instead."

"And is that better? I mean is it better than just killing some rando girl?" She met his gaze directly. "I take it virgin blood isn't something that He wants, considering what you guys to do me."

"No, He just needs life force," he explained. "Doesn't have to be anyone special. Unfortunately, girls are easy targets in the city. Especially when you've got a handsome face." He grinned widely, winking at her.

"Gotta admit, if you wanted to lead me to my doom, I just might let you." She winked back. Gods, she liked being there with him. "So, do you like to run or are you just doing it to see me?"

"I like to run. Mostly because I love doughnuts," he laughed. "You're a wonderful bonus."

She giggled and shook her head. "So tonight..."

"Oh, you know what I'm going to do to you tonight," he smirked. "Needles. Lots of needles. And red ribbon, the color of your blood. I don't know about the others, though. I know Devil is coming to you first."

So Devil was first... "And you? When we play, will you do it without your mask?" she asked and swallowed. Gods, did she want him to work on her as himself. "Or is the kink part of the mask/pact situation?"

"It was part of the kink at first," he replied thoughtfully. "But now...I don't know. I feel like maybe without the mask would be more intimate. What would you prefer?"

"Without," she said with no hesitation. "Can I tell you something?"

"You can tell me anything," he replied, sitting down.

She got up off her chair and went to him, slipping into his lap. "When you first did it, I was scared, but the care... It put me at ease. I have researched, and I have come to grips with the fact that I like it. I like being your little pin cushion; I like what you do to me...and last year it was really good." She blushed and dipped her head, remembering how hard she had come for him. "But it would have been perfect if you'd kissed me after."

"Then I can do that," he agreed, squeezing her close. "Thank you for telling me."

She leaned in and nuzzled his neck. "I like that I can. I like that you want me to," she said softly. "And I like that you do this to me, Leo. I wouldn't trust anyone else to." And that was more than true. Each of them had their things, but to switch it up...she didn't think she could handle that. She heard about women that had just retreated into themselves to escape their trauma, and most would probably call what her seven did to Petra as creating trauma, but she didn't think of it that way. Not that first night, not now. She felt like she was made to find these men, to serve them how they

66

needed. She endured and she was rewarded. Tonight she would get the rest.

After tonight, she wouldn't be alone anymore if she could swing it. She could have Leo *and* Stitches. She could enjoy both—Leo all year and then Stitches these two days? She could see it. Though she could get down with the mask through the year, too. She still didn't understand it all, but she was willing to play to be with them.

"Can I tell you something else?"

"Anything." He was gazing at her with unabashed adoration, and it was quite touching, despite the fact that she knew he was a cold-blooded killer.

"You make me feel safe," she said softly and kissed him, snuggling close, wrapping herself around him. Lord but she wanted hours of making out with this man.

"You know I'd kill anyone that hurt you," he said bluntly when they came up for air. "You're special to me, to us. You are safe within these walls. We might come close to breaking you. We might leave you sore and bruised. But our promise still stands—we'd never hurt you permanently, however much Plague wants to brand his name on you."

She shivered with the idea of that. "I would take it, if it meant I could keep you all," she said softly, knowing she could with him. "Because I know it's not to harm me, but to own me. You all do already." She kissed him again, nipping his full bottom lip.

"We're not going anywhere," he said, looking slightly confused. "We'll be here next year, and the year after. As long as you're willing to fulfill the pact."

She wanted more, wanted it all. "That's the *pact*. I want you beyond that. Life gets lonely when I only feel alive for two days a year."

"All of us?" To her surprise he didn't seem to be averse to the idea. He certainly wasn't freaking out the way Snake had.

She nodded. "You don't think you guys consume my entire life? I can't imagine my life now without the idea of you seven in it."

"Well yeah, but we're also hard on you for the time we have you. Do you think, physically, you could take this every night of the year?"

"Do you think you would want to do this every night? You wouldn't want just...I don't know, to have time with me like we are now? I'm not against living this two-day life every day if I have to. It beats being lonely without you all."

"Probably not," he said after a pause, and she appreciated that he was taking the time to give it real thought. "I don't know how it would work, though. We'd have to talk about it. Maybe weekends. You're going to have to sleep sometime."

She laughed. "Having the seven of you in my life all year...spending time with you...the naughty is a plus. I want to know you, and you know I'm trustworthy. I want this. If I'm the one you come to for this, the one that welcomes it, and I do by the way..." she let it hang. "I want to be with you, for real, and not just as part of your pact, but as more."

"Leave it with me," he told her. "I'll speak to Devil and the others. But..." he trailed off and sighed. "You know it might not to be up to us, right? Just because this works, the pact works, doesn't mean the Elders will automatically approve your entrance into The Order."

"I don't want to be in The Order, Leo, I want to be *yours.*" She cupped his beautiful face. "If I have to join The Order? Sure. If I'm your forever sacrifice, I'm okay with that, too." Leaning in, she kissed him again. They were quiet for long moments before she tilted her head to look at him. "Tell me about you. I mean, I know you like to run, and you like watching me, and sticking needles in my skin, and you like piercings." She palmed him through his slacks.

"You know I like doughnuts and red dresses, too," he joked. "But I have a whole life outside The Order, outside these nights. Would you believe me if I said I own a small pharmaceutical company?"

"Yes, because that tracks," she giggled. "What got you into it? I mean besides the needles?"

"Frustration, I guess," he replied, looking sad. "We're doing research and clinical trials on mushroom-derived treatments for depression. They've known about it since the seventies, but for some reason no one has managed to get a drug FDA approved and it's costing thousands of people their lives every year. I thought I could change that."

Gods her heart...her sexy needle-wielding psycho wanted to help people. The juxtaposition was almost comical. She kissed him. "That is noble and pure," she whispered to him. "I love that. A friend of mine passed in high school, killed herself because of depression." She swallowed down the ache in her throat. "We miss her every day."

"And it's so preventable!" His passion for his work was evident in the anguish in his eyes. "They know it works! The evidence is overwhelming. But we have to tick all the boxes and dot all the I's and cross all the T's. We're closer than anyone has ever been before, though." He took a deep breath and seemed to relax his shoulders by sheer force of will. "I'm sorry about your friend. I know it bothers you that we killed before we met you, but I use the gifts the Dark God gives me to drive the research forward. It's a balance."

"The deaths didn't bother me like you'd think," she said after a few moments. "Like yes, gut reflex? It felt wrong, but it wasn't the death that felt wrong...people die every day for something larger than themselves. It just *felt* wrong." She shrugged. "But when you caught me, I was scared, but it didn't feel wrong. Does that make sense?"

"Not really." He smirked and she swatted him. "But seriously, your lack of self-preservation skills are really quite impressive," he teased. "No fear at all this year, despite how crazy we get."

"It feels...I don't know...right?" She grasped for the words. "Look, I was seriously closed off before you guys, and you opened me up to things that, yes, scare me, but also ended up making me feel so good. It's not like I learned to like the things you did; it's more like I was introduced to things I already liked." She smirked. "I trust you, all of you, because it doesn't feel like I'm like others," she offered. "Death, killing...some people just need to die, and some people enjoy killing. I have done a lot of research on the subject, trying to understand you seven, and I'm not averse to blood, or killing, but it has to feel right, Leo. Otherwise, what's the point?"

"Do you believe in fate?" he asked her curiously. "I didn't, not really, until just now. But I can't think of any other explanation for how we just happened to stumble across a woman that just gets us."

"I...I guess? Honestly, I wasn't sure what happened that first weekend was a good thing at first. Then I realized that I was alive, and happy, only with you."

"You were so cute that first year," he chuckled. "My god...you were like a deer in the headlights. You kept squeaking." She jostled around as he burst out laughing.

"I was thrust into a wild forty-eight hours with seven dudes that might kill me! Before you guys I had only been with two men. Total. I think a little squeaking could be forgiven!"

"Really?" He seemed stunned by that. "But like, long-term relationships? Because you sure knew how to fuck like a champ, even scared out of your wits."

She laughed. "Thanks?" She shook her head. "That might have been just because I knew my life was hanging in the balance? My inner porn star just showed up." She giggled. "But only one was long-term—Ted, my high school sweetheart. He broke up with me in the first year of college. Then there was Lewis. That lasted about a month before he cheated on me as well." She shrugged "After that? It had been...over a year? Yeah, about sixteen months. Between Ted and Lewis? Twenty-four months." She shook her head. "I wasn't popular, and neither of them were any good." She winked.

"They both cheated on you?" His jaw dropped and then his eyes went stormy. "Ted and...Lewis? Their days are numbered. Assholes."

"Ted and I, we were kids. I never thought it would be forever. I was surprised it lasted into college. He's happy now, with a wife, and twins on the way. He was a good guy, and he found what he was looking for. The girl he was with? He's still with her now. Lewis, I never understood why he asked me out in the first place, but..." she shrugged.

"I don't care. He could be Mother fucking Teresa and his days are still numbered. If you haven't figured out yet that we're the only people allowed to hurt you, then you haven't been paying enough attention." His watch beeped and he cursed. "I have to go. It's dinner time with the others and I don't want to get caught in here without my mask." He rose up, lifting her easily, and settled her back in her chair. "Eat your dinner like a good girl and get some more rest. I'll be stabbing you later." He winked and sauntered toward the door.

"I'll be waiting," she offered and watched him walk out, eyes on his fabulous ass. "Be good, Leo," she said softly as he walked out and he paused in the doorway, eyes alight with mischief.

"I think you meant to say 'be *baaaad*, Leo.' You know that's how you love me." With a wink and an air kiss, he walked out, leaving her quietly laughing behind him.

Chapter 8

Snake sat down in his usual spot at the dinner table, waiting for his brothers to arrive. Devil was already seated, too, but he could hear the others moving around in their rooms and someone coming down the stairs.

"You okay?" Devil asked him and Snake nodded.

"Weird vibe this year," he said, unsure how else to put it. "I don't remember her being this sassy last year."

"Yeah, something is definitely different." Devil looked thoughtful and it was on the tip of Snake's forked tongue to tell his leader about the mask thing, but then Goblin walked in and the moment was lost.

"Everything is settled," he said to Devil. "Ghost is on the phone with Stephan right now, and I think we need to see the well here before we see Petra." He looked to Snake. "You good?"

"Yeah, man. You?" Snake wasn't a sociable person by choice. Learning to be around his brothers had been a process, and he'd never stopped being grateful for their understanding. He certainly had more freedoms and alone time than some other groups in The Order allowed their members. Devil might be a killer and a sociopath, but he was a good man to have on your side.

"Five by five," he offered and sat as Ghost walked in.

"Stephan says the well in the Balkans is frothing," he said by way of greeting. "And it's the first time it has done that in over a century. He is pleased." He pulled out his knife, twisting it slowly, the tip pushed against his finger.

"Interesting," Goblin offered.

"What's interesting?" Stitches skidded in, no doubt thinking he was late.

"Apparently the well is frothing," Devil told him. "First time in over a century."

"It's got to be us," Stitches said, taking a seat. "Things are different this year."

Snake stilled in his seat. Yes, things were fucking different this year. Petra had a fucking death wish, playing her silly games with his mask. He wondered if she'd tried it on any of the others.

"If it's harnessing extra energy, then it's positive," Devil said. "The question is whether it will continue to increase year on year."

"Yeah...about that..." Stitches was actually blushing. "I stopped in to check on Petra before I came down. She got some sleep and she's eating her dinner, but she had some interesting things to say."

"Since when have we checked in on her?" Snake demanded. "That's not part of the rules, Stitches!"

"Everything is different this year," Stitches shrugged and, just for a second, Snake felt a bolt of loathing for his brother. His nonchalance would be their undoing one day. "Anyway, she said she wants to stay. She wants more from us than just two nights a year."

"I'm sorry, what?" Goblin said as both Plague and Neon entered.

"What's going on?" Neon asked and looked at each of them. "What the fuck did we miss?"

"Petra just announced to Mr. Big Mouth here that she wants to be with us more than just two nights a year," Devil said, looking as stunned as Snake felt.

"That tracks," Neon said and settled into his own chair as Plague did as well. "When did you see her?"

"On the way down just now," Stitches said, but Snake didn't let him elaborate.

"What do you mean 'that tracks'? Did she say something to you, too?"

"Kinda?" He shrugged. "I mean her mouth was largely occupied when I was with her," he offered with a smirk to his friends, "but she did say something to that effect."

"So she's cognizant and willing this year," Goblin said. "She was willing with us, and now the well is frothing with power..." He looked to Devil. "You think her acceptance, nay, eagerness, is the reason?"

"Maybe..." Devil was frowning, but he didn't seem averse to the idea, and Snake swallowed the turmoil swarming up his gullet. "We need to discuss this with the Elders," he said before anyone else could pitch in. "It's not our decision to make. We all know the pact is an experiment that no other woman has agreed to before."

"Which is why this is so interesting, though I daresay no other woman has been given the option before us," Goblin interjected.

"But there must be some precedent," Stitches said. "Some of our mothers stuck around long-term."

"Mine did," Neon said. So had Plague's and Devil's. Ghost's had died in childbirth, which left him being raised by Stephan alone...which explained a lot about him. "And by all accounts, my dad loved her," Neon offered. "Do you remember growing up? They were all happy. They were all excelling in what they chose to do."

"If Petra is the reason for the frothing, or at least her acquiescence is, then it stands to reason that she could be that all year. Her willing participation in what we do to her can only please Him."

"Some of us came from the orphanage," Snake said flatly. "So no, I don't remember a happy childhood." The happiest memory of his childhood was slicing the throats of the foster parents that had been molesting him. The soft squelching sound still made a thrill run down his spine. Even at twelve, he'd been smart enough to cover his tracks. In hindsight, he obviously hadn't been smart enough because someone in The Order had figured it out and recruited him. Or maybe it was the Dark God himself, watching over His newfound son. Maybe it was destiny.

"Anyway, the veil is only thin enough at this time of year to feed the Dark God," Devil reminded them.

"Unless what's coming from her is strong enough to nourish Him even when the veil falls," Stitches suggested. "If the well is frothing now, only one night in, there's nothing to say they can't harness her essence the rest of the year."

"Nothing to say *we* can't harness it through the year," Goblin said. "Which I'm not averse to."

Neon nodded. "Could we do that? I mean the seven of us? Share a woman?"

"We haven't had a problem so far," Stitches pointed out. "And it's not like we're all home all the time anyway. At least half of us are away on business any given week."

"I am not okay with this!" Snake was trying not to hyperventilate, but this was a level of intimacy he just wasn't prepared for. "She doesn't get to just spring this on us! What the fuck does she know, anyway? She's been with us for all of six nights and that's enough for her to suddenly want the happy ever after? She's delusional!"

There was a shocked silence as everyone stared at him and then Plague cleared his throat. "This isn't going to be a thing that happens quickly, my brother," he said softly. "We'll have to ask permission...discuss it at length with the Elders...decide amongst us how we think it might work. We can make as many plans as you need and give you as much time as you need to make you feel comfortable."

"And if it's not your thing, we can plan around that, too," Devil said firmly. "You don't have to do or agree to anything you don't want to do."

But everything would change. Snake knew that, deep in his soul. They were all in, or they were broken. He would break them. "Do you all feel the same?" he asked, hating that his voice broke. "Given the chance, would you keep her all year?"

"I would give my left nut to keep her," Neon said. "A woman that can handle all seven of us? A woman that *wants* the things we give her? I'm all fucking in."

Goblin nodded to them. "I see her more often than you all do. She's lost all year, until the end of September. Then she starts to come alive. All the rest of the time, she kinda just haunts the world she's in."

"I'm in," Stitches said, as though anyone had been in doubt.

"I'm...interested in the idea," Plague said, with an empathetic look toward Snake.

"I'm in, too," Devil said. "I don't think it would give any of us pleasure to kill her if it all goes wrong, but I'm willing to take the risk."

"She lets me chase her," Ghost said. "I'm *not* giving that up. And if I can mess with her all year?"

"Then I guess I need to get on board," Snake said dully, wondering how to get his head around it. There was time. He knew there was time. He could figure it out. But whatever happened, he wasn't going to be the one that broke the brotherhood.

Chapter 9

Petra opened her eyes after her final nap to a purple and pink scene out the windows. Twilight had fallen and she was due with her seven shortly. She gave herself a mental check of her body and any twinges. None. It was a godsend, that tea, having healed her up, not leaving so much as an irritation.

Leaving the bed, she walked across the room to see what was waiting for her in a large black box. She opened it with an arched brow. "You have got to be kidding..." she said as she pulled the latex nun's costume from the paper. "Good thing I know how to put this on without help." She shook her head, wondering what the point of the gorgeous green dress had been, and walked into the bathroom to get the powder.

Twenty minutes later she was snapping the latex bodysuit between her thighs. The thigh-highs were latex, along with the habit, all black with white bands. Devil was one kinky son of a bitch, but she couldn't deny that wearing the latex made her feel sexy and needy. And this shit was not cheap.

She picked up the small note, written on black paper with a silver marker.

Meet me at the Cathedral.

Thankfully she knew where that was, considering it was Devil's domain. Both her scenes with him last year had been there, defiling the space with cries of need and submission. Tonight, she would unmask the man that had her body thrumming with his need to see her encased in rubber, and she would tell him just how much he made her feel.

She left the room, tottering down to the path on five-inch heels, noticing the stone paths were lit with torches. Night had fallen in her bid to get ready, and she stood in the growing darkness, readying herself. The path meandered into the dark forest, and she took her time, not wanting to work up a sweat, or fall and break something, seeing as the stones weren't level.

Ten minutes after she left the house, she saw the spire, the cathedral lit up from the inside, making the stained glass glow, both inviting and ominous. Steeling herself, she walked forward, and up the stairs to the double doors.

The walk was part of it for Devil, his need to mess with her head front and center, but he didn't realize that while the walk was meant to throw her off, she was eager to see what was waiting for her beyond the doors. Pushing them open, she stepped through.

It was impossible not to gasp at the scene revealed before her. The ruined church was lit up inside with hundreds of black and blood red candles, an unholy fire with the devil at its heart. He waited at the dais before the altar, dressed in black robes. "Come and kneel before me and tell me your sins," he told her, his modulated voice echoing oddly around the building.

She sauntered down the aisle, giving him time to look over her in the get up he had put her in, her hips swaying as she walked. As she made it to him, she lowered herself to her knees, landing on a velvet pillow, and looked up to him with a smile.

"Bless me, Devil, for I have sinned. It's been one year since my last confession."

"And what sins have you committed since your last confession?" he asked.

"I was lazy," she began, lowering her head. "Not exercising as much as I should. And I ate way too much ice cream, because I was lonely." She thought for a second. "And I lusted, over seven men, constantly, to the point where I touched myself more than once. I lied about a dog not being nice, because I didn't trust the person that wanted it. And I had impure thoughts..." she looked up, "About you."

"Your ass would beg to differ about the exercise." There was a flash of teeth as he grinned behind the mask. "But the rest? Naughty-naughty... Before I give you your penance, I think you'd better elaborate on these...impure thoughts..."

She licked her lips and then swallowed, her hands clasped in front of her. "I fantasized often, about you punishing me for my sins," she began, "With the paddle." She shivered, remembering the year before when he had swatted her ass while making her say hail Marys, "And then rewarding me for being your pious little girl." She looked up. "And taking that mask off you, looking in your eyes before I sink to my knees to worship at your altar..."

A low growl rumbled from under his mask. "You can kiss my cock with that dirty little mouth of yours."

She nodded, biting her bottom lip. "Can I look in your eyes when I do?" she asked him, tongue snaking out to run along her top lip. "I want to see heaven when I taste salvation."

"You can look all you want," he told her.

Was he telling her he would take his mask off for her? Either way she was primed, ready for him to inflict his brand of pleasure on her. She looked up at him, waiting for him to move, for him to give her direction.

"I said you could kiss it," he snapped, impatient. "Have you forgotten how your hands work?"

Was it bad that his anger got her as hot as his praise? She reached forward, parting the robes to find him there, waiting and hard. Leaning forward, she placed her lips on the tip and then licked him, tasting the salty precum he had produced for her. Fuck but Devil was beautiful. He was physical perfection, the perfect length and girth, and he flushed so perfectly. Nothing overly red or purple, he had the kinda cock they took pictures of for filthy magazines. She kissed him again, rolling her eyes up as she opened her mouth and laved the underside with her tongue, then licked up to the tip, and kissed again.

He hissed with pleasure and threw his head back, murmuring something under his breath that she couldn't quite hear but sounded like prayer.

Emboldened, she reached forward and placed her hands on his thighs as she swallowed down his perfect cock, and then pulled off, moaning as she did. Fuck, he was perfect. Running her nails across his thigh, she gripped his sac and tugged sweetly as she slipped him back down her throat.

"Tell me...how many times have you come with my name on your lips?" he asked her.

"This month?" she asked, pulling back. "Or this year?"

"That many..." He was amused. She could feel the deep rumble of his laugh as she took his cock in her mouth again. "To be fair, I've fantasized about you a fair few times this year. And God has been good."

She sucked hard, loving the knowledge that he thought about her, and then pulled off. "What's your fantasy, my Devil?"

"I'm living it," he promised her. "Right now."

She shivered, feeling her nipples tighten under the latex, the action slightly painful. "What would it take to absolve me of my sins, my Devil? I am tarnished and I need to be purified." Him standing there, naked under the robe, wearing that mask.... She wanted, needed more. "The body? The blood? Absolution in His name?" she asked. "For him, you sacrifice?" Their parody of the faith had him pulsing in her grip.

"You need to be anointed," he told her. "So stop talking and start sucking."

Whimpering, she sucked him, working him with her mouth and hand like she knew he liked, her other hand massaging his sac, pulling and squeezing at intervals, whimpering when he punched his hips forward, taking him deeper. Her tongue rolled as she got into it, coming up on her knees so she could take him at a more prominent angle, taking him deeper.

"That's it. Take it." He placed a hand on her head, his thumb tracing benedictions across the skin of her forehead, even as he forced his way down her throat.

Tears sprang from her eyes as he would tunnel deep, then hold it there, and she would squeeze his sac and moan as he retreated. It was a dance, one that was making her more and more turned on.

"God...so fucking good," he choked out, pulling out so he could come all over her face. "Now say thank you," he commanded.

"Thank you, my Devil," she moaned and stuck her tongue out, closing her eyes as he anointed her, giving her everything.

He smeared his cum into her skin, dragging it into her mouth and coating her tongue with it. "Now swallow," he commanded, his fingers still in her mouth.

She swallowed, sucking his fingers and looked up to him. "Amen," she said as he pulled them from her mouth.

"Stand up." He reached into the recesses of his robe and produced a wicked-looking knife. "If you don't want to spill any blood, you should stay very still," he warned her. Bending down, he caught the bottom of the dress and slowly, carefully, sliced through it. The latex peeled away from her skin, exposing it to the cold night air.

With a shudder she kept still, but felt it as he nicked her. Heat bloomed inside her, and she bit her lip waiting for his next direction. Her dark priest had her shaking moments later.

"The blood of the sacrificial lamb," he said, noticing the blood with no apology. "Shed freely and without duress." He smeared that across her skin, too, a dark red slash across her lower belly. "Fucking beautiful."

"I am yours, freely and without duress," she repeated after him, bowing her head. "Always, my Devil."

Once the latex was sliced all the way open, he pushed the remnants of it off her shoulders, leaving her standing there in the latex wimple and thigh-high stockings. "Such a sight," he murmured, walking around her slowly, taking in the view. He paused behind her, before sharply yanking the wimple off. The latex caught on her hair, jerking her head back, but before she could regain her balance, the knife was at her throat and his mouth was at her ear. "Would you die for me, sinner?"

"Yes," she said without question. "I'm yours, and at your command, my Devil."

"Right answer." The knife slipped away and he pushed her forward. "Bend over the altar. Face down." He waited until she complied and then bent over her. At first she hadn't realized what he was doing, but then she saw the mask he set down on the altar by her face.

"Nuh uh uh," he warned, shoving her back down roughly the moment she tried to straighten up and look, holding her head down on the uneven stone. "The moment you make a single move to look at me, this all ends. Tell me you understand."

"Yes, my Devil," she said, his voice, true voice, hissing in her ear as she rolled her hips. Fuck, he sounded sexy.

He kicked her feet apart and then strong, deft fingers slid through the folds between her thighs. "You're excited," he remarked, that soft ring of amusement so much sexier in his actual voice. "Not that I doubted you would be. You're a perverse little creature." With his wet hand, he smacked her, hard, and she squealed as it stung and burned. "You mark so beautifully," he murmured. For a few moments there was nothing but a soft rustle of cloth, and then his teeth were on the burning spot he'd smacked and he was biting down, hard.

"Ah fuck!" she screamed and pushed back. "Fuck, yes! Mark me, my Devil. Make me yours..." Her eyes closed and she shivered, feeling her core clench. Fuck, she liked his hands on her, his teeth in her flesh.

And fuck it hurt, but the pain was pushing into pleasure, and quickly. "Gods...please..."

He pulled back. "If you come, this ends," he snapped. "You'll come when I tell you to and not before." She barely had a moment to agree before he sank his teeth into the other pert cheek to mark that, too.

"Fuck!" she screamed and gritted her teeth, trying like hell to follow his instruction. She didn't want this to end. Devil's kink was a lot of fun for her, and their sex was...transcendent. Gods, but she needed to see him, to know who brought her to the threshold time and time again.

He scattered bite marks across her ass until it stung from cheek to cheek, and she knew she would be feeling it when she sat down for days to come, if not weeks. "Such a pretty picture." He admired his work for a moment and then smacked it, making her jump and squeal again. "But you have not quite yet been defiled to the Dark God's satisfaction." He tapped gentle fingertips on her spine as he made a show of thinking. "Hmmm... What to fuck you with," he said. "Maybe a lit candle? Maybe...a crucifix? Hmmm..."

"That beautiful cock I need so badly?" she said, still facing forward. "You can cause havoc with that alone." She wasn't averse to the other things, because she knew that he wouldn't damage her, not this early in the night.

"Not yet. The night is yet young, my impatient little nun. You need to control yourself."

"I'm impatient for you, my Devil," she moaned. "And you teasing me with this," she gripped his mask sitting next to her, "it's the worst torture."

"Why do you think I do it?" he tutted, making fun of her. "Fucking with your head is my life's greatest work."

She moaned. "I'm yours to play with, my Devil," she said and bit her lip. "The candle?" She knew feeling the hot wax on her thighs was going to feel interesting.

"Oh, I wasn't giving you the choice," he said. "I was just thinking aloud."

"So, what is your pleasure?" she asked and rolled her hips, causing cool air to hit her wet thighs.

"My pleasure is that you cease your bleating, Little Lamb, so that I can think." He smacked her again, and then she heard footsteps as he paced around. "Maybe some rosary beads up that tight little ass of yours," he teased. "All this time, I should have been spanking you with a hymn book. Or a bible."

He paced around a little more and then paused. "I definitely think a candle," he said. "I like the element of danger. Will I let it get close enough to burn you? Will the wax sear those peachy little thighs of yours? What size will I use? Some of these pillar candles are fucking huge."

85

"My penance is your choice, my Devil," she whispered, her body strung tight. "I only wish to be absolved in the eyes of my Devil."

"I told you to stop bleating!" Hot wax splattered across the bruised and bitten curves of her ass.

Biting back a moan, she nodded, the wax searing as it splashed.

He ran a trail of it up her spine and it burned like lava. She'd be feeling this for days to come, too. Luckily she'd stocked up on burn treatments after she'd learned how Plague liked to play with fire. Better to be safe than sorry. Her big mouth was always getting her in trouble. She couldn't help it. Another burning streak of wax trailed across her buttocks and then she felt the broad, blunt end of the candle pressing inexorably against her cunt.

Gritting her teeth as not to make a sound, she closed her eyes, enduring what he did, trying hard to not let herself enjoy it.

He thrust it into her, the smooth wax sliding easily against the wet walls of her pussy, almost uncomfortably wide. He had to be using one of the big ones.

A whimper escaped her, and she was unsure if it was a good or a bad one. The burn inside her was there, the stretch something she wasn't really ready for.

"That's it. Take your punishment like a good girl," he soothed, his soft tone belying the way he rammed the smooth cylinder into her.

The praise had her sobbing, grasping at his mask next to her.

"It'll be over soon," he promised, stepping back and leaving the candle deep inside her.

She nodded. "I didn't tell you my biggest sin, my Devil..." she gasped as she felt the wax run down her thigh as she wiggled.

"And what was that, Little Lamb?"

She moaned, closing her eyes. "That I want you, My Devil, and the others, forever. I want more than tonight, to be yours, to endure for you." The words came out as sobs. "Please... Please..." She was so close to orgasm that she couldn't stop herself from begging.

Her body tightened to the point of forcing the candle out, and it clattered to the floor. "You have been a bad girl." There was a shuffle as he made sure it was out and wouldn't start a fire, and then she heard footsteps as he walked away, followed by the creaking of old wood. He had to be sitting in one of the pews.

She could picture it almost, the robed figure in the shadows gazing up at her, splayed over the altar in some unholy vision of the profane. And yet she couldn't see his face. It was infuriating. Briefly she wondered what the punishment would be if she snuck a glance at him, but Devil was absolute. If he said he would stop and walk away the second she broke his rule, he fucking meant it. The desire to turn and see his face was so strong it was mind-bending, but the desire to be fucked, to feel that glorious cock in the aching space left by the candle, was stronger.

Silence fell as he simply looked upon her shame. Outside, an owl hooted softly and the wind rustled through the trees. Something somewhere scratched against the chapel wall. She couldn't even hear him breathing. For a moment she wondered if he'd got up and left. Surely she'd have heard the wood creaking again?

Or maybe he'd faked that. Maybe he wasn't sitting down at all and was standing somewhere nearby, waiting to strike if she faltered. Or maybe he'd just left her there and there was nothing holding her to the altar except her own submissiveness.

"Please." Her whisper was soft, the plea a need of its own. She wasn't sure what she was even asking for at this point, all she knew was she needed.

"Have you suffered enough?" So he *was* still with her, but it was a loaded question and she didn't know what he expected her to answer. If she said yes and he didn't think she had, he would be disappointed and it was anyone's guess what the punishment would be. If she said no, she knew she'd get something even worse.

"Only if you feel I have, my Devil. I am yours."

"Good answer." The wooden pew creaked again and then she felt him coming toward her, the soft slumping rustle of his robes hitting the floor making her heart race.

Biting back a groan she hissed when she felt him near, but not touching. Gods, she wanted to see him, wanted to know him so badly.

Her prayers were finally answered when the thick head of his cock nudged at her entrance.

"Devil!" she screamed and shuddered as he touched her. "Please..."

"Please what?" He was sliding in excruciatingly slowly, strong hands holding her down against the rough stone of the altar so she couldn't push back against him.

"This! Oh, fuck yes, this." She squeezed him with her inner muscles and sobbed. The feel of him inside her, the slow drill into her body, it was driving her crazy. She held the orgasm at bay, wanting so badly to be his good little girl.

He seated himself balls deep inside her with a sigh of satisfaction. "You can come for me now, Little Lamb, and I'll be disappointed in you if it only happens once," he told her and it was all the warning she had before he dragged out and slammed back in, crushing her into the cold stone.

Her body let go, sheath clamping down on him as she pulsed around him, gripping the stone, and his mask, screaming his name out. "Please...more, my Devil... Devil..." Her fingers clutched the mask closer, and she turned her head, eyes closed tight so she didn't see him.

"Put it on," he commanded her without missing a beat. "Cover yourself with the face of the beast and feel his power."

She did and cried out as another orgasm rolled through her, his cock pounding a tattoo inside her body that had her reeling. All of this, so much blasphemy to a god she didn't serve, for a god she did, and the man that brought that out in her. She might not be part of this Order, but she was integral to them, and that caused her to moan and shake. "Devil...fuck, Devil...." Gripping the stone, she came again, her body shattering with the force of it. "Fuck!"

"That is a worthy tribute," he snarled, his thrusts coming impossibly fast and hard as he chased his own release.

"Yes!" she screamed as she felt him falter and push deep, emptying himself into her, jets of searing cum bathing her insides. Panting, covered in sweat, and the man himself, she smiled under the mask she was wearing, her head to the side, and chanced an open eye.

"You can look," he told her, his breath coming in harsh pants. "We're done."

Done? She turned, pulling the mask off, her eyes falling on sinister beauty made flesh. Devil was a fallen angel, dark, with eyes that seemed to glow with unearthly light. Her fingers went to her mouth, tears in her eyes. "Finn..." she said softly, stunned in her afterglow and the need to have him closer. Another man she knew. Another man so close.

"Yeah." His breath was still ragged. "It's me." He huffed a laugh. "You have any idea how fucking distracting you are in tax season?"

"You have any idea how distracting you are whenever you walk into a room?" She pulled him to her, her lips fusing with his in seconds. Fuck, he tasted like whiskey and darkness and all the things he didn't say. Her body thrummed with energy as it pulsed between them. She broke the kiss on a gasp and grinned.

"And here I thought you were lusting for Devil," he teased, "and all the time you had the hots for a lowly accountant."

"My Devil is constantly in my thoughts, but now I don't feel guilty for wanting Finn to bend me over my desk and spank me." She nipped his bottom lip. "Still want that."

"Well...it's complicated and we'll talk about it later, but it's not impossible that we can do that at some point," he told her. "For now, let's get you out of those stockings." He boosted her up onto the altar and rolled them down her legs, tossing them to the dusty floor, even though she knew they must have cost him a pretty penny.

When she was finally naked, he leaned in and kissed her fiercely, a clashing of tongues as they devoured each other. He broke it and helped her down off the altar. "It's been fun," he said, slapping her sore ass. "But now you need to run." He melted away into the shadows under the old pulpit and she stood there, confused for a beat, before his shout echoed loudly round the church. "I said RUN!"

Chapter 10

The torches in the forest stood steadfast in the night as she ran down the lane and into the kirkyard, a smile on her face. Her Devil was wild and sexy, but her dessert was just up ahead. Fifteen feet into the stones, she skidded to a halt when she saw Ghost standing before her, hands behind his back. He was in his hooded Ghostface mask, black pants, boots and a long-sleeved shirt.

"Well, well, well," he offered, modulated voice heavy with sarcasm. She stood there, trembling in the cool night air, and felt her nipples pearl, knowing without a doubt that his eyes were on her.

"Run," he said softly and she took off into the darkness, her feet barely touching the moss-covered ground. She zigged and zagged, rounded a large mausoleum, and another, tearing off between headstones.

She could hear him pounding after her and she grinned, rushing through the trees, doing her best to give him the chase he wanted. Five minutes more and she was stopping to catch her breath, not because she needed to—her endurance had grown since the year prior thanks to her morning runs and such—but it wouldn't be any fun for her volatile lover if it wasn't truly a game of cat and mouse.

He didn't really want her terror in this, no, he enjoyed the chase, the catch, not the fear, at least not with her.

He came into view and she gasped, taking off down the opposite way. Looking over her shoulder, she saw him go left so she went right, not bothering to hide her steps. Ultimately this wasn't a game of kill or live, because Ghost wouldn't kill her.

She ran and darted through the kirkyard, weaving when he would jump out and try to nab her. Left, right, left, hide, sprint. And as she rushed headlong toward a ring of stones, she knew she was being herded. Her heart pumped hard as she skidded to a halt, spinning, realizing she was exactly where he wanted her.

Five angels, grimy, moss and lichen covered, loomed in the darkness. She turned once more, searching him out, and he stepped from behind the largest of the gravestones.

"No escape," he huffed, and she could hear him breathing heavily. Was it from the exertion, or because he knew he was finally going to get a piece of her?

She backed up, one step. Two. He was on her before she could bolt, his hand on her throat with a slight squeeze.

"You knew I would catch you."

"You always catch me," she croaked, his hand squeezing more. "It's the best part."

"Yes it is." He pushed her back, against the praying angel, and lifted his knife. "You aren't wearing anything."

"Blame Devil for that," she said. "He's the one that ruined your fun."

"If I can't cut clothing, I can cut skin."

She shivered at his words, modulated and threatening, but it didn't matter. The idea of it, it turned her on. She had come to trust Ghost in a way she wouldn't any other psychopath with a knife, because of the care he took with her. He wanted to mess with his toy; he didn't want to break it.

He looked down at her smaller body and chuckled. "Tight little nipples. Our victim likes the danger. Or does the victim like me?" he asked.

"Both," she said, arching into his hold more.

"Good answer." Slowly, almost featherlight, he ran the blade down from her collarbone and between her breasts. She hissed at the sharpness, the warmth, then coolness as the blood welled and started to drip. Not a lot, but enough to get him going.

"Fuck, that's pretty." His voice, still modulated, sounded like there was awe behind it.

"What are you going to do about it?" she croaked and he squeezed, making her whimper.

"Oh, I do love that sound."

"Please," she moaned. "Please, Ghost..."

"Oh, don't worry, you will get exactly what you deserve."

Pulling his hand from her body, he lifted her and spun them, settling her in the arms of the wailing angel, her arms up to welcome. He slung her legs over the arms, holding her open, and at the perfect height for him to play with her. And she knew he would play.

Sitting there, blood slowly running down her chest, she arched her neck, and bit her bottom lip, loving the feeling of being exposed to him, the cool night air chilling her heated flesh.

He struck again then, a soft nick just on her right rib, then another on the left, and more warmth trailed down her torso.

"So fucking perfect. Look at those nipples pearl." His modulated voice sounded absent with awe. "Tell me you want this."

"I want this," she said softly. "I want all you give me, Ghost."

"Always?"

"Always."

Forever?" he asked as he ran the knife down her solar plexus, to just above her navel.

"Forever, Ghost."

"And if I kept you..."

She arched. "To chase and to catch and to carve up?" she said softly. "I'm yours, Ghost, to do with as you need."

Taking the knife, he lunged and stabbed it into the tree that was growing out of the base of the Angel, embedding it at least an inch. The power behind the thrust, she knew he was holding back. Still, she moaned and gasped.

And then he was in front of her, sliding his thick cock into her, his head bent down as hers was, watching her body suck him in, the blood reaching her clit, and then lower, trailing down to his cock.

As it reached him, he groaned and gripped her hips, thrusting hard, her body wide open to him. Her back banged against the rock chest of the angel, the sight of her blood, of it now painting his own skin as he fucked her, clearly turned him on even more.

"Ghost, please," she moaned and surrendered, letting him use her, his little blood rag doll.

"So fucking good," he hissed behind the mask and she couldn't handle it. Somehow, his modulator was off and she was hearing his sexy, silky voice. She came on a sob, shaking, the force of his thrusts even harder now, hips like a piston.

Ghost!" she screamed as he gripped her throat, sending her into another climax, his barely restrained violence causing her to grip him like a goddamn vise.

He lost control then, a roar into the night as she reached around him and pulled his mask off. Her eyes saw him in the gloom of the moonlight, beautiful and familiar. His face flashed into her mind, one of the surgeons the shelter used when they had an extremely bad case.

"Dr...Ken..."

Panting hard, he ripped his knife from the wood and held it to her throat. She stared at him, waiting to see what he would do. Would he kill her? Would he end his game?

Their eyes locked and she let out a breathy little moan, her body fluttering around him yet again, and it seemed to bring him back to her, because instead of slicing into her flesh once more, he leaned in and took her mouth in a brutal kiss.

Their tongues tangled. He gripped her hair and head and she felt the knife leave her throat, heard it hit the ground.

Ghost pulled away, eyes glassy, and pulled out of her with a squelch. He smirked, the action lopsided, and then leaned in and kissed her again. She heard him zip up, and then she was being carried to the edge of the graveyard, right to the path that would lead back to the house.

Turning to him, standing on shaky legs, she smiled and he winked, walking back into the darkness.

Chapter 11

Emerson jogged down the steps to their well, intent on seeing for himself if the reports were true. The wells, which were placed in different properties around the world, served as a direct descent to their sleeping god, a way for both matter and energy to make it to him. The well at the Allegheny property was the newest, only coming online in the time of their fathers and, in truth, their fathers had only visited it once.

Originally, they had used the well in the city, in the brownstone that they had caught Petra at, but after that The Order thought it prudent to move all sacrifices out of the city itself, and demolished the building and the well.

A rotunda, the entrance to the space, was open to the south which tracked with The Order's normal architecture. Cobblestones inlaid with their god's divine language ringed the stone well, with a high stone dome over it, allowing for the elements to never reach He Who Sleeps. Datura covered the low walls and ran along the ledges of the four openings, windows to the cardinal points, giving a dreamy look to the place, the scent cloying and not at all unpleasant.

The space was beautiful, as deceptive and deadly as the men that made devotion here. He approached the round well, slightly off center toward the north, giving more space before it, and looked down. He had seen the well in the Balkans, the glowing mass that did not look like water, but oil, sparkles and fog, as it churned further down the hole. Their well was high with energy already, and indeed churning and frothing. He Who Sleeps was dreaming, enjoying what he saw.

Emerson's father had always said that blood sacrifice was paltry compared to what came with compliance and acceptance, and it seemed that was correct. As a group, they had already made seven blood sacrifices before Petra, and they were all high level in terms of energy yield, but nothing close to what they got from her last year. This year, their eleventh, had already exceeded their first seven years combined, and Petra's willingness and compliance...it was far too much of a coincidence.

The glow coming up from the well illuminated the space well enough that he saw Leo as he walked down the stairs. It seemed his brother was intent on seeing the well for himself.

"Is it frothing?" Leo asked, coming to stand beside him and peering over the edge. "Damn...it didn't look like this when we sacrificed this morning. It must take a little while to reach him down there."

"Fucking crazy, right?" Emerson sighed. "But it makes sense. I mean, we all kinda wanna keep her, even Snake, though he can't reconcile that. And she wants us. Maybe that's the difference. Maybe emotion makes it better."

"I absolutely believe that's what's made the difference this year," Leo agreed. "As for Snake, it's not about reconciling it. It's about permanence. He can be with us because we're forever. The Dark God is forever. The Order is forever. Yeah, we'll die one day, but for now he's safe from any kind of abandonment. Petra...he has a point. She's all in. This proves she's all in." He waved a hand at the well. "But she has only been with us seven nights total. It's not a lot of time, even when you know it's right."

"He's been with her least," Emerson said. "So yeah, I can understand it. But if she's got the chance to be with him, with all of us..." He looked to Leo as he leaned against the well. "She's worth the option. Even if she's not seen our faces yet." He swallowed. Lord but he wanted to tell Leo.

"She's seen mine." Leo just said it casually like it wasn't fucking mind-blowing. "I mean, she didn't really give me much of a choice—just yanked it right off my face mid-fuck. I didn't tell anyone because I wasn't sure what the deal was, but Devil seemed down with the idea of approaching the Elders about her, so no one has to die for it."

Emerson laughed. "She's seen mine, too." He grinned. "Ripped it off mid-fuck as well." He laughed harder. "Saucy brat. But it tells me she's serious about playing for keeps with us. She knew she was risking death by pulling that kind of stunt. Which..." He trailed off, shaking his head. "How the fuck did we just happen upon a girl that wants any of this? I mean we are all serious fuck ups."

"Speak for yourself," Leo snorted. "I'm fucking awesome. It's impossible not to notice. Maybe that's why she wants to stick around."

"She said something to me this morning," Emerson looked down at his hand, "that two nights a year she gets to feel alive. We do that to her. She said that we woke something up in her that was needy and needed us." He looked up to Leo. "We need her, Leo. We all need her." He grinned. "You went to her this evening, didn't you?"

"Of course I did." Leo smirked. "I wanted to know what was going on in that pretty little head of hers." He shook his head. "She played a dangerous game. Imagine if she'd tried to pull the mask off one of the others? Snake would have lost his shit. He might even have killed her."

"I think she actually might have with Snake," Emerson said. "He's acting way too twitchy with this, and I mean he's twitchy normally, but..." he shrugged. "I don't think it's us. I mean did you have any idea she did it with me? Fuck, I'm more worried about her exposing Plague or Ghost..."

"I did think Snake was acting weird last night, but I figured it was because the whole vibe felt different," Leo said thoughtfully. "Maybe you're right and she did try it with him. Silly girl. That could have gone very wrong." He took a deep breath and rolled his neck, stretching his arms to loosen the tension in his body. "Now that we've spoken about it and it might be an option, do you still think the others will freak if she tries her games on them?"

"Goblin...nah, he's fucking fiending for her to know him. Plague..." he shrugged. "He keeps everything so close to the vest, I can't be sure. He wants her, though. Remember last year, after his final scene with her when he was waxing poetic about the photos he took of her? But Ghost... He's my brother, but Stephan ensured he's completely unhinged. I don't know." Ghost's lack of female involvement in his growing up, along with being left with an out and out sociopath for a father, turned him in a cross between Patrick Bateman and Billy Loomis.

"Surely if Devil is on board, Ghost won't do anything off the wall," Leo reasoned. "And when we talked about trying to be with her over dinner, he said he was in. So he's not going to completely lose his shit. I don't know. Maybe we should have warned her."

"Maybe. And Ghost's problem isn't that he doesn't want her; he does, desperately. Fuck, you know he's rented that apartment across from her to watch her at night. The problem is he might not want her to *see* who he is. You know his kink is as wrapped up in his chase fantasies as his anonymity." He sighed. "But Devil, if he's in... Ghost will fall in line. The question is, will Devil tell him?"

"He did at dinner." Leo shrugged. "He was pretty clear that he's going to talk to the Elders about it. I'm sure Ghost can figure out some other way to get his kink on. If she thinks she might lose him and, by extension, us, she might stop with the sassy bullshit and actually take instructions."

"True. Though I meant if she unmasks Devil, will he tell Ghost? I mean, she's with them right now." He looked down to his watch. "Just jumped into it with Ghost, actually." Walking over to the east side of the rotunda, he looked out toward where the spire of the cathedral peeked over the trees. Devil had planned his seduction there, and Ghost would have her scared out of her wits running through the graveyards to escape him, probably ending the night in his favorite mausoleum. "I'm going last tonight. Is Plague or Goblin next?" He turned. "Or is it you?"

"Plague is just before you," Leo said. "Snake is next. Then me. Then Goblin."

He nodded. "I'm going to do something different," he offered, "something to see if the energy she gives me is different. Leo, you know I have been thinking about shit a while, and the difference in energy and such, right?"

"Uh...no, you didn't mention that. But sure." He smiled encouragingly.

"My dad...he was convinced when I was younger that there was more to it all than just sacrificing for the Dark God." Leaning against the rock, he settled in. "Since we were inducted and sent out, I haven't been able to put any theories into play, but there's so much we don't know. I remember my father's library, chock full of books and journals from through the ages. I don't know what happened to them, Leo, but I feel like they were taken away so I wouldn't read them. It got me thinking about energy transference, and when we found Petra, about the difference in the energy from a willing woman, one that accepts and embraces who we are and what we do." He walked over to the well, looking down into the frothing mass. "Even if the Elders don't accept it, I think we need to see where this goes past these two nights. I think, and I can't be sure because it's theory, but I think she's a missing piece to our crew. She's..." He struggled for the right word and then chuckled. "She's accepting in a way I didn't expect. I mean she's not averse to our lifestyle; she didn't even fucking bat an eye when I explained a bit of what we are, didn't roll her eyes about He Who Sleeps. She accepted it, and accepted it as something that is true in order to be with us.

"Leo, she's special. I think she's made for us."

"It's possible." Leo moved to sit on the steps. "I mean, I'd be hard pushed to believe in a god and not also believe that He moves in mysterious ways. He has clear power over our lives. It wouldn't surprise me if He brought her to us that night we first found her. Especially since his reach is strongest on those days. But it does make you wonder what the Elders' agenda is. Or how many groups have killed their perfect mates because they didn't offer the choice of death or pleasure."

"Exactly!" Emerson exclaimed. "I remember, my father read that in the early days of The Order, some groups had more than one woman, one woman for each man, but he believed that some groups were so blessed by Him that they were in perfect harmonious balance and only needed one woman to be with them all."

"But why wouldn't the Elders want us to know that?" Leo frowned. "Surely it's safer than killing? Every time someone disappears, law enforcement starts to investigate. Even with all our training about hiding bodies and confusing forensics, at some stage someone is going to slip up. It's the law of averages. And the minute the FBI starts looking hard at The Order, we're fucked."

Emerson looked at him. "The group before our fathers' group were caught," he said with a frown. "And each of them had holdings, millions in assets and accounts. As soon as they were caught, The Order seized all of it. My father, hell yours, never let their assets get outta control to the point they were hoarding millions and I wonder now if it's because they were scared it would make them a target for the Elders. They never did figure out how the group before them slipped up, but it only takes one anonymous call from someone in the know for the boys in blue to start joining the dots, ya know?" He gave Leo a meaningful look. "You know I don't trust the Elders, especially when they insisted on the ancient rites to pass the group from father to son...all but Ghost's father. I don't know if I'm just paranoid, but..." he sighed.

"Do you think they'll refuse to let her stay, then?" Leo asked.

"Frankly I don't care if they do. I would kill the council if need be, even Stephan, to keep her." A cold breeze blew through the rotunda, giving him goosebumps. "And with all my paranoia, it's not something I'm ruling out. I want her; you want her. I believe she completes us as a group." He looked to his friend again. "Don't get me wrong, man, she scratches an itch, but there's urges she won't ever satiate. Will I stop slicing throats? No. Same as you won't stop your needs. But what she's giving us is more potent than the blood sacrifices ever were, and nothing says that that energy can't be harvested year round...except for the Elders. There's so much we don't know."

"What if..." Leo paused, a look of disbelief on his face as though he couldn't believe what he was about to say. "What if the Dark God sent her to us to force us to challenge the Elders? Think about it. We're all stone cold killers and are currently the biggest and most powerful group out there. So, He gave us Petra, knowing that eventually we'd ask the Elders to keep her and that if they say no, we'll burn them to the fucking ground."

"And now we are on the same fucking page." Emerson grinned. "I remember once my father talking about cleansings, and trials decades ago, when The Order was going in the wrong direction and He Who Sleeps intervened directly. We've never seen anyone in The Order getting killed by The Order, aside from our fathers getting skinned during the ancient rites, but there's nothing to say the Dark God wouldn't intervene again if he wasn't happy with the way things are going." He shrugged. "Maybe this is our trial to cleanse The Order." Or maybe they were just psychopaths. Either way, Petra was important.

"I don't know." Leo looked troubled. "I don't know how our fathers did it. If anyone tries to skin me, they'll die in the attempt."

"They were die hards that believed in the system. The only one that questioned it was my father..." he trailed off and frowned. "Shit."

"What?" Leo looked up, surprised by Emerson's vehemence.

"Leo, I need to look at my own journals but..." He swallowed. "I'm pretty sure their sacrifice came soon after my father went to the Elders with his questions."

"So...you think that if Devil goes and asks the Elders if we can keep Petra, they might demand we all sacrifice ourselves to the God?" He shook his head. "They wouldn't. We haven't had kids yet. They can't afford to take us out, not when we're providing enough energy to froth the well. It's one thing to play politics, but The Dark God would be pissed."

"No, I think we are too important right now, and they feel like they have their hooks in deep." He frowned again. "Stephan speaks to Ghost much more since we found Petra. And I feel like he's giving us information, but it might be two-fold. They wouldn't ruin their own luck and good fortune from Him. They do need us; there is no one close enough to our age, or our bloodlines, to take over.

"And it wasn't a fluke that our fathers all ended up with women at the same time. I know they were attempting to ensure blood legacy with us being the next in line. But maybe that sealed their fate as well. I mean, have you ever heard of any group taking the initiative like that? And then we, as a group, find Petra, who is willing and we all want her? You know damn well the pact with her involves pleasure, but it didn't need to. If any of us weren't into her, she would have to endure the pain of it, alone. But we all want her replete and thinking us gods."

"They might not be happy with us only finding one woman," Leo pointed out. "She's not going to have a baby with every single one of us. We don't even know if she wants kids, and you know how important they think blood legacy is."

"Who is to say she wouldn't?" Emerson grinned, the idea of a child with her living rent-free in his head. "But you are probably right in that respect. I just can't help but feel that we are missing things, that it's right in front of our faces." He sighed. "I think we need to get through tonight, rock her fucking world, and then, when dawn hits, tell her we are keeping her."

"Well then we need to speak to Devil," Leo said. "We can't make her promises without our fearless leader on board."

"Well then, let's go and have a conversation while he's still in his afterglow." Emerson grinned.

"I like the way you think, brother." Leo grinned and rose to his feet. "Let's go find him."

Chapter 12

Snake sat in his chair, swimming deep thoughts. Petra would be here any minute. He'd heard her come in and go to her room, and he knew she'd be patching up whatever damage Ghost had done to her, but it wouldn't take long to clean and disinfect the scratches and bandage any slightly deeper ones. And then she'd be here. With him.

He'd been in turmoil ever since they'd had that big discussion over dinner. His brothers wanted her. If he was honest with himself, he wanted her, too. Maybe not for him, but for the way she made his brothers feel. It was impossible not to notice the way they were around her. And Snake knew that deep down he could come to want her in that way...learn to trust her enough to let her touch him...but not yet. He'd seen her in their every day life and while he knew she was professional and respectful out there in the world, in here she was a brat with a big mouth that kept trying to push his boundaries instead of respecting them, and until she learned that wasn't going to fly with him, he wouldn't ever be able to trust her.

So this was it. The point of no return. He wasn't going to lose the brotherhood. They were forever. The Order was forever. And if that meant that Petra was going to be forever, he needed to be honest with her and have a heart to heart. He dreaded it. Opening up wasn't something he did naturally, especially not to people he considered acquaintances, but this was necessary. There was a soft knock at the door and he called gruffly for her to come in.

Padding in softly, she smiled at him sitting in the large chair. "Hi, Snake." She looked him over. "Are you okay?"

It was on the tip of his tongue to snap at her that it was none of her business, but he swallowed it back. Open and honest. Instead, he side-stepped the question. "Things tonight are going to be different," he told her, rising to his feet. "I'm going to talk. You're going to shut that bratty mouth of yours and listen. Afterwards, I'll decide if your questions are worth answering. For now, take off your clothes and get on the padded bench."

She nodded, removed the robe she was wearing and lay down on the piece he pointed to. Eyes on the ceiling, she took a deep breath, letting her hands and arms relax at the sides of her body, the bandage on her sternum in full view.

Fighting every protective instinct he had, Snake took his mask off and set it down on the seat behind him. This wasn't going to work if she didn't see how serious he was. Grabbing the lengths of soft rope he'd set out earlier, he began the process of binding her body to the table, moving her unresisting limbs about.

"I don't know if the others have told you that they intend to petition the Elders to keep you, but they do," he began when her arms were secured. "And that presents a problem for me, because they're my family and I will not lose them. Which means that you and I have to come to an understanding...a way to make this work." He took a deep breath and started on her legs.

"I'm not like the others. I wasn't raised in The Order as a legacy child of powerful bloodlines. I spent my childhood being beaten and abused in orphanages and foster homes, and I was taken by The Order after I killed my first person at the age of twelve." He ignored her soft intake of breath.

"Being raised by Ghost's father was a lesson in brutality. I hope that explains, to some extent, my unwillingness to be touched. My body has been broken too many times. It is now *mine* and *I* will dictate and decide what happens to it. And only with people I trust. And Petra, I don't fucking trust you. You come in here every year with your big bratty mouth, constantly trying to push my limits, and then you go and pull crazy dangerous shit like yanking my mask off. If you want this to work between us, I need you to understand that while your attitude might fly with the others, it doesn't fucking fly with me. You may speak now."

"I... I'm sorry, Snake. I didn't know," she offered. "My attitude is not because of you, or anything past having to protect myself up until this point." She turned her head to him. "I apologize if this year has set you on edge, or my plan has kicked things up. I didn't mean to upset you. I took a shot, Snake...to find a happiness I need. I needed a change; I needed it, or I wouldn't make it to the next year.

"I was raised in an orphanage, too," she said softly, "and aside from the four girls I was raised with, I don't have anyone. Having you seven makes me feel real somehow."

That gave him pause. She'd been in an orphanage, too? He didn't know how to feel about that. If it was responsible for the way she responded to them, that she was somehow fetishizing her trauma, it might not be healthy. On the other hand, maybe she'd had a positive experience, something completely different to what he'd gone through.

"I understand wanting to protect yourself," he conceded eventually. "But it was a stupid way to go about it. Coming in here all ballsy could have gotten you killed. If you haven't learned over the last three years that I have rigid personal boundaries, how can I trust you to learn and respect them going forward?"

"I didn't know." She looked to him again. "You didn't say much to me any of the times before this. I didn't think it was a boundary. I thought you were just uninterested, or you wanted me to show interest. I'm not the best with social cues. I am sorry for that."

"Didn't you ever wonder why I only touch you with toys?" he asked curiously. It was a hell of a big thing to miss...more than a social cue.

"No. Some guys are like that. Some guys...I don't know. You might not have wanted me. The others might have, but you might not have. You also could have been gay, and not interested in women. I just thought it was your kink, to keep yourself removed from me. I didn't like that. I needed to know if you wanted me the way I wanted you, so I did what I did. I am sorry, Snake. I won't do it again. I won't push you again."

"Well it isn't going to happen overnight," he told her. "Today I'm trying something...new. But I'm not ready for you to touch me yet, and probably won't be for some time. If that's not enough for you, then we have a problem."

"It will have to be," she said softly. "I like you, Snake. If we are just friends, I can handle that." She swallowed. "I'm here for you. Do what you want."

"I don't need your permission," he snapped and took a breath. "Sorry. This will take time for me to get used to as well," he said stiffly.

She nodded. "We will learn together, I guess." Her smile was small, but she gifted it to him.

He nodded, too, glad to have cleared the air, but it still remained to be seen if she could control herself while he was vulnerable around her. He finished tying her up in silence and tested his work with a deep sense of satisfaction. "That okay?" he asked. "You can feel your fingers and toes? Circulation is fine?"

She nodded and wiggled her fingers and toes. "No problems."

"Good." He went back to the cupboard to collect the strap-on he'd chosen, hesitating for only a moment before he brought it back to her. Open and honest. That was the aim. He had to be raw with her, and this needed to be done.

It wasn't easy to get the harness on with her already bound, but he managed it, and then it was time. "This is..." He had to clear his throat and start again. "This is the first time I've done this with someone else," he told her.

She looked down her body, arched a brow and then looked up to him. "Never pegged someone before, so this is a first for me, too. I get why I'm tied down, but I'm not sure how this is going to work. I mean the mechanics I get, but not all tied down." She smiled. "But I'm not against it."

"Because I can't trust you not to try and take over in the heat of the moment," he said simply. "This isn't about you fucking me. It's about me taking what I want in a safe environment. And until we know each other better and there is trust between us, this is how it's going to go."

He began stripping out of his jeans, noting the way she eyed his cock with pained hunger in her eyes, but she kept her mouth shut and something in him eased. She wasn't going to make this difficult. He'd prepared well for this session, even though he'd chosen a dick on the smaller side, and didn't feel any embarrassment about removing the butt plug he'd had in and tossing it into a bucket for cleaning.

He took a moment to lube up the strap-on but then everything was ready, and there was no putting it off. Climbing onto the padded table with her, he straddled her body, his knees on either side of her waist, and held her gaze as he sat back and down, slowly impaling himself on the silicone rod.

Watching him, she kept her eyes on his, showing him her acceptance. She bit her lip, clearly wanting to say something, but didn't.

It took him several moments to get all the way down and then he settled there for a second to catch his breath. The fullness was exquisite, but he knew the true pleasure would come when he started moving.

Whatever she wanted to say, he was curious to see if she could keep it to herself or if her impetuousness would force it to bubble up out of her, so he didn't ask. Instead, he took another deep breath and then began to fuck himself on the strap-on, rising and falling slowly at first, but then as he hit the right angle to massage his prostate, he lost control a bit as his brain short-circuited from pleasure. It felt so fucking good...so forbidden...and it had been such a long time.

Her breathing hitched, and she fought a squirm under him, but her eyes stayed on him the entire time, watching.

It was gratifying to him to see the way her nipples were pebbling and her pupils were dilating. She was into this. She might want a more active part, but this was definitely a good start. He picked up the pace until the pleasure was too much and he reached for his cock, giving it the last bit of stimulation he needed to come all over her belly and breasts in thick pearly spurts while his body shuddered and shook. The adrenaline from trying something so private with someone else had made it harder to reach the peak, but the release had been all the more intense because of it. "Fuck..." he murmured, fighting the silly grin that wanted to creep over his mouth. "You look good all tied up and covered in my cum."

"Thanks. I feel good tied up and covered in you, Snake," she said finally, and licked out at the cum that had hit her lip, closing her eyes. "Will you be upset with me if I tell you that was extremely hot to watch?"

"Not at all." He was actually relieved there had been pleasure in it for her, since that was what the sacrifice was all about—the energy they siphoned off her orgasms. Speaking of...he raised himself off her and made short work of removing the strap-on, since it was easier to slide out from under her than it was to put it on. She was obviously aroused, the area between her thighs was glistening under the lights and he couldn't help but feel satisfaction about that. Tossing the used items in the cleaning bucket, he grabbed the Hitachi, knowing from previous experience that it was her favorite, and brought it across to the table. "You want to do it and let me watch, or do you want to stay tied down and let me do it?" he asked softly. "There's no wrong answer or trick question. It's your choice."

"You," she said with a smile. "It's better when you do it. Though..." she gave him a cheeky grin, "Next time we play like this, maybe add a toy to the inner base of that strap-on... It would have been amazing to come with you."

The urge to snap back at her demands rose up in his gorge, but he forced it down. It was annoying that she wanted to make demands and simply assumed they would do it again, when it was his choice. *His* choice. But that said, it was a reasonable request. The energy harvested probably would be even more potent.

"For future reference, this smug, cheeky smirk you have going on doesn't do it for me," he said. "It feels like disrespect, but I'm trying to explain instead of going off on you. But yes. If that's something you think you would enjoy, and if the Elders agree to our request, we can look at purchasing more suitable equipment." He just hadn't been expecting these nights to go this way, so he wasn't as prepared as he should have been.

"I wasn't trying to be smug, or cheeky, Snake. I felt like we connected. I'm sorry if I overstepped with that," she said softly.

He paused again, mulling over her words. It had definitely been a cheeky grin. He was certain of that. Perhaps...perhaps it meant something different to her? Cheekiness as an expression of joy rather than brattiness or disrespect? He didn't know. He would need to speak to one of his brothers to understand it...probably Stitches. He was the most alike to her in temperament. In any event, it was something else that would require adjustment and he would just have to learn.

"It's fine." His voice was gruff but he didn't care. He needed her to come so he could untie her and let her out of here. He needed some time alone to think through the revelations they'd made. He turned the Hitachi on and pressed it to her clit, loving the way she squealed as the sudden shot of pleasured spiked through her.

"Ah!" she gasped, arching as much as she could in the bonds, her body shuddering. Her eyes were on him as she writhed and moaned. "Fuck... Snake..."

Maybe one day. The thought came out of nowhere and threw him for a loop. Could he? Could they? One day would he be trusting enough to plunge his cock into this hot, willing woman? Maybe. But not today. For now he focused on pleasuring her, on moving the vibrator in tune with the bucking of her hips until she shattered, crying out his name as her body strained against the restraints, her throat sounding raw.

"Good girl." He took the vibrator away, not wanting to force her through another two or three orgasms. He knew Stitches had something elaborate set up, so he'd be grateful for the extra time. It didn't take long to undo the ropes and he went over her carefully, checking that

114

none of her joints had been strained or injured. Once he was certain that all was well, he stepped back and gestured for her to get off the table.

"You should go and shower," he told her. "Stitches will need your skin clean."

She nodded. "I...yes. Thank you, Snake." She slipped from the table, standing on shaky legs. She grabbed her robe, slipping it over her shoulders, giving him an awkward smile. It was clear she didn't know what else to say to him.

"I think we can make this work," he said softly as she turned toward the door. "Today was...a good start."

She nodded again. "Sleep well, Snake. I guess I'll see you when I see you."

"Dark God-willing, that will be soon," he murmured, and then she was gone.

Chapter 13

Petra dried off from her shower, refreshed. The scene with Snake had been hot, if not awkward. They would have to work on things of everything progressed, but that was for later. She checked herself in the mirror, seeing the progress. She was already healing, some of the scratches already closed, and the slice down her sternum wasn't bleeding anymore.

Not that she wouldn't wear Ghost's scars with pride. Whatever happened after this weekend, whatever he chose to do with her, because she knew he wouldn't hold back anymore, she would bear it.

And Snake, well, the scars were of a different variety, but they would figure it out together. They had to. It eased her heart somewhat to know that he was invested and did want to work on his issues. All this time she'd thought he didn't like her, but it turned out that he was just in his own world of damage, trying to protect himself the only way he knew how. She'd have to approach him like a frightened colt, softly and slowly so that he didn't bolt or kick out.

But now was for her next appointment, one she had been waiting for. Padding out of the bathroom, she grabbed a robe, slipping it on, and smiled when she saw Stitches standing in her doorway.

"Hey." She smiled and went to him, wrapping herself around him. Leo was comfort and need and desire, and she knew where she stood with him. No confusion or turmoil...just Leo.

"Hey, yourself!" He gave her a wide grin and it was so easy to believe a cold-blooded killer didn't lurk under that open charm. "You smell good."

She leaned in and breathed him in. "So do you." With a grin up to him, she went on tip toe and pushed her lips against his.

"Tsk tsk," he chuckled, pulling away. "Getting ahead of yourself, aren't you?" He smacked her ass, although it was padded by the robe, and stepped back out into the hallway. "You have to earn my kisses with pain. Come down to my room."

He took her hand and she walked with him, enjoying their dichotomy. He was playful, and she appreciated it, but he was also buzzing over what he was planning, and she was both nervous and excited. The pain would be worth it because of the reward. "Will you take pictures?"

"Not me. Plague. You know how much he loves photographing you, so I said he could look in with his camera."

She shivered and smiled to herself. "Okay. And he knows..." she looked and motioned to his face. "Or are you going to do it with your mask on?"

"I'll take my mask off." He opened the door to his room and ushered her in. "I need to see what I'm doing to make sure I don't hurt you." It was bullshit and they both knew it—it wasn't the first time he'd stuck needles in her and he'd never had a problem doing it with his mask on before, but if that was what he wanted the narrative to be, that was what it was going to be. "Get yourself seated," he told her, gesturing toward a massage chair that stood stark and alone in the room. "Robe off. Obviously."

The robe slipped to the floor, and she took in the space as she made her way to the chair. Black walls, the chair, the light above framing the space she would sit. This wasn't Leo's bedroom, but it was his workroom, and as before the space didn't make her feel worried, but grounded. She supposed it was because it wasn't clinical, no white tile and antiseptic smell.

"I am going to make you a masterpiece," he murmured, rolling a small table across that had a stainless steel tray on it containing his needles and supplies. As usual, it was all in medical packaging and sterile. He wouldn't risk her getting an infection of any kind. "I'm going to have to do some prep," he said, rolling a stool over so he could sit behind her, but for a moment he just simply stared.

Looking over her shoulder, she grinned at him. "It's kinda hot how you are looking at me, Stitches." His posture was one of coiled attention, but it was also relaxed, and she knew he was in his zone.

"I'm hot all the time," he told her with a smirk, wetting a cotton swab with alcohol and swiping it over her back.

"Ah!" she started, the cool wetness making her jump slightly. "Was not ready for that!" The drag of the cotton left trails of tingling cold.

"You're lucky Plague isn't here yet. He'd be lighting this shit up like a bonfire," Stitches snorted. "Stop squirming. I need to mark out where I'm stabbing you."

"Yes, Sir." Taking a deep breath, she closed her eyes, feeling the cool points of whatever he was marking her with. "You know, I did look this up, since last year. The art of it...the kink. The first time it scared me, but I came so hard I decided to explore it. I look at it with open eyes now. I mean, when I was younger, I used to sew my fingers together. It's not the same, but...I didn't think I would ever trust anyone to do this, but here you are."

"Well that was fucking stupid," he told her bluntly. "You could have given yourself all sorts of horrible infections. You could have lost a finger or a hand. You'd better promise me you won't do anything stupid like practice this on your own."

"I was a child in an orphanage, with few friends and no one to tell me different. I would never do this now, so you don't have to worry. Only you, Stitches."

"Good. Because if one of us has to come to the hospital because you're septic, you don't wanna know the kind of punishments we'll rain down on you," he told her. She was about to say something else when there was a knock on the door and Plague slipped in, without waiting for an answer. "Right on time," Stitches said, setting down his pen. "I just finished marking her up."

"Nice. Although if I'd been here earlier, I could have photographed the blank canvas without the marks."

"Not my problem, dude." Stitches shrugged. "I told you what time she'd be here. Just do your thing while I do mine." Plague lifted his camera and snapped some shots of her back as Stitches reached for the first needle, peeling open the packet with a small plasticky crinkle. "You ready?" he asked her.

"Yes." Closing her eyes, she waited, wondering about Plague. How would he react to all of this, to her being so accepting, so familiar with Stitches...and what would it mean for them?

"So how did it go with Snake?" Stitches asked as he pinched a section of skin and slid the needle through it.

She breathed out, the slight pain of the pinch sending heat through her body. "I... I think it went well. He...we need to work some things out," she said finally. It wasn't that she didn't trust Stitches; she just felt that what had happened with Snake was between them, and she didn't know if Snake would be okay with talking about what happened to them.

To her surprise, he blew out a sigh of relief and she could see Plague giving a small nod. "Well that's good," he said, placing the next needle opposite the first. "Working stuff out means he's open to it. Did any of the others tell you that we talked about petitioning the Elders?"

"Snake mentioned it. Which is why he wants to work things out," she offered and winced slightly. "Ghost..." she smiled. "He didn't say much, but then he never does. Not even after..." she shook her head. "Well, he didn't say much after I got to look him in the eye." She looked to Plague, to see how he would take that information.

"And Devil?" Stitches slid another needle home. "We told him about your little mask-pulling stunt, by the way. Neon and I. He knows you've seen our faces." Plague didn't say anything, moving silently around the room, the only sound he made being the shutter on his camera.

She giggled. "Any time with Devil is worship. He fucked me over his altar, making me wear his mask, then let me see him." She smiled as she closed her eyes and felt another shard of metal slide through her skin.

"I thought he might do something like that." He sat back to study his work for a second before reaching for the next needle. "You need a break?" he asked as he pinched her skin again. "We're about a quarter of the way through."

"No." Gods, it felt like foreplay to her, and she knew without a doubt that she would never feel like that about this with anyone else. Not Ghost, or Snake or Goblin... Just Stitches. It was just for them...a man that understood something about this she didn't. She was safe with him, at least in this, and it was heady to know.

"That's my girl." He sounded smug, pinching another piece of skin and sliding the needle through. Plague ghosted around them, taking dozens of photographs from every angle, while Stitches worked methodically from her upper back down toward her pelvis, the needles getting closer together the lower he worked. The sharp scratches and the adrenaline were buzzing in her blood, filling her with endorphins to the point she felt almost high.

"Done," he said finally. "You were such a good girl, I'll let you choose the ribbon." From the second tray down on his little rolling table cart, he pulled out a wooden box and moved around to stand in front of her. Cracking it open, he displayed neatly rolled balls of satin ribbon in every color of the rainbow.

She looked them over, choosing a sheer and velvet in black, and looked to him. "Can I choose two?"

"If you want. It'll hurt more," he warned. "The lacing with two is more complex."

She considered it. "The pain isn't the worry," she said finally. "I just thought if there are pictures, I wanted them to be something special. Since this would be a first." Not only, first.

She also knew that Plague liked to shoot in black and white. He'd mentioned it to her once. It made capturing photos of flames a challenge and a wonder. The black ribbon would stand out starkly against her skin.

"It'll look spectacular," Stitches assured her. "Maybe Plague will even give you one of the pictures."

"Maybe," Plague said, still distant as he snapped photos. He had to have taken hundreds just in the short time Stitches had been working. She'd love to know more about his process and how he chose which ones to print, but that was probably a thing to ask during her session with him, instead of taking up Stitches' time.

"You ready?" Stitches was again sat behind her, waiting for her consent to go ahead and lace her up.

She nodded and turned her head, seeing him out of the corner of her eye. "You ready to finish this?" After it was done, he was going to be ravenous for her and she was already ready for him.

"I was born ready," he chuckled and set to work. This time he worked in silence, concentrating on what he was doing.

She hissed, the threading nothing, but the pulling...it tugged on her and while it felt good, there was that burn she wasn't sure she enjoyed.

"You okay?" Stitches paused. "The first ribbon is on. You can take a break if you need to."

She shook her head and gasped, her body thrumming, nipples peaked and rubbing on the leather of the chair. "I'm pretty sure I'm ruining the seat..."

"It'll clean." He sounded amused as fuck and even Plague chuckled. "Cream away, Sweet Cheeks. Just keep still so I don't tear one of these out by accident."

"It's the tugging that's making me squirm, and not because I'm in pain," she gasped. "Fuck..."

"You still have to sit still, my sweet little pain slut." He pressed a quick kiss to her spine between her shoulder blades. "Get your shit together."

The contact had her focusing, all movements ceasing. His lips left a burn on her skin, beautiful and throbbing, almost as much as her back. A steadying breath had her nodding to Stitches to proceed.

He laced the second ribbon up more slowly, interweaving it with the first one in delicate motions that still pulled at the needles piercing her skin. But eventually it was done and he sat back, a sigh of wonder rippling the air across her shoulder blades. "Fucking stunning," he breathed. "This might be my best work."

"I don't disagree, brother." Plague's modulated voice sounded awed as he leaned over Stitches' shoulder to take photographs. "The alignment is perfect." Plague snapped several more photos and then stepped back. "You want me to stick around and take pics of the fucking, or is this a private party?"

"Stick around," Stitches replied. "This moment needs to be recorded for posterity."

His words made her clench and shiver, the tightness of her back sending shockwaves through her being, a pulsing and thrumming, one that had her so needy she was moments from begging him to take her.

"I'm going to warn you now that you really don't want to move," Stitches told her. "If you pull any of these out, it's going to be a fucking mess and you'll probably scar for life. So you're going to sit there like a good girl and just fucking take it, okay?"

He pressed a lever near the floor that raised the seat up from the ground and then when it was the right height, he bodily lifted her and shifted her ass backwards so that it was hanging over the edge of the chair, exposing her pussy to the cool air.

She bit her lip, moaning already. "Please, Leo..."

He smacked her ass, hard, and the resulting jump made her whole back spasm in a flash of exquisite agony. "In here, I'm Stitches," he corrected her.

With a gasp, she nodded. "Stitches...oh fuck... It burns..."

"Good." She heard the sound of his zipper and then the head of his cock was nudging at her entrance and he was filling her, carefully and slowly.

"Stitches...." She moaned and closed her eyes, going completely limp for him. Finally, finally he was inside her and she was so fucking ready, one stroke from him and she would be coming, soaking him. "So good..."

"That's it, that's my little pain slut," he crooned in her ear. "All spiked and strung up and still writhing on my cock like you were fucking made for it."

"You doubt I was?" she moaned, squeezing him with her inner muscles as she panted.

124

"Oh, I know you were made for me," he told her. "You were born for us to break you."

She cried out then, the orgasm rushing through her as he gripped her hips, stars blooming in her vision.

"Okay, stay still," he ground out, picking up the pace and slamming into her, the piercings on his cock rippling in and out of her as he held her hips down tight to the chair.

"That's like telling the world not to turn." She gritted her teeth and tried so very hard to do as he asked. "Fuck... Stitches..."

"That's exactly what I'm doing, my greedy little Petra, but I've got to be careful not to tear that pretty flesh of yours."

"Please, please, please..." she begged. "I'm so fucking close. Your piercings... Please..." she begged, delirious with both pleasure and the swirling pain and heat from the needles.

"You gonna come for me again?" he teased.

"Fuck...so hard..." She moaned and her body let go, the orgasm thundering through her as she as screamed his name into the night.

She squeezed down hard and he groaned in her ear. "Fuck...so fucking tight," he choked out and then he was coming inside her, his full weight bearing down on her hips as he filled her to the brim with hot jets of his seed.

Bliss ran through her for the fourth or fifth time that night and she smiled to herself, knowing Plague had captured it for all of them. "Fuck... Stitches... Amazing."

"Like that was ever going to be in doubt," he laughed, pulling out. "Just rest there for a minute or two. Let me clean up and then I'll get those needles right out." He disappeared, leaving her alone with

Plague for a few minutes, the evidence of their lovemaking dripping out onto the floor.

She looked up to Plague, seeing him watching her, and smiled. "I hope you got good ones," she murmured and closed her eyes, bliss setting in hardcore.

"You know I did," he told her. "The models made it pretty fucking easy." He grinned behind his mask and then his tone sobered. "Since we have a minute, you need to know something. I know you've been pulling masks from the other guys, but you're not going to do that with me, because I'll show you my face when I'm ready to show you my face, and not before. And if you so much as try it, we're done, okay? You've already given enough energy to light up the whole North American continent, so I don't need your orgasms. I can walk away. You hear me?"

She nodded. "It's your choice, Plague. I won't try. Promise."

"Good girl. Well, I guess I'll go switch out this film, so I have plenty left for later," he said as Stitches came back in. "I'll leave you guys to it."

"Thanks, brother." Stitches clapped him on the back and closed the door behind him. "Damn, girl, you made a mess on the floor. I'm of half a mind to get you down there to lick it up. But I don't know when it was last cleaned, so I guess today is your lucky day."

She laughed. "Floors are a limit for me," she said softly. "But you are a god, Stitch."

"You think your limits count on these two nights of the year? That's cute," he teased. "You signed the deal. If I wasn't worried about making you sick, I'd make you do it just to prove a point." He pulled his stool back up behind her and disinfected his hands, the sharp smell of the alcohol permeating the air. "You ready for this?"

She nodded. "Of course. Will these need much aftercare?"

"No more than a trip to get your bloods done," he told her. "It's the same needles." He wetted a cotton swab with the disinfectant and then started pulling the needles.

"And if I wanted piercings...I mean, going forward...is that something you would do?"

"Damn right, it's something I'd do." His hands stilled. "You'd be into that?"

"If you did it, yes. Only you, though. I feel like it would be part of what we have between us, something that's *just* us. I mean, I'm sure the guys would like it, but..."

"That warms my heart." He sounded sincere and she felt the ribbon rippling from her back to fall to the floor as he pulled the last two needles. "Just wait there a sec. You've got some blood spots."

She felt a cool pressure as he wiped them clean and then the prickly stickiness of tiny band-aids as he covered up the worst of them. "Come see me in the morning before you sleep and I'll clean them again," he told her, "but for now, we're done."

"It *was* fun." She turned to him. "Did I earn my kisses?"

"Yes, you did." He gave her a soft, lingering kiss, one that was sweet and belied his deadly nature. "Looking forward to doing this all night sometime soon," he told her. "Not just snatched hours, twice a year."

She nodded. "I'm looking forward to pancakes in the morning with you," she said softly and kissed his lips once more.

Eventually he drew back with a groan. "I'd love to keep you and canoodle like teenagers all night, but you have appointments to keep," he told her reluctantly. "You should head out."

She kissed him once more. "Only because they are appointments I want to keep. I'll see you in a few hours." Her hand went to his face. "Dawn."

"I'll come find you," he promised, sliding her robe back over her shoulders. "I'll see you at dawn."

Chapter 14

Devil was waiting in the foyer when Ghost came in from outside, wiping his muddied shoes on the mat with a fierce grin. Devil tried to match it. The Dark Lord knew he should be in a great mood after what had happened in the abandoned chapel, but the talk he'd just had with Stitches and Neon had soured his appetite considerably. Their suspicion that He Who Sleeps preferred pleasure to pain, or at least a mix of the two, and that the Elders had been covering that up for decades, if not centuries, was sitting like a heavy weight in his chest.

The well here was frothing, too, they said. Petra was giving off enough energy that the bridge to beneath where He slept was literally boiling. The Order raised killers, not lovers. How could they have gotten this all so wrong?

Neon's assertion that his father had possibly been doing research into the energy difference between pleasure and pain and that might have been what got their whole group killed had chilled Devil to the bone. Like the others, he'd sat and watched quietly, trying to keep his tears in and his whimpers down, as his father had been skinned alive before him. The agonized screams that had echoed around the chamber until he had mercifully passed into unconsciousness still haunted Devil's dreams all these years later.

And what had that agony served? If it wasn't what their God wanted? They had all died screaming that day, all except Stephan. And now Devil had to know why.

"I'm guessing from that smirk that you caught her," he said, forcing a grin that he knew looked queasy.

"I always catch her," Ghost said as he pulled his mask off. The man talked little, and went without his mask less. Devil knew that Ghost, Rix, felt he lived two different lives—the one here, where he was free, and the one where he had to play nice in society. "God below...it was sweet."

"It always is with her." That truth curled his lips in a genuine smile, at least. "Do you have a moment to talk, or do you need to go and clean up?"

"Live longer with her scent all over me?" Ghost grinned at him. "I can manage." He was always more chatty after a session with their sweet victim. Ghost looked to him and then frowned. "What's going on?"

"Come to the study." Devil knew it was empty because he'd checked only a few minutes before. They sat down in the comfortable armchairs and Devil sighed. "It's about this situation with Petra wanting to be with us all year round. I have committed to speaking to the Elders about it, but I don't want to go in there blind. They've allowed the pact to stand for three years now, but I know better than to assume that means they're fully behind it. I wanted to know if your dad has said anything to you about it? Or if he's given you any indication which way he leans on the subject? Or if there's anything he's said that we might be able to use as positive leverage when it's time to have that discussion with the Elders."

Ghost frowned. "Stephan..." he frowned harder. "This morning, he texted me..." Pulling his phone from his pocket, he tossed it to Devil. There wasn't any lock on it, not that Devil didn't know all the passcodes they would use. They were brothers, and they shared everything. The phone opened and there were several pictures of Petra bent over a grave stone, one in the arms of the angel in their kirkyard, her legs open, pussy dripping. Ghost grinned. "Think I'm going to have that one framed."

Devil went past the photos and into his messages, opening the thread with Stephan.

S: You have done well. He is pleased. The Well here is high, swirling and frothing. Whatever you have put her through is working.
R: Everything for him, Sir.
S: One more night. The output from the girl must be potent and high, spill blood, as you always do, my son. Give Him a reason to reward you.

"Spill blood?" Devil felt himself frowning and tried to smooth it out before he looked up. "What does that mean?"

Ghost looked him over. "You *do* know how I get down, right?" Devil did. He knew that Ghost's knife wasn't for show. Before Petra, he would carve up their sacrifice, and in his other life, he was quite handy with the scalpel he used as a vet, though he never harmed animals, only people. "A little blood in the mix makes it good for both of us."

"Spilling blood just sounded a bit dramatic." Devil tossed the phone back. "We promised not to scar her, so it's not like you can cut deep enough for a lot of blood."

"He doesn't know that," Ghost said, completely fine with that fact, which said a lot. "All she needs is shallow little cuts to come torrents for me. And I just need the traces of it on myself to finish for her."

Shit. Stephan had really fucked Ghost up if he needed blood to get off.

"So he's on board with the experiment?" Devil asked. "Can I count on his support when I approach the Elders about keeping her?"

"No." Ghost looked to his best friend. "What he knows of this, he thinks it's more pain than pleasure. He thinks we are grooming Petra into a pain slut." He shrugged. "I mean we don't have to do that, since she kinda is, I mean...for us." He set his phone away in his pocket. "I'm all for keeping her, Finn." He used Devil's real name. "The need for her through the year is all consuming. But unless we have her under lock and key, making her suffer? I don't think they are going to be into it. Stephan wants the suffering; he's always focused on it." He sighed. "Look how he fucking raised me."

"Would they know if we did otherwise?" He knew it was a massive risk, but if Petra wanted them enough, she'd play along if necessary. "If we told them that's what we're doing—making her suffer to see if we can overcome the veil all year round, would they ever know that's not what we're doing?"

"Yes and no," Ghost said. "Anything we tell them, they are going to be on the look out for, keeping an eye on. If we don't tell them, go back to our lives like normal, or the normal they are used to, then they won't know. Stephan doesn't have anyone watching us until September, and they end their vigil November third. Finn, what's going on? Why ask me now? I mean you already had your mind made up that you would ask permission. Plague and I were of the mind that it's better to ask for forgiveness than permission, especially with the Elders." He sighed. "She's seen my face, Finn..."

"She's seen mine, too. And the others." Stitches had let that slip early on in the conversation. "She's determined to get under our skin without having a fucking clue how dangerous the game she's playing is." He shook his head. "The others have asked some questions that make me think this might be more dangerous than even I thought at first. Emerson has been digging into his old journals. He seems to think our fathers were killed because they were coming to the conclusion that the blood sacrifices they were making after being with our mothers were causing energy surges.

"Apparently Emerson's dad took his findings to the Elders and a few days later they were all summoned for the final sacrifice." All except your dad. He didn't say it, but the words hung there between them as though he'd shouted them.

Ghost sneered, his mind working through the information. The man was brilliant, and Finn knew the questions would start in moments. "And Stephan got away unscathed, and became an Elder. I always thought it would be your father, since he was their leader. It should have been," he said with finality. "I asked Stephan, after it happened, why he was spared. He told me the Elders had decided it was to be his task to advise us." He frowned. "Which led to more killings, and no mention of us procreating. Finn, our fathers were younger than us when they had us. Stephan is only fifty-nine."

"Why would they choose him to advise us?" Devil rammed the point home. "Neon's dad was the academic. Plague's dad was the most devout. Is it because Stephan was the most easily molded to their will? Or did he play some other part in the dissolution of that group?"

"I honestly don't know." Ghost sighed. "That night, when we were brought in, stood with the Elders and were told it was our turn, I felt nothing except hope that he would leave me be." His voice was quiet. "What he did to me... What he put me through... I thought it would be over. But no, the Elders took *your* fathers and left me with that fucking evil son of a bitch." Ghost's admission was candid and agonizing. It was the first any of them had heard this, and the fact that it was just Devil hearing it wasn't a coincidence. Ghost played it close to the vest because he had to.

"They left all of us with him. Maybe it was by design. We were young enough to be influenced. We were just about to start our own devotions." He looked up. "And we were all at an age that sex wasn't important yet."

"If this goes wrong, how far are you prepared to go?" Devil asked bluntly. He already knew that Leo and Emerson were ready to burn the Elders to the ground. He knew he was ready to do whatever it took to serve his God, and if that meant taking out the people standing in the way of feeding Him all the energy He needed to do His work, Devil would take the mission. But however much Ghost hated his dad, there was still that tie of blood and forced respect.

"For her? All the fucking way. I will never find another woman that enjoys this...wants it. She is solace in a world that simmers in filth. Nothing takes her from me, from us. Even if I have to slit every Elder's throat to make it happen." He grinned, then frowned. "Elders, now that I think about it, I don't remember having seen in a long time." He looked to his friend. "Where are Elder Dumfries, and Elder Gorgan?" he asked of two elders that they had seen at their own fathers' houses before the purge.

"I haven't seen them since...that day." It still choked in Devil's throat to talk of the day of the sacrifice. "Do you think they were killed, too? I'd wondered whose place Stephan took to become an Elder." But you never asked those questions. Their rule was absolute. Or at least it had been until now.

"Something has to have happened to them. I haven't seen any of them since before your fathers died, and aside from my father, I have never had contact with any of the Elders at the Temple. Have you? I mean you should, you are our leader, but my father contacts me." He frowned.

"No, I just get contacts from the group email account or the central line," Devil said. "They never introduce themselves. I never know who's speaking. The only time we ever see them face to face is the ceremony on the second of November every year and even then we don't speak to them."

"Isn't that odd? I mean, Dumfries and Gorgan used to come to our fathers' houses for meetings, and dinner. Hell, I remember seeing them at Emerson's eleventh birthday party." Emerson was the oldest of all of them by a month. Soon after that day, their fathers had been called in.

"I suspect it's because our fathers being friendly with some Elders gave them too much power," Devil said thoughtfully. "If I had to guess from a political perspective, I'd say they're consolidating their power base by becoming less approachable. Removing any idea that it might be democratic and ruling by fear alone. That's possibly why they kept Stephan alive...not just because they could control him, or he rolled on the others to save himself, but because they knew he was the only one that wouldn't raise us in our fathers' image." A rueful smile quirked his lips, despite himself. "And yet here we are, all these years later, pursuing pleasure instead of death."

"Something Stephan has not been on board with completely. And they haven't once asked about any of us having children. That's what's bothered me the most. How does this organization and blood legacy continue if we don't have children?"

"Look at what we're doing," Devil pointed out. "They purged our parents for being trouble makers and now we're bucking the trend by going with the pact instead of killings. Maybe they're hoping our rebellious bloodlines die with us. They've made arranged marriages for other people. And no one knows what happens to our sisters." That was something that had always bothered him. He knew his parents had given birth to a girl before he'd been born, but that was all he knew. No one ever talked about her or mentioned her, and then they were gone and he had no one to ask. "Maybe they raise them in a convent somewhere to be brood mares for other members of The Order. Meek and willing brides under the eye of He Who Sleeps."

"Asking Stephan would be a fool's errand," Ghost agreed. "There are too many unanswered questions, and it's curious that we ended up with a female we all want and are willing to kill *for*, not kill." He grinned. "These Elders, if they are in fact Elders, have their own agenda, my father included. We have to see them on the second, and when we do, I think we need to have a plan."

"I think we need to look at the bigger picture," Devil sighed. Being a politician wasn't something that came naturally to him, but if they were looking at eliminating the Elders, as he feared they were, then they had to take the aftermath into account. The Order would be looking to new leaders, and if they wanted to avoid the mistakes of their forefathers, that new leader had to be Devil. And if this was all carried out in the shadows, behind closed doors, as their fathers' deaths had been, how many groups in five years' time would be sitting and plotting rebellion, as Devil himself was now?

"We have to do it openly and loudly," he said. "No one can deny Petra's power. No one can deny that the well is literally boiling with her energy. Heck, we could take video of the well here. If we openly ask to keep her, in front of witnesses, people will be forced to think and ask questions when they inevitably say no. They'll wonder why the Elders are refusing an obvious power source. And if the Elders are forced to say yes because we've publicly backed them into a corner, you know they'll come for us privately. And we can use that, too.

"We can take all the proof we need—videos or recordings of them declaring us outcasts or whatever and then make it public when we take them down. If we do this all behind the scenes, the way they would, there will always be questions about the legitimacy of our actions and we can't have that. Not if we want to keep her safe."

"Oh, I'm not saying we do it in the shadows. I'm saying we be the killers they fucking raised." Ghost smirked.

"Yes, but we still need to make it legitimate," Devil insisted. "They raised us to be killers, but they didn't raise us to be idiots. If we want this to be one and done, we have to make a show of it."

Ghost nodded. "The fact remains that they want us to give energy through violence, right? Personally, I think we need to show up and just take them the fuck out, because something tells me the coup that was pulled on our fathers, on the actual Elders, needs to be avenged." He frowned harder. "The fact that it's taken 'til now, and a sexy woman unmasking us for us to question..."

"It's a cult," Devil reminded him with a self-deprecating shrug. "Brainwashing is part of the shtick. What's important is that we are waking up. We are questioning. And we're not going to make the same mistakes the current Elders did. If we just turn up and take them out without explanation, what's to stop other groups trying to do the same to us five years down the line? Just because we've joined the dots doesn't mean anyone else will have, so we need to make it obvious." And if Neon's father's books hadn't been destroyed, they'd be able to share his work, too—show The Order exactly how long the Elders had been pulling the wool over their eyes.

"Do we even have names for the Elders right now? Aside from my father?"

"No, but we know they're all going to be there on the second. We must act quickly and decisively."

He nodded. "I just meant that Dumfries and Gorgan, and the others we knew well enough, were blood legacy. They have younger acolytes, or at least they did. Gorgan's grandson has to be at least twenty-three now. I'm saying they could be traced back to blood legacy, but we don't know any of the men on the council right now, except for Stephan. What if they aren't blood legacy? If we make any mistakes, we'll have to keep all the legacy bloodlines safe because that's where they'll retaliate to consolidate their grasp on The Order. Emerson has the family trees..."

"The best way to keep them safe is to remove the threat," Devil said. "Make it clear, open and decisive, and I doubt anyone would retaliate. We don't make mistakes."

"You're right, but I still think we need to find the other families, and I think we need to ultimately share the load. It's clearly not true that violence is the most powerful energy we send below and we can prove that. We can prove that the Elders have lied. If they join us from the start, we won't have to worry about making mistakes. We might even uncover other lies if we all start sharing our stories. Maybe energy transference isn't only set for these two days, maybe it's something the Elders fabricated as well."

"It's possible." Devil shrugged. "I think that's been the way of it since The Order was founded, but that might be tradition rather than truth. Maybe in the early days when the men were allowed to have women around, the Dark God fed on lust all year and these two nights of blood sacrifice were just a bonus feast of plenty."

"It just seems like something that could be a means of control. My father loves control. And now that you say that, I wonder if they're trying to control the Dark God, too. By removing the women, they're starving Him of power and reducing the risk that He is powerful enough to purge them Himself. Do you remember, at all, how things were with your mother?"

"Not really," Devil admitted. "She traveled a lot with work and then she disappeared."

"It's always been me and Stephan," Ghost said softly. "I know Emerson and Jack both remember their mothers, but have you ever noticed that you lost them around the same time? When you were five to six years of age? Maybe that was the catalyst? For your fathers I mean, to start questioning and doing the research. Maybe for mine as well."

"We've never been told what happened to them, either," Devil mused. "Just that they weren't coming back. I know my dad grieved." It was so obvious in hindsight. "Maybe that's why Emerson's dad went down the rabbit hole about energy transference."

"What if..." Ghost sighed. "What if losing my mother was the straw that broke the camel's back, Finn? Stephan has always been a shitheel, and spiteful to boot. Not having her, when his team still had their women... Something feels right in assuming that if he couldn't have her, they couldn't have theirs, either. And that would be a domino drop, so to speak. Jesus...what if all of this is his own design? Why the fuck else would Stephan be named to the council? He wasn't extraordinary. Hell, my family isn't even one of the

139

major legacy bloodlines. We've always been a lesser house."

"Whatever the reason he did it, the point is that he did. We can't undo the past. We just have to make sure it never happens again."

"So we kill them all." Ghost grinned. "She okay seeing your face?" he asked, changing the subject.

"Why wouldn't she be?" Devil smirked. "I'm a handsome fucker and the world knows it."

"Asshole." He grinned. "I mean, considering you work with her..." he offered. Ghost did, too, if indirectly, his practice offering free clinics for the animals at her shelter.

"She wasn't surprised." Devil shrugged. "But she'd seen the others first. I think she'd have been more surprised if I wasn't someone she knew."

Ghost nodded. "Same, though she knows me even less." He grinned. "Having her to play with all year is going to be amazing."

"Well then... Glad you're on board." Devil rose to his feet and clasped Ghost's forearm. "Let's make this happen."

Chapter 15

Stepping into the bedroom, Petra noticed Goblin standing with his back to the door, looking out the window and padded forward. "I am here, my Goblin," she said softly and waited for him to turn.

She was slightly buzzing from her time with Stitches, the endorphins keeping her slightly high. She wasn't sure what she was in for with Goblin, but she was eager to spend the time, and to, hopefully, see him.

The others, so far it had been both nerve wracking and wonderful, and her Goblin...

"Get on the bed," he said and she looked over to it, seeing long swaths of silk tied to the four corners. She grinned. Goblin was going to tie her up? Well then...

She slipped onto the bed, moving to the center, and shed her robe. In seconds she was flat on her back, and Goblin was above her, making quick work of her bonds.

"Now, I know what you are doing, Pet...and this is going to go how I want," he said as he finished tying the right wrist up and moved down to her legs. "Knees up," he said and she did, treated to the long swaths of green silk wrapping around her thigh and calf, keeping her legs bent and immobile. "Gods, I love you all trussed up," he said absently as he leaned back.

She was laid out, arms over her head, hands gripping the green silk, and her thighs open, legs folded on themselves. The cool air of the room caressed her heated flesh and she felt her nipples pearl as Goblin undressed, leaving his mask on, and settled himself on his knees between her thighs, slowly pushing into her.

"Ah..." she moaned and arched, the perfect length of him as he slid inside her... He stopped as she felt herself reach the root of him, and he leaned over her, hands on the bed on either side of her torso. "So fucking good." She moaned.

"Enjoy it while it lasts...the pain will be there soon enough. Well, you will feel uncomfortable," he amended. "See...I don't really want you hurting. But I need your submission to me."

"I'm yours, my Goblin," she said. "I will endure for you."

"Yes you will," he said and gripped her waist as he took her at a very brutal pace. She gasped, sobbed and surrendered to what he was doing to her, bringing her to the edge.

And then retreated. He ran his fingers over her torso, petted her, pressed on her body in different places that made her pulse. Biting her lip, she felt the orgasm sitting, shifting but not blooming, waiting.

"I can do things to you...as you well know," he said, voice modulated, "that can keep you here, just on the edge of coming, on the edge of flying...but it can also cause pain," he offered and pressed the heel of his hand onto her navel. Severe discomfort assailed her for moments. "That's a pulse point...that's a point that can render you incapacitated..." She gasped as the pain shot through her. "Or can send you to heaven." He changed the angle of his palm and pressed again and she almost shot off the bed.

"Goblin!" she moaned as her sheath gripped him, though the orgasm was still sitting there, unchained.

Goosebumps bloomed on her skin and she panted, the pleasure there, but it wasn't an orgasm.

"Tantra can be used for many things, sweet," he said and looked up to her, his goblin mask's attention on her. "Do you crave what I give you?"

"Yes..." she moaned. "I'm yours, Goblin...to use at your will."

He pressed that point again and she shuddered, the pleasure there but once again not an orgasm. She realized then that he was giving her measured thrusts of his beautiful, perfect cock, and it was keeping her there, just on the precipice.

"I know you want to see me...but I want you begging for it. Will you beg for my face...or the orgasm I wonder..."

"Please..." she moaned, looking at him. "The orgasm is hollow without the connection. I need you...please..." she sobbed. "I'm yours, but I want you... You, my Goblin..."

"Fuck," he said and took her harder. "Me? Me?"

"You... Oh fuck..." she moaned as he backed off the orgasm once more. Panting, she smiled at him. "Please...more..."

"More? Of this?" He flexed his hips and she started to feel the pain in her hips and legs.

"Show me... Please... So I can come all over you."

"So sure you are going to like what you see?"

"I like you, Goblin... My Goblin... My sexy fucking Goblin..."

"Not anymore," he said and pulled his mask off, pinching her clit at the same time.

She shattered then, the orgasm twisting inside her as he stared her down with his beautiful golden eyes. She knew him, knew exactly who he was and she cried out, "Jack!" as the orgasm made spots flow into her vision.

And then his cock was gone, and her legs where free and he had his mouth between her thighs, torturing her with his tongue and teeth and she was shaking. Another orgasm ripped through her as he speared her with his tongue, groaning, and then she was on her stomach, Jack's cock inside her again as he took her at a brutal pace.

Sheened with sweat, he gripped her hips, fingers pressing down, creating pressure that didn't feel like it could come from where he was pressing her body. Her core fluttered and he shouted as she felt him shoot insider her, hot and thick, and gods it triggered another orgasm inside her, causing her to moan and...

"What...what happened?" she said. It felt like she blinked but she was not tied anymore, and he was between her thighs, still inside her but she was on her back now, and he had her thighs wrapped around his hips, playing his fingers just around her clit.

She watched as he pulled out and scooped the come that came with him, then rubbed it into her clit and pussy, a smirk on his face. "Waste not want not," he said and looked at her. "Hey, beautiful."

"Hi," she said and licked her lips. "That was... Did I black out?"

He nodded. "Consider it a dress rehearsal...for future play dates." He winked and swiped some of their mingled release on his tongue, and leaned in, kissing her. "God below...you are perfect."

She grinned, the taste of herself and him together on her tongue. Who knew Jack was the kinda guy that liked snowballing?

"Speak for yourself. Yoga?"

He nodded. "We can get into just how bendy I actually am at another time."

"And that Tantra... Jack..."

He put his finger to her lips, and she moved to get it into her mouth to suck on it. He groaned. "Oh, we will see about that soon enough, Pet. You got about fifteen minutes to clean up and get ready." He leaned down and kissed her again. "Be a good girl."

Chapter 16

Petra lay in the large bed Goblin had left her in, smiling to herself. Jack. Of all people. Her bendy Jack was Goblin and boy did he give her every reason to want to see him again, even if he wasn't her Goblin. She felt good, sore, but it wasn't close to what she could be, or should be feeling. The tea, the magic of the night...it was possible their god watched out for her, too, as it was in His best interest.

She turned over to see her fifteen minutes were almost up and sighed, both sad to leave the bed, but excited to see Plague. Her most mysterious of her seven. Tonight, hopefully, things would change. She padded to the bathroom and checked her back, which was healing well and quickly, and the cut on her sternum, which was also not red or inflamed anymore. She grabbed the black robe that had been waiting there for her, padded out into the house, down the hall and then up a set of stairs, to the space she considered solely Plague's.

What was once an aviary, or should have been, was void of anything but scorch marks, its high dome with strategic windows open, both to feed and control her Plague's favorite thing: fire. The ground was warm and she padded into the space proper. "Plague?" she called, wondering which door he would come through.

"I'm here." He appeared from out of the shadows, where he had been kneeling down so she hadn't seen him. He struck a match and tossed it to the ground and the narrow channel that circled the room flared to light. At some stage it must have been for cleaning the run-off from the birds, but now it made a handy circle of fire. She'd smelled the fire gel when she'd walked in but hadn't pinpointed it to anything specific. The effect was spectacular.

Her smile was large as she turned around, stepping on the stones ringed by the fire. Gods, his obsession with fire was devotional, and he understood it in a way few did. He made it beautiful; he made her see it as beautiful. Her eyes met his mask and she bowed to him, softly. "What is your pleasure, my Plague?"

"To paint you. To set you aflame. To make you burn for me in every way." Even with the modulator, his voice sounded raw. "Lie on the table."

She nodded and slipped up to the stone table, lying back. His reverence was infectious. With Plague, she always felt so close to the dark divine he worshiped.

Approaching, he pulled open the belt of her robe with slow, deliberate movements, letting it fall apart and slither down the sides of her body, until she was lying in a pool of silk midnight. She knew it would be a natural fiber and nothing synthetic that might catch fire and stick to her. He had command of all things in this room and nothing would hurt her. Except him. When she had enough skin on display for his satisfaction, he prepared his tools—a small bowl of liquid that she'd guessed over the years was a high-percentage proof alcohol, cotton swabs, a candle and tapers. "Are you ready?" he asked her.

"Yes, Plague," she said softly, her body waking under his scrutiny. The mask held no visible openings, unlike the others, and in a way it was always kinda hotter to her, given the circumstances.

"Good." With a pair of surgical clips he dabbed a piece of cotton wool in the liquid and streaked it across her skin in a twisting, swirly pattern. It felt cold, the icy kiss of winter's first snowflake, but then he held a lit taper just millimeters from her skin and the fire raced along the pattern he'd drawn, a quick burn that raced across the design, tingling and stinging that evaporated in mere seconds.

"So fucking pretty," he murmured. Again, he dipped the cotton and then drew it across her, lighting it and gazing at the flames as they raced across her belly. The next time, he drew rings around her nipples.

"Ah...Plague..." she moaned, the roll of the flames across her skin, the tingle as they burned out... She watched as the flames ringed her nipples and bit her lip as they tightened. She was a kinky little thing, and it was all thanks to the seven. She loved each of the things they loved, but Plague's fire was the most seductive of all of it.

He did it again, mesmerized, before drawing broad swaths of liquid across her until it felt, and looked, as though she were completely aflame. Off to one side, a red light blinking in the darkness showed the camera that was taking photographs of every moment of this and she ached to know what she looked like, laid out this way.

A burning offering to a dark god, on an altar built by a madman. He swirled and burned her belly and her legs, only then returning to the mound above her womanhood, where he drew more slowly and deliberately.

She shook softly, adrenaline coursing through her. It was from the act, not fear or worry. Plague wouldn't burn her, not when she loved what he did to her. The reverence in his motions, careful and precise... She could feel how wet she was getting from his ministrations, and he hadn't even touched her.

He took his time playing with the fire, streaking her here and there, sometimes just holding a burning swab close enough to her skin to give her a rush of adrenaline and a sting of pain before it was gone and he was setting fire to other things. When the bowl was empty, he blew out the candle and dragged her roughly across the

147

stone table toward him, his strong hands big enough to fully encircle her ankles.

The moan that left her lips was guttural, more turned on than she should be, seeing as the man was setting her body on fire. "Fuck, Plague..."

"Yeah," he agreed, parting his robes to free his cock, which had a beautiful curve that she knew was going to hit her in all the right places. "Watch me while I fuck you," he commanded.

She sobbed and bit her lip, nodding as she kept her eyes on his body, how he pulled her farther so she was all but hanging off the edge, his perfect cock lined up with her own body this way. "Fuck, you are beautiful, Plague."

He shoved into her with one hard slide, the channel already slick from her wetness and his brothers' cum. The rhythm he set was punishing, but he still paused to pour the cooling wax from the candle across her belly in splatters of pearly white when he judged it wasn't still too hot.

"Oh... Oh..." Her body arched into the soft wax, and she watched it roll down her body, along the swell of her breast, brushing her nipple. "Plague!" She writhed as the orgasm shuddered through her, deep, reaching and perfect. "Plague..."

"That's it," he crooned, his modulated voice echoing eerily in the chamber. "Come for me."

"So, so good... More... Please, Plague...more..."

"So demanding," he teased, punctuating each syllable with a sharp thrust of his cock.

"I...fuck...I did say please." She closed her eyes as another wave of pleasure hit her. "So fucking good, Plague. I can feel you everywhere."

"Good." He picked up the pace, his skin smacking into hers with sharp cracks that filled the still air, until he too became undone, losing his rhythm as he filled her, with a soft growl of satisfaction.

"Oh god... Yes... Plague!" Her body clamped down on his, and stars burst in her vision, his perfect cock sending her into the stratosphere. Panting, she floated and then drifted down, her eyes open, and watching him watching where they were joined, her lover panting and straining.

He let out a soft chuckle as their breathing evened out and then he sighed, pulling out of her and stepping back, letting her legs drop down so she could sit up on the edge of the table. "I guess it's time," he said, sounding sad, even with the modulator, and she noticed that his hands were shaking as he raised them to his head to undo the straps of his mask. When he finally pulled it away, his striking grey eyes were full of pain and at first she didn't realize why, but then she noticed the scars. The front of his face was unblemished, but starting an inch before his hairline, his skin was a mass of shiny pale scar tissue.

Gods...what he must have gone through. Though it didn't matter to her. He was her Plague, and she was already half in love with him. Instead of addressing it, because something told her he wouldn't welcome it, not until he was ready, she decided to move forward. "Hi." She bit her bottom lip, fighting the urge to reach for him. "I don't think we have met. I mean, you don't only know me from in here?" She smiled. "I know the rest of the guys in some way in the outside world, so how do we know each other?"

"Maybe hearing my real voice might clue you in," he told her, something hopeful in his expression.

She nodded, recollection rolling through her at the deep, sexy timbre, one that when she had heard it, over the phone on an almost daily basis, made things stand up and take notice. Carter, the Animal Control officer she had never met from Philadelphia County. He was her personal hero. What he did for the animals, from closing down fighting rings to sending litters to them from those rings. She knew he was also part of a dog rehab, to help those animals that were exploited. Gods, she loved him for what he did, and now knowing he was her Plague?

"Carter," she breathed. "My sexy-voiced hero Carter." She did reach out then and pull him closer. "It's you..."

"Your hero?" He looked shocked at that, but let her pull him in close. "I thought you'd be annoyed that I make so much work for you guys."

She shook her head. "Every life you save, every time you stop these assholes, you are my hero, Carter, because you care for those smaller than yourself." She cupped his cheek and giggled. "All the girls at the shelter fan themselves when you call because, well, you sound hot as fuck." She grinned. "Good to see that sentiment is true."

"I'm not hot." He pulled away from her. "The Dark God did what he could, and the scars fade every year, but I still have mirrors and two eyes."

"Don't believe me then, but it's still the truth." His face was rugged, full lips she was dying to kiss, bright beautiful eyes, slashes of black for eyebrows, strong jaw and nose. She bet he was beautiful when he smiled. The scars? Personally, she liked them. They just enhanced the sexy dude that knew how to play her body like a violin. "Now, will you kiss me, Carter? Please?"

"Only since you asked so nicely." He captured her mouth in a passionate kiss and swept her up in his arms, almost crushing her body to him, and she understood then how much her acceptance of his scars had moved him. One day she would ask about them, but now? Now was for kissing her hero.

Chapter 17

Dawn was less than two hours away. Carter had sent her off after a few more kisses to her room, and a shower, and there was a robe waiting for her, plush and fluffy with a note to go to the last room on the left, which she knew was Neon's room.

She padded down the hall, intent on seeing her last lover, though sad because he was the last. And while she did know who they all were now, she didn't know where things were going to go after the sun rose, and how things would sit now that she knew.

Oh, she knew she would be discreet with them, and she would keep their secret, always, but leaving them in a few hours...it didn't feel right. Damn it, forever felt right.

Opening the door, she found Emerson, because his mask was on the bedside table, waiting for her in a pair of very thin sleep pants. "Right on time," he said before she was in his arms and he was carrying her to the bed.

"Different..." she said as he deposited her with an oof.

He smiled. "I'm trying something different," he said and shucked his pants, crawling up on the bed to her.

"Oh?" She smiled, enjoying watching how he moved toward her, all controlled violence and grace. She wasn't sure what was going to happen, but warning bells were not going off in her head so, trust was still the word of the day.

Reaching her, he smiled as he looked her over. "Seeing you at my mercy is a powerful thing, and it does things to me, but seeing you here, soft, willing and bright, it's doing something else to me. I got to thinking before, what would mutual pleasure do for both of us..."

"It's always pleasure with you, Emerson," she said. His oral fixation with her at first was daunting, but now, she loved when he used her for his pleasure. "I'm yours to use how you need."

"Tonight, I need to love you, and just as me," he said, caressing her naked thigh.

"Is that allowed?" she said with a frown.

"You don't want that?"

"I do... Very much," she said. "I just don't want that secret wish to ruin this...for you all."

He groaned and she was under him. "It's my secret wish, too," he said and kissed her. She melted into him arched into his naked body as his hands made quick work of the fluffy robe, exposing her to him. Skin on skin, she whimpered and moaned as he lifted her hip and drove into her, fast and hard, and she gasped.

"Em..." she moaned as she kissed his face, shoulder, anywhere she could reach, as he took her, hips rolling. She arched to meet each thrust, their skin on skin contact making everything more...connected. "Fuck, you are so fucking good to me."

"You feel so fucking good, baby." He turned them and she was on top then, his grin finding her. "Ride, baby...don't hold back, yeah?"

She closed her eyes, tipped her head back and bounced on him, his hands rolling up her thighs, her torso, fingers pinching her nipples. "Ah!" she cried out as she came for him, the pinch bringing it to the foreground. And then she was moving, off his cock, his hands on her hips holding her up as he settled her just at his shoulders. "Wha..."

She barely got the words out before he was wrapping his arms around her thighs and pulling her down to his mouth. "Oh God! Emerson!" She shook as he sucked her clit, sending her skyrocketing once again.

"Gods, you really need to sit on my face more often," he groaned from under her. "So fucking sweet..."

Panting, she nodded. "Anything you want, my Neon..."

"No, right now I'm Emerson... Your Emerson..."

"Yes... Fuck yes..." she said and then he was sliding her down his body once more. He rolled them so she was under him and entered her again, she sobbed. "So good..."

"You give of yourself to me, to him?" he said as he loved her.

"Yes..." she said. "For you, for him.."

He took her harder then, gripping her hips, giving as he took, sending her to the stratosphere once again. "Emerson, please... Please..."

Snarling, he changed his angle and she shattered once more, and she screamed into the coming dawn, giving everything 'til it turned into a whisper, tears coming to her eyes.

Emerson was there, kissing her, whispering praise, his hands rubbing her sides, skin...everything a lover would do...everything someone that loved her would do.

"Holy shit," she said as she came down, kissing him, their lips doing a dance her body loved. "Emerson..."

"God below... You are amazing..." He kissed her once more, and then rolled them so he was holding her. "I'm never going to get enough."

Chapter 18

"Leo should be here any minute," Emerson said to her from the bathroom door. Their time together, their appointment was over. Dawn was literally breaking in less than fifteen minutes, and then...then it was very possible she wouldn't see them again, ever.

"So what happens now?" she asked as she slipped from the bed, tender and aching, in severe need of a spa day, but she would see this through. "Normally I'm bundled off by now to the car."

"Clearly that's not happening this morning." He smirked. "You have unmasked us, so things are going to be different."

"How?"

He went to answer when Leo walked in, in his robes, carrying his mask.

"Hey, gorgeous," he said with a soft smirk. "I came to check up on your back. It feeling okay?"

She nodded and went to him, turning to show him. "Whatever is in that tea you guys leave for me helps." Looking over her shoulder at him, she smiled. "See? I'm okay."

Emerson walked out of the bathroom in his own robes. "And she's relaxed, which feels different, doesn't it? Last time, you didn't feel like this." He looked to Leo. "Are the others at the well?"

"They're heading that way," Leo said. "Devil got a call in the office, but the others were on the way down. You heading that way?"

He nodded. "We gotta finish this, don't we? Pet, you wanna see something cool?"

She blinked at them. What happened after they were done with her was a complete mystery to her, so it seemed she was about to see behind the curtain. "I...sure? I mean if you don't think it's a problem."

"Personally, I think you should see this, see what the night brings for us." He looked to Leo to corroborate.

"Uh...sorry, dude, but we should speak to Devil before we just let her come on down. There might be some sort of rule about it." He at least had the grace to look sorry about it.

"Like we haven't broken every rule this cycle?"

"It's okay, I should... I should get dressed and get going." Petra didn't want to disturb the tenuous new bonds she'd formed with both of them by setting them against each other.

"No, stay," Stitches told her. "I'll go speak to him right now. It would be good for you to see this so you don't have to wait a whole year." He grinned and slipped out of the room.

"Emerson..." Petra looked to her lover. "What happens after this? I mean, I know who you all are..."

"And we know you." He grinned and helped her into a black terrycloth robe. It was warm, and fluffy, his scent on it. It had to be his normally. "If you think any of us are going to be able to stay away now..." He shook his head. "You are too important."

"It's nice to hear that, but..."

"But nothing. Things are changing, that's more than clear. I can't begin to understand it or what it means over all, but I trust Finn. His decisions are always in our best interests."

"He's the leader?"

Emerson nodded. "Ever since we were kids. His dad was the leader of our dads' group. He just...I don't know. He just makes you want to follow him. And he's good to all of us. Always makes the decisions based on what's good for all of us."

"And me?"

"I honestly don't know. I know he wants you, same as the rest of us, but things are complicated."

Leo slipped back into the room with a broad grin on his face. "He said yes," he told them. "You should definitely come down and watch this—see what it's all about."

"See? Told you." Emerson winked. "Go with Leo; I'll be just behind you."

Taking Leo's hand, she left the room with him, traversing the hallway and then out into the pre-dawn, the air cool, but not cold thanks to Emerson's fluffy robe. She squeezed Leo's hand.

"You nervous?" he asked her with a grin. "You don't have to be. It's all on us, right now."

"Curious," she said. "It's a constant wonder for me what you guys do after I leave."

"Well, it's nice for us to draw back the curtain a little," he said, sounding genuine. "If you're going to stick around, you should know how and why we do all this."

"I guess I should."

Emerson caught up with them moments later as they started their descent, the stone steps flanked by bushes and plants, night blooming datura which was odd, considering where they were. It was proof that where they were was outside of the norm, magical. Her feet hit the stones, slightly warm, and she was grateful for it.

She saw the flames of candles before them and stopped when the guys stopped in the doorway to a space she hadn't been before. A rotunda, a dome over the space that soared, but wasn't complete, the stars peaking through small slats. Off from center was a circular stone well, moody and glowing light coming from it.

"There she is," Jack said, his Goblin mask off.

The others were all there already, Devil coming down the steps just behind them.

"Come and stand over here." Stitches led her off to one side where she could watch what was happening, but wasn't in the way of the men forming up around the well.

She looked to each of her guys, curiosity and pride filling her. They disrobed, standing in soft black pants, but no shirts, and she noticed each of them had a specific tattoo, a roman numeral for seven, on different parts of their torso. Considering she hadn't seen them all naked, it made sense she was only just noticing them.

"It's time," Devil said quietly as pale light began to filter into the eastern sky. "The God will soon descend beyond the veil. Let us render unto Him that which we have gathered."

As one, they drew gleaming silver blades from sheaths concealed in their pants, and sliced their own palms, without hesitation. She gasped, but they were all fixated on the well as they stretched out their arms, letting trickles of blood fall into the water beneath, which was glowing and bubbling as though it boiled with magic.

"From her blood to ours, to the service of the one God, the true God, He Who Sleeps. Accept this, our Lord, our sacrifice from the blackest night and the eve of all souls. Be nourished by our devotion and grant us, we beg of you, the rewards that you promised in return for our service." He bowed his head and tendrils of light began curling up from the well, coiling around each slashed hand. The men shuddered, some of them closing their eyes, and she noticed that more than one of them was sporting an erection. Whatever the light was doing to them, it was pleasurable.

Sunlight broke the mountain tops, as the curl of magic dissipated, leaving them standing there, the color of the well dimming as the light grew in the sky. She watched as they each flexed their hands, the slice they had made healed. Much like she was after drinking the tea.

"He is pleased," Kendrix said and looked to Devil. "Can you feel it?"

She could feel it, something spinny and sparkly, like sparks from a sparkler.

"He chose luck," Emerson said. "Luck..."

She was quiet while they looked at each other and then walked forward when she was beckoned by Devil.

"What do you mean, luck?"

Emerson smiled. "He Who Sleeps will offer a specific reward for the year ahead. Luck is the most coveted, and the least given. We haven't received it before."

"What did you get before?"

"Growth, and peace," Jack offered. "Those are what are normally given."

"What that means," Leo explained in simpler terms, "is that His gifts will come in the form of luck this year. Lottery wins. Success in the tenders we pitch for. Opportune alignments of things all coming together at the right moment for us to benefit. A new artist to be discovered for your gallery, just as they hit the big time, for example."

"Oh," she nodded, understanding the concept. "That's cool."

Emerson grinned at her. "And it's all thanks to that stunning responsive body of yours."

"And how accepting she is of us," Jack said. "He is pleased because of her."

"Which is a good sign for our approach to the Elders." Devil sounded reassuring, but she'd known him long enough outside of these walls in her day job to recognize the tightening around his eyes as the concern that it was. "Come, you must be exhausted. We should get you home to bed."

"I normally sleep a full day after this."

"We know. We watch you, make sure you are okay," Jack said. "Now...well..."

She looked to Devil and then to Kendrix. "I have to ask. You keep saying you are going to approach the Elders about me. Does that mean I have to wait to see you all again?"

Rix laughed. "Needy little thing..."

"Not needy. I just...things could be different and I like that."

"We're in your life anyway," Devil pointed out. "The only thing that's different is that you know who we are now, so you can approach us if you want to."

She wanted to. Fantasies of seeing her seven danced in her head and she smiled. "Okay. Who is taking me home?"

"That hasn't changed," Devil said, looking sad. "Until you've had formal approval, we can't let you see where we are. But I promise you, we'll be around. Someone will stop by this evening to check on you and bring some food."

She nodded. "Then let me go..." She turned when Emerson grabbed her and kissed her sweetly.

"Sleep well, our little victim."

She giggled, blushing, and heard Kendrix groan.

"Sleep well," Stitches said, and several of the others murmured the same as Emerson took her up the stairs and away to where the black car was waiting.

Chapter 19

Two days later...

"So how was your Halloween Odyssey?" Fiona asked. "I mean, I know you won't really tell us, but we miss you on our Halloween chat."

Unsure what she could actually say for real, she just smirked. "It was a good time, as always."

"Seriously, I don't understand why you just won't tell us what you get up to." Fiona pouted and Carlee laughed.

"Because Pet is getting fucked and she doesn't wanna share." She shook her head. "Girl, keep your secrets; they make you glow."

They were on their weekly video chat, and she missed her friends. Fiona, Carlee and Victoria, the four of them were in four different cities and, for the most part, only had each other. They all worked, or went to school still, as Victoria was getting her Master's, Fiona her Doctorate, and aside from that they didn't have much of a life aside from time with each other.

"So, Vic, how's the thesis coming?" she asked and the conversation changed to that for a few moments, before Carlee changed it to her big contract with the design firm she was working with. It was mundane and normal, and she wished she could tell them about the seven. They already thought she had some kinky lover that had some Halloween fetish, and they seemed to accept it, but who knew what they would say if they found out it was seven sexy as fuck men with severely insane kinks? No, it wasn't time to say anything to them, so she let them speculate.

"Shit, I gotta get to work," Fiona said. "I have class tonight, so don't expect any texts."

"We know." Carlee nodded on the video. "I'll check in once this contract is finished. Should be around Friday."

"So? We good for our meet up next week?" Petra asked.

"Damn right." Carlee nodded again. "I'ma need someone to celebrate with."

"Celebrations all over then. I'll see you guys."

"Love you!" they all said at once before she closed the video call and smiled to herself. Her friends...gods, she missed them. But she had a decent amount to do, considering she went back to work tomorrow.

A knock at the door had her arching a brow. She wasn't expecting anyone, but maybe it was one of her seven. She had slept straight through the previous day, only waking up to pee, and had found lasagna and a salad waiting for her in her kitchen, but she hadn't seen them since.

When she opened the door, it was to find Carter standing there with a take-out bag from her favorite Chinese restaurant and a big grin on his face. "Hey, you," he said, leaning in to kiss her. "I was out this way with work and thought I'd stop by and see if you wanted to share dinner. I'm not interrupting anything, am I?"

She pulled him closer and kissed him again, a grin on her face when she pulled away. "Nope," she said, pulling him into the apartment. "I just got off my call with my friends; you have good timing." She squeezed his hand. "Missed you."

"Missed you, too," he replied, although he looked confused when he said it, as though the realization surprised him. "I meant to swing by earlier, but you know how it is with animals and Halloween." She really did. Every year dozens of pets were scared out of their minds by costumes and constantly ringing doorbells and the occasional firework and ended up running scared.

She nodded. "Gotta be the hero I adore. Come..." They walked into her small kitchenette and she grabbed glasses. "What can I get you to drink?"

"Just a soda, if you have one, please." He took a seat in front of the breakfast bar and it looked like it had been built for him. He was natural here in her space. He belonged.

She handed him a cola and skirted around the table and wrapped herself around him. "So, what did you bring?"

"A mix," he said. "Some beef and broccoli, shrimp with vegetables, crab Rangoon and some vegetable fried rice. I heard that was your favorite order from this restaurant." His eyes twinkled with amusement. Creepy fucker.

"Oh, yeah?" She giggled. "Bet you guys all know what I like to eat from where I order from. Can you use chopsticks?" she asked as she pulled them out of the bag. "Wanna eat at the couch?" The idea of sitting and being comfy while they ate, and hopefully talked, felt more like a date.

"Of course I can use chopsticks." His tone said he could master anything that came to hand, including her, and it made her shiver. "Lead the way."

They set up on the couch, the food on the coffee table, and she settled in next to him as she grabbed a carton of the shrimp and vegetables. "I'm glad you came by."

"Me, too." He settled in comfortably with a carton of crab Rangoon. "When we actually talked about what happened with you at the mansion, I realized the others got to spend a lot more time with you as themselves than I did. It's nice to finally rectify that."

163

She nodded. "Who dropped by yesterday? I was passed out; you guys did me in." She blushed. "And whoever did come by obviously has keys...though I doubt any of you don't have ways into this apartment. I know I should be freaked out about that, but I'm not."

"It was Easton," he replied, surprising her. "He looked in on you and said you were dead to the world. He actually waited to check you were still breathing."

Her Snake. "That was nice of him," she said softly. "So, what happens now? For you guys, I mean. It's all done for the year, right?"

"No, there's still a big gathering at the winter solstice in a few weeks. We all have to go to Europe." He didn't look enthused by the fact. "And this year...well, it's going to be different." He chewed silently for a few moments and then sighed. "It's hard to explain any of this stuff without you knowing anything about The Order, but we're in a difficult position right now. We've generated significantly more energy than any other group and the Elders are going to be pissed about it because, for some reason, they'd prefer we killed for the God instead."

"I can see that," she said softly. "Killing is easy to control. "What we did...do...isn't. Dead lips don't speak. Well-fucked ones can still talk."

"It's actually the opposite," he told her. "Killing and getting away with it is hard. Forensics are getting really good these days and CCTV is fucking everywhere. What we do with you is much easier in comparison. I agree that it's about control, but not that aspect of it. It's about controlling us. If they come for one of us, of course we'd fight it, but if they came for you, we'd burn the world to the ground and spit on the ashes."

She smiled at him. "I meant that killing is something you can or could do without emotion, but sex, indulging, is more unpredictable to the person. It's something I have been looking at. Before you guys, the idea of killing was abhorrent, until I broke it down. I mean some people deserve to die and all, for the things they do to others, and animal, but I can see why your Elders would rather the killing. It's not the act of it that's easy; I mean, you guys were raised to kill, right?"

"Yes, but if you think it's an act that lacks emotion, you don't know us at all," he laughed. "Raising a person to kill means tapping into the deepest, darkest, most perverted parts of them. Killing is a thrill. For some of us it's sexual. For others it's intimate. If I thought keeping you meant I'd never kill again, I'd actually think twice about it. But I know you wouldn't stop me killing rapists or drug cartel assholes, so I can still get my kicks and make sacrifices to the God."

"No, I wouldn't," she agreed. "It is distressing, though, knowing they would rather take the deaths over you guys getting your rocks off." She grinned. "I mean, are they just not supportive of women in general?"

"I really don't know the answer to that." He shrugged. "I don't truly know what motivates them because, on the face of it, denying the Dark God energy is completely counterintuitive. But we believe that our fathers were all killed when they started asking questions about it, so this attitude has been in place and in power for a long time."

She looked at him. "Your dads? Oh, Carter. I'm sorry. Did you know him well? Your dad, I mean?"

"As much as a kid can know his father." He shrugged again, but didn't show any signs of clamming up, which meant the world to her. "He was sacrificed when I was nine, so I never really got to know him as a man."

"Oh, Carter..." She leaned in and wrapped her arms around him. "And your mom?"

"I don't really remember her," he admitted. "She disappeared much earlier on. It's only with hindsight that I'm wondering now if the Elders got rid of her, too."

"That's all horrible." She shook her head. "I couldn't even begin to understand how anyone could deal with that. Knowing you had parents and losing them. All I had were my three friends growing up. You did have the guys, though, right?"

"Yeah. That's why we're so close," he told her. "We were all we had."

"At least you had that." Setting her food down, she scooted over and then snuggled into his side. "Where did you guys grow up? Here?"

"No, there's a compound out in the desert in Arizona where the US headquarters of The Order are based," he explained. "All the kids are raised and indoctrinated there. At least they believe in decent education. It's important to them that we succeed in life."

"You guys are all so diverse in what you do," she agreed. "Any sisters?"

"I don't know," he admitted. "I think at least one of us had a sister, but they're taken away at birth. Only boys are raised at the compound and no one talks about the girls."

"Your moms gone early...no sisters..." She shook her head and sighed, snuggling into him deeper. "So why did you guys end up in Philly?"

"Well, we knew we wanted to stay together, but we have such a diverse group of jobs, like you said," he explained. "This is one of the few places where we can find good gallery space and the rest of us still find good employment opportunities."

"Oh, that makes sense. Easton's work is so dynamic."

"So is mine," he teased her gently. "I wouldn't find big baddies to take down just anywhere..."

"That is true. With Germantown and the Norther liberties with the amount of assholes..." She turned to him and smiled. "You know you are my hero."

"I'm just doing what any decent man with a bit of skill and the right connections would do," he disagreed. "Animals are innocents. They don't deserve to be put through what the scum of the Earth put them through."

She nodded. "It's why I work with the shelter. I wish I could have a pet here, even if it was just fostering. Do you guys have pets? Any of you?"

"I have a dog," he told her, his eyes lighting up. "And Easton has a parrot. You know, because they live for so fucking long..." He shook his head, amused. "Not sure about the others."

"A dog? What kind? What's his name?" she asked excitedly. She filed the info of Easton's parrot away for when she saw him next. "You have a picture?"

"Of course I have pictures." He looked at her like she was crazy. Who wouldn't have pictures of their dog? "He's a Great Dane called Brutus." He pulled his phone out and showed her some photos of a dog the size of an elephant with gorgeous steel grey fur.

"Oh my god, he's beautiful!" she squealed, ripping his phone from his hand. "Carter, he's amazing! Oh my god, look at that baby!" She giggled. "When can I meet him?!"

"I'll bring him around next time I come," he promised. "He usually comes to work with me, but I didn't bring him when I left the house this morning."

"I can't wait to meet him. He's the goodest boy," she declared. They finished eating, and she took the plates and leftovers into the kitchen, then came back, sliding into his lap. "So what do you wanna do? I could call for dessert, or we could go out? Pie? Or..." she blushed. "Do you wanna hangout here and get naked? You know...Netflix and chill?"

He glanced at his watch and looked disappointed. "I should go home," he told her. "I have my team on standby for an op tonight. There's a new club in town and we've heard rumors they're cock-fighting. But raincheck? Next time I'll plan to stay as late as you want me."

She nodded. "I guess if you have to go and play hero... Still." She pulled him to her and kissed him, nipping his bottom lip. "I guess I'll be on the lookout for roosters tomorrow?"

"No, if they're there, then I already have a home set up for them outside the city," he assured her. "But I'm really glad we did this. It's important to me, you know, that you see me now as not just some guy behind a mask. Or some asshole that's all about fucking and fire. I'd really like for us to actually get to know each other."

"Me, too." She nodded. "Dare I hope I can see you more often? Don't get me wrong, I like our phone calls, but this...this is so nice. Spending time with you."

"Sure." His smile was broad and then it faltered. "I..." He took a deep breath. "I can't tell you how important it is to me that you don't see the scars," he told her. "I never wanted to see you before because...well..." he gestured helplessly at his face. "Now that I know you don't care, I'll make a point of coming by."

"Why would I care? Carter, they might be on you, but..." she ran her fingers over them, "they don't change anything. You are still sexy as hell, and your voice is shiver-inducing." She winked.

"The world is a harsh judge," he told her. "You might be the sweetest thing in it."

"Fuck the world," she said and kissed him again.

"Indeed," he murmured, kissing her back and then breaking it off, looking hot under the collar. "I have to go or I'll never leave," he laughed. "I'll see you soon. I promise."

She pouted. "Plan to stay the night." She giggled. "I do make mean pancakes."

"I wouldn't miss it for the world." With one last longing kiss, he tore himself away from her and headed for the door.

Chapter 20

Back at work at the gallery, Petra smoothed down her skirt and fixed her fitted vest as she stood and walked toward her boss. Lorne Miaski was a tall and imposing man, but he never once intimidated her. He had a pleasant smile, a fair way of dealing with people, and he had one hell of an artist's eye. He had been instrumental in starting the careers of fifteen different local artists.

"Ms. Franklin. What's on the docket today?"

She opened her tablet and started to read off the list. "And you have a meeting at eleven, but the agenda doesn't say with whom."

"Ah, yes. No worries on that. Full day. I'll need you to handle the intake for the Reynolds show and I'll need you to take the info..." She listened to him go through his day, basically leaving only two of the fifteen things for himself.

"Wonderful. I'll start on that now."

"You do that." He looked down at his cell phone. "Ah, I have to take this." He walked away, lifting the phone to his ear, leaving her to get on with the laundry list of tasks alone.

The morning rolled by, Petra on the phone for most of it, and in the database updating the four sales that she had facilitated. Three people had come in, two picking up and one looking for a piece of art, but for the most part, it had been business as usual.

Until the door opened and Easton stepped in.

"Hey, you." His grin was as genuine as it was unexpected. "How are you doing?"

"Better now," she said softly so no one could hear it, just him. God he looked good. Jeans, boots, a green Henley, a black leather jacket and that fucking smile.

Gods, he was sexy. Louder she said, "Mr. James. Nice to see you. Can I help you?"

"I have a meeting with Lorne at eleven," he told her. "Now that you know who I am, I have a series of artworks I can show and Lorne called me last week to say you have a sudden vacancy next week. One of your other artists pulled out. If you'll arrange for a porter, they're in my van out the front."

"Of course." She nodded. "I'll have Michael and Gabe bring them in." She called back to their warehouse guys and then looked to Easton. "I'm sure it will only be a few minutes 'til I can send you in." She bit her lip, looking him over. "So what's the new show?"

"You know what? I don't think I'm going to ruin the surprise," he told her, his lips tightening as he clearly tried not to smile.

"Meanie." She shook her head on a chuckle, then leaned against the desk. "You doing okay? Carter told me you were the one to check in on me the other day. Thanks for that."

"Of course," he told her. "I just wanted to make sure you had food. We used you hard. And I'm not a meanie. I want you to experience this artwork without any prior thought or feeling going into it."

She nodded. They had. "Well, it was delicious. And thoughtful."

Lorne came out from his office then to see them standing there. "Easton!" He smiled and shook hands with him. "Tell me you brought the work!"

"It's in the van," he told Lorne with a grin. "Petra has kindly arranged for the guys to bring them in. I think you're going to like them."

As if on cue, Michael and Gabe rolled in a sectioned dolly. They followed the warehouse porters into the exhibition room and watched as the guys added each piece, seven of them, to the easels. They were each wrapped, so what they actually were was hidden.

"Seven? Just seven?" Lorne asked as they stood there. "Should they unwrap?"

"Go for it." Easton gestured for them to go ahead and turned slightly so he could watch her face as the covers came off.

At first she wasn't sure what she was seeing. His bold approach to mixed media meant that sometimes the eye had to adjust the dimension of the image until it coalesced into focus and then...oh, holy fuck...it was her.

On the first canvas, she was literally aflame...a session with Plague. It had to be. Bent over a gravestone. Ghost, no question. The third was harder until she got closer to it, and realized that the shading on her naked body was done with needles. It must have taken him hours. "I've had this collection for over a year now," he was telling Lorne in a conversational tone, but his eyes were on Petra as she stared at her naked body, on display for the world to see.

She swallowed, and then again, trying not to let it affect her. But they were...beautiful. Each of the pieces, one for each of the guys, was her in the throes of passion. Her on her knees, head bowed, habit keeping her largely hidden. She knew it hid the cum that had run down her face after Finn had baptized her. Her tied up in silks, the way Goblin had left her after he'd fucked her within an inch of her life. Her lying on the ground, her face obscured, a hand around her throat as she arched. That was when Emerson had fingered her. And finally, her tied over the Sybian, handprints on her ass.

Memories came back to her and she rolled her shoulders, stifling a whimper and a moan. She looked to Easton and bit her bottom lip.

"This is… Easton, you have outdone yourself," Lorne said. "The light, shadow, composition." He looked them over. "What are we calling this series?"

"Worship." He very carefully didn't look at her as he said it, but the back of his hand caressed the curve of her hip discreetly.

The touch… Snake was actually touching her! Her body clenched and she bit her lip again. Fuck, what she wouldn't give to jump into his arms and rub against him. Not that she thought he would welcome that in the least.

"This show is going to be the most celebrated so far, Easton. To think you have been sitting on these for a year? Don't get me wrong, your other shows have been fantastic. But this? This is transcendent."

"I had a good subject. As a muse, she is…inspiring." He said it casually, unaware of the effect the words had on her. Or perhaps too aware.

"Dare I hope she attends and I can meet the muse?" Lorne asked with a smile. "This show…" He trailed off, shaking his head. "We need to talk price per piece, but…" He whistled softly, still in awe.

Petra looked to Easton then, reaching over her chest to hug her own bicep and taking the opportunity to run her finger across his arm softly, before relaxing her stance. She wanted to talk with him, but everything with Snake was on his terms.

She watched them walk out of the room, leaving her alone in the exhibition, faced with her own memories.

"Ms. Franklin? Are we okay to leave these?"

She looked to Gabe. "Yes. And I think you guys are done for the day?"

"Just the drop off of the seller's piece," Michael said.

"Well then, once that's been installed, take the rest of the day." She knew Lorne was planning to leave as well, which was why he had given her so much of his to do list. And she understood why he'd wanted to handle his eleven o'clock himself.

Alone in the room, she looked over the pieces more, falling in love with them harder. Easton was a talent, but this...he made her look like a goddess.

After ten minutes or so, presumably during which they signed contracts, Lorne and Snake reappeared. Lorne waved her goodbye, but Snake lingered by her desk until they were alone.

"So?" He smirked. "Am I still a meanie?"

"Kinda, but for different reasons." She smiled at him. "They are beautiful. Seeing them, seeing how ethereal you made them, how much movement and care they each had...the effect is overwhelming. Honestly, I would jump into your arms and show you, but we aren't there yet, are we?"

"No. And, honestly, that might take a while. But I'm trying." He looked so raw and vulnerable in that moment.

She nodded. "That's all I can hope for. One day you will let me kiss you for this," she offered. "Thank you for making me look beautiful."

"I didn't make you look anything other than what you are," he told her. "I just captured what I saw."

"Like Carter does with his pictures?" She smiled. "I kinda like being your muse. And I wouldn't mind being her through the year," she said hopefully. "No strings...of course."

"I actually used some of his photos in these works," he said. "I'd like to paint you from life, but a lot of what I do is afterwards. I take the shapes and forms and then I layer them, sometimes for many months."

175

"That sounds intensive, and...fun." She grinned. "I'm always here for that, Easton," she said softly, trying to keep her distance. The man was broody and beautiful and being there with him was in no way awkward. She liked talking to him, wanted to spend time talking about artists, what his favorites were. She took a shot. "What's the rest of your day looking like? Lorne just left and I have a lunch break coming up."

"Well then, what kind of gentleman would I be if I didn't escort you to lunch?" He laughed. "You can tell me about your favorite artists." It was like he had read her mind.

"And you can tell me about yours." She grinned. "Sand and Fog, or Crowsnest?" Both small eateries were close to the gallery, just a few minutes' walk away. Both were out of the way and they wouldn't be disturbed. "Or dim sum?" which was where she usually went.

"Whichever is your favorite," he said with a shrug. "I'll eat anything."

"Even those foods based on dares?" she teased. "Come on."

Fifteen minutes later they were sitting in the back corner of her favorite dim sum place just a block away, their order having been taken for drinks. "They send the dumplings out as they are ready. I told Yuki to bring out non-vegetarian ones since I'm sure you're not vegetarian."

"That's very presumptuous of you," he said, but the creases at the corners of his eyes said he was teasing.

"You are right, but something tells me you aren't...satisfied without a little blood." She winked and then shook her head. "But you are right; I should have asked. I can have her bring just the vegetarian ones out."

"No, I'm good." He shook his head. "Meat is fine. I was just teasing."

She nodded. "I know, but I should have asked regardless. I don't know much about you and what I do know...well, it doesn't really correlate to food. So..." She looked down at her plate and picked up the wooden chopsticks, and started to work with them to get them ready for their meal. She wasn't sure what to say; Easton was so hard to read.

"That's partly why I stuck around today," he told her. "We need time to get to know each other. One day these things will all be familiar. I hope...I hope we can do this again...often."

She nodded. "Me, too. I mean, I know the other guys largely have regular day jobs that keep them busy, but you are the artist and make your own hours. Which is like living the dream, isn't it?"

"It is and it isn't." He shrugged. "When the muse rides me, she rides me hard. I can go days without eating and sleeping, and then I crash. The others have to check in on me."

"The hallmark of an artist," she offered. "I have had to go and check on a few of our regulars when they don't check in...proof of life and all that." She smiled. "But that's part of the genius. And your work is always amazing, Easton. The study in shadow that was your last show was some of the most moving work I had ever seen. I wasn't surprised all the pieces sold in the first hour of the show."

"I was," he laughed. "Talent is not a gift we received from He Who Sleeps. I'm always surprised when my paintings sell well."

"I would think not. I mean talent shouldn't be something given, but inherent to the person. But you have real talent, in a way so few do. I mean some can take a picture, or work with oils. Some can draw. Not me, though. I can't draw to save the world," she teased. "But you can do everything, and it's beautiful. Your talent... You will be remembered with the greats in years to come. And no, that's not me blowing smoke up your ass. You have all the benchmarks of timeless work. I'm just honored I could be part of that."

Yuki came back with several steam baskets and set them in front of them, and then came back with a platter of sauces. Petra thanked her, then opened the nearest one to her and grinned. Veggie Gyoza.

"Mixed media is a journey," he shrugged, refusing to accept the compliments. "That's part of the joy of it. I'm always learning new materials, new techniques." He selected a dumpling and ate it with a small moan of satisfaction. "That's good!" he said. "I'll have to remember this place next time I'm in the area." He ate another one like he was inhaling them. "So what about you? Where did you learn about art?" he asked.

"School," she said. "I always liked it, and it was my favorite course in high school. When I went to college, I majored in art history and restoration. Something that stays with the world, long after the artist is gone, that's true immortality, and it makes the world more rich and layered.

"So many artists, though, they go undiscovered or unknown. Some of the best works out there aren't even signed. I wanted to be a part of that. It's why Lorne is doing the undiscovered talent shows every six months. I suggested it, and after he found Gizzy Baker and Tawret London...well, he's kept it. Neither of them would have had a chance to make it to the big time if they hadn't shown at the gallery; they were too obscure."

"You're a champion of the arts," he told her with a small smile of satisfaction. "It helps that Lorne has a good eye for new talent. People trust his judgment when he says someone is going to be big. He's always right."

"Yes, he is. And I have learned a lot from him since I started working there," she agreed. They ate a few more pieces before Yuki came back with new steam baskets. Opening the next one, Petra grinned. Tofu bao for her and she saw what she knew were pork dumplings in Easton's basket. She picked up her bao and dipped it, taking a bite and gave a little moan, and butt wiggle. "Yummy."

"That was fucking adorable," he snorted. "Do it again."

"Wh...what?" She looked around and frowned. "Bite some bao?"

"The little happy food dance butt wiggle thing. You looked like a newborn lamb."

"Oh..." She blushed. "I didn't even realize I was doing it. Yummy food makes me happy." And few things did before.

"It's lovely," he said with a genuine smile. "We have so few joys in our lives. Seeing someone truly experience them to the full is a blessing."

She smiled, blushing again. "So, why did you become an artist, Easton?"

"At first, it was therapy," he admitted. "There was an art program I was allowed to attend from the foster home. I wasn't into it at first, but it got me out of the house and away from... Well, it got me out of the house. For whatever reason, The Order allowed me to continue when they took me in. They even brought in an art tutor to refine my art when some of my pieces were seen by The Elders. One of them is apparently quite the collector."

She looked to him. "You were raised in the system, too?"

"You knew that. Unless you weren't paying attention during our session?" he teased.

"I did, but I mean, full on system. When were you out? We didn't discuss it. Myself and the girls, we were all in 'til we graduated from high school and went to college."

"The Order took me in when I was thirteen. The others were all around the same age." He ate more dumplings. "Did you never go into foster care?" he asked curiously. "I wasn't ever given the option to stay in a home."

She shook her head. "The orphanage kept all of us. We never had the opportunity to go to a home. We all were just there. Though it wasn't like the orphanages you see in movies. It was a huge old Victorian, something like twenty bedrooms, on land just outside of town. We had the Matron, and a few caregivers that came and went, but aside from the Matron we didn't have anyone for too long."

"Did they send you out to school?" He seemed fascinated by the idea, and maybe a little jealous.

"Eventually," she said. "We all started school after our second grade year at a preparatory school, though I don't know how, considering it was a prep school, you know? We were told we had benefactors, but we never met them or anything. When we went to college, we all got some sort of scholarship, though we did work our asses off for them."

"You were lucky," he said softly, some darkness in his eyes that showed itself in the lines of his whole face. "I'm glad for you that your experience was like that."

"It wasn't great. I mean, we didn't have much interaction beyond each other. The Matron was a hard woman, and we learned early to stay out of her way. Holidays weren't a thing for us, nor birthdays, or anything. We were just kinda...kept alive and allowed to learn, if that makes any sense? We didn't have much of anything else." She looked to him. "I take it your experience wasn't quite puppies and rainbows." She didn't like the haunted look in his eyes. "You don't have say or anything..."

"Trust me, your experience is a dream compared to what I went through," he told her. "But in many ways, I'm glad you don't know better. I'm glad the...darkness that touched me never came to your door."

She shook her head. "I'm sorry anything awful happened to you, Easton." She swallowed. "But if you ever wanna talk, I'm here to listen. I might not have had the same experience, but I understand about trauma. Like I said, it wasn't perfect, and I lost people along the way." She thought of Kimberly and her taking her own life. "Fighting demons alone... Just know I'm here for you, regardless. No judgment, no blowback. I'm just here."

"It's enough that you know it happened and that there are consequences," he said with a shrug. "I might overcome them one day. I might not. Either way, I'm prepared to try. For you. For my brothers."

"I'm here for you if you ever need me," she offered as Yuki brought them more food and refills on their drinks. Whatever he went through, she was sure she didn't want to know the details, but she would listen and witness for him, if it helped him. Deciding to change the subject, given the way he was looking at her, she said, "Carter told me you have a parrot?"

"Yes, an African Grey called Niobe," he said, seeming relieved at the change of subject.

She smiled. "Are you kidding? That's so cool! Is she a good girl? I know some Greys can be mischievous. How long have you had her? Does she get along with people, or is she a one guy parrot?"

"She's a show off," he said. "Whenever the others come over, she tries to sing them arias." He grimaced. "She's a terrible singer."

She giggled. "Oh yeah? But I bet she loves you." She sighed. "I always wanted pets. We couldn't have them growing up and most places won't allow them in the city." She smiled. "Do you spend time with her at home, or at your studio? Or is it both the same place?" she asked shyly.

"It's hard to describe," he said with a frown. "They're separate buildings, but there's a caged aviary between them and Niobe can move around as she pleases. But I'll often shut her out when I'm working, because the chemicals I use are bad for birds. I can wear a respirator. She can't."

She nodded. "You're a good bird dad," she offered with a grin. The information he had given her reminded her of a few different buildings in Old City, which wasn't so far from where she lived. "I hope I can meet her at some point. I love birds."

"I'm not a good bird dad when I'm painting," he reminded her. "And believe me—she lets me know about it! I'm sure you'll get to meet her at some point. When the Elders have approved our union."

She smiled at that. "And if they don't?" she asked seriously. "Honestly, if they don't approve it, do I just get cut loose?" Or killed. If that was it, well, she would do it, having had some happiness in it all. But it wasn't what she wanted. She wanted lunches like this every day, and dinners with Carter, yoga with Jack, runs with Leo... She wanted her men...the only ones that mattered to her.

"If they don't approve it, they will die," he said coldly. "You do not cross men like us and live."

She wasn't prepared for that answer and the surprise showed on her face.

"You knew we were killers," he said quietly, after checking to see no one could overhear. "Why does that surprise you? You've accepted us. All of us. To men that have had our families ripped from us, when you're all we have left that is soft and sweet and good, we hold onto it."

She smiled at him. She hadn't realized she meant anything close to that to any of them, but for Easton, the most aloof of her seven, to say it...she knew it carried weight. "I just..." She didn't know what to say to that, but tried. "Hearing you're cared for as such, when you haven't really been cared for in your entire life is...daunting. I know the other guys all want me. And you...well, you have your own thing and I'm okay with that. But I didn't ever expect that kind of outcome." She looked up to him. "That is my want. To be with the people I want to be important to, the men that are important to me." Even if they were killers and psychopaths, she wanted her seven. And it seemed they wanted her, too.

"I think it goes beyond want," he mused. "I think we all have a human need for acceptance, however damaged we are. You are the one person outside the brotherhood that has seen all the darkest and most perverted parts of us and yet, somehow, you still accept us. Even want us, for some reason. You have terrible taste in men."

She chuckled. "No, I have wonderful taste in men." She picked up one of her dumplings and offered it to him. "All seven of you feel like mine. You have since that first few nights, even though I didn't understand it then."

"I'm still semi-convinced it's trauma bonding," he teased when he'd finished chewing. "You know, like in action movies where the guy and the girl go through something awful and then they get together at the end."

183

She arched a brow. "Me, too...and the crazy ones like *Natural Born Killers* and *The Doom Generation*?" She grinned. "What about horror?"

"This could still end up with everyone dead," he conceded with macabre humor.

"Maybe. As long as it doesn't end up like a Disney animated musical. Something tells me Niobe would steal the show."

"Toss up between her and Brutus," he replied with a smirk. "The dog is guaranteed to win hearts. Even I like him, and I'm not a dog person."

She giggled at the mention of the large dog. "I can't wait to meet him, either. Carter showed me pictures of him the other night. He looks like the goodest boy."

"He's very well trained." He set his chopsticks down. "I'm stuffed. Is there more to come?"

She looked to Yuki and made the cut off motion, then looked to him. "Not anymore. You can eat, though! And you tried everything. I like that."

Yuki walked over with a small tray and the bill, and Petra clapped and grinned. "Ooh, thank you, Yuki." She looked to Easton. "Do you like mochi?" she asked as she handed Yuki her card, then picked up the piece of gooey ball. "It's not ice cream; these have sweet ube inside." She offered him one and took a bite of her own, closing her eyes, doing her little butt dance and moving her arms softly like she was dancing as she chewed.

"I like watching you eat mochi," he laughed. "Too cute."

"It's so yummy." She finished her second bite, doing her hand dance when she did. Sweet, refreshing and yummy. She blushed slightly at the look Easton was giving her.

"Here you go, Petra. You and your friend have a good day, yeah?" Yuki said as she came back with the slip to sign. She smiled at Easton.

"You, too, Yuki. Tell Hami that it was amazing today." Petra signed the slip and pushed her chair out, standing. "I don't want this to end, but I need to get back and finish my day," she offered shyly.

"I'll walk you back," he said, and she wasn't going to argue.

Philly was quiet now that the lunchtime rush was over and she was more ready than ever to finish her day. "So what's the rest of your day looking like? Working on something new?"

"I'm actually taking Niobe to a concert." He looked embarrassed. "There's a famous countertenor in town and he's doing a private show this afternoon for a handful of guests in the art world. I explained how Niobe adores opera and he was, in his words, 'just tickled pink' by the whole thing and 'thrilled to meet her.'"

"That is the coolest thing I have heard," she said as they stopped at the gallery. She unlocked the doors and opened them, letting him walk in with her. "It sounds so fun! I hope you and your feathered little date enjoy it." Setting her bag down, she turned to him. "And I'm hoping I can see you again soon, yeah? That was the best lunch I have ever had."

"Now I know you're blowing smoke," he laughed. "You eat at that restaurant all the time. But sure. I was going to email the contracts for the new show to Lorne, but I'll stop by with them instead. And next time it'll be my treat."

"I meant that it was the best lunch because I was there with you, Easton," she said shyly. "I never go with anyone, so it was really nice to spend time with you. And if you would let me, I would hug you for it." Honestly, keeping her hands to herself was maddening. He constantly looked like he needed comfort and she ached to give it to him.

"I'm not there yet," he said softly, but he didn't look uncomfortable expressing that, which was a start. "I think... I don't fucking know. I'm driving blind here. I just feel like I need you to know more of me before I'm in a place I can take that step, you know? Like maybe you need to see my home and meet Niobe or something."

"Are you inviting me over?" she teased. "Or you could bring Niobe to my place...or...I don't know..." She wrung her hands. The wrong words might break the fragile bonds blooming between them and she didn't want that in the least.

"I can't invite you round yet. Not until Devil has petitioned the Elders. There are rules." He sounded apologetic. "We've already broken a ton of them just by you knowing who we are. But maybe you could meet Niobe. I was thinking of getting tickets to a show next week and she usually comes with me. What do you think? Would you like a night out at the theater?"

She blinked. A date with her Snake and his favorite girl? She nodded, slightly dumbstruck, then shook herself. "I...yes. I never have been."

"Really?" He looked astonished and then a bright smile took over his features. "Well then, I'm honored to make it happen. I'll text you the details." He glanced at his watch and sucked in a breath. "I have to go. Be good. I'll message you this afternoon."

Gods, that smile. "You, too. And stay safe, yeah?" She just stopped herself from reaching out to him.

"Always." And with a smile and a wave, he was gone.

Chapter 21

Yoga on Fifteenth and Pine was hopping as usual. The class she had taken for about a year now was always full with drop-ins, and today was no different. Slipping into the studio, she set her stuff down and put her sneakers away, grabbing her mat and her water, and made her way to the left side of the class, away from the windows.

"Hey, Petra, nice to see you back."

"Ah...yeah. Last week was crazy with work and I had my annual Samhain trip," she offered to Keezie, the instructor.

"Did you have a good time?"

"I always do," she replied with a smile.

"Trips feed the soul," Keezie said with a grin. "We should get some wheat grass juice and talk sometime."

"Sure, that seems fun," Petra said. In the time she had been taking the class, not once had Keezie asked her to hangout. "We can talk later."

Keezie smiled and walked back to the front of the class and Petra sat on her mat, smiling as Jack laid his down next to her.

"You aren't honestly going to go out with her, are you?" he asked with a grin.

"No, probably not. Still not sure why she asked me."

"Because she's gone through at least seventy percent of the girls here," he said softly to her. "Finally worked her way down to the Ps..."

That gave Petra pause. "Now I know you're talking shit. Keezie has a boyfriend."

"Which is why she's not hitting on me." He grinned. "Not that I would, her boney ass does nothing for me. I much prefer bitable and bounceable asses." He winked.

"Corman up there is for you then," she offered to him and nodded to the dude up front.

"You know your ass is the only one I wanna bite. Still pissed D got the honor first, though he is our leader so..."

She laughed. "So now that I know you and I get to be yoga friends?"

"Yep. And I can keep your virtue all ours and away from Skeezie Keezie."

"Like it was in danger of being anyone else's..." she murmured and they both settled down as Keezie started the class.

Seven positions and they were in downward dog, Jack looking over to her as Keezie walked the room talking.

"Your mindful practice needs to be centered," she said. "Your form perfect to reach your intentions." She walked behind Petra and placed her hands on the small of her back, pushing her down, correcting her. "Ooh, Petra, there's some tension there..." she said as she walked away.

Jack smirked. "Tension she wants to release..." They stood and did another three positions, then were sitting cross-legged. "What are you doing after this? Wanna get a beer?"

"After yoga?" she said, eyes closed as they did their breathing exercises.

"Unless you wanna take her up on the wheat grass and cunnilingus."

Petra snorted back a laugh. "I don't think that's the situation. Maybe she just wants a friend."

"Maybe she wants to shove her fist up that perfect pussy," he countered. "Which I will not let happen. You wanna get fisted, you come to me, or Neon..."

Turning her head, she arched a brow. "You guys wanna fist me?"

"What? No...well, maybe Neon does... I'm just saying we can handle all your needs." He winked. "Full service."

"And then some," she offered as they were instructed into the last section of their session. Quietly she lay there, focusing on her breath, and the man lying right next to her. If she didn't know for a fact that Jack was a fucking psychotic lunatic, she would never guess. He was beautiful and friendly and didn't put off any of the red flags some of the others might in public.

"Namaste," they heard Keezie say and the studio started to move, the session ended. Sitting up, she smiled at Jack who was watching her move with his own grin.

"I tell you, now getting caught watching you isn't a bad thing."

"It wouldn't have been before," she said as she rolled her shoulders.

"But before I was an unknown and didn't even talk to you," he said as he helped her to stand. "And you were infatuated with seven men."

"Still am," she offered as Keezie walked up.

"I wasn't aware you and Jack were friends," she said by way of greeting.

"Oh...yeah, we weren't really 'til recently," she offered.

"Her boyfriend is my best friend," Jack said with an easygoing smile.

"Boyfriend? Ooh, you have been holding out on us..." Keezie said, clearly not as excited about the guy as she sounded.

"Well, we aren't really friends. Why would you know?" Petra asked.

"We could be, though," she said. "You always seem so involved I didn't want to bother you but...your vibe has always drawn me to you."

189

"Uh huh," Petra said.

"Yep." The woman was back to being sunny. "Listen, why don't I call you and we can have that hangout, yeah?"

"Ah...yeah, sure," Petra said and Keezie smiled again, triumphant.

"Great! I'll text you later!" She waved and walked off, a bounce in her hip as she did.

Jack wrapped his arm around her shoulders. "You tell me that's not a woman trying to sound the dinner bell."

She rolled her eyes. "You're my boyfriend's best friend?"

"Well technically, yes." He whispered, "I mean I'm also your boyfriend...but you belong to my six best friends so...not a lie."

Boyfriend. Seven boyfriends. She smiled. "Just a stretched truth."

"Umm...yes. We can call it that." He let her go and they walked out of the studio. "Though make no mistake, Stitches finds out about her interest in you, he will mail you her heart in a box. He doesn't share well." He winked.

"So you are saying I can't have female lovers?" she asked as they started down Fifteenth.

"Do you want them?" Jack countered.

"No, but I'm trying to figure it all out."

"I would think seven lunatics with very specific tastes would be enough for that tight little body but...I can tell the guys..."

"Nothing." She laughed. "I didn't peg you for the jokester."

"One of us has to be," he suggested. "So...where to? That beer?"

"I was going to go home," she offered. "Have a shower, take a nap, I'm on at the shelter for the overnight tonight…"

"You feel like company?" he asked as they crossed the street.

"Is that allowed?"

"I don't care if it is. No one is watching us, or you right now."

"Easton said something about not allowing me to come round to your places…"

"Probably because his place is a mess. Not a shit hole, mind you, but he's an artist and it bleeds into everything."

"Something about the Elders…"

"Fuck those guys. But I wasn't asking to bring you to my apartment on the Parkway. I was asking if you wanted company in that shower and the nap…maybe even tonight."

"Don't you have things to do?"

He nodded. "You. If you want to."

"When would I ever say no to you, Jack?"

"Not yet…probably not ever." He turned to her. "Come on, sexy. You're all relaxed from the yoga but I think a couple orgasms are just the thing to send you into that nap right. What do you think?"

"I think if it's your bendy ass giving me the orgasms I'm counting myself lucky."

"We haven't played in the Kama Sutra pool, have we?" he teased. "Oh, the things I wanna show you," he said and wrapped his arm around her, steering her toward her street.

She couldn't wait.

Chapter 22

"We will be arriving in Philadelphia in about thirty minutes, sir."

Emerson looked up from his notebook and smiled at his steward. "Thank you, Yale. Seeing the family this week?"

His steward nodded. "Yes, sir. And thank you again for the generous time off."

"Nothing to thank me for. I'm not traveling for a few months, so..."

"Yes, but paid leave is...generous."

"Honestly, think nothing of it," he said, the matter closed. With Petra in Philadelphia and the main concerns of his overseas businesses handled, he was largely free to put all his energies into wooing their girl. He was behind, well, not as behind as Kendrix was, given the man's proclivities, but he needed to step it up.

Gods below, he never thought he would be in this situation, certainly not three years ago when he had found that passage about the pact...

"Now this is fucking interesting."

Emerson walked into his living room, book in hand. They had a few hours before the annual blood sacrifice, and it was rare they were all together otherwise, but after seeing the entry in the diary, he needed to show his brothers.

Jack and Rix looked up to him as he plopped down on the wingback chair across from the rest.

"What's interesting?" Finn was cleaning his mask in his usual chair by the fire.

"Well, I was going through my dad's old journal," he began with a grin. *"I mean there's some wild shit in there, as you know. But this...apparently there's like this, dad says 'pact'? An old tradition where a woman*

is given a choice, become a willing sacrifice and endure, or death."

"What does that mean exactly?" Jack asked. "What? She just walks in and says, 'hi, I'll let you willingly torture me?' Who does that?"

"Well, no, it's not like that." Emerson frowned. When he had found the journal, half hidden behind a bookshelf in his own bedroom, he had been fascinated by learning about his father, and his father's group's life. Their sacrifices were involved and he had felt closer to him just knowing they were on the same path...except for his own mother, who was mentioned several times in the journal, then...wasn't, but that was farther down the pages.

He flipped pages and started reading. "Amelia Robinson could have been the one," he began. "Beautiful, sexy, and she ticked the boxes...or so we thought. She had found interest in all six of us, and after a long discussion we decided to ask her...fill her in on everything, because she could be the one."

"Wait, they told an outsider?" Easton's jaw dropped. "And what does he mean, she was interested in all six of them? Weren't they all with your mothers at that point?"

"Does he explain the pact?" Finn spoke over Easton's confusion.

"Kinda?" Emerson said and moved more pages. "Okay, it says here, 'A female of grace, bred for both pain and pleasure, will beguile those that worship, bringing more to the well everlasting.' So under that it says he did research on the subject, and it turns out back in the day there was the option of a pact, where one woman would become the conduit, a sort of balance as the sacrifice, where pain and pleasure are indivisible. Basically, a woman that could take the pain and convert it to pleasure would feed He Who

194

Sleeps." He looked to Easton. "I don't actually know when this was written, if it was before we were born, or during our childhood."

"Of course he couldn't just write it in plain fucking English," Carter snorted. "But it does sound fun. Imagine getting to fuck some chick with all our perverted kinks two nights a year. Normally we have to pay for the specialist shit."

"Wait, this was a thing they offered the people they killed?" Finn tried to clarify. "Fuck all of us and get hurt doing it, or die? And they thought this woman might take them up on it?"

"Apparently. I mean..." He started reading again. "Apparently this Amelia was dating all of them..." he read through. "And they gave her the option. She apparently freaked, then decided that while she enjoyed fucking them all, she wasn't into the secondary..." he looked up. "It is written like they treated her like a girlfriend...odd, right? I mean are we allowed to do that?"

"I doubt it," Easton said at the same time as Finn shrugged. "Things were different back then. Maybe they had an arrangement with her to service the needs that Carter here pays for." He nudged Carter with a grin. "Perhaps she was a submissive of some sort. Who knows? But it's interesting that it said it was in place of the killing. Does it say what happened to this Amelia chick?"

"They sacrificed her two nights later," he offered. "She said no, they had no reason not to go forward with what they planned...death or not." He pulled a face. "Imagine that. A woman that actually would take both sides of it?" He chuckled.

"No such fucking thing," Rix offered. "There is not woman in the world that could handle what the seven of us do."

"We have to start offering it," Carter said to a chorus of groans from the others. "Oh, come on! It's tradition! Don't you want to see the look on their faces when they try to think it through? It's going to be funny as fuck!"

"It's not supposed to be funny," Easton said with a prim tone. "We're here to serve the Dark God."

"Nothing stopping us enjoying it, though, brother," Carter said cheerfully. "Who doesn't like to play with the food a little?"

"You're sick," Finn snorted. "I love it."

"Agreed," Rix said, with a savage grin. The man loved any sort of game.

"I'm in," Jack offered.

Emerson shrugged. Either way the sacrifice would be done. Who cared if they fucked with the woman's head a little beforehand? She was just bones and meat anyway, energy to feed him. They rarely knew anything about their victims past their names...their conversations with them nothing past them begging. So this would be interesting.

"Let's do it," Finn decided. "It's tradition, after all. What could go wrong?"

"Speaking of chicks... We ready?" Jack asked

Rix nodded. "No change in her routine. Easy snatch. House is ready and so is the courtyard."

Emerson grinned. He might be the least psychotic of the group but he relished these two days. "Well then, let's saddle up, yeah? We have much to do and only a small amount of time to do it." He let his thoughts wander to the possibility of a woman like that. Their fathers thought they had found her, but were wrong, and it was clear that it was an option...why had things changed? Didn't really matter, they knew what needed to be done, and it would happen.

For the good of He Who Sleeps.

And now look at them. Three years in to a pact with a woman of worth. It was heady. Originally they had been joking with her, of course, and never thought she would say yes, but when she did...it was like a switch had been flicked.

Their two nights that year had been...brutal for her. Literally with no idea what it was they were stepping into, they faked it well, and she endured everything they did to her, and there was some freaky shit going on simply because they could, but she had walked out on her own two feet. Afterwards it was a mad scramble to find the priests and figure out what the fuck they were actually doing, and what, if anything, could fuck with their sacrifice.

"Hello?" Emerson called as they walked into the courtyard of the Grecian villa that housed the Oranari, their Order's scholar priests.

Three men dressed in black robes with silver symbols around the hem filed out of a set of double doors, and stopped just past the stone arches. The bowed their heads.

"They Who Sacrifice," they greeted them. "Welcome."

They had made their way to Greece, the seven of them intent on speaking to someone that might have insight on what they just did, and what it meant for their future.

"How can we be of service?" the one in the center asked, his voice deep, but quiet.

"As we mentioned on the phone, a sacrifice accepted the pact and we were woefully unprepared," Finn said respectfully. "We are hoping you can teach us the traditional ways so that we are better prepared when our sacrifice returns to us next year." He

paused, uncertain. "She does return to us next year...?"

"He is pleased...but He could be generous," the one on the left said. "A clock set in motion."

The one on the right lifted his hand. "Come, we will explain..."

They followed the three Oranari into the inner sanctum, a room with floor-to-ceiling books, with several long tables and stations in the center. They were the three heads of their Monastic order, but there were several adepts and lower brothers that were in residence, but they rarely saw visitors.

"The female," the one in the center began. "She took the pact, willingly, yes? No coercion?"

"Yes," Finn replied. "The choice was offered, explained and accepted, inasmuch as we knew what to offer, anyway. We only had loose terms from an old document we found."

"And where did you find this information?" the high Oranari asked. "The pact isn't something that is...common knowledge.

"My father's journal," Emerson offered.

"Seems they missed one," the third said with what sounded like amusement in his voice. Emerson arched a brow.

"Missed one?"

They waved him off. "She agreed to two nights, to endure?" they asked as one. Damn it, that was weird.

"Yes," Jack offered to them. "And she did."

"And she is unspoiled as of now."

Emerson nodded. "Yes."

"Then what is it you wish to know? As with everything, you are They Who Sacrifice, and we can answer a question for each of you. Be mindful."

Finn paused, clearly trying to get his words in order before he asked his question. "We are unclear how the transfer to the Dark God works," he explained, very carefully not making it a question. "The book was not clear on any ritual aspect of the pact, just the basic concept of it. We dripped her blood into the well, but that was a guess based on our understanding of other sacrifices we have made. If there is a means and method to maximize the sacrifice given to the God, can you describe it to us?"

The High Oranari looked pleased. "In options past, before the modern age, when He was closer to mankind, and dreams, she would have been branded an eternal sacrifice through devout ritual. Sadly, that is no longer possible, as He has retreated deep."

"Energy must be transferred through the flesh, though whose is...negotiable," the second said. He looked to them all. "This day and age is too volatile, and something this precious, it would fall to Those Who Sacrifice in order to ensure potency."

Emerson looked to Finn. There was information there, but there was also doublespeak. He took his shot. "You are saying we must be the ones to transfer the energy." He nodded and it was something he figured, as they had the connection to He Who Sleeps. "Were we wrong in having her offer her blood to Him?"

The third answered. "Not wrong, crude, though with your limited information, it was the best you could do. He was not offended, and while there is power in the blood, there is more in the essence."

"How do we act as channels?" Carter asked, blunt as always. "And cut the bullshit fancy talk, guys. Please. I have all the respect in the world for you, but if you want us to do this properly then you need to speak plainly."

The third looked to him. "As she would have had to be...branded into service, you all will be in her place."

The second smiled. "In this day and age, a tattoo would suffice, one that ties you all together, it's also the most optimal way to ensure His essence is inside you all." Holding up a hand, he went down the hall and returned in moments with a small vessel in his hands.

"Inside resides His essence, bound in smoke and ash," the High Oranari said. "It will be mixed with the ink to tattoo."

"Then let's do this." Finn nodded with grim purpose. "Where do you want us to set up?"

"Are you absolutely sure this is the route you will take? Once you do, things change," the High Oranari said.

Emerson looked to Jack who blanched. "What...what changes?"

"Your ability to feed him," the third said. "Sacrifice must be through the female you chose today." He walked forward to them and walked around their physical bodies. "There is enough of her still inside you to bind the pact. How you go forward once it is done, however, is on you."

"Are you saying that if we choose pleasure, it is only her own going forward if we do this?" Kendrix said, interest in his voice. "Or ours as well?"

"There must always be balance, Lord Kendrix. Essence comes from the lowering of the aura, and potent essence is both the Yin and the Yoni. He prefers a balance there."

"But then what role does the pain play?" Finn asked, giving up on the one question rule since they weren't giving full answers and he wasn't leaving until they knew everything. "That was the one aspect *of the journal that was actually pretty clear—she must hurt as much as she must find pleasure in it."*

"And what happens if she nopes out or dies in a car crash?" Easton asked, speaking up for the first time. "Life isn't guaranteed. She could walk in front of a bus tomorrow for all we know. Just because she accepted the pact this year doesn't mean she isn't scarred mentally from it and would rather die than come back next year. Does that mean we're all fucked?"

"He has a point," Finn agreed, his sudden fire to get the tattoo extinguished. "Do we have to get the tattoos now? Can we watch over her instead and then come back, say next July, for the tattoos if it looks like she's okay?"

"And you still haven't answered all our questions anyway," Carter pointed out. "You haven't told us what the tattoos even do. Do we have to give blood? I'm not jumping into this with both feet until I know everything."

Emerson looked to Leo, who had been extremely quiet through all of this. "Leo? You okay there, man?" As their most...emotional of the seven, he was always a wild card, from his decisions to his kinks.

The High Oranari sighed. "Lords, we are but servants to His will, we can only answer what we know, and admittedly what we know is steeped in the times they were conceived in. Truth is we do not know what would happen if she died in an accident of the modern world's making.

"In the past, she was protected by her sacrificers, and Him as well, becoming a Daughter of the Blood. It has been a very long time since that has happened, and as to her mental capacity to accept this, that is for you to decide. Surely you will not allow her to live her life without your influence, however hidden?"

201

"Of course we can be in her life," Finn said. "Some of us already are, which is kind of weird. I knew I recognized her from somewhere—she's the receptionist at the gallery I'm the accountant for. But I'm not going to get into fate right now. The point is, we'd need to be right there next to her to prevent accidents, and she'd notice that. If you say the God is distant and can't protect her, why would we take the risk?"

"The pact binds completely her to him, her to you, you to her. The tattoos with her essence involved, and you are all rolling in that, would extend safeguards to her. I do not believe he would allow for his Eternal Sacrifice to be harmed."

Number three looked up from a book he had picked up. "It was only after the age of Those Who Sacrifice passed and a new group was instituted in the past that the woman was released from her service."

"That could easily be another twenty or twenty-five years," Easton pointed out. "None of us have even been called to breed yet. Does it have to be a legacy group or can someone else take over?"

The High Oranari smirked at him. "Is she not a woman you would want forever as a victim?" He chuckled. "It is written that certain women are made for this, they were, back in the times of high belief, anointed early through our old customs, and raised to become. It has been many, many ages since that happened. If you found, or were gifted a woman that would make your sacrifice dynamic, different and...a return to the old ways...would you not take it?"

"I'm not sure that's what my brother was getting at," Carter sighed. "The kind of pain we give is a lot. As she gets older and her skin gets more fragile, she's not going to heal as easily from bruising or scratches.

It could get debilitating for her, taking that kind of damage in her late forties or fifties."

"Exactly," Easton agreed. "She's no good to us broken."

"Sadly there is no precedence for that, either, given how long people lived back then as well," the third offered.

"Though, by your own fifties, you should have passed the torch to a younger group," two said.

"Are there any accounts of what happens to the woman after they left the service?" Emerson asked.

"Three," the third said.

"And?" Kendrix asked.

He just smiled. "Do not believe answering that at this junction would help your cause," he offered. "After your fourth year, ask this again, should this experiment continue."

The second went to a shelf and pulled a book, starting to look through it. "Lord Easton," he said, "your question about legacy is a no. Technically you are not legacy, though you must have some old blood for him to accept your sacrifices."

"So we can retire her and ourselves at any time?" he clarified, letting out a sigh of relief when the priest nodded.

"Well that seems a whole lot less terrifying all of a sudden," Carter snorted.

"I still think we need to watch her," Finn cautioned them. "We need to be sure she can handle it."

"Provided others are able to pick up the good work," the Head Oranari said. "Which isn't a problem as there are at this point up to six almost of age. My suggestion with your Eternal Sacrifice is to keep her safe, and to seal this pact with the tattoos as soon as possible. The more of her still in you, the deeper the devotion each year."

By the second year they were ready for her, and for what would be the maximum output for he whom they worshiped. She had taken it, not with resignation, but curious intent, and in some instances, true enjoyment, her gifts to them energy and slaked lust.

Gods, they had lusted over her...each of them had lost a little bit of their minds to her that second year, where she not only endured but was amendable to what it was. And now, post fourth sacrifice year with them, she was as infatuated as them, if not more so, and down for all of it. Did that make her a little crazy, a little off? Absolutely, but he had decided he didn't want it any other way.

The woman was perfect for all of them, even Easton with his hangups. It was like she was a true gift from below, a woman that spoke to their collective darknesses, but also their souls as a kindred spirit. She was rare, and the priests had made that very clear.

She needed to be protected and he was going to be damned if they didn't do just that. Sadly, being away since their weekend had left him largely on the outside, aside from a few texts and a very sexy video chat two days before. Only a few more hours and he would be back in the mix. Thoughts turning to what he was going to do when he saw her stopped as his phone rang. Stitches.

"Leo..." he said softly by way of greeting. "How's it going?"

"Pretty good, brother! And you? When are you coming home?" Even with the expensive phones and relays, he still sounded slightly muffled.

"Touchdown is less than an hour. How's our little sex pot?"

"Surprisingly domesticated for such a wild little savage," Leo laughed. "She's been enjoying time with the guys. Carter took her dinner, and I know she's seen Easton at the gallery."

Odds were she saw Jack at her yoga seeing as it was weekly. "And have you been meeting her for her morning run like normal?"

"Of course!" Leo snorted. "Like I'd miss out on it."

He laughed at that. "So, for the most part we have all been keeping her occupied. She did seem happier on the call we had."

"Yes, but in less perverted ways than our annual fuck fest," Leo laughed. "We're just letting her get to know us. Really know us. Peeking behind the curtain, so to speak. That's actually why I was calling." There was a pause and Emerson heard a can being opened in the background, followed by the gurgle of several long swallows. "It's your birthday soon. I was thinking we could plan a weekend away somewhere with her. Spend some time all together that isn't in the service to the Dark Lord."

It wasn't something they normally did, ever since they turned eighteen they didn't really celebrate birthdays...or anything really. But if it was a weekend with her...he smiled to himself. "My dad's place in Chesapeake is still empty," he offered. "And I recently had it upgraded. Safe house and all. Big enough for all of us, and her, and secluded enough as well. Also, Elders think it burned down." It wasn't a secret that he didn't trust them, and that Stitches was right there with him.

"That sounds perfect," Leo said. "Leave it to me then. I'll order in some food and drinks. Can you take care of the travel?"

"We can take my Denali," he offered. "Unless the guys wanna drive by themselves. You know Rix when he doesn't have to play sweet, helpful vet would rather drive his Ducati..."

"I suspect Carter will want to take his bike so Brutus can come along," Leo said thoughtfully. "And you know Easton isn't going to sit in a crowded car for that long. More space in the Denali for champagne then, I guess."

And presents for their girl. It might be his birthday, but there wasn't a better gift than that woman. "Just gotta make sure she can take the weekend. I will have the place aired out and ready for us soon. You going to mention it to her? I mean it would be super ego if I'm like 'hey, Pet, come to my birthday party. There will be cake and ice cream,'" he laughed.

"Sure, I'll call her this evening when she's home from work," Leo said. "I don't think she'll have a problem taking it off. Her boss at the gallery owes us plenty of favors and the shelter is a volunteer thing. I'll make sure all the others are free, too. You know she's going to pout like fuck if someone can't make it."

Emerson grinned at that. Gods, how the hell did they get so lucky? "She totally will...but honestly, I wouldn't wanna do this without all of us. We are a unit, especially when it comes to her. Seeing her individually is smart, it strengthens things, but it wouldn't be right without everyone. And I'm going to be honest...I like seeing her eyes light up with all of us."

"She seemed really into the multiples this year," Leo agreed. "It'll be fun to see how she plays when it's not all set up and pre-planned."

"I have no doubt this is going to turn into some wild shit." He laughed. "And it will be interesting to see how much of her we retain this weekend...to see if it is true that it's just Samhain weekend that we can worship and tribute for Him."

"Yeah," Leo sounded thoughtful. "It would almost be worth coming back to the city to sacrifice right afterwards, just to see what happens. I mean, I'm not saying we should do it every time we have a wild orgy, but a few times a year, maybe? If it works?"

"You know I'm down with whatever works. Finn and the guys would be, too." Hell, he thought she would be okay with it as well. "I mean if it works? Knowledge is power."

"Power is power," Leo snorted. "Okay, brother. Get yourself safely on the ground and I'll go start organizing this shindig. I'll catch you later."

"Stay safe," he said as he hung up. Visions of their girl at his father's house, dug in like a tick, at home in the space, hit him. The idea was heart warming and he realized that this woman had her claws in him in ways he didn't think were possible. He would have to see her, and soon.

"Sir? Please strap in..."

He grinned. "You got it."

Chapter 23

Petra locked her apartment door with a smile on her face. Things were good. It was almost a ten days post Halloween fuck fest and she felt like life was on the right track. Her guys were attentive, texting her, calling, meeting up with her through daily means. She was happy, constantly smiling, giggling or laughing. Such a change from who she had been before this Halloween. It was freeing, and wonderful.

But things didn't really change, aside from being with her guys. She still went to work, still worked at the shelter, still talked to her friends. Yoga had gotten more fun, regardless of their instructor's now obvious interest, and her phone calls with Carter sexy and naughty, and her video chats with Emerson, who was out of town, were dirty as hell.

Walking out of her building, she stepped down the front steps, and smiled at the woman that ran the market just past her building. "Good morning, Franny!"

"Hello, Ms. Franklin," the woman said.

Sunshine filtered through the trees, and she set her bag higher on her arm and slipped her sunglasses on. It was a beautiful and brisk day, and her thoughts ran to the weather for the coming weekend. Thoughts of enticing one or two of her guys to a picnic or maybe Reading Terminal Market danced in her head as she walked and she was stopped suddenly. Looking up, she smiled.

"Oh, Officer Douritz! I didn't see you there! I'm sorry, I was in my own head."

"It's quite all right, Petra," he said with a grin. "How are things? You all good? Did you enjoy your weekend away?"

She gave him a tight smile. "I...how did you know I was away?"

"I just didn't see the usual signs," he shrugged as though it were nothing. "I almost always see you running in the morning or your lights on in the evening when I'm on patrol. You get to know your beats pretty well. Things stand out when they're different."

"Oh." She smiled more genuinely. "Yes, it was restful and restoring," she said. "Was the neighborhood rowdy for the holiday?"

"Halloween is always crazy," he chuckled. "I thought at first that maybe you were hiding from the trick or treaters, but I don't think that's your style."

"Oh no, I love the holiday. It's honestly my favorite day of the year." She brightened. "I need to head out. Have a good day, Officer, it's going to be a beautiful one today!" She waved and started down the street.

"You, too!" he called after her. "Stay safe!"

Safe? She was more than safe with her guys...well, safe from the rest of the world. The walk over to work was easy and without incident, and she stopped at the bakery, grabbing some donuts and bagels, as well as a carafe of coffee for the staff, but frowned when she got in. No one was in.

"Lorne? Mike? Gabe?" she said as she walked through the main gallery toward the back. Where was everyone? "How the hell are the doors open?" she mused as she stepped into the back offices.

"Come into my parlor..." Finn teased her from behind Lorne's desk. "It's just us today. He's gone to view a collection and the porters have the day off."

She smiled and placed the parcels on the table then ran over to him, jumping into his lap as she hugged him. "Best surprise," she said as she leaned in and kissed him. "Missed you," she said softly.

"Missed you, too," he growled, openly inhaling the scent of her hair with a satisfied sigh. "You smell so good. I hope you haven't got any work planned today."

"I have some emails…" she teased. "But no." They weren't open to the public today, as they had specific days that they were closed just for internal work. Without Lorne and the guys there she didn't have to do a damn thing, aside from Finn. "What do you have in mind? I mean, don't you have things to do?"

"I only have one thing to do today, and that's you." He had a wicked grin on his face and she couldn't help but laugh. "I'm going to fuck you on every available surface I can find, and when you're all nice and hot and sweaty, I'm going to fuck you up against the window and leave the print there as an art installation for everyone to see."

Shivering in his lap, she squirmed slightly. "So today's agenda is orgasms? You want brekky first? I got donuts and bagels," she quipped and ran her hands down his chest. Finn was dressed for work in black pin-striped slacks, wing-tipped shoes, black shirt and grey tie, but his sleeves were already rolled up, something she had only seen on their weekends.

"I find it's always a good idea to start the day with a healthy shot of protein," he teased, boosting her up onto Lorne's desk.

She arched a brow at him and leaned back. Gods, the look in his eye was savage and naughty and she was going to ruin Lorne's desk blotter just looking at him. She was counting her lucky stars she decided to wear thigh-highs instead of hose then, because she knew how interested Finn was in lingerie…though this wasn't latex, he would have to make do.

She was also thanking her stars she didn't wear a pencil skirt today, opting for a knee-length black Peter Pan collared cotton dress with a more flirty skirt. Her shoes were black five-inch bootie style with large organza bows lacing them up. She had felt adorable and secretly sexy because of the thigh highs, and now, her naughty Finn was going to reap the benefits.

"What have we here?" he murmured, flipping her skirt up over her thighs. "It's almost like you came prepared." He traced a finger down the inside of her thigh where the seam of her thigh-highs met her soft flesh, tickling with his light touch, and she laughed. "And lace...my, my. I do fucking love lace."

He loosened his tie and then paused, thinking better of it, before taking it off altogether and asking for her hands. He bound her wrists together, the silk pressing into her skin, and then gave her a dark look. "Those will stay over your head, or there'll be a spanking that will leave you sore for a week. Am I understood?"

She nodded. "Yes, Sir," her breathy answer belying how turned on she was. She wanted to be his good girl so much, though a vicious spanking from her sexy Devil was not really a deterrent. "I woke up wanting to feel sexy. That's why the thigh-highs..."

"You're always sexy," he replied bluntly, fingers roaming across the small expanse of black lace that was the only thing separating him from the slick wetness of her need. "I think I might keep these. They're pretty."

"Bra is pretty, too," she said, her breath hitching. "I love the feel of lace...almost as much as latex." She winked at him. "Though lace is more forgiving and feels naughty on the skin."

"I'm gonna dress you in everything," he promised her. "And then I'm going to have the best time peeling you out of it. But for now..." He curled his fingers under the lace and dragged it down her thighs, rolling his chair back to get them all the way off, before tucking them in his pocket for later. "For now, I just want my breakfast."

"What...oh!" she gasped as he pulled her forward, gripping her hips, dragging her to the edge of the desk, causing her to lie back. She threw her arms over her head like he asked and arched. Fuck... Finn and that wicked mouth...

He took his time, exploring her with the finesse of a classical musician, teasing notes from her throat that she didn't know she was capable of. The languid strokes of his tongue were at once both tender and merciless, allowing her no escape from the pleasure, either over the precipice or back from it. The man was a fucking maestro with that tongue. And he was in it for the long haul.

"Please... Please, Finn..." she whined. "It's so fucking good..." She gasped again and arched, needing more from him. Gods, he was a goddamn magician, his mouth weaving a spell she loved. If she had her way he would live between her thighs. Man both kissed and fucked like the devil. Her Devil.

He ignored her, taking his sweet time, before finally adding fingers to the mix, sliding two of them deep inside her while his mouth focused on her clit.

"Finn!" she screamed as the orgasm tore through her, making her shake and shiver. "Fuck yes, yes, yes!" Her body clamped down hard on his fingers, pulsing and throbbing. It was good but she needed more of him. "So...fucking good..." she panted.

"That," he said, leaning back and wiping his mouth on the back of his hand, "was just the first of many. How do you feel about breakfast now?"

She giggled and moaned. "I love when you have breakfast," she said and wiggled slightly. "Your mouth is a lethal weapon, Finn..."

"I'd better not have fucking killed you with it," he said. "Who else am I going to eat donuts with?"

"Leo?" She giggled and sat up, offering him her arms and the tie. "And bagels...don't forget bagels."

"Do you see Leo here right now?" he demanded. "It's just us. All day."

And she was grateful for that. She hopped off the desk and then laughed. "We are going to have to buy Lorne a new blotter," she said, and then looked at him. "You did that...well, I did that but it was your fault." She grinned and tottered over to the boxes and grabbed the donuts, bringing them back to her lover. "What's your favorite? Glazed, chocolate? Boston crème? Jelly? Cruller?"

"You bought all of those and bagels?" He blinked up at her. "I know Lorne doesn't pay you enough to be feeding the whole crew like this."

She shrugged. "Dozen donuts and a dozen bagels. I do it on occasion, when I'm feeling saucy," she offered. "I did think everyone would be here...and honestly if they were there would be like three left total. There's also a carafe of coffee because Lorne's idea of coffee is sludge."

"I do like a girl that comes prepared," he chuckled. "Do you need a protein shot, or do you just want to dig in with the rest?"

She smiled and stood in front of him once more, then sank to her knees. "You know damn well my favorite thing is worship and tribute." She bit her bottom lip and reached for his belt, already seeing his erection pushing against the thin suit material.

"I don't know...you seemed pretty into the donuts just now," he teased.

Her smile grew as she caressed him through his pants, and looked up at him. "You going to come down my throat?"

"I'm going to come everywhere you'll let me," he said. "But for now, yes, your throat will do."

"You know I'm your little cumslut, Finn." Pulling the zipper down, she freed him and gave him a sweet lick, then swallowed him down, slowly, her tongue petting him as she did.

"Jesus fuck..." he breathed, letting his head fall back in the chair as she worked his cock. "I'm not the only one with a magic mouth."

His praise spurned her on, sucking hard as she gripped his thighs. She loved the feel of him in her mouth, loved that he wanted the worship, and she was eager to give it to him. She whimpered, her own body waking as she sucked him, getting wetter by the second. But fuck, she wanted him, wanted to drink him down, wanted to make him growl for her.

And growl he did, holding nothing back as he shot his load, creamy spurts filling her mouth to almost overflowing. "Yeah...definitely the best way to start the day," he managed, his grin lighting her up inside.

Swallowing him down, she looked up to him. "Would that I could do it every morning," she said and climbed into his lap, tucking his cock back into pants. "So...protein...now I think I need some sugar."

"You could have this every morning...soon," he promised her quietly, not bothering to put himself away. And why would he, when his cock was that perfect? "We just need to approach the Elders about it and then we can discuss a more...permanent arrangement."

"Well, you will forgive my poo poo of the Elders. Don't see why a bunch of dudes get to decide if you guys get a willing woman that wants all of you," she said cheekily. "Though I suppose it's better than being without all of you like it's been." She leaned in, inhaling his clean scent, and nipped his throat. "I'm greedy. I want you always and immediately."

"Being one of us is...well, it's complicated." He nuzzled her gently and then reached for a coffee. "We're killers. We're secretive for a reason. We wouldn't literally get away with murder if we didn't have strict rules and protocols. It might not make sense to you from the outside, but the system is designed to protect us from the law."

"I know that...I'm grateful for it. Otherwise, I might never have had this," she said softly. "And I know you guys probably think this is all Stockholm Syndrome...it's not. Nothing in my life made sense until that night I found you guys. Nothing. And when I'm not with you it feels...I don't know...wrong. Like it's not supposed to be the way of it. Like there's a vice around my lungs, and when I'm with you, or any of them? It eases and I can breathe fully."

"Trust me, none of us think it's Stockholm Syndrome," he assured her. "We feel the same way. Just took us a little while longer than you to figure it out."

"Dudes usually have block heads," she teased. "I wanna know you. I want..." She looked up at him. "Don't get me wrong, Finn, sex with you is transcendent on so many levels...but I want to know *you*. I wanna know what makes you smile, your likes past the naughty things we do. I want to be yours, and for you to be mine."

"That's why we've been spending as much time with you as we can," he pointed out. "And I know it's supposed to be a secret right now, but I think Leo and Emerson are cooking up a little trip for us all. But don't you dare let on that I said something when they surprise you with it, or you won't like the punishment I deal out." He gave her a long, level stare until she nodded and zipped her mouth closed. "But it'll be over soon. We see the Elders next month."

"Jack mentioned you guys would be leaving for the holidays," she said softly.

"Yeah. Maybe next time we could try and get back before Christmas. I mean, obviously it's not a thing we celebrate. Jesus has fuck all to do with the Dark God. But it would be fun to spoil you rotten."

She nodded, quiet. "The winter holidays have never been something I looked forward to, so it's not a big deal. I'll be working at the shelter for the holiday this year, since I don't have family except the girls, but they are all elsewhere so it works. Will you guys be back by New Year's?"

"Yes. And that we can definitely celebrate together. We can all drizzle you in champagne together."

That got a giggle from her. "That sounds fun...but only if you guys lick it off." She pulled back and looked at him. "Only winter holiday I used to like was Thanksgiving. What do you guys do for that?"

"Whatever you want us to," he said with a grin.

"Really?" she asked. "You guys don't normally have plans?" Her mind started running through what she could do.

"Well, no. We like to cook but we've never had much to be thankful for, you know?" He grinned and sipped his coffee. "Now we have you and we can be grateful in all the ways."

"Hmmm. Seems you should be thankful for his grace, and his favor," she offered. "But I kinda like that you are thankful for me." She smiled. "I'm thankful for his grace and finding you all..."

"We sacrifice to show our thanks," he shrugged. "What better way to prove your loyalty to someone than killing for them? He knows we serve. He doesn't need some made up day about genocide to know we are thankful."

"True. Though I don't do the thankful for the way things happened and why. I enjoy cooking for it. I haven't in a long time. The girls and I used to do it. It was the only guaranteed time we could be together so... These days, though, not so much."

"We should redesign it," he said. "Make a tradition. Something we do every year. We could maybe even choose some sort of fancy ass meal to cook instead of dry turkey and pumpkin schmuckery. We can have gifts. Maybe even a little ritual or some shit like that. Let's really mash it up and make it something fun."

"I do make a really good turkey," she quipped. "And so much food...the girls would have to take it home. Something tells me we wouldn't have that problem." She nodded to herself. "I'ma cook this year for you guys. And I will be dessert. But I do like the idea of a little ritual..."

"And gifts," he said firmly. "You're getting gifts whether you like it or not. You might even have help in the kitchen. Snake has Michelin star skills. He just doesn't bother very often."

"Easton can cook?" She was impressed. "Well then, this is going to happen." She grinned. "You said they had a surprise for me... Let's have a surprise for them then."

"We should all be around," he said. "It's a public holiday after all. We just need to find a venue. We don't all live together." He looked shocked as something occurred to him. "That's going to have to change," he murmured. "We'll have to start looking for a place big enough for all of us."

All of us...was she considered in the all? "What about the house in the mountains?" she asked as she shifted, straddling him. "You guys don't live there at all? Or is it just used for the weekend?" She grinned.

"It's just for the weekend. You wouldn't want to live there full-time...trust me." He shuddered. "We're all accustomed to a better standard of living than that."

"Ah...it is a grand old house," she offered, hand going to his groin. She palmed him, and squeezed. "Jack mentioned he lived on the Parkway, where are you? Old city? Center city? South Philly? North?"

"I'm in the old city," he told her. "In one of the brownstones off Locust that got renovated a couple of years ago."

Nice area. Way nicer than where she lived. Her apartment was nice, but all her guys were wealthy and it showed. "Oh, that's a nice area. You are near the park," she said and squeezed him, grinning as he thickened in her hand. Fuck, he was perfect. She shifted slightly and pumped her hand down his length.

"I'm coming in that soft little cunt of yours this time," he told her softly. "I've missed being inside you."

She shifted again and sank down on him, sighing. "I missed you inside me, though this is...different." She moved slowly, loving the feel of him, the long deep strokes at a languid pace. "Oh...Finn...fucking heaven..."

"I'm a twisted fucker and I have my kinks, but I don't have to be like that all the time," he told her, strong fingers dimpling the flesh of her hips. "I'll take you to church when I want to, and I'll make you into a shocking modern art piece, but sometimes I just want to look at you while we...fuck." He'd been about to say 'make love.' She was sure of it.

"I love the way you take me," she said and shuddered on a downstroke. "But I need this, too...this...connection." She gasped as he wrenched her down hard. She pulsed around him. "I love your kinks,

Finn. And I love feeling you inside me like this...it's holy in its own way."

"It is." He was coming undone, color rising in his cheeks as he rose up into her. It was so fucking hot that he was still in his suit, the soft, expensive fabric sliding against her thighs.

Fucking at work was something she never expected to do, but boy if she could have this every day... "Mmmm....you feel so fucking good..."

"Damn right I do," he smirked, his breath starting to go ragged. "No one else fucks you like I do."

"No...fuck no..." she moaned and shuddered, the orgasm punching through her calm. A gasp left her as she shook for him, her arms around his neck as she started to ride him harder, faster. "Oh fuck... Please...please..."

He braced his feet against the floor and slammed up into her, again and again, dragging her orgasm out as he chased his own, until finally he came with a soft grunt, shoving it into her with inelegant rhythm as he milked it out.

Panting, she slowed, a little moan escaping her. "The fucking best." She hissed and ground down onto him, feeling them pulse in tandem.

"Let's not tell the others that," he whispered, his breath teasing the shell of her ear. "They might get jealous and that would ruin a good thing."

"You all fuck me the best, just in different ways..." Well, except Easton. She kissed his neck. "But you are the bestest." She giggled and nipped him. "My sexy work distraction."

"Distraction?" He raised an eyebrow. "I'm your job today, Petra. You'd better work hard."

"The hardest. I meant that you coming in before this was always a distraction...the thoughts that ran through my head about you..."

"Then I guess we'd better see how many of those we can make a reality today," he chuckled. "But I could do with a bagel first. This is going to take some serious carbs."

She giggled. "I'm kinda afraid if I slide off you we are going to ruin these pants."

"Fuck it." He shrugged. "I'll call a car to take me home. No one is going to see them."

"Well then..." She climbed off his lap, pouting at the loss of him and pulled her dress over her head, leaving her in just her bra, thigh-highs and heels, his cum trickling down her thighs. She turned and walked over to the boxes. "Cream cheese?"

"And bacon," he said mildly, watching the slick run down her legs. "New kink unlocked. I need to buy you a dozen pairs of those stockings."

Looking over her shoulder she grinned. She felt naughty, and sexy, and the look on his face had her body clenching. "I won't say no to that. I love stockings. They always make me feel naughty." She grabbed his bagel and a donut for herself, biting into the sweet goodness, the jelly shooting out and onto her chest. "Oops!"

"Oops?" He burst out laughing. "Like you didn't do that on purpose, you little minx. If you wanted me to lick your tits, why didn't you just say so?"

She laughed and shook her head. "Would that I was that smooth. I literally bit the wrong end." She showed him the hole that they made to put the jelly in. "But apparently my mistake is your dessert."

"Give a man a chance to eat first," he laughed. "And then I'll come for that jelly with pleasure."

"You will need your strength," she said and wiped the powered sugar from the corner of her mouth. "I plan to be demanding today, since I can be." Leaning back on Lorne's desk, which was seriously defiled, she might have to buy him a new one since it was only going to get worse, she finished her donut in silence, and watched as Finn had his own breakfast. "Coffee? Or there's juice in the fridge..."

"I finished my coffee. I'll just have some water. Keeping you occupied is thirsty work." Getting up to fetch himself a glass, he used the opportunity to unbutton the top of his shirt and shrug out of it, tossing it across the back of the office chair when he returned. "Don't get too comfortable on that desk," he teased. "I wasn't kidding about fucking you on every flat surface we can find. I wasn't kidding about the window, either. Speaking of...I hope the front door is locked?"

She nodded slowly, taking in the beauty that was Finn without a shirt. Gods, could he be hotter? Licking her lips, she gave him a sexy grin. "Of course it's locked. I'm a damn good assistant." She winked. "And you are edible."

"Still hungry?" He shoved his open trousers down his thighs. "Feel free to feast..."

Gods, she loved how cocky he was, how sure and in control. Men like that did not look twice at her before, hell, both her exes weren't anywhere close to dominant...but her seven, they lived there, even Leo with his sweet nature with her. She was on him like a shot, this day getting crazier as she went to her knees in front of him, her body and her need for him like she was a different person.

Before the seven, sex was something that happened, but now, it was a thing, it was everything because they wanted it, and she wanted to please them. She was constantly horny, and had been since that first weekend, her body always alive and alight and needing, but now, now it was getting what it wanted, and she couldn't get enough.

Gripping his hips, she slipped her lips around him, tasting them both as she laved and sucked his generous length.

"Fuck," he breathed, his eyelids fluttering closed before he forced them open to watch her. "You're so fucking good at that."

"I aim to please, Finn." She grinned up at him and licked him again. "Apparently I have always been good at giving head." She slipped him back into her mouth, relaxing her throat as she took him deeper.

"I don't want to imagine you doing this to anyone before us," he growled darkly, a hand fisting in her hair. "And if we haven't fucked you often or hard enough to erase any memory of other guys, then we need to step it up."

She pulled off him again. Looking up, she closed her eyes at how he tugged her hair. "I haven't thought of them in a long, long time," she said honestly. "They were my awkward past; you and the guys are my future, Finn...the only thing that matters to me."

"Good. Now go bend over your desk out there and show me that pretty pussy of yours. I want to rail it." He let go of her hair and gestured to the door leading out into the gallery. Luckily the blinds were still down since she'd never gotten around to opening for the day, but there were gaps in them that passersby could see through if they stopped and pressed their faces to the glass.

Possibly being found out was a turn on she realized as she sauntered to the desk and bent at the waist, opening her legs just a little, and angled her hips so he could see just what she was working with. Looking over her shoulder she grinned. "Like this?" Gods, she felt powerful, and sexy and wanted so badly just to please him. What would it have been like to just meet this man, if the world was different? Well, if the world was different, she wouldn't have the other six then, would she?

"Stay right there. The guys need to see this." He grabbed his phone from Lorne's desk and snapped a photo to send to the others. "God, you're fucking sexy. Cum dripping down your thighs and still desperate for more." Tossing the phone back onto the desk, he kicked his trousers all the way off and stalked toward her.

The idea they would all see her like that... Lord, she loved it. She shuddered and bit her bottom lip, the cool air in the showroom giving her a shiver as it passed over her wet thighs.

"I love that you're so fucking needy for us," he told her, coming up behind her and wasting no time fitting his cock to her entrance and sliding in. "But after this I'm going to need a small break. I'm looking forward to watching you sitting here in nothing but your stockings and my cum writing emails like you're not our dirty little princess on the desk I just fucked you on."

She shuddered and squeezed him from the inside. These games with him... Her phone rang, and she reached down into her bag, grabbing it, and set it on the table. "Kendrix," she said on a moan. "Should I answer?"

"Of course," he laughed, thrusting into her hard enough that she almost knocked it off the desk trying to answer it.

She hit the button and moaned. "Oh fuck..."

"Listen to those sweet cries," he said. "Dirty little slut getting railed at work."

She moaned again. "It's so good..."

"Of course it is...little cumslut. I am about to go into surgery and you send that photo..."

Her phone vibrated and she looked. "Mm... Leo is calling, too...video..."

"I want video. Go give him a show," Rix said. "See you soon, baby."

She switched over to see Leo, eyes starry in the video.

"You started without me?" he grumbled. "Rude." He set his phone back so she could see where he was sitting and the fact he already had his pierced dick out and was stroking it. "So fucking hot."

"Fuck..." she moaned and pushed back at Finn. "Finn's been taking care of me all morning...." She licked her lips. "Is that for me?" She gasped as Finner fucked her harder.

"It's always for you," Leo groaned, eyes fixed on his screen. "Always and forever, cupcake. Any time and any place you want it. Fuck..." In the tiny thumbnail picture of herself, she could see Finn behind her grinning devilishly as he pounded her.

"Hey, Leo, you fucked her ass yet?" he asked and Leo groaned again, picking up the pace at which he was stroking his cock.

"Not yet. Why? You gonna get it ready for me?"

"Maybe. It's so tight...so perfect...so virgin. I might just thoroughly defile it myself."

"And what do you think of that, cupcake?" Leo asked her.

Anal was not anything she had ever wanted before, but for her seven? Nothing was off limits, and she knew they would make it so good for her. "Anything you want... I'm yours..." she moaned and bit her bottom lip again as Finn took her harder. "Oh fuck...I'm going to come.."

"What do you reckon, Leo?" Finn smirked at the camera. "Should I let her come?"

"Nah, I'm not quite there yet," Leo smirked right back. "Pull out. Let her cool down a little." Finn burst out laughing, but he did as Leo suggested, leaving her squirming on the desk, a hot, horny, dissatisfied mess.

"Damn you both..." she said and pouted, her body sitting on the edge of need. "This isn't fair..."

They both burst out laughing and Finn shook his head. "You wouldn't think she'd already come several times this morning," he said and Leo snorted.

"Greedy little slut." From anyone else it would have sounded bad, but he said it with so much affection it wasn't offensive at all. "How does she feel, Finn?"

"She's so wet she's going to have to put down towels if she wants to get any work done today," Finn said, trailing a finger through said wetness and leaning over her to show it to the camera. "But I haven't worked her up into a real sweat yet." He smacked her ass. "Tell Leo what I'm going to do to you later when you're all hot and sweaty," he instructed her.

"He's going to fuck me against the windows..." she shivered. "And I can't wait. Though I might lose my job after that. We both might...and get arrested." She giggled.

"Please tell me you're going to do it with the blinds up like some sick performance art," Leo pleaded but Finn tutted.

"And let other men see her naked? No. They can see her body print afterwards, and if she can't keep her mouth shut there might be one or two that stop and look in the gaps, but otherwise this is all for our viewing pleasure."

"You going to video us?" she asked, wiggling her hips as Finn ran his fingers over her waist and hips. "Show the guys?"

"Video? I might just stream it live on a group call," Finn chuckled. "I'm sure it would make all their days."

She nodded. "Even Easton?"

"Girl, Easton wants you just as much as the rest of us," Finn assured her. "It just takes him a little while to let people in physically."

"Trust me, he'll be jacking off just like the rest of us," Leo said crudely.

Before their last nights together, she might not have believed him, but then she remembered watching her Snake jack off while she was on the Sybian and realized that he might enjoy the show as well. "I want..." she said, her body starting to cool. Honestly, this was the best day of work ever.

"Tell me what you want, sweetness," Finn encouraged her. "In detail."

She swallowed and looked to Leo, who nodded to her, hand still on his cock. "To put on a show for them," she said first. "I need to come; I need to touch...be touched. I don't know why, but it's like my body is just a ball of need."

"Define touch," he instructed, stroking a finger down the length of her naked spine and making her shiver all over.

"I want to be wrapped around you, and you me. All of you..." She swallowed, closing her eyes as she relaxed, and spoke what she felt. "Covered in blood, and cum and...you... I just want..."

"I don't know what you've done to her, but she seems to have forgotten how to talk," Leo teased. "Maybe you should just stop and let her try and go back to work."

"You do and you won't like how I act," she said to Leo on a grin. "No more blow jobs..."

"Spanking for impertinence added to the schedule for today," Finn noted aloud with a grin. "Don't worry, brother, I haven't broken her. She's just a little fuck drunk." He smacked her ass and then pushed his cock back into her.

"Ah...oh yes...fuck..." she moaned. "That's exactly what I need..." She shuddered as her body squeezed his. "So perfect. More...please..."

"With pleasure. Watch and learn, brother," he snarked at Leo as he went at it hard, crushing her hips into the desk and sending it shaking.

Her body shook, her hands holding on, her eyes on Leo as he tugged at his cock, the metal in it winking in the light. "Finn..." she moaned. "Leo...fuck, I want it in my mouth."

"We can make that happen," he promised her. "Soon," Finn agreed.

She lost it then, her body clenching around him as she surrendered, shattering with the force of the orgasm. "Fuck yes!"

On the screen, Leo was coming, too, the idea of fucking her mouth while Finn fucked her pussy clearly doing it for him, too. Finn was the last to come, holding her down to the desk as he filled her with a satisfied growl.

She panted, closing her eyes and licking her lips like she could taste Leo. "So fucking good. Thank you..."

"So polite," Finn teased. "I love it." He pulled out of her and grinned. "I'll let you say goodbye to lover boy there. I'm going to clean up."

"You are wasting that..," she said to Leo as she watched his cum drip on his hand. "I love watching you come."

"Well, some inconvenient little madame isn't here to clean it up," he pointed out. "I love watching you come, too. You make the cutest little face." He grinned into the camera, reaching forward to pick it up. "Go clean up. I'm quite sure he's left you a mess."

She nodded to him. "You coming over tonight, or am I cursed to wait 'til tomorrow morning? In which case I might just toss you into a bush..."

"I can come over tonight, but I'm fairly sure Finn will have fucked you into a coma by then and the last thing you'll want or need is more dick," he laughed. "But it's up to you. Send me a text later, okay?"

"What if I just need you?" she said softly. "These morning runs are the worst kinda tease. We haven't had time together otherwise..."

"Then I'll be there," he replied, letting his humor soften and fade out. "I'll bring food. Let me know when you're on your way home and I'll meet you there."

She smiled. "That's the right answer." She grinned. "I'll see you later." She blew a kiss at him.

He blew a kiss back and cut the call, leaving her with a warm feeling.

She sat up and turned to see Finn walking in with a water. "Hey, baby..."

"Thought you might be thirsty," he said, setting it down next to her. "I put some extra towels out in the bathroom if you want to go clean up."

She smirked. "I thought you wanted me to ruin my chair while writing emails," she teased.

"Not going to lie, knowing I'm in and all over you is a major fucking turn-on," he admitted, "but also I care about you and don't want you to ruin your favorite office chair or anything."

She blinked at his words. He cared about her. He said it. She shook it off, filing that away for later, so she could unpack it, and smiled sweetly. "I see your point." She walked over and kissed him softly. "I'll go freshen up."

Chapter 24

Leo was sitting on the step of Petra's building when she rounded the corner and had to swallow his laugh. She looked half asleep and was walking very gingerly. Poor thing. Finn had obviously gone to town on her. Still, she smiled dreamily when she saw him sitting there and he rose to his feet to kiss her cheek. "Here, let me take your bag," he offered, taking her things and scooping up the bags of food he'd brought with him.

"Such a gentleman," she said and took his arm. "Surprised you're not in the apartment..."

"That wouldn't have been very polite," he said, as though butter wouldn't melt in his mouth even though he knew damn well the idea had crossed his mind more than once. But he knew she'd be tired and sore, and the last thing she needed was a shock from finding someone unexpected in her sanctuary. "I went to the Middle Eastern deli near my place for dinner," he told her as she let them both into her place. "I didn't know if you'd want hot or cold, so I brought enough to feed the five-thousand in the hopes there's something in there you'll eat. Why don't you go and take a shower and I'll get this all set up?"

"Perfect. Though, Leo, it wouldn't have bothered me if I had walked in and found you in my place. I mean, I know Rix has a key. I figured you all did."

"Well yeah, but we like to do creepy shit with them, like checking in on you when you're passed out from being fucked into a coma," he laughed. "Who wants to do normal stuff like pre-warm dinner for you?"

She laughed. "Noted...though it would be sexy to walk in from work to find you waiting in bed for me." She winked and walked off into the bathroom. He heard the shower turn on and then splashing. It was clear she was in and enjoying it.

He laughed quietly to himself as he began warming up food. So demanding, their little minx. She never knew when to stop. She might think it was sexy to come home and find him in her bed but it was almost like she'd forgotten how extra he was. There'd be rose petals and chocolate and candles fucking everywhere, and she'd regret having to tidy it all up the next day, especially since the sheets would need washing, too. Maybe more than one set.

He set out dishes of mezze and flatbreads, before adding kefta and grilled lamb and eggs poached in spicy tomato sauce. There was couscous and grilled halloumi and fresh tabbouleh... He'd probably gone totally overboard, but it was all fresh and he was glad to know she'd have food for the next few days. He'd just finished setting up the table when she returned, looking fresher and less tired than before.

Dressed in lounge shorts and a tank top, clearly no bra, she smiled at him as she pulled her hair up into a bun. "It smells yummy," she said. "What's vegetarian? I'm not really sure about what it all is."

"Everything except the brochettes, those are kefta," he told her. "You can eat everything that's not on a stick. This is lemon-flavored rice wrapped in vine leaves. This is a whipped feta spread. This is aubergine with fresh garlic and sesame paste. This is grilled halloumi with warm sun blush tomatoes. This is..." He continued listing all of the dishes and what was in them until her eyes were glazing over, and eventually he just made her up a plate with some of everything and let her taste it.

"Ooh...yummy," she said softly and smiled. "This is perfect...good choice." She leaned in and kissed his cheek. She did a little food dance in her chair and closed her eyes as she chewed. "So how was your day? I mean after you came like a firehose?"

"Not bad," he replied, settling into his chair now that he was sure she was okay with his food choices. "I don't think I need to ask how yours went..."

"It was the best workday ever." She giggled and sipped her drink. "You making headway with work?"

"Yes and no." He set down his fork and sighed. "I have meetings with my lawyers next week. We're getting some pushback from big pharma over hospitals hosting our studies. Antidepressants are such big revenue earners because people take them for sustained periods of time. Us finding a 'cure' for depression," he quoted it with his fingers, "takes a big chunk out of their bottom line. So they're leaning on hospitals and clinics to refuse to participate in the study. If we can't legally persuade them to back off, we'll have to start looking at setting up our own clinics in collaboration with private practices that actually have their patients' best interests at heart instead of lining their own pockets." He shook his head, but then remembered a couple of good pieces of news and smiled at her.

"Our neuroscientists had a breakthrough, though. One of the reasons the FDA has dragged their feet over approving these drugs as a treatment is because we've never been sure how they work. We were aware it had something to do with neural plasticity, but my team have developed a new technique to actually watch it happening in real time in mice and it's incredible. We also got approached by a university this week looking to run research on using the EMDR technique in conjunction with psilocybin low and micro-dosing, so that's exciting, too.

"It means new funding, new staff, new grants we can apply for... But best of all, if it works, it will be an incredibly effective treatment protocol that can be offered at lower cost than expensive psychiatrists and long-term medications." He cut himself off and forced himself to pick up his fork again. "Sorry. I got carried away."

"No, it sounds fabulous! Why *wouldn't* I want to hear about your team saving the world? And with what He has given you this year, I think you are onto all good things." She smiled. "I like listening to you talk about it. It feels...normal and domestic."

He chuckled. "I've never been normal and I'm probably more feral than domesticated, but it is nice to just hang out with you. It's true." He paused, chewing thoughtfully. "It's interesting that He Who Sleeps lets us use the gifts He gives for things like this. You'd think that a God that feeds on murder would be all for chaos and destruction and misery. Yet here we are, making art, curing depression, rescuing animals... Sometimes I wish we could actually communicate with Him for real, you know? Ask Him if this is really what He wants or expects from His followers. You should ask Finn his theories on gods sometime. When he's not being a kinky fucker, he actually has some pretty deep thoughts about them."

"Theological conversations? That could be enlightening," she said and then was quiet for long moments. "You know, I think that He allows for this because of balance. But is He truly dark? I mean, humanity is not of use to Him if they aren't in a measure of comfort. You need a baseline from which to hurt someone. If they're already in pain, a little bit of torture isn't going to do a whole lot. And animals? Honestly, any god that would willingly hurt innocents..." She shook her head. "Humans are not innocent. Animals are."

He snorted. "If you really think that, you've never met a goat. Cantankerous little fuckers, every one of them. They're cute when they're babies, but the minute they get big, they're out to destroy you and everything you love."

"Yes, but they are innocent. They don't harm like humans do. They *are* assholes, but it's their nature, given to them by nature. Humans are corruptible. Goats just *are*." She smiled. "Goat eyes freak me out."

"I think if you have enough sentience to have a sense of humor, which goats definitely do, and a desire to prank the people that feed you, which goats also definitely do, there's some wickedness in there. And yes, they have freaky eyes. Little weirdos." He shuddered.

"Anyway, the gist of Finn's deep theories about any organized religion is that barely any fraction of it is actually based on, or endorsed by, the god or gods that inspired it. We know there's a God. We have proof of it. So, you know, it stands to reason that other gods exist, or at least they used to exist. But the god-human axis is inherently corrupt and it has the *telephone* effect of errors getting magnified down the generations. I guess what I'm saying is that, theoretically, The Order might be as wrong about the Dark God's needs as the Christian Church is about their faith."

"Oh yes...tenets , unless given directly by the god, are the wants and desires of man. We could go into that all night. My friend is a theology student, doing her master's right now," she offered. "Her thesis is on organized religion and its need for human control."

"Obviously they have some things right, or we wouldn't be able to feed Him," Leo said, really enjoying being able to have an intelligent conversation with someone outside their little brotherhood. At work it was all science this and money that. He was too driven and, of necessity, too secretive to have many friends. The Order was like a jealous lover.

"They knew the tattoos would work, so that we don't have to bleed you. But what's really interesting is that tattoos have been around since the ice age, right? But up until we asked about it and the ritual tattoos were suggested, they used to brand Order members who found someone that agreed to the pact."

"Control?" she suggested. "I mean control through despair, and agony, and pain. It's the same they did with the inquisition." She paused as something occurred to her. "Oh, you need to meet Victoria. I mean, I can talk about this to some degree, but she knows so much." She grinned. "Is it possible, and forgive me if it seems farfetched, 'cos I am not initiated, but is it possible that there has been sinister workings with the need for control in your order for longer than you think? That they have their own agenda? How did you guys find out about the tattoos?"

"Oh, I'm quite sure that's an aspect of it. And I'm certain the Elders have mostly their own power on their agenda. We weren't even supposed to offer the pact—it fell out of common use and we only stumbled across it in an old journal and thought it would be funny to try it. We never saw you coming, that's for sure." He laughed again, shaking his head at the craziness of it all.

"We didn't have a fucking clue what we were doing, so we went to the Lore-Keepers when we got back from that first year with you. It's this little group of priests that are supposed to just guard the history and traditions of The Order and they're supposed to be completely impartial."

"Maybe they are? I mean they probably don't mean to hold shit away, but they aren't going to offer information, which probably keeps them safe as well."

"The priesthood is sacred. Even the Elders respect that," he disagreed. "It's hard to explain to someone who didn't grow up with it. For an Elder to make an assault on the priesthood would be the worst kind of blasphemy. Any member of The Order would kill them on sight. And when we asked about the pact, they gave us the knowledge and the tools to use it, even though it was probably some Elder or other that decided to retire it as an option."

"Which is what I mean. That they won't volunteer the information in their arsenal until asked about it," she said. "But I can see how that would work. It's all very interesting. I mean as a mortal woman that is just...taking this all on faith." She looked to him. "And I have faith."

"Their function is only to teach when asked," he shrugged. "I suspect back in the day, it was expected that the Elders would take the teachings of the priests and spread them. But yeah...thanks to human fallibility, the Elders went their own way. But if they do something expressly against the teachings of the first priests, the current priests have the power to strip them of their power and their skin. They are the judge, jury and executioner. The Elders can skirt the teachings and maybe retire them, but they can't go directly against them. Anyway, you'll learn all this when you join up. And I'd be surprised if you didn't have faith now that you've seen the well and the magic rising out of it. You can't argue with your own two eyes." He blinked. "Unless you're looking at an optical illusion, in which case fuck your eyes."

She grinned. "I'm not saying I have faith in Him. I have faith in you, and Easton, Jack, Finn, Carter, Emerson and Kendrix. I have faith in who you are together, and who you are with me." Finishing her food, she sat back. "Today has been awesome. Fuck fest at work, dinner with my favorite needle happy lunatic, wonderful conversation..." She smiled at him. "Though

237

Rix said something about seeing me soon." She shivered.

"Yeah, I was supposed to ask you about that." He'd forgotten in all the talk of other things. "It's Emerson's birthday next weekend. We're planning a weekend trip away. You're coming."

"I am?" She laughed. "And it's Emerson's birthday?! Why didn't he say anything? Oh, I have to figure out a present."

"We don't celebrate birthdays," he told her. "Not since we lost our parents. Until now, anyway. We thought you'd enjoy a weekend away from the city with all of us together. So it's been arranged with your boss at the shelter and the lanky dude at the gallery and we'll pick you up at lunchtime on Friday."

"Ooh, I'm in...and where are we going? Seven of you for the weekend!" She grinned. "A girl could die from that kinda attention." She winked and giggled.

"You've survived four so far. I think you'll be fine," he chuckled. "As for where we're going, that's a secret and you can pout all you want. I'm not telling you."

"It's okay, I trust you. And I have a secret of my own," she teased.

"Oh God...you're not pregnant, are you?" His stomach lurched even as he said it with panic that they'd have to rush to buy a house and get a nursery set up and figure out lawyers to protect the kid and...and...and... "It's too soon," he blurted out. "We don't have a house ready yet."

She laughed. "Oh no, no I get the shot," she said. "Not that you guys have seemed to care either way. All of you but Easton coming inside me at any chance. I mean, don't get me wrong, I enjoy the fuck outta it, but no babies. At least right now." She blushed.

"We should talk about that, though," he said, his racing heart starting to settle now that he knew they didn't have to leap into overdrive to get her settled somewhere to incubate. "Kids are probably going to be on the menu for some, if not all, of us, at some point. Do you want kids?"

"Before meeting you guys? No. I mean, I didn't have a family aside from the girls, and my upbringing wasn't...ideal." She looked to him. "But now? Yes, especially with you all, if you wanted them."

"We do," he said, a soft smile lighting him up inside now that the panic had settled. The idea of keeping her barefoot and pregnant and constantly horny wasn't a kink he'd known he had. He needed to make an appointment with a doctor to get himself checked to make sure he was firing some good little swimmers. Get ahead of the curve. He wanted to be first.

And what a child she'd have...beautiful, strong, intelligent. He was completely caught up in the daydream until he noticed she was smirking and brought himself back down to Earth.

"Did you have enough to eat?" She'd cleared her plate but hadn't gone back for seconds and he wasn't sure if that was because she didn't like it or if it was because he'd loaded her up the first time round. "I did bring Greek pastries for dessert, but you don't have to eat any more if you don't want to."

He'd also brought some of the fabulous ultra-creamy Greek yogurt, with honey-coated walnuts from the deli, too, but she might like that for breakfast instead so he didn't mention it.

"It was super yummy, but I could go for some tea," she said as she stood. "And a cuddle on the couch?" She grinned. "Maybe something sweet?"

"I make a pretty good hot chocolate," he offered, trying not to think, as he always did, of Easton. God, he remembered when his brother had joined them...a damaged, half-feral and quiet little ball of explosive rage that had never known kindness or leniency. Leo had always been the most carefree of them and for some reason that none of them had ever been able to nail down, that angry little boy had gravitated toward him. So Leo had tried. He'd tried to interest him in sports or in books or in any one of half a dozen hobbies, but the first time Easton had ever opened up to him, it had been over a thick, creamy hot chocolate that Leo had learned to make from some chef on the TV, with real dark chocolate.

He'd put a cup in front of Easton, who'd sniffed it suspiciously as he did with most food, and then he'd sat there glowering like an incoming storm until Leo had taken a sip from his own mug. The look on his face when he'd tasted it for the first time had been nothing short of magical. It was such a simple and easy thing and yet, for a kid that had never known love or sweetness or the smallest of treats, it was everything. The memory still gave Leo a little frisson down his spine even now, all these years later.

"You look like you remembered something nice," she said to him, drawing him back to the present.

"Nice but sad," he admitted. "I was thinking of Easton when he was a kid. He loved hot chocolate. I haven't made it for him in years."

"You should make it on this weekend away then. Maybe he will love it."

"I will." He swallowed the unexpected lump in his throat. "So what do you say? You want one now? Do you have chocolate in the house?"

"I'm sold. Not sure I have everything in the house for it, but I'm totally game."

"I can make it work," he told her. "Come on. You'll have to show me where things are."

Twenty minutes later they had found all the ingredients, or made do with what she had in the fridge, and were sitting on the couch together, Petra snuggled into Leo's side. It felt domestic and perfect, and she smiled up at him.

"It's amazing, and you are amazing, Leo. Thank you for tonight."

"Any time," he said with a soft smile. "I like hanging out with you, too." And he meant it. She was funny and a great conversationalist. There hadn't been a single awkward silence, even though he knew she was exhausted from her day of epic dicking. "You just let me know when you're ready to sleep, and I'll tuck you in," he offered. "You must be wiped. Finn can be a demanding kind of guy."

"Finn was super fun. You all are," she agreed. "It never feels like a chore with any of you. I'm always ready, and while you all wear me out, it's nothing a good sleep won't fix." She smiled. "Will you stay tonight? Wake up with me to go running?"

"Of course! But no funny business," he said, internally acknowledging the sadness. "The last thing we want is for you to get a UTI from too much sex." Maybe in the morning, he thought. Perhaps he could persuade her to skip the running in favor of other more horizontal workouts.

"Obviously." She giggled. "I was just thinking sleeping and waking up with you would be a fantasy. Been a really, really long time since I slept through the night with anyone...though usually it was with the girls when we were scared of the thunder."

He would bear that in mind. The next time there was a storm in this area, he'd be in her bed come hell or high water. "I'm not going anywhere," he promised her. "Why don't you go do whatever it is girls do to get ready for bed? I'll text one of the others to drop off my running kit for the morning."

She leaned up and kissed him, sweet and chaste and perfect. "Okay, back in a flash."

He texted Carter to ask for his running kit and to let the others know where he was and that he was staying, and then used the rest of the time to clean up the kitchen. He'd brought dinner, and he didn't want to leave a mess behind for her to clean up. When she reappeared, he grinned and hung up the dish towel he was using. "You mind if I have a shower?" he asked.

"Of course," she said as she stood there in short frilly shorts, and a tank top that said sleep like you own it. "I'm going to finish my hot cocoa and then slip into bed...and wait for you to join me." She grinned. "Towels are in the cupboard."

"I was going to ask if you wanted to watch," he laughed. "I'm not averse to putting on a bit of a show."

She licked her lips and nodded. "Dinner and a show...I like it."

"I'm no Magic Mike," he admitted, figuring it was better to manage her expectations now, "but I've got moves."

"Seeing you wet and soapy is more than enough, though I want a slow dance for Emerson's birthday weekend."

"You got it," he promised. "I'll practice and everything." He loved that they could joke around like this. He knew he had a good body and that she was really into his piercings, but sex should be funny and silly as often as it was serious and intense. It was a good sign for the future that they could play around.

"Good. Now go get soapy in the rain locker. I wanna see that water running down your sexy body." She walked forward and slapped his ass in his slacks. "Be a good boy for Petra." She giggled.

Her sassiness aggravated him as much as it turned him on. "Don't treat me like a dog," he told her. "You won't like the consequences."

She grinned. "Never, my love," she said softly. "I was just teasing you."

"I worry sometimes that you forget who we are," he admitted, simmering the mood down a little. "We're cold-blooded killers. All of us. And we can be cutesy and sweet and whatever the fuck they call it in romance books these days, but each of us is only a hair's breadth away from the kind of violence you have nightmares about."

"I don't forget who you are, Leo. I know you all have a hair trigger, but I also know that I can tease you and you know it's just teasing...and sometimes I tease to get spanked. Sue me. I like your hands on me."

"And what if I don't want to spank you?" he asked curiously. "What if the only thing that's going to soothe the violence is piercing or tattooing you? The rules about permanently marking and maiming went moot the moment you decided you wanted us outside the pact."

She turned and wrapped her arms around his waist. "Then I take what soothes you, Leo. You want to pierce me, suspend me? Tattoo my skin with your name, or other things? I'm okay with that. I'm yours. I'm all of yours, and I signed on for all of it, Leo. I know you don't really believe it but..." She smiled. "I want this. Being with you seven, it's the only thing that's ever felt right, truly right in my life. If I'm destined to bleed, to endure for you? I will."

"We're going to break you," he said with a certain sense of savage satisfaction. It might be a while coming and she definitely wanted it, but they would break her on the blades of their desires and she'd come for them while they did it. It was so fucked up and glorious all at once.

"Then you break me," she said softly. "That feels right, too."

How did they get so lucky? She was so perfect for them in every way. "Maybe one day we'll bring you over to our side," he joked. "Teach you how to inflict pain and go out and kill someone."

"Maybe," she agreed. "Though don't get me wrong, I could take a life if I had to...might not be clean, but I could." She snuggled close to him. "You need that shower, love. Come on..."

"Are you saying I stink?" He laughed, following her down the hall. "So fucking rude..."

"No, I am saying I wanna see this sexy body wet." She grinned over her shoulder. "And then I want you to hold me in the bed, and that's only going to get done if you shower."

"So demanding," he teased. "I'm here for it. Show me the water and find me a towel and I'll make all your wet dreams come true." He waggled his eyebrows, loving the way she creased with laughter, even as he started stripping to get in the shower and her cheeks heated with lust. This had definitely been the right choice.

Chapter 25

"There she is!" Carlee said from the other side of the screen. "Girl, you look... I'm not sure how you look." She grinned. "You look seriously satisfied."

Petra nodded. She was satisfied. She had woken up with Leo, had some perfect morning sex, and then lazed about in bed another hour with him before he left for work. No running, just cuddling. And it had been one of the best days of her life.

"That's the face of someone that's been thoroughly fucked," Victoria said, squinting at her screen. "Spill it. Now."

"It's been an...intense twenty-four hours," she admitted. "I'm sure you guys don't want the gory details," she teased.

"The fuck we don't. You know how long it's been since I got laid?" Carlee said.

"Not as long as I've been dry," Fiona said mournfully. "I'm starting to think mine might have closed over. So yeah, we need the details."

"Cobwebs... I'm pretty sure I got bats up there. It's like a cave." Carlee laughed. "So let us live vicariously through you, cuz it's obvious it was one hell of a dicking...unless you have switched sides?"

Petra shook her head. "Oh, it was dick," she said and smirked. "A few, actually."

"You had a gang bang?" Fiona gasped, her eyes alight with curiosity. "You dark horse! Tell us everything!"

"No...well... No, a threesome," she cocked her head and looked up squinting, and then frowned. "Nothing more than that yet," she offered.

"Yet... Pet, what are you into? Are you...are you seeing two guys? I mean clearly you have been with two but are you..."

"Seven," she said softly. "Seven men."

"I'm sorry, I think I misheard that," Victoria frowned at the screen. "It sounded like you said seven men."

She nodded. "I did. Seven amazing men." She smiled wistfully.

Carlee, who had her tea cup poised at her mouth moved, and dumped tea into her lap. "Ah, fuck!"

"What the fuck?" Fiona was staring at the screen, her jaw dropped. "Seven?"

"How?" Victoria screeched. "Stop this coy shit and start at the beginning!"

"What the fuck?" Fiona whispered again.

"Starting at the beginning..." She laughed. "That's a bit of history there." She shook her head. How much to tell them? "Well, I met them three years ago. Halloween weekend."

"Hold up, that's what you are doing Halloween weekend? Seven hot dudes?" Carlee had recovered enough to be indignant. "Fuck beans, how the hell is that fair?"

"Wait!" Victoria was literally screeching. "You've been fucking seven guys for three years and you're only just telling us about it now?! What kind of shitty friend does that?!"

"It's a cult, isn't it?" Fiona said, sobering. "That's why you didn't say anything. You've been inducted into some cult that passes you around like a sex toy."

Petra scrunched up her nose. Fi was closest to the truth. "I mean...*I'm* not in a cult," she offered. "And I'm not passed around as a sex toy." Okay, that was stretching it.

"There's a 'but' coming," Fiona sighed. "And that's probably exactly what you would say if you were in a cult. Do you need an intervention?"

"No *but*," she offered. "I met them three years ago, and we got on, and we get it on, no strings," she swallowed, "before this year once a year...Halloween."

"So what happened this year?" Carlee asked.

"We all decided we wanted more."

"Okay, but...how did you guys get together?"

"It was a party here."

"Since when do you go to parties?" Carlee frowned."

She shrugged. "My first year here, I went with a friend..." She smirked. "She left after a bit, and it was kinda cool...they were masked and all. It was very *Eyes Wide Shut* really and there was not one chance I wasn't going to miss out on that." Okay, it wasn't completely the truth, but it wasn't a lie.

"And they're all just okay with it?" Fiona was frowning. "You managed to find seven guys at one party that don't mind sharing?"

"What the hell kind of parties are you going to?" Victoria was still screeching. "And why didn't you invite us?"

She laughed at Victoria. "Girl, it wasn't like I found this shit on my own." She looked to Fiona. "They are friends, brothers of a sort. Grew up much like us...together, and alone and they...well, they share things. Me being one of them."

"Okay, this sounds like a goddamn romance novel, but they aren't hurting you, right?"

Define hurt? she thought and then shook her head. "No. I wouldn't be in this three years if they were," she offered. "I mean I'm clearly a deviant, but I don't have a death wish."

"It still sounds like a cult," Fiona said doubtfully. "A bunch of guys growing up together and alone and sharing everything? How is it not a cult?"

"What difference does it make?" The decibels were coming down but Victoria was still clearly overexcited. "How does it work? Do you have massive orgies? Do they fuck each other as well? Details!"

She laughed again. "No orgies, they aren't like that, they are all hetero, but they have learned that one between them all keeps them bonded." She smiled. "As to how it works? Well, I have time with each of them and it's...well, it's delightful. I'm something different for each of them, and they are something different for me." She smiled again, wistful. "You know it's refreshing to have a man be something, not all things? Like if he's something, he can't drop the ball on the other things, making him so very good at being that one thing."

"Not even one orgy?" Victoria looked disappointed. "Well, fine, I guess. You do you. I'm still pissed you didn't tell us this before."

"No orgy yet." She shook her head. "We have had limited time together up until this point. Though we have a weekend away coming up. One of them has a birthday and we are going away for it, to celebrate properly. As to why I didn't tell you guys," she looked to each of them in turn and then shrugged. "I didn't know how originally..."

"And now?" Carlee asked.

"Now I need you guys to know, because they are precious to me, and things are going past some naughty, kinky sex."

"I knew it! Tons of kinky sex!" Carlee fist pumped. "Spill."

"It's not that simple," she offered.

Fiona was still staring moodily at the camera, obviously unsure about the situation, but Victoria had no such reservations. "Why are you being stingy about the details? Do they have dick measuring contests?

What are their names? Are they employed? Any of them have funky kinks? Piercings? Tattoos? You're killing us here!"

"Dick measuring contests...not that I know of. Names? Leo, Emerson, Easton, Finn, Carter, Kendrix, and Jack. Employed? Yes, two of them own their own companies, one's an artist, one is an accountant, and three of them work in animal welfare," she started.

"Well don't stop there," Victoria said, making a gimme-gimme motion.

"Kinks? Well, let's see...there's the fire kink, which is really hot...and the toy kink...the oral kink. Ooh and one of my guys has a real hard-on for blaspheming." She giggled. "Another likes to chase me like he's a movie slasher..."

"Okay, now I know you're just making this shit up," Victoria said. "That kind of stuff doesn't happen outside of books."

"It does in my life." She smirked at her friend. "One of my guys is into piercings, too."

"As in he has them or he wants you to get them?" Victoria asked.

She grinned. "Both. His kink is very specific...you remember that time we went to the fetish show, and they did the workshop on erotic needling?"

"You let him stab you with needles?" Fiona was definitely unhappy. "Some guy you picked up at a party and have only met three times? How are you all being so cool with this?"

"Fi..." She sighed. "Look, being with them I have been able to explore things...things any vanilla guy wouldn't dream of...things that I have found that I like. Honestly? Back then I was interested but where the fuck was I going to explore that? He let me explore that with someone that knows how to do it right."

"Don't give me that face," Fiona replied primly. "I'm just worried about you. Are you sure he's being safe? Do you know how he stores and sanitizes his needles? How do you know he's not sharing them around his other fuck buddies and giving you hepatitis? Someone has to ask these questions."

"She is kinda right," Victoria agreed reluctantly. "But you'd know if he wasn't safe, right?"

She nodded. "Fi, I'm not dumb. He's always safe and everyone has always been tested." She smiled. "I'm safe, and I'm happy."

"Well, I wanna know how I could be happy," Carlee said. "Seven men sounds like a lot but..."

"Yeah, where do we sign up for the sex parties?" Victoria demanded.

"In your cities? I don't know." She laughed and shook her head. "But honestly, you guys would get into something like this? Really? I thought you were one man kinda girls."

Carlee scoffed. "You kidding? College I was less into dudes and more into girls." She grinned. "Though I did enjoy the occasional orgy, and before you even disapprove, Fi, they weren't with the shitty jocks. Goth boys had all the skills."

"Lay off it," Fiona snapped. "I don't have a problem with fucking around, or with orgies for that matter. I've done my fair share of non-vanilla snacking. You don't get to judge me as a prude because I'm worried that one of our best friends let some guy she only met a couple of times stick needles into her. I'm allowed to be worried, and frankly I'm concerned that you aren't."

"Hey, now," Victoria soothed. "No one is saying you're a prude—"

"That's exactly what Carlee was just implying!" Fiona interrupted her. "She literally just said 'before you disapprove.' We're not just talking about sex here.

Needles have consequences. I couldn't care less who you fuck around with or how many dicks you want to take at a time or in which holes, but the minute you start introducing foreign bodies into the organ designed to protect you from infections, you should all be asking questions. You wouldn't go to some skeezy back-street piercing parlor, would you?"

"Sometimes I forget you're a biologist," Victoria admitted. "I don't think you're a prude, and I'm sure the others don't, either." She gave the camera a quelling look. "We know you're just looking out for Petra."

"Leo owns a pharmaceutical company," she offered. "He's working on some amazing things having to do with depression. He knows about skin, and blood, and needles. I wouldn't ever let someone touch me if they didn't know what they were doing."

"That's all you had to say," Fiona said, nodding. "That's okay then. So...this birthday weekend? Where are they taking you?"

"Yeah, and will there be cell service?" Victoria asked. "Just in case..."

"Leo didn't say. It's supposed to be a surprise." She smiled. "It's our first big time together, all of us. It's Emerson's birthday, and he and Leo are the ones that made the plans. I'm really excited about it. I mean, spending time with them for a few days without jobs in the way. Leo and I run each morning, and I get to see Finn at work, but..."

"Wait, you work with these guys?" Victoria's jaw dropped. "They're just...out there normalling...like the normal people?"

"Yes, they are normal people." She shook her head. "Easton is an artist, Finn is actually the accountant for the gallery. Carter? He's actually the head of Animal Control, and Kendrix is a brilliant spinal surgeon for animals," she said proudly.

251

"That's..." Fiona frowned but bit back whatever she'd been about to say. "Small world..." Victoria shook her head wonderingly. "It's almost as though it was fate or destiny or some romantic shit like that."

"Fate..." Carlee said. "I never discount fate. But were they there before you knew them?"

"Honestly, not all of them," she said. "Finn had worked with me, but we never interacted. Same with Easton, since you know in the beginning I never really saw or spoke to any of the artists. Jack started going to yoga at some point after we met. Same with Leo and me running together. Carter and Rix, I never once met them beforehand, though I had spoken to Carter on the phone. I didn't know him, never met him before. And Kendrix, I didn't know him at all before this, though I knew of him, the director of the shelter claiming he was a boon to the shelter, helping them."

"None of this makes any sense." Fiona sighed. "These guys are all regularly in your life, but you only all get together once a year until now?"

"And how the fuck did you keep a straight face when you walked into work after the first fuckfest and realized you'd been nailing the accountant?" Victoria was back to hysterical screeching. "Oh my god! I'd have died!"

"You gotta learn to play the game. I mean it wouldn't do if Lorne knew..." She smirked, throwing aside the fact that they were masked when it happened. "And Finn has the blaspheming kink."

"When do we get to meet them?" Fiona asked, still subdued. "Will they be around when we get home for Christmas?"

"Unfortunately, no. They go back to the school they attended and grew up at for the solstice, but it's possible they might be here," she offered. "I was told that New Year's I have plans..."

"Then perhaps a virtual get-together," Fiona pushed. "If these guys are everything you say they are to you, you'll want them to meet your best friends."

"Of course I want that, I just don't want them interrogated," she teased. "You guys are my family, not just my friends. I just want everything perfect when it happens. Right now we are trying to figure out this dynamic on a more permanent level, and what we mean to each other, you know?" She smiled. "And I know it's different, and isn't something people would largely accept, but it makes sense for us."

Carlee nodded. "When you are ready... But we want pictures..."

"Pictures of what?"

"Dicks, of course!"

"No thanks." Victoria's face screwed up. "I don't mind hearing about them, or who has the biggest one, but I don't need pictures."

"Agreed. I've had enough dick pics for a lifetime," Fiona shook her head. "Besides, when we do meet them I don't want to know what their schlongs look like. That would just make everything awkward."

"You sure? I could send a worksheet of dicks and pictures and see if you can match the dick with the guy?"

Victoria snorted. "While that sounds hilarious, maybe we'll save it for your bachelorette party."

Petra giggled, the idea of a bachelorette party, of marrying those guys... "Deal. I mean I don't need you to be jealous." She winked.

"It's been so long since I was with a guy that I don't think I'd even care about dick size," Fiona laughed, lightening up finally. "I'd just be grateful."

"Besides, if they're big enough to look really impressive, the guy really has to know what he's doing with it, otherwise it's just uncomfortable," Victoria pointed out.

"They know." She giggled and blushed, her mind going to both Rix and Carter. "Gods, do they know."

"Yeah, yeah, rub it in why don't you?" Victoria shook her head. "Actually kinda selfish if you ask me. The rest of us out here in the desert of eligible men and you just snap up seven all to yourself..." Her smile said she was joking but there was a tiredness there. It was true none of them had dated in a while and there was a serious dearth of decent men. The dating scene was a nightmarish hellscape from which few escaped unscathed and attached.

But ultimately was she any better? Seven killers, ones that could snap on her in a heartbeat. But that was the beauty of it, wasn't it? The danger of it made their time together sweeter. Did she think she would service them? Yes. Did she think she would do it unscathed? No, but it didn't matter. She loved them. And she had a sneaking suspicion they all loved her as well.

"Okay, but the biggest question is...would you want seven?"

Victoria appeared to give it some sincere thought. "I think I'd take three," she said finally. "I think that's the optimal amount of man I could take."

"Four," Carlee said. "They can keep each other busy." She laughed.

"You know, I think I'd be okay with just two," Fiona said. "That's enough to keep me satisfied and keep on top of the house chores."

Petra shook her head and sighed. "The three of you are hopeless. But I should go. I'm almost late for work, and Vic, don't you have to get to class? What is this, your last week of TA duties?"

"Yeah." She fist-pumped. "Have a great day at work, chica. And no more secrets, okay?"

"You know, this wasn't exactly a secret..." she hedged. "But yeah. No more secrets. I love you guys."

"Love you, too, doll. Slap a few asses for me." Carlee winked. "Call soon, yeah?"

"I'll send you all the updated calendars," Fiona said, ever the organizer. "Love you, guys. Be safe."

She switched off with a wave and sighed. Telling them everything was going to be hard, but this was a good start.

Grabbing her bag, she slipped on her shoes and left, her mind on her guys.

Chapter 26

"Good morning, Officer Douritz," Petra offered as she walked up to the gallery. The police officer was standing in front of the gallery window, and nowhere close to his beat, which was supposed to be her side of Broad Street.

"Petra..." He seemed transfixed by the very obvious sweaty print of her tits on the glass. Finn had insisted on leaving the blinds open in that section to display her wantonness to the world. Kinky exhibitionist fucker. "I saw the security grate wasn't fully closed and came to check that everything was okay." His jaw clenched as he glanced back at the window.

"Oh." She smiled. "I didn't know you lived this close enough to notice something like that. As to the grate, my boss had an installation started last night, apparently it needed to dry a bit," she offered, looking at the prints of her body.

"This is artwork?" He looked deeply uncomfortable. "Who made it?"

"Not sure. We have a show coming up, one of our regulars, and the work is kind of...erotic I guess. My boss is very avante garde these days, I believe this is part of the marketing," she offered, very sure she never wanted the man before her to know it was her.

"You should perhaps wear heels," he told her abruptly, turning away from the window. "It's exactly your height. Wouldn't want anyone thinking you're the model."

"Oh. I guess it is. Normally I do wear heels, today is warehouse day," she said brightly. "Can't climb ladders in heels and it's not safe to wear no shoes on the catwalks," she said of the building behind the show room. "Much to do. Are you just going into work yourself?"

"Yes, I was just heading out to patrol when I saw the shutters." He straightened his uniform. "I'll get going, then. Have a great day."

"You, too, Officer! Stay safe!" She waved and went to the door, opening it with the code, and entered, locking it behind her. Lorne would be in shortly and as much as the comments from the cop amused her, she didn't think Lorne would buy the same story. Needing not to get pulled up in the drama, she grabbed the Windex and some towels and set to work cleaning it off.

Fifteen minutes later she had cleaned off the windows, much to her own chagrin, and Lorne was coming through the warehouse doors.

"Morning, Ms. Franklin, how was your day yesterday? We have a ton of things to get inventoried."

Four hours later she was getting off her knees and arching her back, cracking it in the process. Everything was done, Lorne's extensive list of new intake cataloged and inventoried and she was in need of a glass of wine and a soak.

"Ms. Franklin? I need to head to the parkway, Glitter Franz is scouting a location for the installation..."

"It's fine, Lorne. You coming back later?"

"No," he chuckled. "Glitter wants me to meet their agent..."

She nodded. "Well, have fun."

"You, too, and enjoy your weekend off."

She nodded as she watched him walk out, and then stood, sighing.

"How much will you love me if I offer to massage that aching back for you tonight after a luxurious soak in the hot tub?" Leo's voice came from the front door of the gallery.

"Us," she heard Jack say as she turned to them both. "Hey, beautiful girl."

"So much," she offered and skipped over to them, kissing them both.

"No yoga with Keezie this weekend." Mischief danced in Jack's eyes. " Our yoga instructor wants to make our sweet girl scream."

"She can take a ticket and wait in line," Leo teased. "And she only gets to do it if we can watch."

"Funny, I mention my exes and you wanna murder them. Skeezie Keezie wants to fist me and you are all for it," she teased.

"I didn't say I wouldn't kill her afterwards," he pointed out. "She'd technically be an ex after."

"Ugh, she is not worth hiding the body," Jack said. "And I'm pretty sure she would give her an STI, then where would we be? A full course of antibiotics and a miserable Petra..."

"True," Petra said. "No reasons for antibiotics needed."

"So how was your day, beautiful?"

She shrugged. "Aside from showing up and one of the cops seeing my boob prints on the window..."

"I'm sad we didn't get to see it," Leo laughed. "And I'm going to tattle to Finn that you cleaned it off. I'm looking forward to watching him punish you."

"It will be worth it. I mean, could you see Lorne getting all pissy about it? Then he would know me and Finn defiled this place in every possible way. He would never leave us to work alone again. No, thank you." She shook her head. "Though I do admit it was weird having to come up with a story to the cop that asked me."

"You know him?"

She nodded. "He's a beat cop on my block. He lives over this way apparently and saw the grate not down, so he investigated, as cops are wont to do..."

"Well, I guess I'm glad that someone is looking out for you," Leo said. "The law is generally useless, but in this case, one more pair of eyes on you can only be a good thing."

"Yeah, but when that pair of eyes is figuring out that it's my tits on the window..."

Jack chuckled and chucked her on the chin. "Probably gave the guy spank bank material for weeks."

"You want us to kill him?" Leo asked. "You know...for laying eyes on your tit prints?"

"Well, no. It just was uncomfortable...I mean, he's a cop." She shrugged. "So just the two of you picking me up? I assumed Easton would..."

"Ah, but Easton has been here before," Jack offered. "We haven't so..."

"Well, to that logic Carter and Rix should be here, too, and Emerson."

"All of who are already on their way to our destination."

"Well I gotta grab a bag."

"All taken care of." Jack winked. "And there are actual clothes in the bag we packed for you. Not just frilly sexy things."

"Against my protests, I might add," Leo laughed. "I voted for total nudity, but the birthday boy said no."

She smiled. She hadn't seen Emerson, and was eager to, considering they had only had phone and video time. "Don't worry, love," she told Leo. "For your birthday I'll go completely starker's the entire time."

"I'd like that in writing," he said seriously, despite the twinkle in his eye. "I need to be able to hold you to that."

"You know I would never deny you, Leo. Any of you."

"Birthdays could be fun going forward," Jack quipped.

"Oh, I have no doubt whatsoever that you'll make all our birthdays very special," Leo said, glancing at his watch. "You about ready? The car will be here any second. Can we help you lock the place up?"

She nodded. "One of you can make sure the back grating is closed. The other? Make sure the warehouse is empty of people. I can handle the showroom," she said and they set to work. Mere moments later they were all in the showroom and they were ushering her out to an SUV parked in front of the building, the windows blacked out. She locked the door, hitting the code in, and the grating came down, clicking into place. "There. All done."

"Well then, my lady," Leo rubbed his hands gleefully. "Your chariot awaits."

Chapter 27

The Chesapeake Bay house was beautiful, old stonework and eaves, a place that felt like it was holding its breath until they all walked in.

"And you grew up here?" she asked Emerson as she looked around the splendor of the grand foyer. Aside from the house they used during Halloween weekend, she had never been in a place that grand, but this placed seemed happier, and homier.

"'Til I went to school with these miscreants," he offered and wrapped himself around her. "And on occasion small holidays away. Do you like it?"

"It's beautiful. Feels calm...and loved."

"Well, if nothing else, my father loved this place. I was actually born here," he said softly.

"And you bring me here for your birthday?"

"No place I would rather be, with you and them. We are going to have a real good time."

"And we are safe here?" she asked.

"As kittens." He grinned then looked to the six of them that were standing around the foyer. "Pick rooms, yeah? I get the master, obviously, and Pet is sleeping with me."

"How is that fair?" Jack said.

"Because I'm the birthday boy." He winked at his friend. "But that's only if she wants to."

"Of course I do."

"I'm taking one with French doors," Carter said in a tone that brooked no argument. "I'm not traipsing through the house any time Brutus wants to go out." The dog was on his heels as they headed toward the rooms at the back of the house.

"Guess that leaves most of us upstairs then," Finn said with a grin.

She watched the dog go, still not having been introduced to him, but knew there was time. "There are enough bedrooms, right?"

Emerson nodded. "Enough for everyone and a few more." He squeezed her sides. "Come on..."

The lot of them walked up the main staircase, and broke off from each other on the second floor, each making their way down different halls, Emerson and Leo guiding her down the main one.

"Double doors at the end are ours," he said to Leo. "The two on the left are bedrooms, third on the left is one, too," he offered as they walked and stopped at the double doors. "Though I have a feeling largely this is where the magic is going to happen this weekend. Well, bed-bound magic."

"Bold to assume..."

"Assume nothing. It's my birthday and if I want my best friends, your boyfriends, to run a train on you in here, I'm going to have it." She shivered and he chuckled. "Hey, Leo, she likes that idea."

"Was there ever any doubt?" Leo paused at the room closest to theirs and then stepped back. "Knowing how noisy she is, I think I'll maybe put a room between us if I want to get any sleep at all this weekend," he chuckled.

He chose the next door down and let himself in, slinging his bag onto an unseen bed with a cheeky grin.

"Amateur," Finn shook his head. "Some of us came armed with earplugs to be close to the action and still get some sleep."

"Am I the only one that isn't completely overthinking this?" Easton was standing in the hallway looking at them like they'd all lost their minds.

"Don't tell me you didn't look which rooms have south-facing windows in case our beauty here lets you paint her from life," Finn said and Easton had the grace to look sheepish.

"Maybe. But at least I'm gentleman enough to be thinking about activities other than fucking all day, every day." He turned to Petra. "I'm not saying I'm not going to be involved in the fucking when it happens, but if you want a break from it, I'll be in that south-facing room over there," he told her, pointing a thumb over his shoulder.

She laughed and extricated herself from Emerson's hold and went to Easton. "It's a date," she offered and touched his arm, which he allowed. She considered it a small victory. "Now, why don't you all go and get settled then. I'm going to take a shower...alone...and then what?"

"Dinner," Easton said. "It's already being set up by the caterers. Go shower." He winked. "Get comfortable, sweetness. It's going to be a long night, yeah?"

Fifteen minutes later she was out of the shower, dressed in a long-sleeved wrap dress, bare under the dress to her toes. Emerson had left it out for her, with the simple ask of "Please" on a handwritten card, and she obliged, leaving her hair free as well.

Padding from the room, she made her way down the stairs, loving the feel, the energy in the house. And stopped as she spied Carter and the large dog coming from the other side. She went to her knees and smiled. "Look at you, you beautiful baby!"

Brutus sniffed her hair and then her face and then glanced back at Carter, who was just waiting patiently.

"It's okay, boy," he murmured. "You can say hi."

Brutus swung his enormous head back to her and, without warning, swiped her from chin to temple in one sweep of his long, wet tongue.

She giggled and smiled, huge. "Oh, look at you! Hello, you big boy!" She looked to Carter, covered in dog slobber but she didn't care. That was what wet wipes were for. "Will he let me pet him? I would never presume..."

"Sure," Carter smiled easily, clearly comfortable with her being around his dog. Brutus was the size of a small horse, but seemed to have a gentle nature and was clearly well trained. "He's a total softie," he added as she reached up to pet the sleek, grey coat before her. "He doesn't like people touching his feet, but we've been working on that, haven't we, boy?"

He scratched Brutus' head and the dog gazed up at him adoringly. "His groomer is his second favorite person in the world and we've come up with a plan so she can clip his nails without him pulling," he explained. "He's not bad or aggressive with her. It just takes ten times longer than it has to because someone doesn't let her hold his paw for very long."

"I can see that. There was one dog at the shelter a while back that had the same phobia," she said. "They can work through it, though I'm glad he's such a good boy. Brutus, we are going to be good friends," she said to the animal. "Do you like blanket cuddles? I do..." She scratched behind his ear. "Such a good boy." She looked to Carter again. "He's amazing. And so are you." She got to her feet and went to him kissing him sweetly. "Thank you for bringing him."

"I knew you wanted to meet him, and he loves road trips." Carter shrugged self-consciously. "It seemed like a good idea all round."

"Hmmm..." she hummed and snuggled close to him. "Where is everyone? Emerson mentioned dinner, but we didn't get a tour of the place," she offered, her hand going absently to the dog's back to pet him.

"Yeah, it's getting late. I figured he wanted to get food into everyone before he got six hangry brothers and one hangry girlfriend," he teased. "Come on, the dining room is this way. I'm sure you'll get the tour afterwards."

They walked down another hallway and ended up in a large room with a decently long table, set for eight.

"There she is...and looking fucking edible," Emerson said. "That dress is temping as hell."

She blushed. "You picked it."

"I did. So? Shall we eat?" He pulled out the chair next to him.

Leo's stomach grumbled loudly and he burst out laughing as he entered the room. "I hope they're catering a whole feast out there," he said, taking a seat at the table. "I'm starving."

"You're always hungry," Easton teased, taking the seat next to Carter and turning his attention to Brutus. "Hey there, big guy," he said quietly, getting a huge head snuggled into his chest as he scratched behind ears and stroked flanks. They were clearly familiar with each other and just as clearly adored each other.

"Why didn't you bring the bird?" Jack asked as he and Kendrix said down, the latter's eyes on her, intense and brooding. She hadn't seem him since they got back, but their calls were...intense.

"She doesn't like travelling and there wasn't enough room in the car for her equipment," Easton explained. "She's okay. My housekeeper is staying over to keep her company. She's going to have a whale of a time."

"Since we're talking animals and I know you all have the impulse control of raccoons on meth, I'd like to remind everyone to please not feed Brutus from the table," Carter announced as the others all arrived and took seats. "He's a good boy and he doesn't beg, but I don't want him to pick up bad habits from you horrible lot."

267

She smiled. "Understood. No snacks for the puppy." She winked at him.

With everyone seated, the food started coming out, and Emerson looked to her. "I had the chef make yours special, since you don't eat meat."

She nodded as they brought out a plate of large portabella, farrow and spinach. "Oh, it looks yummy." She looked to Emerson's plate to find the same meal but with steak and smiled. "It's lovely."

"Before we start, a toast..." Jack said as glasses of wine were brought to the table. They all raised theirs. "To Emerson. The oldest of us, the smartest, though I dare say I'm better looking." He flashed her a wicked smile. "Happy birthday."

"Well now you've done it," Leo said after the toast. "If you're going to start a pissing contest about who is the best looking, we'll have to put it to our lovely queen here to decide. What say you, cupcake? Who is the most handsome of us all?"

"Hmmm..." she said and sipped her wine, mulling it over. "You are all smoking hot," she said evenly, "made hotter by the things you do, and how you treat me. But you all have the top spot in different categories..." With a grin, she looked down at her wine. "And they are all equal for me. Though, my friends asked about each of your dicks. I couldn't comment there." She took another sip of her wine and giggled to herself.

"Someone gave you lessons in diplomacy," Finn chuckled. "That'll teach Leo to be an idiot."

"Hey, I'm all for a dick measuring contest," Leo said right back, unperturbed. "I'll slap it on the table right now." He stood up and started unbuckling his pants.

"Don't take it out unless you're planning to use it." She giggled.

Kendrix didn't say anything from his spot, just pulled out his knife and started spinning it on his finger.

"Same with you," she said to him. He gave her a savage grin, but said nothing.

"So you told your friends about us? All of us?" Jack asked.

She nodded. "This morning, actually. It was quite the conversation." Looking to Finn she declared, "not really diplomacy, more you all tick different buttons for me, but you are all sexy to me, and you all get me, and keep me wet."

"Leo, sit down and stop being a prick," Finn sighed. "I heard your stomach rumbling earlier, so you're only spiting yourself by messing around."

"You're all just scared I'm the biggest," Leo smirked, zipping up and rebuckling his belt to sit down.

"What are you? Five?" Easton rolled his eyes.

"No one wants to listen to you peacocking," Carter told Leo. "Petra was about to tell us about her friends and what they think of the situation, so shut up and let us listen."

"So what did they say?" Jack pressed.

"Well," she began, "after a bit it was really positive, but from the off they were...well, surprised I guess the word would be. Fiona..." She giggled. "Was like, this is a cult, isn't it?" She mimicked Fiona's voice. "And then Carlee and Vic were both wanting to know about dicks and sex and how naughty you guys are." She blushed. "But a girl can only kiss and tell so much."

"But you told them there were seven of us?" Finn asked.

She nodded. "I did."

"And they were just...cool with that?" Easton's voice made his disbelief clear. "They didn't even once question your sanity?"

She laughed. "I did say Fiona asked if it was a cult, right?" She looked at her sexy artist. "They were not super cool with it at first, or the fact that I told them we have had a standing Halloween date the past three years."

"Makes sense. Normal girls in normal society," Jack offered.

"Not normal, I mean they are my friends and clearly I'm not normal. But more like it's what's expected of them. One dude, maybe two to be scandalous. But Seven? Carlee was all for it, but she's a deviant like me." She giggled. "Vic and Fi are more reserved about it, and that's okay, but they wanna meet you guys, make sure you're not serial killers." She smirked and then snorted. "As if."

"Uh...I think technically you only have to kill three people to qualify as a serial killer, so by that definition, we actually are serial killers," Carter pointed out.

"Awkward," Leo snorted. "Sorry, ladies, we're exactly the things you're worried about."

"And yet you're more than that. All of you." She looked to each of them in term. "And also, they are only worried because they have been conditioned to worry about those things."

Emerson nodded. "Society thinks it's bad so they have to look out for those things. It's nice they are about you like that. If they were raised like us, it wouldn't matter to them."

She nodded. "I was teasing you guys. I know you are, and I don't fucking care. I mean I get it, they are worried for my safety, but I'm not."

"Even with that lunatic kicking about?" Leo pointed at Rix.

She nodded and licked her top lip, and he returned the favor before saying, "She loves all the things I do to her."

"Yes, I do." She winked.

"Sexy little deviant," Emerson offered.

"I'm not sure I'd want to meet us in a dark alley," Carter laughed. "You have zero sense of self-preservation. It's as impressive as it is concerning."

"I mean..." She shrugged. "I don't think it's that. Don't get me wrong, if any of you walked out of a dark alley and crooked a finger, I would be following you back into the darkness, but if someone else did? I would run. With you guys, it's not self-preservation."

"Please don't say it's destiny," Easton's nose scrunched up as he said it. "One of these idiots will start pretending to be Sean Connery and claiming there can be only one."

"And blood is a bitch to get out of the carpet," Finn agreed.

"No one is swinging swords with Brutus in the room," Carter said and Leo laughed.

"What about dicks? Can we swing those?"

"Again, are you five?!" Easton looked exasperated but was saved from saying anything else by the first course coming out.

"I'm not saying destiny at all," she offered, winking at Leo's cheeky words. "And none of you are the Highlander. If anything, He Who Sleeps is the Highlander," she offered as she picked up her fork. "I am saying that even the first time, it didn't feel like I was in danger with you. I told Emerson this."

"She did."

"And Leo." She nodded to the lunatic across from her. "Standing there with the lot of you in your masks, it was daunting, and a bit frightening, but it felt like opportunity, and not like I was a hair's breadth away from checking out for good. That feeling stuck with me."

271

"It does kind of feel like there was something at work, though," Carter said thoughtfully. "I know a couple of us talked about it, but the odds of finding a woman in that moment who wouldn't freak the fuck out is astronomical. Billions to one."

"And yet here she is," Rix said with a savage grin. "So we shouldn't waste her..."

She didn't want to think about them leaving for the holidays, to get permission for this to happen for real. In her eyes they were already forever and anyone that tried to stop that, she would hurt. She wasn't losing them.

She smiled at her most volatile lover. "I don't think you guys ever would."

They finished eating in silence, each of them thoughtful and pensive, at least until the staff came in, took away their plates, brought in a cart filled with desserts, and then bowed to Emerson. "Happy birthday, sir. We will take our leave now. We will be back tomorrow for breakfast."

"Thank you. And safe home," he said as they closed the door. "Now the real fun can start."

"I'm so fucking over plates." Leo shoved his aside with a wicked gleam in his eye. "Anyone else feel like eating some of that birthday cake from bare naked skin?"

"As usual you got the right idea, though..." He looked to her. "Only if she wants it."

She nodded. "All of you?" She looked around the room.

"The table is certainly big enough," Finn said, sliding his plate away to the end of the table.

"I'll just put Brutus in our room," Carter chuckled, standing up and heading for the door, the enormous dog at his heels. "The last thing we want is for him to get the wrong idea and try to join in."

"Total drama," Jack agreed. "Or worse, he might think we are hurting her in a bad way."

"She does make some...interesting vocal choices in the throes of passion," Leo teased.

"Depends on how you play that instrument," Rix said, his eyes on her.

"We all know I'm the musical maestro," Finn said.

"He does play me like a violin," she offered.

"Is that a challenge?" Emerson asked.

"If we've all got to take turns this might get pretty boring." Leo feigned a yawn. "How about we all just lick her at the same time and see what kind of sounds she makes?"

"Someone grab her. Look at her, she's all but vibrating in that seat. Bet she's soaked that dress thru," Emerson said. "Toss her on the table..."

"Maybe not toss," Carter cautioned, re-entering the room. "First person to land her in the hospital for throwing her around on solid wood furniture gets a solid right hook from each of us."

Emerson chuckled and picked up a large pillow. "Better, Carter? I always enjoy my dessert presented to me on a silken pillow."

Petra giggled and looked up at them all. Hungry gazes and high color in their cheeks. Guess the idea of her as dessert was really doing it for them. It was doing it for her.

"What do you say, Petra?" Finn took a long swallow of his wine. "You want to stand up and take that pretty dress off and let us eat off you?"

In response she did stand and untied the tie at her waist, letting the soft material slip from her body. She was naked, proudly, feeling both sexy and wanton with the looks on their faces directed at her.

"Sweet hell..." Emerson growled.

"Get on the table," Finn commanded softly as the others shoved platters of desserts aside to clear a space.

She climbed up, knee on the table as she heard Jack swear, sure he was getting an eyeful of how wet and needy she already was, and crawled over to where Emerson was still seated, the silk pillow in his lap. She turned so she was settled on her ass on the table in front of him. He grinned.

"Sitting that perfect ass on the table is not in the cards tonight," he said and lifted the pillow. "Will someone please lift our little victim up so I can put the pillow down?"

"With pleasure." Leo lifted her up so that Emerson could slide the cushion underneath her, settling her back down gently.

"Would you look at this," Emerson murmured. "So fucking perfect," he said before grabbing her ankles and wrenching her legs apart. "She needs some sweet adornments...but nothing on that perfect pussy." He looked up. "Agreed?"

"Whatever the birthday boy says," Finn said mildly.

"Agreed," Leo nodded righteously. "No sugar-induced yeast infections here, thank you very much."

"But chocolate everywhere else?" Carter said, more gleeful than she'd heard him in a while.

"Oh, go nuts...make sure she's sticky with a lot of things," Emerson said, heat in his eyes. "You ready to be our plate, sweet girl?"

She nodded, shaking softly with anticipation. "Any rules?" she asked.

"Do you think we need them?" Finn asked her. "Don't you trust us?"

"With everything," she said. "I just didn't want to hear that I get to be the plate and I can't come."

Emerson laughed. "My birthday...have I ever stopped you from coming?" He caressed her inner thighs, eyes on her pussy. She felt her core clench.

"No..."

"Then that's your answer."

Ever the showman, Leo jumped up onto his knees on the table, the wood barely groaning under the weight. "I claim the head!" he declared with a grin, daring anyone to challenge him as he pulled her shoulders back and settling her in his lap.

With a giggle she looked up to him, and arched a brow as Jack handed him whipped cream and a strawberry. Jack, with another can of the cream, started spraying sections on her stomach, lines and little balls of fluffy cream. She looked down to Emerson who was watching his friends with a feral grin on his face.

"This might tickle," Carter warned, leaning in to swipe a tongue up her side to catch some cream that was melting from her body heat.

"Ah..." she arched at the contact, the heat of his tongue sending zings of feeling through her. Never had she had this...the attention of so many, so many that wanted her. Emerson chuckled as he slid a finger into her waiting heat.

"Ah fuck, she's fucking drenched. Does the thought of all of us on you at once turn you on, Pet?" Her core clenched on his finger. "Oh, fuck yes, she likes that..."

She looked to Finn and Rix who both had hooded gazes, carrying over dessert toppings from the cart, and Jack who was still happily dotting her with cream, and then to Easton who was still sitting in his chair.

He wasn't making any move to engage, but the way he was looking at her...it was hungry. The raw, naked feeling in his eyes was so conflicted, like he wanted to join the others but something was stopping him.

Gods, she wanted her Snake so badly. Wanted him to be with her, to connect with him so badly. And outside of the bedroom, they were. He had been calling, they had their date coming up, but the disconnect... She smiled at him before Rix gently, so gently turned her face to him and leaned in, kissing her.

Gods, the man could kiss, and she arched as he pinched her nipple. "Pay attention to us," he said softly against her lips, pulling back.

Her body was a mass of cream and sauces and fruit, and as she caught Emerson's eyes from between her thighs he winked and lowered his mouth to her.

"Ah!"

"Back off." Leo shoved Rix none too gently. "I said her head was mine." He coated his thumb in cream and swiped it across the seam of her lips, before pushing it into her mouth. "Suck it clean," he commanded.

She did, hearing Rix chuckle, then the heat of his mouth on her breast. She sucked Leo's thumb, licking around it, like she was sucking his perfectly pierced cock. Emerson was weaving magic between her thighs, his tongue and fingers playing her, making her body string tight.

She moaned around Leo's finger as Jack bit her belly softly, sucking and licking the cream off, Carter on the other side. She knew they would leave love bites there. And Finn...where was her Devil?

She found out a few seconds later when one of the legs hooked over Emerson's shoulders was lifted in strong hands and Finn trailed a slick, chocolate-covered strawberry up her calf.

She looked up to Leo who was looking down at her, and sucked hard at his thumb as she arched, everyone's mouth's on her at the same time. The sensation of lips, tongue, fingers, she let go of Leo's finger as she cried out, her body rolling through a stellar orgasm. Emerson groaned before pulling away.

"Fuck, you taste better than all that sweetness...honey and peaches and..."

"Ambrosia," Jack said.

"Spice," Rix said.

"Fuck that poetic shit," Leo groaned. "Stop wasting all that tongue wagging and give her another one." With a grin, Finn shoved Emerson's face forward, back between Petra's thighs. "You heard the man. She isn't screaming names yet. Get to work."

She felt Emerson chuckle against her before he sucked hard on her clit, causing her to arch again. Jack and Carter held her down by her pelvis, keeping her immobile and she cried out as she felt Rix bite her other nipple.

Tender, she panted and closed her eyes, Leo's hand on her throat, holding her there, but not squeezing. She gasped and writhed beneath them as the pressure in her body built, and broke as she felt Finn's lips just at her knee. She screamed Emerson's name then, two fingers hooked inside her, pressing viciously on her G-spot.

Shaking and moaning she rode through it, and she opened her eyes seeing Easton still sitting there, watching her.

He licked his lips, adjusting himself in his trousers. "You having fun over there?" he asked her, his voice raspy.

She bit her lip and reached for him, desperate for that final piece, her Snake...her dangerous asp...willing to drown in his venom.

Reaching across the expanse of wood between them, he caught her hand in his and squeezed it tight. Vulnerability flashed in his eyes before he snarled, "I asked you a fucking question." She knew he was

277

covering up his awkwardness and discomfort, but he had willingly touched her. Was still willingly touching her, despite the storm of emotions boiling across his features.

"You should answer him," Carter said gently, quietly, none of them looking at where their most broken brother was touching her.

"Yes...but I need you," she said honestly. It didn't matter if he left her then, her body was alight, all her men touching her in some fashion, and she gasped as another orgasm rolled through her. "Fuck!"

Chapter 28

Emerson stole through the house, the grandfather clock in the main hall chiming out four AM. Something had woken him, and the need to be elsewhere in the house was strong, problem was, he didn't know where he needed to be.

And this was the only reason why he wasn't still lying in bed with Petra, wrapped around her warmth. Because something woke him. The sooner he figured out why the sooner he would be back between the sheets, and slipping into his willing little concubine.

The house was quiet, the guys each either sleeping in their own rooms, or, if they were Leo, passed out next to Petra as well, and Brutus wouldn't leave Carter's side unless something was amiss in the house itself.

No Brutus.

And the pull on his senses was still there.

He made it through the second floor, and then down into the kitchen, the idea of getting something to drink high on his mind as well. Some water would bring clarity, he expected, and padded to the fridge, grabbing a bottle of water. Standing in the dark, he opened it and drank it down, sighing after he drained half the bottle.

This house was so important in some ways. It was the closest he ever felt to his father these days, being here, with the same phantom scents, the wood polish and the squeak of the floorboards. When he had passed, for a long time Emerson didn't set foot in the dwelling, and it was only after his twenty-first birthday that he had received a letter from his father's solicitor that the house, along with funds to keep it up and running, were his, as well as the stipulation that no one but his own team knew it existed.

So he had sent word to the Elders that the property had burned down. Since then they hadn't even asked about it. He had found it weird they did before his twenty-first, but after, and his announcement, they had stopped pretty much all contact regarding his father.

Of course, they had no reason to believe he was lying about it. He, like the rest of them, were good little soldiers, doing the God's work, worshiping as they saw fit to teach them. But he didn't believe that was true anymore. Oh yes, part of it was true, the proof was in the pudding, He Who Sleeps kept them in favor, and they were reaping the fruits of that. But it always felt hollow.

Until he had read his father's journal. And now...now they weren't flying blind but...

Leaving the kitchen, he padded to the study, where his father had spent so much of his time, entering the room on a sigh. It felt the most like him in this room, and for so long he had avoided it. It was too emotional, and he still hadn't worked through losing his father, losing all their fathers the way they did.

The space was filled with old furniture, old books and a massive desk he gravitated to, thoughts of Petra bent over as he railed her high on his mind. He ran fingers across the wood, and then walked around it, seating himself in the large wingback chair, turning on the small desk light.

The staff had done their job keeping the space up to date and clean, even making sure his father's leather blotter was perfect and in amazing repair, but clearly original. He ran his fingers along the edge of it and it shifted, his eyes going to the newly exposed wood. Something was scratched into the wood.

Frowning, he pushed the blotter back, revealing a symbol carved into the wood, a circle within a circle with a line bisecting the far edge. The carve was smooth, as if someone had touched it repeatedly, as if lovingly. He followed the carving, once, twice, and then smiled to himself as he let his finger pull to the edge of the desk and then frowned, feeling it catch on something...round.

He pushed on it, and felt it catch, heard a click and a panel in the wall, just under the closest bookshelf, unhinged.

"The fuck?" he said as he turned and sank to his knees, opening the hidden door. He reached in, and pulled out a thick envelope, two books, and several journals. Blinking, he brought them to the desk, setting them out in a line.

Clearly someone didn't want this stuff to be found. And he knew, without a doubt, it was his father. "Shit, Dad..." he said as he opened the envelope and began to read.

I knew you would find this one day, and if you are reading this, then I know there is still hope for you and for your group. Things are not what they seem in the organization, and I only hope that you have found this in enough time to save yourself, your children and the boys you have bonded with.

Holy shit, he thought and kept reading.

I write this on the eve of my death...something I cannot change, and knew was coming. Something didn't feel right, and because of that, I took these steps. If you are reading this, it means that I'm dead, so is my team, and these documents might be all that's left to help you all. Journals no one knew I kept, three books with rites no one knows exists anymore, because they were deemed heretical for the knowledge inside. Knowledge that brings us together, closer to

Him than they want. Knowledge that threatens what they want.

My son, the best parts of me, know that I left you with the knowledge to make things right. What you choose to do with it will decide if we did the right thing in giving in. We were not strong enough to take that next step. But you all may be. Everything is here that can help you, well except the woman you need to bring it all together.

Trust no one but your own friends, your brothers. And listen for His voice in dreams. Know that He protects you...and He sees so much more than they let on.

I love you. I loved your mother. I always will. Love isn't a handicap. Make it right.

He blinked. Blinked again. "Holy shit."

The urgency he was feeling started to dissipate and he smiled. He did see much, didn't he? Attributing this to His influence, he gathered everything up, and set it in his normal arrangement for research. He set a fire in the fireplace, and turned on the lamps around the place, opening a drawer to find pencils and legal pads, and settled in. He would read, and figure out what exactly his father was talking about, hopefully having some answers before they all woke for the day.

Riddles, and a mystery...and possibly a way to keep their lady. It was the best thirtieth birthday present he could have aside from already being there with her.

"Happy birthday to me. Thanks, Dad," he said softly and settled in to read.

Chapter 29

"Jesus, has he been in here all night?" Emerson looked up from his notes to see Rix smirking at him. "You realize Jack has that sexy as fuck woman tied to your bed right now, right?"

"And you're not up there?" he asked his friend.

Kendrix snorted. "You know that ain't my scene...though it *is* yours."

It was, and it was just fucking tough noogies that he wasn't involved. "Well, it's good they are keeping her busy. We gotta talk." He looked to Finn and Easton. "Shit hit the fan."

"That sounds serious." Finn sobered immediately and pulled up a chair. "What's going on?"

Emerson nodded to the books and the packet on the table. "Read the letter," he offered to Finn as Rix started looking at the books.

Finn scanned the paper and then handed it to Easton, his lips drawing a thin line. "Summarize the rest of it for me," he said, eyes fixed on Emerson.

"Well, you know how we have been talking about how things aren't right?" Rix looked up to him and then to Finn. "They aren't. Dad's journal I found was only the tip of the iceberg. These there..." he laid hands on the two journals to his right, "have information..." He swallowed, trying not to get choked up, "Information on how things before they died were different and what my father saw as wrong due to our own rites."

"What do you mean?" Rix asked. "This book reads like stereo instructions."

"Well that book, brother, details how having a single female for a group to worship with brings not only favor, but abundance...and independence."

Rix frowned. "Something we think we have but don't...but our fathers..."

"The Elders they had were more hands off, and allowed for the different options of faith."

"Options of faith?"

Emerson nodded. "Our mothers were an option. Petra is an *option*. Blood sacrifices are an option. An *option*."

"Emerson, get your shit together," Finn sighed. "Stop waffling and get to the point. What do you mean by 'an option'?"

"Sorry, Finn, this is fucking crazy to me." He swallowed. "These were options. Killing all year is an option. He Who Sleeps would rather...varied energy, but his favorite is feminine."

"We knew that, that's why we sacrifice a woman..."

"We didn't *have* to. We could have had since the beginning what we have with Petra now. Our fathers, remember seeing that they tried to find a woman for all of them? And failed? But they all found women to marry, have children with...and perform personal rites with." He looked to them. "Their large sacrifice was blood, but the rest of the year, it was sex. And the veils...they aren't as heavy as we have been led to believe through the year. He watches...he savors what we do." He sighed. "And I think that because we have been all but starving him of variety he stopped speaking to us."

"What? I have never..."

"Nor I. But my father details here how He sent my mother to him...how He sent all our mothers to them."

"You're waffling again." Finn held up a hand to pause him. "Let me get this straight; our fathers were feeding the God all year round by gathering energy from our mothers? That's always been an option? We could have been feeding Him all year round with Petra since day one?"

He nodded. "Yes, individually and because it's Petra, as a group. The energy we raised last night...the spike when Easton touched her..." He shook his head. "But we have been led to believe that blood is what He craves, and *only* what he craves. Why?"

"Control," Rix said. "Fuck."

Emerson nodded. "This journal, it shows how our fathers were led to our mothers, after the attempt to find a central female failed. My father writes that each of them were given visions through dreams of our mothers, and followed the feeling to find them in waking life." He picked up the book closest. "And this book? It tells of why and how females born to our order are kept separate, as not to create bonds...because they serve a purpose, too. To become mothers, and in some cases a central female for a group. They were never to be sacrificed; they are the feminine divine for He Who Sleeps."

"Wait," Easton spoke up for the first time. "You're saying that Petra might be...one of us? She was raised in an orphanage."

Emerson shrugged. "I don't know. It's possible. We need to ask her about where she was raised again, about what happened the night she found us." He sighed. "Each of our mothers were of the blood, raised elsewhere. My father says my mother, Francine," he chuckled. "I never knew her name," he said absently. "Says she was raised on a commune outside San Francisco. Finn, your mother Daphne was raised in an artist collective in Canada." He looked up. "Each of the mothers were raised in alternative societies. Rix, your mother Kimber, she was an orphan." He looked to Easton. "And I don't think you being brought in was an accident."

"That's monstrous," Easton whispered. "They farm them like fucking dairy cows, bringing them in when

285

they're ready to breed. And they did this to me? They...they..."

"Everyone, shut up," Finn was frowning. "I need to think this through." Rising from his seat, he paced back and forth across a rich rug that muffled the sound of his footfalls. "This doesn't make any sense," he said eventually. "What do the Elders have to gain by weakening the God when they gain their power from him?"

"Honestly I don't know, Finn. The control, though...that makes sense."

Rix leaned back, looking thoughtful. "Controlling what he gets, keeping him at their mercy... Yes, they do gain from him but...He gives but He doesn't take away. Each of the new Elders, even my father, are captains of industry, politicians, fuck, isn't Hartford a fucking gun runner?" He shook his head. "They don't need more power, only to maintain what they have and ensure none surpass them."

"Man has a point," Emerson said. "And East..." he looked to Snake, "it says here all the mothers were aware who they were, what they were raised into. It wasn't anonymous. And not all females from where they were raised were called to serve. Many worshipped Him on their own, in their own female led rites. Much like the school we went to. By all this information, my father wrote out they were loved, and in love, and never coerced into being with our fathers." He smiled and looked up. "They had normal courtships, actually fell in love, and those actions served His purpose as well..."

"And the Elders just decided to shit all over that?" Easton's fury was clear in every line of his body. He was almost vibrating with the force of his rage, his muscles tense and strained. "They just killed your parents for the hell of it?"

"For control," Emerson said. "And yours, I think. Well, your mother. My dad wrote that they finally found a fallen heir, but I can't find anything past what's written here about it. Your name, and where you were found, and the..." He swallowed. "State of you when you were finally brought in." He held up a finger as he began to read.

"Visholu found the fallen heir two days ago, and I fear we were too late. We still aren't sure how the hell he was spirited away, or how Glynnis ended up at the bottom of a ravine, all we know is he's been traumatized, but exhibits much of what his blood gave him. Eye for an eye, those that harmed him are dead by his hand, as is proper, though on a personal note, Easton should never have had to deal with any of that. He is resilient, and I hope his future is filled with the love and care he should have had, as part of our order."

He looked up, gauging his friend's mental capacity. "There is more, if you want to hear it. Not much but..."

"Of course I want to fucking hear it!" Easton howled. "You have no idea what I suffered! You have...you had...the fucking..." He was hyperventilating and couldn't get the words together, terminating instead in an inarticulate howl of helpless and primal rage.

"Brother," Finn approached him, palms up, as though gentling a skittish animal. "Breathe. Brother, breathe. We're with you and we will raze everyone that had anything to do with this to the ground. I give you my word on that. They will suffer. But we need to be clever about this. Destroy it at the root. We need to figure out what happened and who was involved and for that we need calm." He didn't know who was more shocked when Easton fell into his arms, crying like the broken child he was.

Emerson got up, followed by Rix, gathering around their fallen friend and brother, and wrapped themselves around them both. They weren't normally so tactile, but in this case it was needed. He felt horrible, always had about what Easton had endured, but if there was a way for true vengeance...

It was long moments before they let him go, and he leaned up, looking at Emerson expectedly. "You good?" he asked and Easton nodded. "Glynnis Ambrose was your mother. Daughter of Elder Harnis Ambrose, who was murdered the night your mother and you disappeared. It doesn't say who your father is, though they think he wasn't of the blood, and took you and Glynnis..." He got up and went to the journal.

"They had a lead, some guy from the town the Ambrose family lived, but he didn't make it far. They found him in a motel, overdose. No you, no Glynnis. They found your mother a week later. They think you were taken from them both. They think someone killed Glynnis, and staged your would-be father's death and sent you into the world. I'm sorry, brother. Glynnis and the Ambrose family were third cousins to Rix's family, which is why you were placed with Stephan. Though my father thought you should have been placed with Finn's family." He looked down. "And Finn's father fought for you. Stephen would have none of it." He shook his head.

"Here's the big thing. Dad thinks it all started with you. All of it. Because after Ambrose died things started getting strange, and others started either disappearing or other Elders were being appointed. It was slow at first but by the time you had been delivered back to us...a lot had changed.

"Here," he continued, coming to sit with them all on the floor. "Dad references a Dark Path, one the priests warned over. A prophecy, where seven would gain the knowledge, the power to lead, to bring order to our Order." He flipped a few pages. "The Dark Path would emerge when some would try to stop that though certain...situations, one being the birth of a brother not solely of the blood." He frowned. "The Book of Prophecy... Rix, hand me that green book!" he said as things started to come together. "Thank you. The Prophecy of the Seven, here it is." He began to read.

"The Seven will usher in a new age with He Who Sleeps, anointing their age with knowledge, and wisdom and untold power. Lo, beware that of the Dark, the quelling constriction seeking power above all else, for the few, not the many.

"Six of the Blood, a seventh that marries the waking world and that of his own blood. A conduit to His Direct Divine becomes the bridge to everlasting."

He looked at them. "Now, I have no fucking clue what it means, but the three that went after Easton took twelve years to find him. Visholu, Tannet and Frane. They inducted Easton into The Order as soon as he had been born, and were honor bound to find him, but the tie to Him was weak because of the half blood, and those working against this."

"Hang on," Rix said, chatty and clearly annoyed. "We are part of a fucking prophecy?"

"Apparently. I hadn't gotten through everything by the time you guys came through. You know my process, I skip pages and take tidbits then follow the fucking bread crumbs..."

"Then keep following because right now, people gonna die at Solstice."

He nodded. "Dad says that when Easton came back, brought by the Warders, that's what the priest's called the three, the Elders, well some of them were happy and I think those were the ones that were killed. The others, the assholes in power now, weren't and oddly they were the ones that insisted Easton be placed with Stephan, citing blood ties to physical family, but really 'all our blood is the same, and serves him,'" he read from the journal. "It was then Dad was approached by the priests to hide this book, and write these journals with everything he knew. I don't think they realized he didn't know everything."

"Fuck."

"Apparently, and this is underlined, 'our seven are the seven of the prophecy, as all of us are the same age, and the culmination of seven high families, full bloodlines, aligning the stars.' I think they would have been the seven but Ambrose had a daughter, not a son, so the next generation was us...all seven of us. Three days after this journal was written, they went to their deaths."

"Okay." Full of nervous energy, Finn was pacing again now that Easton was calm enough to be seated. "It's fairly obvious that the Dark Path is the way we've been raised to only kill. That's pretty fucking dark. And according to this prophecy, we're supposed to fix it. So my understanding is that we're supposed to destroy or remove the Elders insisting on the death-only path. I fully expect the priests will be on our side, given that they've supported the pact thus far. What I can't understand is why the Elders didn't shut us down when they knew what we'd started with Petra."

"Maybe they don't know," Easton said into the thoughtful silence that followed, his face still pale and ravaged by grief and shock. "All this time we've assumed the priests and the Elders are the left and right hand of The Order, but if the Elders are actively weakening the God, they're directly working against the priests, who exist only to support Him. Has anyone here actually told an Elder explicitly about the pact? Anyone?"

They all shook their heads, realization dawning that The Order didn't function as they had thought it did. "They must be wondering how we've gathered so much energy the last couple of years," Finn said. "The priests must know about the prophecy if they told Emerson's dad about it. They wouldn't have asked him to record it and hide the journals if they didn't expect us to find them at some point. So they'll be with us, but I'm guessing the Elders don't know about it at all. If they did, they'd have tried to kill us already."

"What are we actually talking about here?" Easton asked, looking up at Finn. "I mean, I'm going to kill all the usurping bastards that killed my family and left me in hell, but what about the rest of The Order? Who will take over from the Elders? Will the others even support us if we're the only ones that know about the old ways?"

"We need to speak to people." Finn stopped pacing and turned to Emerson. "Finish reading and make a concise summary of the information. We'll get everyone together this morning over brunch and talk about it as a group. We act as one. We make decisions together. And then if we need to gather support, we'll start contacting people we know and trust. We have a little time before we leave. Let's use it wisely."

Emerson nodded. "There's a lot of information here, I mean my dad's journals only have so much but these books... And we need to talk to Petra, ask about the orphanage, what she knows about it. Dad's journal names where our mothers came from, maybe we start looking that up. It's clear they aren't even a thought to the current regime, unless they took them out?"

"Those are questions for a later date," Finn said firmly. "Right now, we need to focus on securing our position and keeping Petra safe. We can worry about the women when the Elders have been removed."

"Killed," Easton said flatly. "Not removed. Killed. I want them skinned alive the same way they did your fathers. Stephan included."

"Amen there, brother," Emerson said on a sigh. "No survivors."

Jack, Petra and Leo took that moment to walk in, Petra looking entirely fuck rumpled. "Theres the birthday boy," she said and smiled at him, then looked around. "What's going on?"

"Emerson here has been dishing out the revelations left, right and center," Finn told her with a rueful grin. "But there's no point in him repeating everything all over again without everyone here. I've asked him to make a summary while we go and get brunch and then we'll have a group meeting."

"A war council," Easton said somberly.

"War? Sounds like fun." Leo flashed a grin, ever the cocky bastard. "Come on then. To the kitchen! I'm in charge of waffles."

Chapter 30

It was getting really cold outside, but that didn't stop Brutus from bounding joyfully across the lawn after the balls Carter was launching from some contraption he'd brought with him, and Easton had followed them outside, the fresh air bringing him some clarity.

It was too crowded inside, too busy with all his brothers and his thoughts at once. Carter felt quiet and safe.

"How are you holding up?" Carter asked him quietly and Easton sighed. He was still a mix of boiling rage and sadness that he didn't know how to put into words.

"It's going to take some time to process it," he said honestly. "Finding out about my family after all this time... It's a lot. And I guess I hadn't realized how much I still felt like an outsider. Realizing that I *am* one of you...that I was born one of you...my whole world view and sense of self is fucked."

"I get it." He didn't. Not really. But Easton would never say that. He just appreciated the support. Behind them, he heard the door open and turned to see Petra stepping out to join them wrapped up in a thick coat and an enormous scarf.

Her smile hit them both, sweet and nonjudgmental. At brunch they had talked, bringing everyone up to speed, well the more abridged version. She had listened, and shed tears but had remained silent through it, as if she knew there wasn't much she could say. And since she had been there, a comfort to all of them, if silent.

"Either of you want coffee or cocoa or something?" she asked. "Leo is in the kitchen making some and I figured I would see."

Cocoa sounded wonderful. Leo hadn't made it for him in years. "I'll take a cocoa," he said, "but I'll drink it out here. I needed some peace and quiet."

"I'm good, thanks." Carter shook his head. "Brutus is going to be chasing balls for another half hour or so until he tires out."

She nodded. "I figured. Back in a flash..." She walked back inside, coming back out a few minutes later with a tray of cocoas and a blanket over her arm. "Here, Easton," she said as she set the tray down on the small table and handed him the cocoa. "I hope you don't mind, but...can I play, too?" she asked Carter with a smile. "Or if Easton wants to snuggle on the couch here, I did bring a blanket."

"Sure," Carter said, showing her how to launch the ball while Easton tried to figure out if that was girl code for her wanting to snuggle on the couch but having to make out it was his idea for some reason. Women were complicated. The whole concept of snuggling was alien to him. It wasn't just that he felt weird about having someone in his personal space. No one had ever shown him that kind of affection.

He didn't know what to do. On one hand, this weekend had been about breaking boundaries for him. He'd pushed through his fear and anxiety and allowed himself to touch and be touched. But he felt on edge...one baby step away from a meltdown. How much was too much? Would this platonic contact trigger his violent feelings?

He didn't want to hurt Petra, not outside of a scene anyway, but he sensed that she was trying to get closer to him, wanting to be let in, and keeping her at arm's length would hurt her, even though it wasn't his intention. He stood there uncertainly, watching as she and Carter launched the ball and played with Brutus, laughing and joking.

He envied Carter the ease he seemed to communicate with everyone around him. He wished he could be like that. One day he would. When all of this was over, he was going to find a good therapist. He had to if he was going to be the kind of man that Petra deserved. He had a lot to work out.

"Brutus is the best," she said softly as she approached him and took a sip of her cocoa. "Though I'm excited to meet your lovely parrot."

An image flashed through his mind of her with Niobe sitting on her shoulder, their heads bent together as though they were sharing secrets. He'd have to sketch it later. The image was adorable. "I'm sure she'll love you," he said awkwardly. "Look, Petra, I'm not good at this like the others. I'm not...well...socialized, I guess. When you say you brought a blanket in case I want to snuggle, but you know I don't like physical contact, is that your way of saying you want to snuggle?"

"I know you are feral, Easton, and that's okay," she offered. "You know how I feel about you, but I don't want to push you, or make you feel upset so..." she shrugged. "I feel like I should leave the ball in your court, so to speak. Let you know I'm interested, and want these things with you, but not pressure you into it. I don't want to be a burden on you or your mental wellbeing." She gave him a small smile. "But yes, I very much want to snuggle under the blanket with you. If you don't want to, it's okay, too. No offense taken."

"Then let me know you're interested. Don't let me try and figure out if there's some sort of secondary message." He quirked a lopsided smile. "I'm not the sharpest tool in the box, and the only experience I have with women, aside from you, is killing them. If you want to snuggle, say you want to snuggle, and then I'll decide whether or not I'm in." Piece said, he sat down

295

on the seat and tried to make himself comfortable. "We can try it, but I'm not making any promises, okay?"

Her smile was huge, bright and perfect, and she nodded, settling in next to him, but not too close. "At your speed, Easton," she said as she pulled her knees up and under the blanket she was settling. "And I'm sorry, I'll try to be more direct with you going forward. I just didn't want to make you feel like I thought you weren't...I don't know." She shrugged, clearly trying to find the words.

"I know you're into me," he said. "You don't need to try too hard. I promise you I'll get there. I was just..." He swallowed, unused to being so open and vulnerable by choice. "I was just thinking that when this is over and we're back home, I want to find a therapist. I've never been to one before. I think I should. I want to be a better man...the kind of guy you deserve. And I know that takes work."

She leaned in. "Can I tell you something? I loved therapy. I love therapy now." She smiled. "I don't actually see someone anymore, not since I met you guys, but I do work from the tele-app. But without it I wouldn't really be where I am right now. Therapy is cleansing and I'm proud of you for wanting to. It's the first step." She smiled and patted his shoulder, clearly wanting to do more. "You okay? I mean I know today has been a veritable shit show, and life altering in some massive fucking ways..." She blew out a breath. "For all of us."

"I'm not okay," he admitted. "I found out this morning that my whole fucking life is a lie. That the people I thought were supposed to be my leaders, the guys I look up to and respect, dropped me off in an orphanage to be abused for my entire childhood."

She nodded softly. "And they will die for their bullshit. As is proper. You deserve every piece of revenge, to be coated in their blood, because each of them deserves to die horrible vicious deaths. I can't...I can't even begin to know what you went through, and I know it won't make it better..." She turned her head to him. "But my heart hurts for you, Easton. All I want is to hug you, and help make you feel better one day."

"I'm making progress," he said, actively forcing himself to relax into the seat next to her and feel her warmth. "I've been practicing. Small touches. I thought you'd noticed when you were dessert last night."

She giggled. "Holding your hand... It was...it made it that much better...but I'll admit it makes me greedy for more time with you. You know what I want? Quiet time with you. Intimacy in the carnal sense is good, great and I'm down, but...I want the small hours, the ones where we don't have to touch, just be together. Spend time in the same room, in our own heads, not having to talk, just be," she offered.

"We can do that," he agreed, "and maybe...well...if you want to, you could maybe come to therapy with me. It might be easier for you to know parts of my history if I have someone to help me tell you."

She blinked at him "I...really? I would be honored to go and be your support." Her little finger touched his own under the blanket. "Thank you. I mean, really."

"I know I'm not like the others," he said. "I'm not warm or affectionate. I can't just fuck you anywhere and everywhere like the others can. But that doesn't mean I don't want you. It doesn't mean that my feelings run any less deep than the others'. I know you've doubted me, but I hope you know I'm trying."

"Easton, we never have to have sex if that's what you need to feel safe with me. We all have different needs. I want us to be right, you know?"

"I want to do that with you, though!" He hoped he didn't sound as agonized as he felt. "I want us to fuck

297

like bunnies! I just can't seem to get out of my own way. It's like the moment someone touches my bare skin and I'm not in control of it, I get these violent flashbacks and I can't break out of them on my own. I know it's PTSD, but Carter helped me do some research, and there are some great treatments out there for it now. I just need you to wait for me and know that I'm trying."

She nodded with a smile. "I will, and I know you are, Easton. It would be sweeter knowing we waited." She giggled. "And when it does happen, it will be so worth it. One step at a time, yeah?" Her little finger ran along his softly, a tease to let him know she was there, and wanted to be.

"I'm working with Carter." He blurted the words out before he could overthink it and tried to ignore the way his cheeks heated with shame and embarrassment. "He's always felt safe to me. He's so calm. And I thought maybe we could work out together what the worst triggers are. Maybe you could...I don't know. Maybe you could help. Would you feel comfortable with that? Talking to him or watching us be together, I mean."

She grinned. "Hell yes, seriously hell yes." She leaned in farther. "He brings out the same in me...makes me feel safe. Even before I knew him, our play never scared me, I felt safe with him so I understand why he feels that way to you. He's calm...he's centered. It's something I love about him."

"It wouldn't scare you to see me freaking out?" He had to know. She obviously cared about him and it was hard to see people you care about suffering.

She was silent a few moments, seemingly mulling the question over. "I honestly don't know, but I'm willing to try, and to endure to help you, Easton. You are so fucking special to me...so important to me."

That warmed him in ways he didn't know how to put into words. "I feel the same about you," he told her. "I'm sorry I threatened to kill you when you took my mask off. I freaked out."

She chuckled softly. "It's okay. I expected something like that, taking that risk and all. But thank you for apologizing for it. And I'm sorry I did it. I mean I'm not sorry I did because we are here but...if I had any idea..."

"How did Carter react the first time you saw him?" he asked curiously. He'd often wondered since they'd been unmasked, but hadn't found the time to ask his brother. "I've never really paid much attention to his scars, but I've seen the way people react to him in public. He doesn't go out much." He tamped down a swell of rage on behalf of his friend. People were shallow and cruel.

She gave a wistful smile. "He actually unmasked himself. And when I saw him...and I knew him...it was like..." she blushed hard. "Carter is my hero. What he does, how he takes up for the animals and makes sure they are safe... Someone that loves animals that much... He had my heart before I knew it was him. But seeing him, knowing he was my Plague..." Biting her lip, she thought a bit. "He was surprised I was so okay with it. And I don't even notice them. What happened to him isn't what he is, isn't who he is. I know who he is and I love him for who he is, not what he looks like, though he's sexy as fuck." She giggled. "And it's the same for you. What happened to you isn't what and who you are, Easton. I see you, just like I see him."

"I think it's easy to say that from the outside," he said thoughtfully. "From the inside, it's shaped everything that we are. Everything I suffered made me a killer. It brought me home to my family. I am filled with so. Much. Rage. And yet that pain and fury is what makes me a great artist. And Carter...his burns taught him patience and compassion. But the medical malpractice suit on his behalf made him extremely wealthy. It shaped his entire life. And his kinks. He knows more than anyone what it is to burn. He wouldn't be able to do what he does, or be your hero, if he hadn't been scarred so horribly as a child. We are both the sum of our suffering and always will be, even if the people around us don't fully understand the way it's shaped us or our lives."

She nodded, thoughtful. "I see, and I can appreciate that. Still doesn't change that you both are men I feel so drawn to, so comfortable with. Since the beginning. I mean I was scared, but it was an apprehensive kinda fear...and then a fear that I wanted. You know, I have been thinking about what Emerson said, about their moms and such being raised in this..."

"Yeah? You said your orphanage was pretty decent." He wanted so much to ask her if she thought she might be a lost Order member, like him, but he didn't see how that could have happened. It wasn't The Order orphanage. She'd have known. And unless she was another legacy bloodline the priests had tried to hide from the Elders eliminating every family that stood in their way, it didn't make any sense that she'd have been taken and hidden somewhere different.

"It was. Safe, but largely kept apart for a long time. 'Til high school at least. I mean we went to specific schools as girls, but then once high school came around, something changed, and I remember something changing because me and my friends were never allowed to hang out with other kids really..." She looked to him. "'Til high school. It was like, one day the ladies in charge were like 'we have to get them ready for the world' and started letting us go places alone, and to the movies and to school. It was weird." She took a sip of her cocoa.

"Maybe it was some sort of orphanage policy?" he suggested, still considering the idea that she might be Order and not know it. "Were they Catholic or something? One of those religious places that keeps you sheltered?"

"No. I mean we went to the prep school, but there was no religion behind it. Looking back it felt like a finishing school, and then when we were of age for ninth grade, we were told it was going to be the public high school for us. Vic, she thought maybe funding for us ran out, but...can't help but think that there were reasons for that." She sighed. "We always thought it was weird we were all but unleashed on the world when our hormones were raging, and we had no idea how to deal with boys really...our socialization learned through each other and of all things etiquette classes, though much of that kinda was shit in real life, you know?"

"That is weird. To be so sheltered and then suddenly let go." He shook his head. Maybe it was just coincidence. He should probably let it go. And yet something just wouldn't stop niggling at the back of his brain. "What was the name of the orphanage?" he asked. "Maybe if they're low on funding we can look into it and help them. They did such a great job with you, it would be nice to pay it back and make sure no kids go through what I went through."

"Seasons House," she said. "It wasn't billed as an orphanage, but we were all there and orphans."

"Seasons House..." He made a mental note. "And remind me again where exactly it was? If it's a private entity rather than a state-run organization, we could still become benefactors."

She considered that and smiled. "It's in Ohio, a little town called Epiphany. When I left for college and all someone told me it was a paper town...you know, the ones that are added to actual maps for copyright traps?" She grinned. "I mean it was a town of like five thousand at most but it was mostly an aging population. Pretty sure the place is down to like three thousand people now. It's been a while."

"Do you know how you got there?" He pushed for more information, alarm bells still dinging somewhere in his mind that there would be such a well-financed orphanage in such a tiny place. "Seems kind of weird that there would be enough orphaned kids in such a small place to warrant having a whole orphanage."

"I wasn't from there. I don't think any of us were," she offered. "I remember taking a car ride there...myself and Matron Angela, as well as two kids...babies actually." She frowned. "Two little girls that cried a lot in the car. I don't remember how I got in the car, but Matron Angela took us to Seasons house and I met my friends." She frowned again. "And before you ask, I must have been three? Yeah. Me and the girls were all three...there were babies, too, and some would come, little girls and or babies sometimes, but after a while we didn't have any new people. It was just us."

"All girls?" He had to admit that it stung a little bit to talk about her experiences. If not for a random twist of fate, he could have been shipped off to some private institute instead of suffering the hell that he was delivered to.

She nodded. "Never any boys. We saw boys, knew what boys were, I mean we watched TV and all. But it wasn't 'til high school that we were around boys. And none of the women that worked with us were married or lived elsewhere." She looked up, as if thinking. "All together there were twenty girls, and seven matrons

302

when I was there. Now...now I just don't know. Been a long ass time since I was back." She frowned. "I don't think I have been back since I left for college."

That was an extraordinary amount of staff for such a small number of wards. They needed to look into this place. Was there some way The Order could have spirited away that many girls over the years without the Elders knowing? And why? Why would they have done it? Petra had been taken as a three-year-old. That was long before their fathers were killed. And yet...if there was a prophecy about the seven of them, it was possible there was a prophecy about her, too.

She was the central figure that triggered the coming war, after all. They needed to speak to the priests and threaten them until they got some straight fucking answers. They needed to tear this house apart, too. It was possible there were more hidden books lying around. Emerson's dad had been a smart man. He wouldn't have left all of the information in just one place in case someone other than Emerson had discovered it. He'd found the first journal, the one that mentioned the pact, somewhere completely different.

"That's a thoughtful face," Carter said, coming over to them with Brutus in tow. The dog was panting heavily, his sides heaving from exertion and his breath misting in the cold air.

"Yeah, Petra was telling me about her orphanage, where she grew up. Something about it just seems...off."

"Off as in we should investigate it?" Carter asked, and Easton was grateful that he didn't question his sanity or hesitate to back him up.

"Maybe," he hedged.

"You guys think something is up?" she asked and hummed. "What are you thinking Easton?"

"I don't really know," he admitted. "It's just something we talked about with Emerson...about how our wives almost always come from The Order. Like there's something hereditary in us that makes us a good fit for this life. Which made me wonder if you were somehow also an Order baby and somehow ended up at a random orphanage instead of one of The Order facilities, because the odds of finding a woman like you in the wild were billions to one. But the way you describe it, so many matrons to so few children, and so isolated and remote... I'm wondering if The Order is actually running an underground orphanage that the Elders don't know about and I can't make any sense of it."

"You think they were hiding kids from the Elders?" Carter frowned as he mulled it over. "But why? I don't know the details but Petra was there for a long time before our dads were killed."

"That's what I'm stuck at," Easton agreed. "Maybe I'm way off. Maybe there's nothing strange about it at all. Maybe it's just some rich person built and funded a private orphanage and overstaffed it out of the goodness of their heart."

She shook her head. "I don't know. We never met anyone, we never had any important people come through...and didn't you guys say that growing up you had things you learned, rites and all? Didn't Emerson say something about the other facilities having their own rites and such? We didn't have any of those things. I mean we didn't celebrate any big holidays. Well, Halloween was always fun for us, dressing up, making pies and such, candy hunting on the grounds with flashlights..." She smiled at the memory. "But the winter holidays, like Christmas and yule...we didn't do. We didn't have a tree, didn't get presents, didn't celebrate birthdays, though Thanksgiving was always a thing."

"See, that sounds like The Order," Easton said. "Even the shitty orphanages I went to celebrated Christmas with a cheap plastic tree. Getting the kids to make ugly-ass paper decorations was a great way to shut them up. There's definitely something off about it."

"I'll look into it," Carter said. "If there's a link to The Order, or anything nefarious, you know I'll find it." Easton did. Carter's ability to find things about people and places bordered on the supernatural. It helped that he had the best equipment and an incredible grasp of hacking skills, but he also just seemed to have a nose for it.

"But we never had things we did that could be considered rites. Didn't you guys have like, devotionals or something?" she offered as they looked to see Jack walk out.

"Hey, guys. What's going on? You all look really serious."

"Not serious," Easton hedged. "More curious. But Carter's dealing with it. What's up?"

"Just wanted to make sure you guys weren't popsicles out here." He grinned. "And our girl was warm and toasty."

"She's fine," Easton said, kind of offended that Jack would think he wasn't caring for their girl. Jack knew him better than that.

"I'm coming in." Carter shivered. "Brutus is done playing and it's definitely cold out here."

"Maybe we should all go in," Easton suggested. He'd finished his hot chocolate and the temperature was dropping. And he wanted to speak to Emerson about finding other journals.

"Good, cuz Leo is in the kitchen making a massive amount of popcorn for a movie. Finn and Rix are just finishing up their campaign on CoD." He winked at her and Easton and then followed Carter into the house, leaving them alone.

"So? Movie time?" she asked as she turned to him. "Can we still snuggle on that massive couch?"

"Of course." He didn't even have to think about it. Perhaps he'd be okay after all.

Chapter 31

"So what are we looking for again?" Petra asked as she walked through the enormous house.

"Journals? Hidden books, anything that looks outta place?" Jack answered as they moved into the library room.

"You guys really think Emerson's dad hid more stuff?"

"He was too smart not to," Finn said. "He had no idea what would happen to the house after he died. And if it had been emptied, the desk would have been sold or destroyed."

"Granted, I didn't find this shit from snooping," Emerson said as he walked in.

"What does that mean?" she asked as she started pulling books out.

"I don't know. I woke up, and something pulled me from that warm bed with you, sweetness...it was like a need, excitement. I don't know. But I made it into the study and the feeling got more intense until I found the cache that opened the bottom of the wall."

"You ever get the feeling that He Who Sleeps is significantly more active in our lives than we think he is?" Leo said, and while his tone was joking, it still made everyone pause for a moment.

"I mean..." Emerson began and shook his head. "Dad's journal said He visited others in dreams...it stands to reason that if we *are* the seven, and she *is* the woman..." He looked to her. "That He is guiding us."

"Then we are simply instruments of His will," Finn said. "The coming annihilation of the Elders *is* His will. He wants the old ways restored."

"That's a safe bet. Safe bet that he sent this sexy woman to us as well," Jack offered and kissed her on the head before moving off to search another section.

"Emerson," Rix said. "What's the plan for the house... here I mean?"

Emerson shrugged. "I was told to keep the place safe, like a safehouse. The Elders think it was burned down, as I told Leo." He looked to Kendrix. "Unless you told Stephan."

"I haven't told him anything. Not that he asks about my life or my plans...only really contacting me when it's time for the big devotions."

"Then it stays between us," Finn said firmly. "This is a secret only we know, even when this is all over. The God might be on our side, but that doesn't mean the Elders don't have people hidden in every rank of The Order."

"Amen to that," Carter agreed fervently. A safehouse would benefit them all, especially if they could keep their Petra there.

"I think that was dad's intention. So..." Emerson said as he pulled the last book off his shelf. "Nothing so far. Maybe..." He grinned. "Maybe we ask for help?"

"From Him?" she asked, intrigued. "How?"

"Well.." Emerson grinned. "He responds to several things...perhaps an offering?"

"Of pain?" she asked softly.

"No. I think of pleasure," Emerson said. "Something to sweeten Him?"

"Fucking typical," Finn snorted. "You search one shelf and you're already focused on fucking. I swear you're like a fucking teenager."

Emerson laughed. "Your brain went to fucking, mine didn't."

"What do you mean, if not that?" she asked her grinning lover.

"I did say sweeten Him, I didn't say satisfy Him," Emerson offered. "Something to let Him know His efforts with us, I mean we are all in agreement that He's the reason we are all here, right? So something that lets Him know we appreciate what He sent us."

"And what's that?"

"A kiss?" he offered, "From each of us, to our sweet little victim."

"If you're really that bored with searching, go and entertain Petra somewhere else," Easton sighed. "Did you forget we declared war on the Elders? Remember? The guys that killed our parents? That landed me in that shitty hellscape? There's a time for playing and this ain't it."

"It's not the worst idea he's ever had," Leo pointed out. "A little extra energy from us might give Him enough power to communicate across the veil."

"Then go and fuck her properly," Easton snorted. "A kiss won't do shit. Finn's right. Emerson just wants to dip his wick while the rest of us get on and do the actual searching."

Emerson shook his head. "I... I honestly didn't..."

She shook her head. "It's okay...maybe that's not a good idea," she said, looking at Easton. She knew he wasn't ready to kiss her yet and was surprised Emerson had even suggested it. Her Snake wasn't exactly touchy-feely with his brothers, either. "Maybe not now." She went to another lower shelf and started to pull books out. She wasn't getting between them in this. Easton, her sweet damaged Easton would always be the hold out 'til he was ready not to be. She had to respect that, although it made her wonder if the rest of the guys knew he had never willingly kissed her.

"Maybe energy isn't a bad idea," Jack pointed out. "And no, I'm not suggesting we run a train on her. There has to be other ways to manifest. I mean we were taught blood, we have learned sex...maybe there's other ways? Personal sacrifice? Other acts... I can see why Emerson suggested a kiss, it connects two people, with connection comes manifestation, but..."

"You know what would really help with that kind of knowledge? Finding more books," Easton snapped and Finn placed a hand on his shoulder.

"Easy there, brother. I know you're hurting, but we can look and have a conversation at the same time, okay?" Easton didn't look happy, but he just shrugged and went back to searching shelves, methodically moving books and tapping the side and rear walls of the bookcases.

"I think we might be limited by transference," Finn said thoughtfully when he was sure Easton wasn't going to lash out. "During the festival weekend, we absorb the energy using the tattoos and then pass it to the God by dripping our blood into the well. Raising energy with Petra here is all well and good, but how do we transfer it? There isn't a well here. Can we drop blood anywhere? It was something I was going to speak to the priests about when we see them next—how the energy was transferred to the God in the old days when He was feeding all the time."

"This would all have been a lot fucking easier if those wrinkly old bastards had told us all of this when we asked," Leo said sourly.

"Maybe they had to be sure that Petra is the one?" Finn suggested, his tone still thoughtful. "I mean...I don't know. You're the one that's read the books we've found so far, Emerson. Has there been anything about how the feeding works?"

Emerson stopped his search and then turned and raised a finger, and walked out the room. Rix arched a brow at her and then Finn. "I hate it when he gets like this."

"This happen a lot?" she asked Rix.

"It did in school. His research meter would go off and he would do shit like this then come back and have some info none of us had come across. Bookish asshole."

She laughed and shook her head. "I mean him saving the day right now..."

He walked back in with the second of the two journals. "Blood!" he said with a triumphant glare.

"Whose?"

"Ours," he offered and looked to them. "Journal said it was through blood it was transferred. Here..." As pleasure and pain are two sides of a coin for him, with one should come the other to be whole. Francine has me paint my blood over her heart. It works when I haven't christened her with my essence." He looked up. "I'ma say that means when he didn't come inside her?"

"So it's some kind of feedback loop?" Leo queried. "We build the pleasure, take it from her, and then somehow giving it back takes it from her and gives it to the God?"

"Then why did we need the wells at all?" Finn asked. "Is it less potent to cover her in blood or something?"

"I don't see anything in here about a well, at least outside of the main devotions of the festival weekend," he offered. "It is possible that we don't need it if it's a full circuit. I'm also working off the information given...and both participants were of the blood." He looked to her. "We don't know if she is."

"So basically you don't know anything," Easton snorted, going back to searching shelves. "Maybe it's a way to test it," Leo said, with a look in her direction that she didn't know how to interpret. "Maybe if it works, we can confirm that the orphanage is a secret Order facility?"

"But how are we going to know it works?" Carter spoke up for the first time. "Even if the God does give us some sort of signal, there's no way of knowing if it's because of something we did or if He's pissed that we're fucking about instead of looking."

"We aren't fucking about," Rix said. "And Leo's suggestion bear's weight. What do you propose?"

"I'm not proposing anything," Carter shrugged. "It was Emerson's idea. I'm just testing his hypothesis with reasonable questions.

"No, I meant Leo... You think there's a way to test it?"

"I'm the fabulous of this sorry outfit," Leo laughed, "not the brains. I just thought that if it worked we'd know she's Order, but Carter has a point. I don't fucking know how we test if it worked or if He Who Sleeps is just fed up of waiting."

Sitting there, she smiled. Seeing them interact, even if it was arguing...

"Pet? Baby, answer us something..."

"Okay?" she said to Jack.

"When you found us, how did that happen? Like, what was going through your head?"

She cocked her head, thinking. "I... Well, I was walking home from work, and changed my direction, going down the street you guys were on."

"Is that something you normally do?" Emerson asked. "Take different routes?"

She shook her head. "Now, sometimes, but then? No. I was literally just here in the city for a short amount of time, less than two months."

"Interesting. And why did you move here?"

She shrugged. "Philly seemed interesting. Small city feel but big city opportunities. It has a huge art scene, but less competition than New York, but also...it felt right to move here." She chuckled. "I remember trying to figure out where I was going to move to and Philly just popped into my head."

They all looked at each other, before Jack spoke again. "And you finding us..."

"Right...so, I changed direction, thinking it would be a better route. I mean it was..."

"Depending on your view..."

"Well, yeah. So, when I saw you guys carrying the girl in, something pushed me to follow." She swallowed, thinking back and then frowned. "Seeing her there, I...I didn't like seeing her there."

"Because you are a good person," Emerson added.

She shook her head. "No, it felt wrong...like it wasn't supposed to be *her*. Not jealousy, because what kinda lunatic...but it felt wrong."

"So now we get to the deeply philosophical questions," Carter said. "Does the God speak to people outside The Order?'

"It's possible? I mean isn't it bloodlines that matter, not the fact that they are in an organization? Blood remembers, blood transcends," Rix said.

"I've never really understood any of this," Leo admitted. "I know there are the seven legacy families, but why are we more important than the others if it's all about blood? I'm sure there must be other bloodlines as old as ours in The Order."

"Because our blood is purer," Emerson said. "Technically there's thirteen legacy families, the thirteen that He anointed and blessed when he walked the earth." Emerson looked to them. "Though I understand there's more than that, families that sprang from individuals he called after, once he had slept." He sighed. "Regardless of religion, it's all dogma. But suffice to say that it's a safe bet those sitting at Elder spots are not part of the original thirteen, aside from Stephan."

313

"But if He called families after, how do we know that He didn't just call Petra?" Carter asked, shaking his head. "I think that whole line of questioning is just going to have to wait until I can look into this orphanage and figure it out once and for all. If she is Order, then it's fine, and we can all carry on as one murderous little family. If she's newly called, then we induct her into The Order when the Elders have been deposed."

"Killed," Easton corrected, not even turning around.

"Carter's right," Finn said. "We could talk ourselves round in circles until dawn and still not figure out if our beauty here is Order or not. But if you want to try kissing and bleeding, Emerson, be my guest."

Emerson shrugged. "Just ideas, guys. Trying to be proactive."

"We aren't getting anywhere all being in this room, well except on each other's nerves," she offered and got to her feet. "And it stands to reason that the study and library would hold much but nothing that he wanted to hide. I'm going to the kitchen to get a drink."

"Maybe splitting up is a good idea," Finn agreed with her.

"Hold up," Carter made them both stop. "What if we're thinking about this backwards? Am I right in thinking that every time we've been touched or contacted by the God, it's either been at night or while we're sleeping?" The others looked at each other and shrugged. "I wonder if that's because the veil is thinner at night. Or maybe we're more susceptible in a dream state. Completely aside from the question of Petra's origins, what if being in some kind of altered state would allow Him to contact us more easily?"

Jack looked to her and then to the group. "Meditation? I mean it could get us to that more altered state. Skeezie Keezie talks about transcendence through both meditative states and euphoric states, though I think the secondary might be because she wants to nail Petra..." He grinned.

"Well then maybe a couple of you could go and meditate? Or take a nap?" Finn suggested.

"Well that depends on if Easton thinks that's the best use of our time." Jack teased.

"At least Carter is using some kind of logic, based on empirical evidence," Easton shrugged, moving onto the next shelf. "Do what you want. There might not even be anything else here to find. Just leave me out of it."

"Technically I was using evidence-based ideas as well," Emerson said as he leaned against the bookshelf. "We are dealing with a God here, one we all worship, and I kinda think that while Carter is right, science and this world is not the answer...the spectral is," he answered matter-of-factly. "Maybe a melding of it." He looked to Carter, then to the rest. "What do you think?"

"Isn't that exactly what I just suggested?" Carter asked. "An altered state of consciousness would be considered spiritual by a lot of people. Many indigenous cultures use drugs to attain that level of communion with their spirits and deities. The two aren't mutually exclusive."

"True," she said. "I don't think we need mushrooms or anything..."

Emerson smirked. "So, a nap? Who is coming?"

Rix, who had been on the top of the ladder on the bookshelf, jumped down. "I'm going to go check the attic." He went to her and kissed her forehead. "Have fun." He winked and walked off.

"I don't sleep in the day, but if you guys don't have any luck, I'm okay with hitting the weed later," Easton chuckled. "I keep a small stash for when the creative

315

juices aren't flowing. I'm guessing that might be altered enough."

"Were you high when you painted Petra?" Finn asked curiously.

"Hard to say," Easton shrugged. "Each artwork takes weeks or months. I might have smoked once or twice during the time I was painting them, but I have no idea."

That was interesting to her. She smiled at him. "Good to know I'm a muse when you are high." She winked and then sighed. "I'm going to get my drink, then I think I'm going to go and sit in the solarium and try this meditation thing."

"Good luck." Easton winked at her. "I'll be here, probably still searching all these thousands of feet of bookshelves."

"I think we need to stop looking in books, and figure out if there's more hidden caches around the house," Jack said and looked to Emerson. "You know of any secret passages or rooms?"

Emerson shook his head. "I didn't know about his little hidden vault in the wall so..."

"There must be blueprints somewhere." Carter slid the book he'd been paging through back onto the shelf and headed for the door. "I'll go boot up my computer and see if I can find the planning applications or who the original architects were. This place isn't that old. They might still have the original floorplans."

"I'll head out to the hardware store," Leo said. "If we need to measure rooms against plans, I'd rather have one of those laser tools."

"Wow... Leo, using your brain instead of your balls...I'm impressed," Easton teased him. "But good thinking."

"Well then that's a plan." She smiled. "I'm off. If you find anything..."

"And if you figure anything out..." Emerson said with a smirk.

Chapter 32

Somewhere in the house a clock chimed softly and Carter glanced at the time on his screen, sighing when he realized it was one in the morning. It had taken him hours and an exorbitant amount of money to get the original architectural plans for the house. The firm that had designed it was still in business, but they hadn't digitized their records from before they went online so he'd had to pay for them to find and scan these old drawings.

Luckily they were in good shape and he'd been going over them, but there weren't any hidden passageways or rooms built into the design and he couldn't see any obvious missing space from memory. It was a good thing Leo had been to the hardware store for the laser because it looked like they were going to have to measure the rooms and see if anything didn't add up.

He was about to close the laptop and go to bed when he heard a creak on the landing upstairs, followed by the very obvious sound of someone descending the stairs. Rather than call out and risk waking anyone else up, he quietly closed the laptop and headed toward the door. Out in the lobby, Rix was shuffling slowly across the space, his eyes open but completely vacant.

"You okay?" Carter whispered, but Rix didn't acknowledge him at all, even to glance in his direction. His movements had none of his usual grace or speed and after a couple of seconds, Carter realized that his brother had to be sleepwalking. Sliding his phone out of his pocket, he messaged Emerson to come downstairs as quietly as possible, and he set off after Rix to try and figure out where he was headed.

The sleeping man walked into the kitchen, heading straight for the walk-in pantry, opened the door and stepped in. For several long moments he simply stood there, shoulders slumped, breathing deeply, and then he startled and jumped back, crashing into a shelf of canned goods as he flailed about.

"Easy! Easy!" Carter soothed, just as Emerson appeared in pajamas pants at the door. "You were sleepwalking."

"That's fucking new!" He hissed and looked around, his normal calm façade crumbling. Kendrix was never so pure as when he was awoken from sleep. That was when he allowed himself to be a man, not the thing his father had wrought. "Where the fuck are we?"

"The walk-in pantry," Emerson said with a frown. "You got a craving for Fruit Loops?"

Kendrix scowled, his mask sliding into place. "I was fucking sleeping, asshole. I don't know what the fuck is going on."

Carter was mentally scanning the plans he'd just been looking at and frowned. The space did seem slightly smaller than it had been on the drawing but it was hard to tell. He stepped back and looked at the hallway, trying to figure out the junctions of the rooms.

"This backs onto the understairs cupboard," he said absently. That would be an easy space to alter without it looking any different on the plans. "And you could easily shave a foot off the kitchen and the library without it being obvious because of the cabinets and the shelving making it hard to measure. We can get Leo down here to measure, but I bet if there's a secret room or cache, the door is in there. This has to be the God guiding you."

"What were you dreaming?" Emerson asked.

Rix bared his teeth. "I don't dream."

"Be that as it may..." Emerson looked around. "We need the rest of them? Who is sleeping with Pet?"

"No point waking them all up if it's nothing," Carter said, stepping past Rix into the pantry and studying the joints of the walls.

"Well Rix was brought here, so let's work on the idea that Rix knows?" Emerson said and looked to their friend.

"How the fuck do you propose I do that?"

"I don't know, maybe calm down and feel?" he asked. "When I found the cache, I was just moving on autopilot...the feeling..." he shook his head. "What do you feel, Rix?"

"Cold," he said immediately.

"This room isn't cold," Emerson said and looked to Carter. "Feel for a draft."

"There's no basement on the plans," Carter said, tapping the back wall. "Maybe there's a staircase behind here...aha." He pressed a small section of the wall and it sprang forward to reveal a small handle. "Interesting." He took his phone out again and switched the light on. "Let's go." With a grin back at the others, he turned the handle and the whole back wall of the pantry swung open into darkness.

"Hold up, Indiana," Emerson said. "Why are you not feeling cold?" He looked to Rix. "Are you still feeling cold? Clammy? Wet?"

"The fuck?"

Emerson sighed and shook his head. "God influence, speaks in half answers," he said. "Cold, clammy, Wet... Could be walking into a watery room..."

"No, not clammy, not wet...just cold. And yes, still cold."

He looked to Carter. "Lead on, Doctor Jones..."

"Your concern for my wellbeing is so touching," Carter teased, giving him a sappy grin. He ducked under Emerson's swat and headed into the darkness, descending some concrete steps that led down in a steep spiral. "Anyone see a light switch?" he asked.

"It wasn't concern for your wellbeing. Finn would have our nuts if something happened." He laughed as Rix grumbled behind them.

"I'm not touching anything..."

Emerson laughed. "Is there anything to touch? Carter, shine that over this way," he said and pointed. "Light switch?"

The light glinted off a chain hanging against the wall and Carter shrugged. "One way to find out." Before either of the others could stop him, he reached over and pulled the chain. There was a click and a metallic pinging sound, and then a lightbulb buzzed into luminescence. "Bingo!" He reached the bottom of the stairs and stepped into a large, cold room lined almost entirely in massive stones.

"Root cellar?" Rix asked, standing at the bottom stair.

"Maybe? Though I didn't know it was here, and there's no stores here," Emerson said. "What else do you feel?"

Rix frowned. "Nothing."

"So we are either in the right place or the wrong. Though I doubt He Who Sleeps would play hot and cold with us."

"I'm wondering if this is some sort of secondary cover in case someone stumbled onto this room," Carter said thoughtfully, peering around. Going back to the stairs, he poked around a bit and then whooped triumphantly. "Yes!"

There was another click and then the grinding of heavy machinery as whole sections of the floor slid away and islands of shelves began rising out of the ground. "Holy shit!" Carter breathed. "We've hit the motherlode. Even if the Elders tried to clean this place out, they'd never have discovered this."

"My father..." Emerson said as he stood back with Rix. "Where the fuck did he get these books?"

"No idea," Carter said cheerfully, studying the nearest bank of books. "Some of these are old! Look at this!"

Rix walked past them and went to a farther side of the stacks.

"What?" Emerson looked to Carter.

"The Origins of He Who Sleeps," Carter said gleefully. "The priests would give their nutsacks to get their hands on this!" He paused. "Unless... Do you reckon your dad might have stolen these from the temple? Or that the priests maybe gave them to him for safe-keeping during whatever happened all those years ago?"

"Either is possible," he said with a frown. "Rix, what are you doing?"

Rix turned to them with a book in hand. "Rites and Observances," he said as he opened it. "And they are not the rites we learned. Like at all." He looked up. "The feminine..." He slumped then and went to his knees, gasping.

"Rix..." Emerson said as his friend shook his head, as if shaking off cobwebbing. "You okay?"

"What the fuck?" Rix frowned. "That felt weird."

"The God is maybe still connected with you." Carter put the book down and went across to Rix. "Damn...you're looking pretty pale there, brother. Maybe it's time to wrap this up and go find the others."

Rix frowned. "I think I need a drink..."

"Water is just up the stairs," Emerson said.

"No, an actual drink, being puppeteered about is not my idea of a good time."

323

"Drunkenness is an altered state of consciousness," Carter smirked, helping Rix to his feet. "I'd stick to the OJ, buddy."

"I didn't say get drunk...have you ever known me to get drunk?" Rix argued with him as he helped him up the stairs.

"Alcohol is a drug," Carter said seriously. "If you're feeling under the influence now, I promise that a shot of tequila isn't going to help."

"Not under the influence, more like someone was moving my body against my will."

"That doesn't sound like a lot of fun," Carter admitted, turning off the lights as they headed back up the stairs. "On second thoughts, maybe we shouldn't go and wake everyone up right now. It's almost two in the morning. Maybe we should all just go to bed and come back to this bright and early. Those books aren't going anywhere and we know where they are now. What do you think, Em?"

"I think we have been flying blind for three years," Emerson offered as they hefted Rix up the last stairs. "And I think we have a limited amount of time," he sighed and threw himself into the chair closest to him. "We have what...a week 'til Thanksgiving...and then three 'til we need to be in the Balkans for the festivities? What amounts to a month to figure out how to keep her safe...how to keep us all safe and bring Him back to His glory."

"I know, but there's no point in burning ourselves out by working every hour in creation," Carter told him. "You'll be better able to assess all this when you've had a few hours of sleep. You were up most of last night, too. You're no good to us or Petra when you're half dead from exhaustion."

"He's right," Rix said. "We only have so long left here, Car, at the house. Our lives are calling Monday morning, and after that...aside from this asshole who can be playboy of the year and just research everything, the rest of us have jobs, jobs we need to go to to keep up appearances." He looked to their friend. "Easton is on his frayed edges..."

"What about a compromise?" Carter suggested. "We box it all up tomorrow and ship it to the city so we can go over it in our downtime. Hell, I can stay behind on Monday and hire a van and drive it down myself if necessary. I can put the bike in the back with the boxes."

"I don't think we should bring it outta this house," Emerson said. "He went through a lot of trouble to hide it from them..." He shook his head. "And if we succeed we can't let them fall into the wrong hands. We still don't know who we can trust, aside from ourselves. Go...go to bed. We found the stash. Tomorrow we spend as much time as we can to read and go from there." He looked to Rix. "Aspirin. It's what helped me after my little tête-à-tête with Him. I will go crawl into bed with her, sleep a few hours so Carter doesn't lose his shit. I'll set my alarm for four hours, and then I'm up and working on this."

"Okay." Carter was relieved. He understood the urgency, was feeling it himself, but they both looked dead on their feet. At least they were all here and could split up the search between them. If it came down to it, they could take photos of the pages instead of trying to read everything and take the digital copies. A promise of four hours sleep was good enough.

Waving them off up the stairs, he went to his room where Brutus was sprawled across most of the bed, despite knowing full well he wasn't supposed to be on there. Still, Carter couldn't fault him. The mattress was incredible. With a rueful grin, he stripped off, pushed the dog aside enough to actually get under the covers, and settled in for what would be a very short rest.

Chapter 33

"Where is the wine?" Petra asked as she settled on the large cushion on the ground in front of the low table covered in books. Six days after Rix, Emerson and Carter had found the hidden library, they were settled into a rental house in the northern Liberties, officially celebrating the feasting holiday. It was after dinner, Petra creating one hell of a meal for all of them. Now, she was relaxing in the living room while Leo and Carter cleaned up the kitchen.

Since finding the books, things had been slightly different. Emerson was focused on figuring out what exactly the right course was, and her sexy psychos had, for the most part, become less so, though she had a feeling that that wasn't who they all were at their core. Learned behavior wasn't inherent behavior.

And her guys seemed to be enjoying it all.

"Here," Rix said and poured more of the crisp white wine into her glass.

"Thank you. Now where were we?" They had been working on everything since they got there the afternoon before, between prepping for the meal and sexy bouts of indiscretions.

"Emerson was waffling about the history of The Order," Easton said, sounding distracted. He'd been flicking through one of the books the guys had brought from the Chesapeake house, despite Emerson's protests. There had simply been too much to read and they didn't have enough time to go back there before they left for the Longest Night ritual.

"He does love to waffle," Finn teased. "But seriously, has anyone found any more recent records? We still haven't figured out why The Order included killings in the first place. It doesn't sound like that's what it was all about at first."

"I don't waffle. I love waffles," Emerson said. "There is a big goddamn difference."

Ignoring her cheeky lover she looked to Finn, who was sitting imperiously in the large wingback chair, a glass of scotch in his hands. "Finn and I were looking at a book earlier..." she began, remembering they had only got so far before he had put her on her knees, and slipped inside her, making her read to him. The book had been forgotten soon enough, but she had found a specific passage. "And I did find one thing... Easton, hand me the yellow book there."

"Sure." Easton passed her the book she asked for, setting aside the one he'd been flicking through so he could devote all of his attention to her.

She opened it and flipped through a few pages. "Here... Okay, so," she began to read. "When the solar eclipse was in Draco, Brother Garbi received a devotion, one mired in blood." She looked up at them and back down. "To which, blood is the life," she frowned, "This isn't Dracula, ugh, and it shall bring life to him."

Emerson frowned. "The eclipse in Draco was around a hundred and fifty years ago."

"It's disturbing that you just know random shit like that off the top of your head," Leo said, coming into the room and sprawling in an armchair near the fire.

"So it's really recent," Easton said, sounding shocked. "The Order is thousands of years old. Are you telling me they've only been including killings over the last two centuries?"

"No, I'm saying that it has been largely killings for the past two centuries," Petra said. "This book says that blood rites were a natural part of the worship, but it was in balance with life rites, and those included..." she flipped through another few pages, "births, sexual rites and the rites of abundance." She read through a few more. "But a lot of those rites were tedious and were left to the female side of the group. It was when Brother Garbi had the devotion about blood that all life rites were given to the women. And males started with blood." She sneered. "So apparently because the life rites were too involved, they got rid of them. Because they were lazy?"

"That's fucking interesting," Emerson offered. "And I didn't just know that about the eclipse. Google is your friend." He shook his tablet at them.

"What is kind of interesting is that a lot of those rites involve blood," Leo pointed out, being serious for once. "The ascendance to womanhood, the birthing of a child, the loss of virginity... All of those have some element of bleeding to them. I wouldn't be at all surprised if there were monthly rituals to be done, too."

"They ever do anything like that at the orphanage?" Easton asked curiously.

She shook her head...then stopped. "Well...no...but when we got our periods for the first time, each of us, there was a special dinner." She looked to them. "And flowers given to us, as well as pomegranates."

"So if it's the blood that's important, not the life or the death, killing isn't necessary?" Easton pressed, looking pale.

"We don't know that for sure," Finn soothed, trying to calm him down. "We know that our sacrifices have been feeding Him all these years."

"But nowhere near the amount of energy that He gets from the small drips we make after a night with Petra," Easton persisted. "It's all backwards. Sex is about life. Blood is about life. What if we were never supposed to kill and it was all just some huge fucking misunderstanding?"

"I'm not ruling that out," Jack said as he walked in, bringing more wine, and some water with him. "Is it at all possible that it was not only misunderstood, but willfully done?"

"What do you mean?" Emerson asked.

"I mean things changed when this Brother Garbi had a devotional, right? What if he did have it, but interpreted it how he wanted to, to gain power?"

"It's possible," Finn shrugged. "The priests are supposed to be impartial and absolute. If he was in charge of the Lore Keepers at the time, they might not have questioned his 'revelation.'"

"How could they not?!" Easton was on his feet, full of rage and sorrow. "How could they not question a total about turn from something that had been working for three thousand years?"

"Times were different then," Finn said, leaning forward, ready to move if Easton exploded.

"Brother, no one is saying that killing is inherently bad," Leo said calmly, his tone belying the fact that he was also poised to spring. "Some of the people we've sacrificed have more than deserved it. You had every right to kill those fuckers."

"You don't get it!" Easton's eyes were filling with tears as he hissed. "If those lazy fuckers hadn't decided to do away with the women, and if this fuckwit Garbi hadn't been on a power trip, I wouldn't have been in the orphanage and I wouldn't have had to kill those fucking assholes! Your fathers would all still be alive! We'd have had mothers!" His voice broke and he abruptly spun and left the room.

Petra leaped to her feet and ran after him, leaving the guys to argue, searching Easton out. She found him pacing in the study. Stopping dead in the doorway, her heart hurt for him. Any of her other guys, she would have gone to them directly, to comfort them, hold them, but Easton...

To her astonishment, the moment he saw her, he fell into her arms. "My whole life feels like a lie," he wept. "I don't know what to do. I don't know how to feel." His tone was so agonized her heart broke all over again.

"Easton, if I could take this pain from you, I would. Devour it, and hold it I would. No one deserves what you have been through." Tears fell down her cheeks, her arms around him holding him tight. Gods, it felt so good to hold him, like a switch had been flipped and an ache was gone, an ache she didn't even know she had been nursing.

"I wouldn't wish this on anyone." He was burrowed into her, face in the crook of her shoulder, so his words were muffled.

"Of course not. You're a good person," she said softly, running her fingers through his hair. "Doesn't mean I wouldn't take the pain for you. Because that is what you do when you care for someone."

"I just can't... I can't..." He howled in rage and grief.

"I know. I know, baby, I know," she said softly and kissed the top of his head. Her poor perfect Easton. He needed to grieve, needed to come to grips, because he wouldn't survive, they wouldn't survive without him.

"What am I supposed to do?" He wept, his whole body shuddering with the force of his grief.

"If I was a normal person I would say to forgive...to work through it... But I'm not normal, and neither are you, my love," she said softly. "And I know whatever we do won't fix things, won't fix you, but whatever we do, we do it together. I won't let you drown alone, Easton. I promise."

"How am I supposed to tell a therapist any of this?" he said helplessly.

She saw his point. "I don't know, love. None of this is normal...so maybe we don't approach it like normal people."

"I want to be better," he told her, pulling away finally, his face blotched and tear-stained. "For me. For you. The others. I thought I could fix this, but the more we learn, the worse it gets."

Taking his face in her hands, she looked him over. "Easton, I don't know what do to make this better, aside from you guys killing every last one of them, and then maybe we...maybe we can work on it together, to heal you, to try to make things better." She gave him a small smile. "It hurts me so much to see you struggling so bad, knowing it's an enemy we can't really face. I'm going to do everything I can, try everything, to ensure things get better."

"You'd do that for me?" The look in his eyes was so lost. "Even when I can't...be with you like the others can?"

"I told you, Easton, there are plenty of ways to love someone...and it doesn't have to be physical. Being with you is all I want, however you feel safe. I love you, Easton, it doesn't hinge on anything but you being you."

"How can you love someone as damaged as me?" he asked, completely bewildered.

"How can I not?" she asked softly. "And no, I don't have a savior's complex or anything like that. I don't think I can change you or save you or fix you. I just want to be here for you, to love you because you deserve to be loved, Easton, and I very much want to be the person to do it."

He broke down again, hiding his face behind his hands, hunching over as though everything in his core ached.

Everything inside her broke for the man in her arms, the need to avenge the child he was, the man he became, all because of the way others treated him. Whatever she would do, could do...an idea started to form. She wasn't sure if it was even possible, but the idea rolled around her mind even more. Holding him, she let him cry.

"How's he doing?" Carter's voice came from the doorway behind her, speaking softly. "You need a hand?"

Knowing Easton had said Carter and he had been working on something, she nodded and put out her hand, so he came to the two of them. She didn't speak, her arm around Easton's middle, holding him tight.

"How are you doing there, brother?" Carter asked gently.

"Not great," Easton admitted. "I don't know how to process any of this."

"None of us do," Carter said. "I know I'm not the only one feeling like my whole life has been a lie. Or feeling this overwhelming rage for my parents. For all the families they've destroyed with this bullshit. All we can do is make them pay and then we have a lifetime together to try and put the pieces back together."

"And we will," Petra said to them both. "I promise."

"I'm sorry." Easton pulled away from them completely and tried to dry his face. "I'm ruining the weekend. We should go back to the others."

"No rush," Carter said softly. "Take your time."

"You guys go on ahead." He was closed off now, turning away. "I'll be fine. I'll come through in a few minutes."

She sighed. "Okay..." She let Carter pull her to her feet, giving him his dignity. "But if you need..." she left it hanging. "The only way any of us can help is if you let us. I love you." She smiled at him and felt Carter squeeze her hand.

"I know. I love you, too. I just don't want to go back in there looking like a half-cooked tomato." He glanced back at them. "I'm fine. I just need to calm down."

She smiled back at him. It was a victory in her eyes. "I expect a cuddle when you come back," she offered and they walked out and down the hall, Carter holding her hand still.

"Don't ask for more than he can give," Carter said quietly, pausing her in the hallway. "He was okay to be touched just now because his distress overrode his fear, but making 'expectations' of him when he's still trying to get out of his own head might be counterproductive. You have to wait for him to come to you."

"I know. And I also know that Easton needs direction from me. He told me if I want something, to tell him. I would never punish him for anything... We have an understanding, him and I. And I would never ever expect something he wasn't willing to give."

"Then consider your words," Carter said to her. "You just told him you expect a cuddle. Not that you want one, or you'd like one. That you expect one. Words have power. This is a long road to recovery for him, and it needs to be handled with care. Expectations are..." He sighed, looking tired. "You know, that's not my story to tell. But Stephan had many expectations of Easton and none of them were pretty. You should encourage him to open up to you about it."

"Understood." She nodded.

"Good. Then let's get back to the party." He smiled and kissed her forehead.

Entering the living room, she saw Leo and Jack had pulled out desserts and were eating from the pies themselves, spraying forkfuls with whipped cream.

"Look at the two of you." She giggled. "Aren't we supposed to be researching?"

"No," Finn said firmly. "This is supposed to be a holiday weekend. Enough of the books and the theories. We should be stuffing ourselves silly and relaxing. Things will get serious soon enough. There's time to figure out the history lessons afterwards."

"Amen to that," Leo said, stuffing another piece of pie in his face with a broad grin.

"You want some pie, baby?" Jack asked, brandishing a fork full of pie at her. Sitting, she let him feed her. "Open," he said and she did, and he sprayed cream into her mouth. She squealed and then laughed.

"That was a lot!"

"I think you have taken a bit more than that in your mouth," Emerson commented from his seat at the couch.

"Damn right, she has," Leo smirked.

"Jerks." Shaking her head, she grabbed her wine glass, Rix filling it back up. "Well, dinner is done, desserts are being demolished..."

"There are two more pies in the kitchen," Jack offered helpfully around a forkful of pie.

"So what else to do?" she asked with a grin.

"What would you normally do?" Emerson asked.

She shrugged. "With my girls? Drink a bunch of wine. Play some stupid game like Truth or Dare or Never Have I Ever or cards..."

"Please tell me we have a copy of *Cards Against Humanity*," Leo said, perking up. "I'm going to make you laugh so hard you'll never recover."

"I didn't bring any," Emerson offered. "Do any of us own that?"

She shook her head. "I didn't bring any, either. We could watch a movie?" She wasn't sure they were really the kinda guys to play Truth or Dare with, and certainly not Never Have I Ever..

"I'm not sure..." Leo made a face. "How are we all supposed to snuggle with you at the same time? There's only one of you and seven of us."

"Then I guess it's Truth or Dare," Rix said with a smirk.

"You sure you're ready to go down that particular rabbit hole, cupcake?" Finn said with a grin.

She arched a brow. "I wasn't the one that suggested it."

"Um, you did mention it."

"But I didn't suggest it," she insisted. "And anyway, you do realize that a game of Truth or Dare is not going to hold up to what we normally do, right?"

"Sounds like a challenge." Rix smirked.

"Personally, I'm all up for chasing you all around the garden while you're naked, but it's maybe a bit cold," Leo sighed.

"We kind of suck at group activities," Carter laughed. "What about Charades? That doesn't require any equipment, and we could do it in teams."

"How is it that Finn's the leader, but you're the daddy?" Easton laughed, coming into the room.

"No one is chasing her anywhere but me," Rix growled, desire flashing in his eyes.

Shivering slightly, she settled on the chair and a half alone, pulling her legs up to settle under her. She looked at Carter. "So should I call you Daddy? That going to be a thing now?"

"You can call me whatever you want, Princess," Carter said, heat in his eyes.

"And I'll chase whoever I want," Leo snarled right back at Rix. "Try and fucking stop me."

"Easy, boys," Finn said calmly. "Put your dicks away. This is a party, remember?"

Easton groaned. "You had to go and mention dicks, didn't you? Now Leo is going to—"

"Dick measuring contest!" Leo crowed, getting to his feet and reaching for his belt.

"How many times has he tried this now?" Carter asked Finn conversationally.

"Too many," Finn sighed back. "Sit down, Leo. There's pie on the table. No one wants dicks in the pie."

"Fine. Whatever," Leo sat down grumpily.

"Yeah, it's not that kinda party," she agreed with a giggle. "If it was I would have figured it would be a dick in the mashed potatoes."

"Do not give him ideas," Emerson groaned.

"Leo baby...your hog need some attention?" she purred in a tease.

"When does it not need attention?" Leo answered. "If I could have you bouncing on it all day every day, I'd—"

"Get pretty raw and land both of you in the ER with cystitis or some shit like that," Carter interrupted. "And you wouldn't want to do that to our girl now, would you?"

"No...Daddy." Leo smirked and the others burst out laughing.

"You are both terrible." Shaking her head, she winked at Easton. "So we sitting here just insulting Leo all night?"

"You know," Emerson said with a sly smile, "I think Petra should answer the age old question. I mean, since Leo isn't going to stop with the measuring..." He looked to her. "Who is the biggest?"

"I know dudes don't wanna hear this but size isn't everything...and it's not the size, it's how you use it." Taking a sip of her wine, she smiled into the rim.

337

"That's a shit answer," Leo snorted. "But I'll let you get away with it because I know you're just trying to protect everyone else's feelings."

"No, I'm actually not trying to protect anyone. You guys are volatile and wild and slightly crazy but not one of you has any kinda issue with what you are packing." She sipped again. "Each of you are quite proud of it...some more than others..."

"Yes, we are all of those things...and competitive." Emerson pointed to the rest of them.

"Fine. So ask me specific questions. I'll answer." This could be fun.

"If you had to describe each of us in one word, what would it be?" Carter asked.

"Person or cock?" she offered. "Cuz those are different answers I think. Well, for the most part."

"This is me," Carter chuckled. "I'm not interested in anyone's dick but my own."

She hummed. "True. Okay..." She pointed at him. "Thoughtful." She winked and pointed to Jack, "Fun," Leo, "wild," Emerson, "romantic," Finn, "naughty," Rix, "dangerous," to which he gave her a savage grin, and to Easton, "complicated."

"Seems fair," Carter shrugged. "What did you see the future looking like when we get back?" Easton asked her curiously.

"Us together, whatever that looks like," she answered without thought. "I'm not interested in being without any of you, and a life without you now is not an option. Any of you. You all tick boxes for me, and I hope I do for you as well."

Jack nodded. "Goddamn right you do."

"I guess what I meant is do you see us all in a big house together like this, or having different roles in your lives?" Easton clarified. "Because it might be nice to talk about real estate before we go. Have plans to look forward to that aren't just killing and fucking, you know?"

She nodded. "I didn't know a big house was in the cards for us, though if I'm honest that is a dream for me, to be with you guys, make a go of it with you. But I wouldn't push any of you to do that."

"It's not a hardship." Emerson smiled indulgently.

"We'd actually talked about it," Finn admitted. "I think it's safe to say that we'd all be happy with a centralized place where we can have you all the time."

"But we might have to get it custom designed and built," Carter explained. "Brutus needs space. Easton needs a studio with good lighting. A few of us are going to need offices. That's going to be hard to find, even in a city this size."

"And we should talk about what you want," Finn said. "In an ideal world, if you didn't have to work and could do anything you wanted, what would you do?"

"I...what?" She looked at them, considering their words. Not having to work? That was insane. "I...well, I guess I would keep doing what I was doing. Helping animals, working with beautiful art." Catching Easton's eye, she blushed. "I love what I do, I mean I didn't have weird ass parents pushing their own agenda on me. I do what I love...the art, the animals... If I didn't have to work, I would still do it all, because it brings me joy. In a perfect world I would want to help more animals, and make things safer for them."

"And a family?" Emerson asked.

"Aside from you guys? You mean kids?" He nodded. "Yes. Of course. A real family." She sighed. "What brought us together doesn't change how badly I want happily ever after with you guys. Is it normal? No, but who of us is?"

"Well that's good to know," Finn said, grinning. "Extra rooms for kids. Check."

"And maybe enough space out back for an animal sanctuary," Carter joked.

"Oh, that would be lovely." She beamed. "Well maybe not in the back yard, but close..."

Emerson was fiddling with his tablet. "Twelve acres just outside the city in Bala Cynwyd..." He shook the tablet at them. "Perfect for a massive house, already equipped with a barn and its own forest." He looked up at Rix. "Perfect for a bit of chase."

Rix chuckled and shook his head, but winked at her, causing her to blush. The thought of being chased again sent a shiver through her body. Rix was her most volatile lover, so over the top, from his chases to his home invasions...gods...it worked for them.

"Sounds good to me," Easton was grinning. "Add it to the short list and send me the link. If it's still available when we get back, I'll book viewings for all of us."

Leo was also looking at his phone. "Pretty good road links from there into the city," he approved. "Do we know any good architects?"

"I might be able to handle that," Emerson said. "You guys remember Damon, graduated with us from the school?" He referenced their school in Arizona. "He isn't involved in the organization, and would understand us wanting a place created to our specs."

"You have friends you grew up with that aren't part of the faith?" she asked.

"No, he's part of the faith, but he's not part of the inner circle. He's from a lesser family that gets the favor through personal worship, but not through group rites. I don't think he ever belonged to a group."

"Maybe that's part of the reason The Order is keeping Him starved," Carter speculated. "I'm not defending those assholes in any way, and they're all going to die, but what if they want The Order to stay small and for the likes of Damon to only get a taste of the power he could be receiving? Keeping the power base tight and unnoticed."

"Maybe," said Finn, "but it's up to Him who joins The Order. Not the Elders. Anyway, Damon is a great choice. Let's hit him up. He's good, so he's going to be busy. And wherever we buy, we're going to either have to build or carry out major renovations."

Emerson nodded, pulling his phone out as Jack looked to Carter. "That's a valid concern. There are many guys we went to school with that aren't inner circle, hell, remember Xander Cade? Remember he was slated to be part of a crew and then wasn't. I can't remember why, but... It was soon after that we were given free rein over the fall rites. You know, I don't think another group has been created since we were. With the amount of men we graduated with, there should be groups feeding Him in every major city, but if the Elders have made it that way..."

"We need to have a long talk with the priests when we've taken over," Finn said. "And I know it's a lot to put on you, Emerson, but I was wondering if you'd put together some sort of educational package or presentation to send out to all the members about what's going on. Summarize what we've learned and what's going to change. Maybe think about putting together an Order-wide library for anyone to read and use. I think part of how this was allowed to happen is the fault of those assholes at the temple keeping all the knowledge to themselves."

"It was on the list, so I'm glad we are on the same page," Emerson offered. "Considering I have the least amount of shit to do daily this works."

"Em, what is it you actually do?" she asked him.

341

"I oversee nine companies my family has a vested interest in. Majored in business management and here I am." He winked.

"You can have a team," Finn told him. "Anyone you want. I don't expect you to do this alone."

"Obviously. If I need you guys, I'll ask. Though, Carter, I might need your data miner friend. I have an idea about the accounts, too."

They talked about their plans, Petra settling in to listen to it all, and smiled at Easton who was sitting on the other big chair. He looked better, and she felt better about everything with him. Their conversations flowed down the track of preparations, and she drifted off, listening to the quiet rumble of her men's voices as they planned to take over the world.

Chapter 34

Petra stepped down to the street with a smile on her face and a spring in her step. Thanksgiving had been amazing with her guys, and while she was dreading them leaving for the Solstice, she was looking forward to the few dates she had lined up with them before then, not to mention the surprise meet ups they were enjoying doing.

They had been home four days from the holiday trip and she had been surprised by Easton at work for lunch, Jack and Leo at her apartment bringing Italian, and Finn taking her to the night show at the museum.

And today, today was a trip to meet Leo at the coffee shop, before she went to the gallery to help with the boxing of a show that was heading to New York.

"Petra!" Officer Douritz greeted her as she came down the steps from her front door. "How are you? I didn't see you around over Thanksgiving. Did you go away?"

She nodded, a bright smile greeting her. "With friends. How was your holiday?"

"Friends? Where? I thought your friends usually came here to see you," he said, frowning.

"Oh, we rented a house a bit farther north since it was easier for all of us to converge and pay a cleaning bill," she laughed. "I hope your holiday went well. No baddies out on these streets keeping you from turkey and pumpkin pie?"

He brushed it off with a laugh. "It's all part of protecting and serving," he told her. "We miss out on holidays so that you can have a safe one." He paused and she thought he was going to let her pass, but then his gaze narrowed. "You noticed anything up in the neighborhood lately? I've been seeing a lot of unsavory-looking guys visiting your building."

"Oh! No... Um...a few co-workers have popped by recently, but not that I'm aware. Maybe someone new moved in?" she said slowly, though the comment rubbed her the wrong way.

"Uh uh...co-workers from the gallery or the shelter?" he asked. "If they're going to be visiting you at home, I could run background checks on them for you?"

"Both actually, one of them is the head Animal Control officer, though what are you implying?" she asked, her smile not reaching her eyes. "You think I don't have a good sense of people?"

"Of course not." He clearly realized he'd overstepped the mark because he cleared his throat. "I'm just looking out for my people. This is my beat, you know?"

"Of course!" she said with a nod. "Well, I'm going to be late. Have a great day, yeah? So much to do today! They are moving one of our biggest shows to the sister gallery in New York!"

"I'll wave if I pass by," he said with a broad grin, moving aside to let her pass. "Have a great day!" He stood there and waved, watching as she headed down the street. Because that wasn't creepy at all...

Chapter 35

"You guys on the way?"

Petra nodded though Jack couldn't see her. "Yes. Just had to get the crate all loaded up. You guys already there?"

"Just waiting on Carter and You. None of us are looking forward to seeing you off."

"Don't you mean me seeing you off?"

"Same thing."

"But when you guys get back, I'll be welcoming heroes."

"Yes, you will. Okay, see you at the airfield in a bit." He hung up as Carter slipped into the car.

"All set?"

"You should see the side-eye he's giving us," Carter laughed. "He hates the crate."

"Brutus baby, I promise...won't be long," she said to the back of the SUV as Carter pulled away from his curb and pulled out onto the street. "Jack said they're just waiting on us. And thanks for letting me watch him this week. We need bonding time."

"Just don't let him sleep in the bed, okay?" Carter laughed. "I don't want him picking up bad habits while only Mama's home."

Mama. She blushed and giggled. "Don't worry, Brutus, you can get the couch," she teased. "So you guys ready for this?" They had been prepping for this for weeks. After finding the information they had during the birthday, and then what else they figured out at Thanksgiving, then further when Finn and Emerson had visited one of the high priests...there was so much they had uncovered and Finn had been a monster trying to make sure that at the end of this, they won.

345

"Of course we are," he said easily. "We've been planning this for weeks. Finn's a smart dude. You don't have to worry about us, Petra."

"But I do worry, Carter." She grabbed his hand and squeezed. "You figure out about my orphanage yet? I know you were looking into it. I wanted to tell you, I asked my friends about stuff, see if they remembered anything that might help."

"Honestly, I couldn't find much about it online," he said. "Which leans toward it being Order. I'm still following the trail of shell companies, but I figured that it would be easier to just ask whichever Order accountants are still alive when the purge is over. Did your friends remember anything?"

The conversation came back to her quickly. They had been talking the night before, since all their plans for the holidays had fell through, too many life things happening at once that they couldn't collectively get away for longer than a few hours, so their meeting was to set up their Xmas Eve gift exchange virtually. It had turned into the four of them sitting around their living rooms with a bottle of wine each, courtesy of Vic, catching up and reminiscing. "They did. We talked about...remember when I mentioned what they did when we got our periods?"

"Yeah?"

"Well, Carlee remembered something that I think the rest of us blocked out. She said that one of the matrons collected phials of our first blood. We all remembered the flowers and the pomegranates, but Carlee, she remembered one of the matrons having each of us sit, and collecting our blood straight from the source, so to speak, and..." She swallowed, this was the thing that freaked her out most. "She remembered them saying that this would have to do because virgin blood wasn't an option for us."

346

"Virgin blood?" Carter frowned, not taking his eyes off the road. "I wonder what they meant about it not being an option. I'm guessing they were sending some kind of blood sacrifice."

"Well, that's the thing... After Carlee said it, Fi was all 'I remember that, and I remember one of the matrons saying that this class won't get offered.'" She frowned. "If we were Order, and I found you guys through him... Carter, it means my friends are, too, and we have all been cut off from Him."

"Maybe not," Carter shrugged with a quick glance across at her. "You said it was a decent place. And you've all done okay for yourselves, which is pretty good considering you're all orphans and the cost of living is prohibitive. You have your dream jobs and the others are studying. Maybe He's been watching over you all this time."

"It's possible," she agreed. "What will you do while in the Balkans?"

"Normally? Or what's going to go down this time?"

"This time. I mean I assume things aren't going to go like they normally go. Did Emerson get through to Damon? He wouldn't be there, right?"

"No, only the groups tend to go to these things," he said. "And yeah, things will be different this time. We don't want to run the risk of pissing off the big guy, so nothing is going to happen until after the ritual. He'll get what's His and then we'll get what's ours."

"The ritual for the Solstice?"

"Yeah. There's robes and chanting and ritual bleeding into the well. You know. A regular night out on the town." He smirked.

"With you guys it is. Tell me, do the Elders bleed, too, or just the sacrifice group?" she said, something tickling at her brain, something remembered just on the edges. "The thorns..." she said absently.

"Everyone does. But it's not a big palm slicing thing. We all use those little finger prick things. It only takes a drop." He glanced across at her again. "What about thorns?"

"Oh..." she said and shook herself. "The matrons, they would have roses around during the holidays...and eucalyptus and lavender grown in the greenhouse...and they always pricked themselves on the thorns. I remember that, and they would always say it was nothing."

"You think they were sacrificing somehow?" he asked. "Makes sense. Something else to ask them when we get to the bottom of this. The place is still running."

"Is it?" she offered. "Maybe I should contact them, see how things are."

"If they didn't tell you when you were there, I don't think they'll tell you anything now," he said, shaking his head. "Certainly not over the phone."

"No, well I wouldn't ask them, silly." She laughed. "Could you see it, 'hello, matron, this is Petra Franklin, tell me, do you all worship a sleeping god?' The scandal!"

"I doubt they even keep records there," he told her. "Just in case there's ever a raid or something."

"It's possible. I mean the only things we have from there are our school transcripts."

"They'll ship everything to HQ. I'll look into it while we're there," he promised.

She squeezed his hand. "Well good. I trust you to do what's best, and to ensure all of you that things are good. But promise me you will all come back. Knowing what happened to your fathers..."

"We're coming back." His voice had gone the howling cold of an Arctic winter. "They have no idea what's coming and we've done the groundwork. We're not going to be alone out there."

"No?" she asked hopefully.

"Not even close." He reached across and grabbed her hand, squeezing it reassuringly. "We're going to be fine," he promised her. "I know it's scary for you, but we know what we're doing. Besides, do you really think anything is going to stop us coming back for you? They can drag us through hell and we'll still come back."

She smiled at him with that. "And I the same with you all."

They turned the corner, the SUV ambling up the drive to the private airfield toward the hangar and the plane, and the six men standing just inside the open doors. Didn't they just paint a stunning picture. They pulled to a stop, and suddenly Leo was right there, opening her door.

"Evening, beautiful," he grinned, his face lighting up as he escorted her out of the car with a sturdy hand. "I wish we could take you with us."

Leaning in, her lips met his softly. "I don't. Not unless it was safe for all of us. Just come home to me, yes?"

Jack and Emerson were there then, pulling her into embraces, whispering pleasantries and words of solace to her. She kissed them each softly.

"Promise to stay safe," Jack said. "We still have access to the feeds in your apartment from the cameras."

She nodded. "Are they on record?" she teased. "Might have to give you guys a little show."

"As much as I'd love that, distractions could get us killed," Finn said with real regret in his eyes. "We'll let you know when it's all over and maybe then we could have a victory dance."

She nodded. She was kidding, of course, about the little show, but seeing her guys in survival mode, knowing what they were going into...she put on a brave face for them. "Please, just promise that you will take care of yourselves and each other. I mean coups don't happen every day, right?"

"Don't worry on us. They did raise seven brutal killers," Kendrix said to her.

"And some of us have military training," Carter reminded her.

"We've also got friends," Leo pointed out. "We're not going in alone. They don't know what's coming and Finn made us run all kinds of drills. It's going to be a fast and brutal strike and we'll be fine."

"I promise that we'll call you as soon as it's over," Finn said, pulling her into a hug and kissing her forehead. "You have my word."

She nodded and snuggled close to her love. "Of course, just remember to be my Devil," she looked to Carter, "my Plague," Leo, "my Stitches," Emerson, "my Neon," Rix, "my Ghost, " Jack, "my Goblin," and finally to Easton, "my Snake."

Rix went to her and pulled her into a hug, kissing her forehead. "Stay safe."

"Yeah. Don't make us have to spank you for being naughty when we get home," Leo whispered, hugging her tightly and making her laugh.

Carter was the last to break away and head for the plane. "Look after my boy," he told her, holding her close. "And let me know if he gives you any grief. He'll test boundaries. He's too smart not to."

"He won't be a bother. He's my sweet boy." She looked to Easton who seemed to hang back and smiled. "Be safe, love," she said softly and raised her hand at him.

"You, too." He blew her a kiss. "Love you!" he called back over his shoulder. And then they were gone.

She stood there, watching the plane taxi, then lift into the air, her heart leaving with them. She had only a few days to endure, to wait and hope they returned. Brutus' heavy bark pulled her from her reverie, and she sighed, making her way over to the car, to return to the city and life without her guys.

Chapter 36

Three days later, three days closer to the guys coming home to her, and Petra was all but crawling out of her skin. It felt like she had lost a limb, the depressing feeling of being alone, with the seven of them, turning her into a ghost haunting her own life once more. Brutus was there, and a welcome distraction, but it wasn't the same.

Though the dog was very in tune with her, cuddling, giving her kisses. He cared, and she loved that the giant moose of a dog was like a big baby for her. He was the only thing keeping her grounded...well, that and work.

Her boss at the gallery was not excited at first with her bringing Brutus to work with her, until the dog scared off a vagrant that had been defecating at their back door. After that, Brutus came back in to a new massive bed by the heater in her main office, and it was comical to see him dragging it everywhere she went. Cuz he was not leaving her alone, taking his charge very seriously, but he was going to be comfortable, damn it.

Bringing Brutus to the shelter had been a welcome thing once she told the director she was watching Carter's dog. Everyone was so in awe of the man (just like she was) that Brutus was being treated as a king. There, he was more relaxed and was a boon to the animals that had come in. His calm demeanor had put several of the sick and hurt animals at ease. She was going to have to talk to Carter about him doing therapy work at the shelter.

"He has really taken to those puppies," Wilma, the shelter director, said as they looked on to Brutus passed out on a massive bed in the office, seven six-week-old puppies asleep on him and between his massive paws. Petra took a picture of it, so she could show Carter later, and smiled at Wilma.

"He's the best. So good with the bunnies that came in, too. They felt safe with him."

"Much like you do with his human, yeah?"

Petra blushed. She had told Wilma that she and Carter had been seeing each other, after the last call they had had, officially, just after Halloween. They were all so enamored of him that Wilma had given her blessing immediately and deemed Brutus the shelter mascot, though he was going to get a new designation soon enough—shelter protector.

"Carter call yet?"

She shook her head. "He's in Europe, some town in the Balkans for a family thing. Time difference is a mess, but we have texted," she lied. "He's going to love this picture."

"I'm sure. You keep him, Petra, the man is a wonder, and so selfless."

He's also a brutal killer that has only parts of a conscience, she thought with a wry smile. Instead of voicing her thought, she said, "I am never giving this one up."

"When does he come home?"

"I think the 23rd? Something like that. I was told he would be home for Christmas." She grinned.

"Ah, young love. It will be nice to have you spend the holiday with him."

"I'm sorry I won't be able to do the Christmas eve overnight."

"Nonsense, Petra. You need to have a life, too. You have done it three years now. Jerry can take the night, he already said he wasn't going back to Wisconsin."

"Still, I feel..."

"Nothing!" Wilma waved it off.

"Hey, Wilma?" Taggert, the kennel tech, said as he came in. "Call on the scanner, we are getting intake in five."

"What is it?"

"Sounds like dogs, puppies."

Petra smiled. "Ooh, more friends for Brutus. I'll go and grab them, can you get the intake ready?"

Wilma and Taggert nodded. It was part of her job, and she was close to ending her night. This last intake, a walk home with Brutus and another day closer to seeing her seven.

The idea of her guys high on her mind, she walked out, clipboard in hand, into the loading dock area where the trucks came in for intake and frowned as she saw a truck there, lights on, but no driver.

"Hello? Wilma is ready for intake..." she said as she turned and gasped.

He'd been waiting behind the door, masked and dressed in dark clothing, but it wasn't one of her guys. She barely had a split second to react before he'd grabbed the back of her head and pressed a mask to her mouth and nose, flooding her airway with something harsh and chemical smelling.

Struggling, fear gripped her as she tried not to breathe whatever it was in. Who was this? Were they from the organization? Why was this happening?

No... No... Brutus...the guys... Fuck...

Darkness took her in moments.

Chapter 37

Kendrix sat with his father, schooling his face to the blank unreadable mask his father preferred. Three days at headquarters was too much time, and he was itching to get back to his lovely victim.

They had been met at the airfield by Stephan, which was unusual, and had put them all on alert. His father had been pleasant enough, speaking of the best energy harvest they have had, thanks to them, and that they were celebrating something huge at Solstice, which at this point was only hours away.

The Elders had congratulated them, citing that their group had made the impossible possible, that the expenditure of their time and their energy was creating more of a froth than they had ever seen, and that they knew it would take time, but it was all coming to fruition.

Emerson had thought they meant the whole killing as a focus they had pushed on all of them, and they were all very sure the Elders didn't know anything, especially when Elder Coupa asked them what they did with the girl they had been torturing for "His glory."

"The changeover will go into effect on the first of the year," Stephan said about the money he was funneling into Rix's practice from his own businesses. "I know you are doing well, son, but you could be doing better. This will ensure it, and give you more time away for worship and tribute. Numbers need to go up. We are expecting a thirty-five percent increase of devotionals for the new year's first quarter."

Rix nodded. Stephan wanted him to hire on a few other surgeons to his practice and to "go on sabbatical" so he could go elsewhere in the world, to train new groups in killing to make sure no one got caught. He now knew that was absolute horse shit.

"It is as you say, Father." He looked down. "We have a meeting with Finn and Elder Ponta, if you will excuse us?" He looked to Easton, who was still working through the information that Stephan wanted him to set up shop on the west coast, to work on his craft there. It was plain as day they wanted to split them up, to "maximize" favor for the God. But they knew what that was...

"Of course. We will see you at the celebration tonight." Stephan dismissed them from his sight, picking up his glass of port. As a unit they walked out of the room, in no rush, masks of indifference still on their faces.

It wasn't until after they got into the quiet hallway of their section of headquarters that Rix looked to Easton. "They are trying to split us up, which means they either know, or they are convinced that the deaths are what's making things better and they want more instances of it."

"Not here. My room," Easton said, clenching his jaw. He was right. Anyone could be watching.

He nodded, Easton was clearly shaken, and in truth, so was he. They made it to Easton's doors in moments, slipping through as he texted Finn and the others to meet them there. They needed to know.

"They are on their way here," he said as he threw himself on the large chair in Easton's living area.

Easton was shaking, but he didn't know if it was with fear or rage. "They know something," he said, pacing around as they waited for the others. "They must do."

"Either that or," he sighed. "They honestly think their idea of death only is working finally and they want us split up to maximize the carnage. Which would ultimately end in our deaths when someone slips up.

Thiry-five percent in the first quarter...that's..." He shook his head.

"And why? Why are they pushing for so many more members?" Easton shook his head. "That's dangerous as fuck. There's something else going on here. We're not the only one with plans."

He nodded his agreement as the door opened, Finn, Leo and Jack walking in. He knew they would come in waves as not to draw attention. None of them were dressed for the night, either.

"What's good?" Jack said with a frown. "Because I just spent a lunch with Elder Morkan and he just told me he wants me to start killing year round, and start at seven for the first quarter."

"Yeah, we just heard some bullshit from Stephan," Easton said. "They're actively recruiting, and they want to split us up. None of this makes any sense."

"It's weird." Leo frowned. "Why up the kills in the first quarter? They say the veil isn't thin enough early in the year so what's the point of killing more?"

Rix frowned. "Because they lied to us and the veils are the same all the year. They want us more entrenched in the death side of it, and I don't doubt Damon and his friends will be called in next, since they are the next closest devotionals group we could have." He shook his head. "Something is going on in the ranks that they are digging in like ticks to this death focus."

Emerson walked in with Carter then. "It's not just that. They are turning this into a full on death cult, and I think they are setting us up as Martyrs."

"Splitting us up so they can pick us off one by one." Finn shook his head. "This changes things."

"Well at least they made one fatal error," Carter said, sprawling in one of the chairs. "They told us before they announced it to everyone else. We can cut it off before it grows arms and legs."

"And let the guys know," Emerson added. "Forewarned is fore-armed."

Rix sneered. "So what do we do?"

Emerson's mouth opened to answer him when Carter's phone started buzzing. They all looked to him.

"It's...the shelter." Frowning, he answered the call. "Yeah, hi, Carter here." He went so still that he could have been made of stone and his face paled. "What? When? Did you report it?" He swallowed. "I'm not in the country right now. Can you keep him until I get back? I'll call when I have flight details."

"What happened?" Finn asked as Carter hung up.

"Petra's been taken." Carter's face was still white. "Video footage of the back porch shows some guy in a ski mask knocking her out and putting her in a van. They've reported it to the cops."

"Fuck!" Finn swore viciously.

"We have to go and find her!" Leo sprang to his feet. "What the fuck are you all doing still sitting here?"

"We haven't done what we came to do," Finn told him. "If we go now, they make the announcement and we get broken up."

Rix rolled his shoulders and stood up. "I don't know about you but I have had it with the bullshit around here. They want killers...let's give them killers." He grinned savagely. "Emerson, tell them what you found last night."

Emerson looked to them. "I didn't wanna say yet without hard evidence..."

"What is it?" Jack offered.

"Elders are expendable, or so the priests said when I questioned them last night. They are not the head of the organization. We, as the main devotional team, are. Elders were put in place to guide, but everything was supposed to be through us. It was around the same time they stopped with the dual devotionals that Elders went into power."

"Fuck." Jack shook his head. "So all Elders?"

"I think these fucks took it too far. Those from our father's time were largely in a guidance capacity. And all Elders before our fathers were once a devotional team."

"So we kill them all." Easton said it quietly, but his voice didn't waver. "Tonight."

"Put the word out," Finn said quietly. "Everyone we pre-gamed needs to know it's going down tonight."

"On it, boss." Leo was practically vibrating in his skin as he headed for the door. "The sooner we get this done, the sooner we can all go home."

"And fuck up the world of the asshole that took our lady," Rix said. "And if I find out that it was one of these fucks, I'm burning the world down."

Jack looked to Finn and then to Emerson. "Em, how will this affect the Solstice sacrifice? Is this even a thing?"

Emerson grinned. "It's a thing, but not tonight. It's got a window, as long as it happens before Midwinter, there will be no repercussions." He looked to Finn. "We kill everyone tonight that is a problem, get on that plane, save our girl, then go to the mountain house...and worship." He grinned. "And I have a better rite for that, too."

"I say we drain every last one of those fuckers into the well," Finn said. "Sacrifice made."

"Ooh, that's perfect," Jack said. "Though we need to come back to the better rite." He winked. "How long?"

Rix turned from his friends and rolled his shoulders once again, pulling his fingerless gloves from his pocket and slipped them on. The situation was tense but they did tense well. Was it going to be sloppy?

Probably. Were they going to have the element of surprise? Absolutely. They had already spent too much time there as it was, and they were only moderately closer to the answers they needed. The original plan was to keep a few of them alive for answers but answers weren't as important as their lady being safe.

So first they burned down the organization, and then they burned Philly to the ground to find her.

Chapter 38

Petra opened her eyes, blinking several times as the world around her came into focus. Head swimming, she came to consciousness with the events that put her into this position fresh in her mind. No bleary confusion. No, she knew that she had been taken, just not where or by whom.

And she knew her guys were a world away. If she was lucky Wilma would call Carter and they would come, but until then, she needed to be smart, listen and wait, because it was entirely possible she was going to have to try to save herself.

She wasn't a hero, but damn it, she wasn't a coward, either, and while her guys each had a specific set of skills, she didn't doubt for one fucking second she couldn't open someone's veins to get to safety...in fact, she was counting on hidden viciousness to deal with this, along with calculated patience.

Checking her surroundings, she realized she was in an apartment, untied, and completely clothed, and she was lying on a couch. Sitting up, she looked around, noticing the brown drapes drawn on the windows, the overlength pooling at the floor. The couch was brown, too, as was the chair, and the carpet a pristine tan. The place looked like an earth tone nightmare. No color, no life, all brown, all drab. Where the fuck was she?

As she heard a door open, she turned to see who it was.

"Oh good. You're awake." It was that fucking cop. "I brought you some breakfast and a couple of aspirin. I figured you might have a hangover." He set a paper bag and a bottle of aspirin down on the coffee table next to her.

"You... Why am I here, Officer Douritz?" she asked carefully, not planning on eating anything he left for her. Asshole drugged her already.

"Because I can't trust you to keep yourself safe," he said with a soft smile, as though it were the most obvious thing in the world. "You're hanging out with these dangerous guys. I'm keeping you here to keep you safe."

She frowned. "I'm sorry...dangerous guys?" She shook her head, wanting to know how much he did know. It wasn't going to matter, by the end of this this asshole would die by her hand or one of theirs, forfeiting his life the second he took her.

"I've looked into those guys hanging around you, sniffing after you like street dogs. One of them was a suspect in a double murder." He shook his head. "You're my girl, Petra. I can't let you get hurt by those animals."

"I'm sorry, I'm your what?" she asked and frowned. This was what she got for being friendly. Truly no good deed went unpunished. "Officer Douritz, I don't even know your first fucking name, and let's not even forget you're like what, ten, fifteen years older than me?" She didn't mind older men but this was fucking ridiculous. "This isn't fucking happening. You can't just abscond with someone."

"Don't be like that," he said, frowning. "You know that's not how it is with us." She opened her mouth to protest and he loomed over her. "Shut up and eat your breakfast, bitch." When she flinched, he straightened up with that sickly sweet smile again. "I got your favorite coffee."

Jesus fucking Christ, split personalities ahoy. The Petra she was before her guys would have flinched at the action, but it just fucking annoyed her now. This guy thought because he was bigger than her he was imposing? As if. She got chased around the woods by Kendrix and he was twice the size of this asshole, *and* he had a massive fucking knife.

"Why would I trust anything you gave me? Honestly. And what do you intend to do with me? I will be missed, Officer Douritz, as I'm sure you will be, too, considering your job," she hedged. "So, what's your end game here, just kidnap me from my life and what?"

"Because I love you." His face was starting to darken with anger and before she knew it was coming, he slapped her hard enough to send her sprawling on the sofa. "Now eat your fucking breakfast. And don't bother trying to escape. Everything is locked until you learn to be a good girl."

Getting off the ground, she felt everything in her snap. "Oh, fuck this. You seem to think I'm this *good* girl...well, joke's on you, asshole, I only play one on TV! And if you checked into my guys then you know that they are not the people with whom to fuck. They will find me, and when they do there won't be enough left of you for them to ID." Her gaze on him was unwavering. She was not going to be this man's anything, and if he tried to touch her again she would make him very fucking sorry he was alive. "Touch me again, *Officer* Douritz," she sneered, exaggerating his designation. "I fucking dare you."

She'd underestimated his speed and dexterity. She was on her front with her arm twisted behind her and the cold steel of handcuffs closing around her wrist before she could blink. "If that's how you want to play it," he told her, wrenching her other arm behind her back and cuffing it to the first one. "I tried to make it easy on you, but if you're going to be silly about it, you'll soon learn." Leaving her squirming on the floor, he attached a chain to the handcuffs and the other end he padlocked to a radiator bolted to the wall, dragging her so that she was close enough. "And you can just fucking go hungry. I'll be home in two hours."

"Fucking asshole!" she spit at him. Oh, she was going to feed him his fucking eyes.

Chapter 39

Emerson growled as he paced the cabin of his Learjet, seething with rage. Normally the one to keep the clearest head, right now the high from their insurrection in the Balkans was waning, the anticipation of finding the dead man that put hands on their girl starting to ramp up.

"Em, calm down and go get fucking changed. You're still fucking covered in blood and getting off the plane in the States is going to cause a problem," Jack offered.

"I'll get changed once we have a fucking plan. Car? East? You guys find anything yet?"

"Maybe." Carter was frowning at his screen. "There's nothing else from the cameras around the shelter, but this one guy has been casing her building a couple of times a day for weeks now. I never noticed the pattern at first because he's a cop, so I figured it was just his beat, but he's been doing walk-bys out of uniform, too."

"He's been hanging around the gallery, too." Easton turned his screen so Carter could confirm it was the same guy.

"He's a cop?" Finn crowded in to look over their shoulders at the screens.

"Maybe." Carter shrugged. "The uniform looks legit, but it could be a fake. I know a couple of guys at that precinct that I've worked with before. I'll reach out and see if any of them can identify him."

"Don't tell them why, though," Finn cautioned and Carter rolled his eyes.

"I'm not a fucking idiot," he replied. "I'll let you know when I get a response."

"Baby steps," Jack said. "Now what?"

Rix sneered from his spot across from them. "I think we need to talk about what's going to happen when we catch this asshole."

Emerson nodded. They needed this handled so they could know she was out of any danger. At first they had thought the organization was involved but they learned quickly that wasn't the case. Now, with all the insurrection Elders dead, Stephan included, the priests were in charge in the Balkans, and they had counseled handling this business quickly, because He Who Sleeps would require an audience.

If they didn't get her back unspoiled the world was going to burn, and screw Him and his sleepy ass.

"We kill him. I would say slowly but..." Emerson offered his brother.

"Anyone else think he's in for it with our girl?" Jack asked. "She's no shrinking violet."

"He's going to die, but we need to plan this carefully," Finn said. "If he is a cop, we can't just disappear him. Not without bringing down some serious heat. This needs to be flawless. No evidence. No accidental appearances on private cameras. No witnesses. Yes, this is Petra and we're all in primal rage mode, but I need you all to park your feelings and get your heads in the game until we have her in hand and him in a deep dark hole somewhere."

"He gets sacrificed," Emerson said with clarity. "Taking what's ours, what's *His*..." He shot a meaningful look at all of them. "We do this like we do a devotional."

Jack nodded. "Except we do it as a team."

"And when we take him, we take him quickly, quietly and invisibly," Finn said. "Even if his cop buddies think he's a douchebag, they're going to be all over this with a fine-tooth comb."

"He is a cop," Carter confirmed. "Just had a response. It's an Officer John Douritz. I'll start looking for an address."

"Emerson, touchdown in twenty," they heard as his pilot, another member of The Order and one of his oldest friends, called through the doorway. "Providing we are still going to the airfield." He knew exactly what was going on, and was all in with helping get them there. "Don't need to do some helo shit?"

"I think the only one of us rated for that is Carter," he said dryly. "Yes, take us to the airfield."

"Carter might be the only one rated but I would chance it," Rix said.

"No. We need to plan this," Finn said firmly. "No half-assing. We find out where he lives. We do recon. Then we go in and smoke him."

"Obviously, Finn..." he looked at their leader, seeing the worry and fear. "Airfield, Mark, no missteps."

"You got it, boss."

Jack sighed. "Anyone have eyes on her apartment? Perhaps we need to talk to the friends. They do know about us," he offered. "Though don't let Em call, lord knows what's coming out of his mouth." He frowned. "We should have tagged her. I knew we should have tagged her."

"None of us saw this coming," Carter said quietly. "There's no point beating ourselves up about it now."

"I'm watching her apartment and there's been no sign of movement since she disappeared," Easton told them. "I've been over all the footage."

"I don't think we should bring her friends in," Leo spoke up for the first time. "It's just more people who know about what's going down and will need an explanation when the guy disappears. She was definitely taken. There's no need for them to know about it."

Jack nodded. "Just trying to be proactive."

Emerson could feel how raw they all were, but he also knew they would be ready, and would get her back and everything would be...well, it would be over. He wasn't sure what they would be getting back, but Jack was right, she was a handful and there would be no way she would be there without a fight and causing this asshole one hell of a problem. Thank god Rix taught her how to use a knife. He just hoped she knew they were coming for her.

"Found it," Carter said and Emerson knew it was the address.

"Well then, let's figure this shit out, and go get our girl, yeah?" Jack said. "Em? Go get changed, yeah?"

Nodding as he felt the plane start its full descent, he walked into the back cabin. Good thing they brought their masks with them, because he had a feeling they would need them.

Chapter 40

The clock on the wall announced another hour down, and with each hour she was there, alone, she was seething, and of course plotting. Just thirty-two hours in this house, stuck to the radiator, and the asshole had left her a jar, a bottle of water and another sandwich of which she wasn't eating. She had drank the water and, because she didn't fucking care, used the jar for the bursting bladder she had. If nothing else, she could use it as a weapon if needed.

But now, she was at the point where she was hoping her guys were on their way. She wasn't stupid, they were in Europe, and if they knew, and something inside her felt they did, it was going to be a while 'til they found her. She was going to have to be savvy, and smart, because while she was hoping on her guys, she was possibly going to have to figure out how to save herself.

So...thirty-two hours. If it worked out as the past thirty-two hours, Officer Douritz would be back soon. And she was going to have to deal with shit. He had been more pissed off the last time he showed up, which was about four hours ago, and oddly she still didn't know his first fucking name.

Hearing the sound of the lock, she frowned. Asshole was early.

He came in with a broad smile on his lips, but it quickly fell when he saw the untouched sandwich still lying there and storm clouds gathered in his eyes. "You didn't eat." He sighed, shaking his head. "Do you want an IV and a feeding tube? Because that's where you're heading with this."

"No. If you want me to eat, bring me something that is packaged," she offered. "Sorry, Officer Douritz, but I'm not going to trust what you give me since you kidnapped me. I mean honestly, where is the lie?"

"I wouldn't hurt you." He was getting angry again. "I only drugged you to make sure you wouldn't hurt yourself on the way here. Now that you're safe, you need to eat!"

"I will. If you bring me packaged food," she countered. "And yes, I'm actually hungry, but Officer, you have to kinda see. If you want me smart, I'm being smart." The reason was sound. "So don't get mad at me for telling the truth and keeping myself safe."

"On this, you're just being petty," he snapped. "I brought you here to save you and you're just talking yourself in circles. Eat the fucking sandwich or I'll make you eat it."

"So this is how you treat someone you love?" She shook her head. "Or is it that you think If I eat that sandwich I'll accept that love? I'm not stupid, Officer. You want me to be good, I want packaged food. Threatening me isn't going to endear me to you, either." She went on. "You clearly have all the power here, stalking me and bringing me here. Allow me this then? Something packaged. I don't give a shit if it's a fucking protein bar, you want me to trust you?"

"I don't fucking care if you trust me," he replied bluntly. "I just want you to obey me. And if you won't do that of your own free will, then I will beat obedience into you. You will serve me as a wife should serve her husband."

"In what year?" she asked. "Is this 1950? Or Victorian England?" she asked. "I need to know what I'm supposed to be doing. And dude...really, why me? I mean you're decently attractive," not a lie, "why me?"

"We have a connection," he replied, rolling his eyes as though she were stupid. "And there's no point giving you the rules right now since you can't even follow the simplest of basic fucking instructions. Really, Petra."

He shook his head, disappointment in every line of his face. "I thought you were smarter than this." He stalked away, heading toward his bedroom where, if the previous night was anything to go by, he'd change into street clothes and then go and crack a beer and make himself some food.

Asshole wasn't even on this planet, was he? She looked to the bologna sandwich and sneered, she didn't tell him she had pulled the meat out of it, and had it wrapped around her hand, getting her hand greasy, to help her slip that cuff off when she needed it. He also didn't have to know about the straight pin she found under the radiator, which she was planning to stab into his eye when given the chance.

But right now, she had to wait...and watch...and be patient.

Looking up to the ceiling, the open beams done in a rich chocolate brown, dusty but well kept. She could smell the scents of oil soap. She could see the place was well taken care of, but not completely. He had specific things...like the floor was swept and not sticky but it wasn't gleaming. And the walls were clear but the paint wasn't fresh. The furniture was clean but older, and the kitchen wasn't updated but there was the scent of cleaners.

She needed to figure this all out. He was selectively proud it seemed, and she needed to be able to capitalize on this.

Night had fallen while he was showering and changing and the shadows were creeping across the floor. He hadn't left the light on for her when he came through on his way to the kitchen, all freshly washed and comfortable, and she hated him all the more for it, but it meant that her eyes were adjusted to the gloom well enough to see the face popping up at the window and ducking down again. It had looked an awful lot like Leo.

Were they here? Hoped surged in her chest as she stared at the dark space, hoping he'd give her some sort of sign. She only heard the clicking of the lock at the front door because she was on high alert, but it sent her heart racing. It had to be them. No one else would be breaking into a cop's house in the night.

Slipping her wrist a little in the cuff she felt the give go, and slowly pulled free, changing her seat, so whatever was going to happen, she would be ready for. Free of the metal, she rolled the straight pin into her hand, and pulled the jar he had left her closer, as she was not discounting any of her possible weapons.

The asshole was in the kitchen, the water on as he muttered to himself. He didn't hear the door slide open, nor did he see the two bodies that melted into the shadows of the room. But she did. The gleam of scales, and the bone white of the ghost she knew so well.

Swallowing, she went on red alert, ready for whatever was going to happen.

More shadows streamed in behind them, heading to other parts of the house. She could have told them there was no one else around, but she didn't dare make a sound. Besides, knowing them they'd have checked anyway. They were thorough, her men. They didn't leave a threat at their backs if they could help it.

Leo slipped into the room and came to her side, eyes anxiously checking her over in the near dark to make sure she wasn't injured. His eyes narrowed at the chain and if he hadn't looked murderous before, he certainly did now. He made a hand gesture to the other two and they crept toward the kitchen where their unsuspecting victim was sizzling something on the stove.

Gods, she was glad to see them. She wanted to jump into his arms and fall apart, but there would be time for that later. Right now, she was pissed.

Pulling both her wrists up, she showed him she was free and then pointed to the sandwich and then shook her head, letting him know she had not eaten anything. And she was slightly weak, but something else was happening inside her, a thrumming, as adrenaline started. They would not let what happened to her go unpunished.

Jack in his Goblin mask came into view and she watched as Carter and Emerson, his mask not lit, stood in the shadows close to her. Which meant that Easton and Rix were with that asshole, but where was her Devil?

He stepped out of the gloom with a finger to his Devil mouth and then offered her his hand, helping her to rise. She did, wobbly as she had spent a lot of time on her ass, and smiled to herself as Leo was right behind her, holding her steady. Devil's fingers went to her cheek, where she knew the bruise bloomed from where he hit her. The rigid stance of her Devil told her so much, but she had her own ideas.

"You okay?" Jack murmured to her. She nodded. "We need to get you out."

"No," she said, voice barely a whisper, but they heard her. "I am staying and I'm going to scare the shit outta this asshole."

She looked beyond, seeing Easton and Rix just outside the bright glow of the kitchen lights, and rolled her shoulders before she walked forward, and into the light. She stood there, quiet, behind the asshole cop, and got ready for war.

"Officer Douritz," she said softly, knowing the asshole would turn around when he heard her voice.

"You little bitch." He turned the burner off and spun toward her, ready to swing.

She ducked and stepped back, knowing her guys were there, behind her, waiting to see what she would do.

"Wonderful thing to say to the woman you wanna wife up," she said and rolled her eyes, just out of his reach. "Ah ah... Don't take another step, shit bag. I got out of your shitty cuffs, you don't think I wouldn't have a plan..." Standing her ground, she felt the slide of something heavy into her back pocket. So much for the pin idea, she thought as she put her arm behind her back and gripped the handle of the knife. Rix.

"Now we are going to have a discussion about how to treat women...though I don't know why I'm going to bother, you won't last the hour..." And they would see to that.

And then it all went to shit. Apparently, the fucker had a concealed holster in the small of his back because one second he was holding a spatula, the next he had a gun pointed at her face. "You're only wife-material when you've learned your place," he sneered, "and I haven't even begun to start beating that into you."

She smiled and shook her head. "My place is anywhere I wanna be," she said defiantly, "with my Seven." She felt them step forward, and heard the cock of a gun, though she didn't know who was holding it. "Not with anyone else. And you done fucked up."

"Put the gun down," Devil said, his voice deathly quiet and the cop swung the gun toward him, only for Leo to casually snatch it him from his hand in a move Petra had only seen in movies.

Officer Douritz put his hands up, backing toward the stove as he searched for a way out of the situation, but there were too many of them. "I didn't know you were this much of a whore," he spat at her.

"I'm happy to surprise you," she said with a smile. "My guys are...well, a bit pissed you had the audacity to even consider this...touching what's theirs." She felt Emerson wrap his arms around her waist and pull her to him, holding her close, the brightness of his mask hitting at the corner of her eye. "And I owe you for that slap..."

Douritz reached for the pan behind him and, had he been faster, the cast iron would have made a formidable weapon. But Carter was faster and laid him out cold with a single punch that Douritz didn't even see coming.

"String him up," Devil said. "I left the rope and the buckets by the back door."

"You ready to kill your first man?" Carter asked her quietly as the others began to move, dragging Douritz into the living room and preparing to string him upside down from the beam.

Was she? Not remotely. "Honestly? I don't know. Fucker deserves everything he gets, and he needs to pay for what he did."

Emerson walked up behind her. "Are you okay?"

She nodded. "Physically a little malnourished, but if you're worrying about my mental health, I'm peaches, baby."

The beams groaned, sending dust sifting down over the three men hauling Douritz up by his feet. He woke up just as his hips were leaving the ground and began to thrash about like a fish caught on a line.

"Don't bother," Leo told him harshly. "This is inevitable. Accept your fate."

"Fuck all of you!" Douritz screamed, his face going beetroot with his efforts.

"So, love? You going to take the final step?" she heard Rix say as they walked over to where the asshole was strung up. "Not going to lie, seeing you slice his throat is going to get me super hot."

She giggled at her ghost-faced lover. "Is it the blood or is it me?"

"Both. You know that."

She looked to Emerson who said, "If you don't, it doesn't change anything. You still belong to us."

"And we're more than happy to do it for you," Leo told her. "You don't even have to watch. I can take you out to the car and we'll sit out there while we wait for the others to clean up."

Sit there? She giggled. She knew damn well Leo would be on her and keeping her focused on him and the things he was doing to her. And it wasn't that she didn't want it, she did, but this...this was important, and she wanted her guys to know she was all in with them. Killing a predator wasn't a problem.

"We need to do this," she said instead. "I need to do this with you."

"One more step," Rix said, clearly enjoying this.

"Don't worry, love, this whole things won't be in vain."

Carter stepped up behind Douritz and held him still, yanking his head back so that his throat was exposed while the cop screamed and thrashed.

"Do it quickly," Finn advised her softly. "And you'll need to press harder than you think you will. No hesitation. You've got this." He squeezed her shoulder and stepped back.

She walked forward, Rix behind her now, hand on her stomach, leaning down to her. "Be a good girl, baby...send this fucker to hell."

She stepped away from him, brandishing the knife her insane lover had given her. "See, Douritz, you fucked up picking me for your little fantasy...bringing me to this hell hole, stalking me... The only ones allowed to stalk me are my Seven." She went to him and smiled at him. "And you won't get a second chance to do it right." She looked to Finn. "Is this for Him?" she asked of the God. "And is there anything I need to do to make this a devotion?"

"No, we'll do that part when we take the blood to the well," Finn told her. "You just do what you need to."

She nodded. "Of course, my Devil." A step, and she heard the asshole whimper, realizing he was seriously in deep shit, and struck, putting more that she probably should have behind the slice. Flesh and muscle parted, Blood started to fall in a curtain as the gurgle of air left the body. It went slack, and she panted, watching the life fall, the light die in his eyes.

"Such a good girl," she heard as Rix gathered the knife from her hand and someone pulled her into a kiss.

"Let her watch," Carter said to whoever it was. "This is important."

The blood fell into a bucket, drained quickly, the cut she made more than sufficient for the task. "Very good control," she heard Rix murmur from her left. "Couldn't have taught you better myself."

Eyes still on the macabre scene, she said, "How did you guys find me?"

"We tracked him," Carter said, gesturing to the body, which had stopped twitching now and the arterial spray had slowed into a steady stream. "We caught him scouting your apartment a few times and connected the dots."

"I never expected this. He was always nice, talking to me, and others on my block. How are we going to get away with this? He's a fucking Philly cop for fuck's sake."

"Leave it to us," Finn soothed her. "We have a plan. You head out with Rix and Leo and the rest of us will clean up this mess." He looked at Leo. "Make sure she eats and drinks and if she needs medical attention, you know who to call."

"Yes, boss." Leo saluted and put an arm around her shoulders, guiding her away from the body. "Let's get you out of this shit hole."

Chapter 41

Settling into the large couch in the living room, Petra looked at the room with new eyes. Last time she was there, she was a victim and they were her psychos. Last time she was there, she was a vessel for His energy, a sacrifice for his glory.

Nothing had changed, of course, aside from the fact that she was theirs now, fully, they were hers, accepted and more. And instead of standing there, waiting for their attentions, she was settled between two of her men, waiting on the others to tell her what had been going on.

The whole unpleasantness of the insane cop had been over two days now. Leo and Rix has gotten her through the first six hours, taking her from that shit hole in South Philly to her apartment, then to Wilma to get Brutus. Of course, she had asked a lot of questions.

"Petra...honestly, what happened?"

She sighed and shook her head. She couldn't tell her the truth, but a semblance of it. "Carter, you know his job...well, he pissed off the wrong people. Closed the wrong fighting ring..."

"Say no more! I figured it was something like that. You all right? I mean physically, mentally?"

She nodded. "Carter and his friends got there in time."

"Daresay whoever it was is not with us anymore?"

"No...they have slipped this mortal coil..." she answered.

"Good. When my husband was alive, these situations were weekly. Once he passed my life got quiet but...I never forgot that madness. Carter isn't one of the bad guys, though...it will be okay."

They had made it to the devotional house in the mountains shortly after ten AM, Rix and Leo feeding her, and then passing out with her in the bedroom she normally slept in, citing keeping her safe. It wasn't a problem for her, having missed her guys, though she did miss their attentions, she had been exhausted.

The others had shown up a few hours later, smelling of accelerant, dirty and exhausted themselves. They had eaten, and now, they were all sitting in the living room together, and she was keen to learn about what had been going on.

"Now that you are safe," Emerson said as she snuggled into him. "And we aren't completely losing our minds trying to get back to you, things can progress."

"We need to go back to the Balkans," Finn said. "After we've finished up here, I mean. We need to go back and finish what we started. I don't entirely trust the priests to run the place."

"People must have questions," Carter agreed.

"Well what happened?" she asked and Jack took up the story, what drove them to up their timetable, her, and the fact that the people in charge were making moves, big moves that could destroy the organization forever.

She listened as he recounted their actions, swift and decisive, the whole insurrection taking all of an hour. Their allies, friends from school and those that felt things were off, and there were many, helped and aside from the assholes on the puppet council, was bloodless.

"Finn went to the priests then, who had been waiting in the rectory, and told them we needed to save you. They agreed, and we left, saved the day, and here we are."

She smiled.

"Now...are you okay? I mean really okay?" Emerson asked. "No... I know you feel okay but killing someone is life changing."

"I'm okay. I have had rest, and food, and while I know this is going to be something I'm going to have to face, that's for later." She looked to them. "And I know you guys will be there for me."

"One thing that might come in handy..." Easton looked a bit uncomfortable. "I spoke to the priests when we arrived and asked for some...spiritual guidance. Turns out that counselling and therapy is actually in their remit, so...you know...if you want help, it's there. They said they'd be happy to work with me virtually."

She smiled at her sad lover. "That sounds great actually. I mean it won't be like we have to hide anything from them," she offered. "We could go together, when you're ready. So, what else?"

"Well, we did a bunch while there. Carter and I went to the priests about your orphanage, and to get a clear look at what that whole thing about the women and the sisters were," Emerson said to her.

"What did you find out?"

"A lot, actually. My dad's journal was right, but the priests have said several of the communes had gone dark a while back, though they still maintain that He was getting devotions from his Feminine."

"We thought that maybe once we'd finished up over there, we could come back here and actually go and speak to people at the orphanage," Carter said. "If any of the original staff are around, they could tell us why they went dark."

"Why go back before that?"

Rix looked at her. "The priests want to meet you...and see what bloodline, if any, you belong to."

"They can do that?"

383

Emerson nodded. "Apparently."

"So I'm coming with you?"

"You didn't think we would leave you behind after what just happened, did you?" Leo looked at her like she'd gone crazy.

"I don't know. I mean it's very possible you could split up and some go and some stay with me and Niobe and Brutus." She smiled. "They get to come, too, right?"

"Niobe can't fly," Easton said regretfully. "But her sitter will stay with her while we're not here."

"And Brutus can definitely come," Carter agreed. "I'm not sure he'd forgive either of us if we left him alone again."

Pouting at Easton, she said. "But I get to spend quality time with her when we come back, right? Promise?"

"You have my word," he told her and then smiled brightly. "Besides, she has a really long lifespan. You'll literally have decades to spend with us when this is all over."

"Enough talk of pets," Finn said with a gentle but tired smile. "Let's get this sacrifice out of the way and try and have an early night. Emerson booked the jet for tomorrow morning. The sooner we get there, the sooner we can come back home again."

"Okay... I mean that sounds good. I'll go get ready for bed."

"Bed nothing. Baby girl, this is your devotional," Rix offered. "This isn't happening without you."

"Oh..." She brightened. "I get to come."

"You get to *offer*," Emerson said. "As our devotional, you have the honor of offering to He Who Sleeps. If you are part of the organization, then you need to know how to do this."

"I'll go grab the bucket," Leo offered. "I'll see the rest of you down there."

"Thanks, Leo." Finn rose to his feet and she watched him worriedly. He looked exhausted, they all did. Planning the coup and all the international travel with the accompanying jetlag, plus the effort required to kill a man and cover it up...it was no wonder they were all tired. Maybe the God would give them all a bit of an energy boost to get through the next few days.

The trip down to the well was quick, and she made it a point to walk with Finn, holding his hand. She missed her Devil, missed them all, and she needed to reconnect. "I'm a little nervous about this," she said as they made it to the stairs. "What if it isn't accepted? What if..." *I'm not accepted*? She didn't finish the thought with words, leaving it to hang in the air.

"He sent you to us." Finn looked down at her in amusement. "Why on earth wouldn't he accept you when He was the one that gave you to us?"

"I don't know..." She fidgeted. "I was so worried before...that I would never see you again," she offered. "Now that I'm here, I'm just worried."

"Well stop," he said gently. "This is meant to be. You were born into The Order, I think, and you were brought back to us. We're not leaving you again. Besides, it sounds like you've already made offerings of your first blood."

"And it's not like He doesn't already know your energy," Carter pointed out from behind them. "We've been feeding it to Him for three years."

She nodded. "Still kinda...scary."

"Nonsense," Rix said as he walked by and pinched her ass with a wink. "Get to it so we can all turn in."

She looked to Finn. "Okay, how do we do this?"

"Same as we did when you watched after Black Night," he told her. "Except this time instead of us cutting ourselves, you can dump what's in the bucket in there."

"Okay..."

They set up, them around the perimeter, this time with her at the center. Words were spoken, and she felt the tickle of power at her navel, sighing as it went from a tickle to a blanket, and further, making her body tingle.

"For you," she heard Finn say, and she stepped forward and tipped the blood into the well.

"For you," she whispered.

Much as it had the morning after Halloween, tendrils of smoky light began curling up out of the well, reaching toward her. "It's okay," Finn said, steadying her as she automatically backed away. "Let it touch you."

Steeling herself she stood there, waiting. The tingle of magic grew, and as the smoke touched her it turned electric, the air charged around her as if her hair would stand on end from the static. But no static came. The caress of power was innate, and she felt it inside, as well as out, a small moan slipping from her lips as her body thrummed with energy and needed release.

"Just let it roll through you," Finn said gently. "Don't fight it. It's a gift." Tendrils of light started reaching out to the men as well and Finn smiled as he reached out a hand to the one nearest him, letting it curl through him.

"I feel so much better," Carter groaned quietly from behind her. "I didn't realize how tired I was."

"It tingles..." She gasped. "In odd places..."

"Don't worry, love, we will help with that later," she heard Jack murmur.

Soon the space was filled with tendrils that glittered and pulsed with unearthly light and she was sighing, allowing it to suffuse her. And then she felt it, a heartbeat, deep and thrumming, off from a human's, a weird cadence, not a falter but a rhythm that had its own origins.

"I....can you feel that? Is that Him?"

"Yes, it is," Finn confirmed. "He's pleased."

"He should be after all the blood He's had this week," Leo said drily and amusement tingled through them all.

"Joy," Carter realized aloud at the same moment they all felt it. "He's gifting us joy. That's a new one."

"It's a new era," Finn reminded him.

She laughed, feeling a tear run down her face as she did. Joy... Joy never felt this good, this pure. She looked to her guys, and smiled at each one. The tendrils receded from them then, feeling came to her, wrapping her in a thick embrace. She felt the pressure around her heavy but not at all unpleasant, before it pulled back and slithered back into the well.

Falling to her knees, she let the tears fall, happiness and the feeling of being so small in the face of something so awesome coursing through her.

"Kind of overwhelming your first time, huh?" Leo said, coming across to her to help her up.

"I didn't get joy," Easton blurted out. "He spoke to me. I didn't get joy."

"What?" Finn turned to look at him but Carter was closer. "What did He give you instead?"

"I don't know how to explain it." He just stood there, tears pouring down his face as he struggled to find the words. "It just...it doesn't hurt anymore," he stuttered out. "The memories...they don't suck me in. I can... I can..." He broke off again and Carter hugged him, looking over his head at her and the others.

"I think what he's trying to say is that the God has taken the power of his memories to help him heal," he explained, with a meaningful look at her.

She crossed to him and Carter, unsure of what was to happen, how to even approach her sweet Easton, but she wouldn't let him be there alone. He needed to know she was there, all in, for everything.

"He told me that what stops him from engaging in physical contact is the flashbacks," Carter explained to her quietly. "The moment someone touches him, he gets sucked into the bad memories and he doesn't know how to get out of it. If that's not happening anymore..."

The conclusion was obvious. He'd be able to initiate actual physical contact with her. Even though he still needed to work through therapy to deal with his trauma-trained behaviors, his memories would no longer have the power to come between them.

Biting her bottom lip. she nodded and stepped forward. "East..." she said softly, reaching for him. If they could be together...if they could...

"I'm a bit overwhelmed," he sobbed and then burst out laughing because obviously.

She followed suit, pulling him to her and hugged him tight. He didn't stiffen, and she let out a heavy breath as she laughed with him. Looking up to her guys they were all smiling, in awe, and looking hopeful.

"A true blessing," Finn congratulated. "We should go and celebrate."

Chapter 42

Petra stepped foot through the doorway of the main building of the Balkan compound with fresh eyes, and hope suffusing her. "This place is fucking massive."

Emerson nodded from her left. "This is where most things happen...though apparently it's not our original compound and temple."

"And where is that?"

"No idea. Maybe the priests will finally give that info up." He smirked.

The foyer of the building was huge, two large stairways on either side of the room leading to a second floor and then another two, leading to a third. Five men walked from the left into the main foyer.

"And you return with precious cargo," one of the guys said and went to Finn, shaking his hand. "The well is frothing, and the priests are pleased." He looked to her. "Welcome, Devotion." He bowed his head.

"This is Damon," Emerson said to her. "He's building your house."

"Oh... Hi. Pleasure."

"It is. You are a revelation," he offered and looked to Finn. "Everything is cool, but we have a problem...found something."

Finn sighed. "Why am I not surprised? I have a horrible feeling we'll be finding messes left by those fuckwits for years to come." He shook his head. "What did you find?"

"A cache of information, books the priests didn't even know about," Damon started, "and Vincent found accounts, tons of them. But the biggest thing? We found what amounts to a fucking harem."

"I'm sorry, what?" Emerson said. "A harem? Of women? Here?"

Damon nodded. "Youngest about fifteen."

Petra looked to them, eyes wide. "I'm sorry, a fifteen-year-old girl?"

"Among others, yes."

"What the fuck?" Easton had gone pale and Carter squeezed his shoulder. "When were they found?" Finn demanded. "Do they need medical assistance? Were they without food and water?"

"About six hours after you left. Bradley did some of his drone magic, and noticed lights coming from a section of the older compound area that was supposedly not in use. We took a team down, found four rooms of women, well fed and pissed off as hell." He grinned. "Abernathy went in, checked who would let him. They are in good health, and the oldest, a woman named Hadley, wants answers. I told her what I could, and moved them all to the east wing."

"How many women, total?" she asked.

"Forty-seven. And two are pregnant."

"What the fuck?" This time it was Carter who swore. "Do we know which Elders are responsible?"

"It doesn't really matter." Finn stepped in before Damon had to answer. "For there to be that many, they all had to know about it. Especially if they've been bringing them in from the women's compounds."

"Does this mean we have to clean house at the women's compound, too?" Leo asked uneasily, none of them really looking forward to skinning a bunch of old ladies alive. "If they were collaborating?"

"Only one way to find out," Finn said grimly. "Lead the way, Damon."

Petra took Finn's hand as they walked and squeezed. "We will figure this out."

Damon walked them to the east wing, and then to the middle rooms, and knocked. "Hadley? It's Damon. New management is here."

The door opened, a woman around her age looked them over and then settled on her, eyes wide.

"She's not here for..."

She shook her head. "No...oh no... I'm here of my own free will with my guys," she said. "I'm Petra."

"Come on in," she said after a few moments, seemingly believing her.

The room itself had several older women there, and the two pregnant woman, as well as two younger looking girls. All looked wary, and several also looked pissed off.

"Are your needs being met?" Petra asked them.

"Damon and his team have been most agreeable," one of the women said. She had an English accent. "It's true then? You are the lot that murdered those assholes?"

"My guys did." She introduced them all to her Seven.

"You are a devotion," one of the women said. "I thought that had been done away with."

"You know about devotions?" Carter glanced at Finn, who shrugged.

"Look, as you've probably figured out by now, the whole male branch of The Order has been led in a bit of a different direction the last forty years, give or take," Finn said. "We're trying to put that right, thanks to He Who Sleeps sending us our Petra here, but you know how the priests like to talk in circles and frankly our boy Emerson has a lifetime of texts to try and wade through, so we're pretty much clueless.

"Why don't you tell us how you ended up here and what you think has happened, and we'll work from there?"

Hadley sighed. "Told you no one knew." She shook her head. "Let me guess, you didn't know about her, didn't know about the female side of the organization?"

They nodded in unison. "Well then, let's sit and talk, yeah? Because this is going to blow your mind."

"Don't get all dramatic, Hadley," the English woman said. "Let me, since Hadley is all drama and anger." She smiled. "Ardith, by the way, that's my name. So each of us were brought here, against our will, after our safehouses had been cleansed, and burned. Between us, we all came from seven houses, collectively. Devonshire," she pointed at herself, "as well as four others, and then there was San Francisco, Maine, Manitoba, Temecula, the Blue Ridge Mountains and some god forsaken swamp in Louisiana. We were brought here because we were all thoroughbreds." She snorted. "Bloodlines."

"The prophecy," Carter said quietly. "This must be why they were trying to break us up and get kids from pure bloodlines. They must have found out about it."

"How long have you been here?"

"Some of us over seven years...a few only three."

"And how many children were born?"

"Eight," Hadley said. "That number will be ten soon."

"And how many were fathered by Stephan?" Rix pulled up his phone and showed Hadley, who sneered.

"Two."

"Boys?" She nodded. "Where are they?"

"Arizona I believe...where you all were."

"And the girls?"

Hadley went ashen and shook her head.

"Fuck," Rix growled. "Well, that fucking rapist is dead, along with the rest of those assholes."

"It wasn't rape," one of the girls said. "Some of us did it willingly. It was safer..."

"Sweetheart, coercion is still rape," he said dryly.

"Yeah, we're gonna need all the therapy in here," Leo sighed. "Those priests had better know their shit. They're gonna be busy."

Finn nodded. "Well, you're safe now. You have your own free will. You don't have to stay stuffed up in here if you don't want to. You're welcome to go back to your compounds and rebuild."

"There isn't anything there, I mean they came in and took what they wanted." She looked to Petra. "And just how are you with them...?"

"I don't know. By His grace, I guess," she offered. "Did you ever hear of a compound in Ohio?"

Hadley shook her head. "I don't think so. I was fifteen when I was taken from Manitoba."

Ardith shook her own head. "Devonshire was closed off from everywhere. Our matrons," Petra looked to Finn. Same word, "they said we were the safest, that He Who Sleeps had given us amnesty from the world, and we would be liberated, and given as devotions to those that would cherish us. Three days later they were trying to get us all moving to leave." She shook her head. "There was twenty-six of us there, and eight matrons. Now, it's just us five left from that house."

"I think it's time to see the priests," she said to Finn. "We need to know before we go further."

"Then let's go see the priests," Finn said, rising to his feet. "Thanks, ladies. We'll be back later."

Chapter 43

"Devotion," the priest said as he walked into the foyer of the temple to greet them, bowing his head and one knee.

"Hi," she said and smiled. "You can just call me Petra."

"Lady Petra," the priest corrected. "And sons." He nodded to the rest. "I see you were successful."

"We were," Rix said. "And clearly came back to bedlam. Now, before we go any further, answer me, did you know about those women?"

"No, Kendrix. None of us were aware of what was going on."

"In your own compound."

"No, in the compound that was deemed unsafe for anyone to use after the earthquake almost forty years ago."

"You didn't think to consider?"

"Why, sir? We couldn't see the buildings at the lower vantage just under us. We deeply regret..."

"How did He not know?"

"That we do not know. Our vision of the feminine has long been murky...though he chose to keep much of what was going on away from us. We believe that he didn't trust us, and he shouldn't have. So much happened under our watch, so much we couldn't stop. We have much to atone for," he said solemnly.

"You can start by answering questions," Emerson said.

"Let's take a seat." Finn gestured to one of the big conference tables the priests sometimes used for teaching. "This is going to take a while and I know Emerson is going to have questions about a retraining program for everyone in The Order when we've handled the immediate problems."

They all settled in and the priest turned to Finn. "Please, on behalf of the Priesthood, allow me to offer our deepest apologies for letting it get this far. I fear we have been too long caught in a bubble of our own making; lost in the study instead of the teachings. We tried to make it right, with you and the Lady Petra, but it was not enough."

"What's done is done." Finn shrugged. "All we can do now is focus on how to get ourselves out of this mess and what to do going forward. Tell us what you know about how the female half of The Order works. I know you said that the visions have been cloudy, but surely you know the history? The things that were deliberately kept from us?"

The priest sighed. "Brother Kildare would be best to explain," he said and pulled out his phone. A moment later another priest walked in, older, one of the Relics. "Sons, Lady, this is Brother Kildare, the oldest of our order."

She nodded to him and he bowed to her. "Devotion," he said with reverence, and then slapped the other priest upside the head with a deceptively frail hand. "I told you this was going to happen. Now you listen to me." He looked to the others. "Sons, an honor to meet you all, finally. I taught your fathers," he looked to Emerson. "Especially yours. Did you know he was to become an Adept before he was called to serve?"

"What? I didn't even know we could..."

"Of course not, why would you know of the opportunities they didn't want you to know about?" He huffed and sat in the large chair. "Ooh, much more comfortable than the one I have. Eustace..."

"Of course," the other priest said and started tapping on his phone. It was clear there was both reverence and deference to the older priest by the other. "You shall have one in your chambers after this."

"Too right. Now...what are we talking about? And let's be focused about it, or I tend not to be." He looked them all over.

"We know nothing about the women's side of The Order," Finn said bluntly. "That needs to be rectified. How did the two halves used to function together? What is the God's preference? What trainings do we need to integrate into the packages Emerson will be rolling out when all this is settled?"

"And what do you know of their compounds?" Carter added.

"A lot of questions there, boys," Kildare cackled and shook his head. "This religion functions like any other, two sides, the feminine and the masculine, both sides having their place. Before the insurrection, something I could not change being one man, and one of the Lore Keepers, mind you, both sides worked in concert. Devotions were through the feminine, through both toil and pleasure, as you have seemed to bring back." He looked to Petra." And with your blood, no wonder he is pleased."

"So, you're saying our order works like priests and nuns?"

"In a fashion. More like we, the priests, learned and kept the rites, while the women, the matrons and the priestesses, prepared the feminine for his love." He smiled. "He Who Sleeps is a lover before he is a destroyer, something those assholes never understood. Oh yes, the power from destruction was vast, but the power from the feminine was bigger, more malleable, and more loved."

"Why would they have us only kill then?"

"Why else, dear boy? Control. They could control what he got, and keep that which was purer for themselves. Each of them had wives, and they used them as devotions, though they didn't have Order wives, not all of them."

"Son of a bitch," Rix said. "They all but killed off the feminine to keep themselves in the power?"

"Killed? No, more like scattered them. The compounds, thirteen of them around the world...well now, there's six," he sighed and then slapped Eustace again, annoyed, "were created to nurture the feminine, to teach them that being a devotion was a life of love, privilege and reverence. That their men, their masculine, would protect them, and each would become a conduit to Him and they would prosper."

"Why all this in the first place?"

Kildare smirked at her. "Because if He wakes, the world would end."

There was a moment of shocked silence and then Finn rubbed his eyes. "Okay," he said tiredly. "So in order of priority, we need to get the women's compounds back up and running. Then we need to roll out a complete education reform for every member, that's mandatory. After that, I'd like to convene a ruling body that's a collaboration between us, the women and the priests to be sure we never stray so far away from His word again. Does anyone else have any suggestions?"

"No, but I do have a question," Carter said respectfully. "Who will be in charge in the interim? We all have jobs and lives back home in the US." Finn shrugged and put the question to the table.

"I would stay on as a liaison, but I have Niobe at home," Easton said regretfully.

"Does the seat of power have to be here?" Leo asked, turning to the priests. "Or could we temporarily redirect all questions and matters of ritual to our place back in the States?"

Kildare considered them. "You, as the purest blood, with the devotional of purest blood, are and have always been in charge. The Council of Elders have never been in charge, not until the regime change." At which he slapped Eustace upside the head again.

The man shook his head. It was clear by his own admission he was involved through neglect but it was also very clear it wasn't only him. Still, he took the abuse from Kildare as if it was his due.

"You have always been in charge, and the seat of power has always been where you are," he offered. "It was how he was able to find your devotional for you. She was there as well." He smiled. "This compound was for us, the priests, the knowledge we hid and coveted, the magic we nurtured for Him."

"Magic?" Jack said. "We have never heard of magic."

"It resides in all of you, gifts of his bloodlines," he sighed. "I forgot you do not even know the truth of it. Long ago, when the world was different, young and wild, He Who Sleeps was awake, causing much strife for those that dwelled on the surface. It wasn't his fault, of course, he was wild by nature, chaos incarnate, and he needed tempered, gentled so his nature didn't destroy the world.

"Then he met Gaia, a woman of purity, who understood him. She gentled his nature enough for Him to gain followers, the first thirteen. Their family followed, and created The Order. Gaia and He lived and loved, and eventually she, being mortal, passed. He, having mourned his love, and knowing she was finite, as gods only get one love, chose to sleep, dwelling deep, where dreams lived, where he could be with her."

"Holy shit. We have never heard this," Emerson said, eyes wide.

"The thirteen, they are your ancestors, and they had helped to keep him happy for a long time."

"And the recent elders?" Rix asked.

"Only your father was of the original bloodlines. The others," he spat. "Charlatans and wannabes who believed they deserved more. He doesn't give like that, and when they realized that, they punished him. And in his sleep, he reached out and sent your devotion to you. As many had through the years, you are Gaia, and they are Him," he said to her finally. "All groups should be like this, individually or as a group. He has been starving on the violence. He needs love. And he rewards love."

"Wait, back it up a few moments..." Carter was shaking his head. "You just said that Petra was a pure blood, too. How do you know that?"

"I am the oldest living priest left, Carter, I have magic in *me*," he offered and then gave them a sly smile. "Though I do not know which family she belongs to personally. Would you like to know?"

"How?" Jack asked.

"It's a simple devotion, in the room of names," he said. "Eustace, have the vault opened and readied. Come," he said to them, "we will see, yes?"

Emerson stood. "You're of the thirteen, aren't you?"

"I'm pure blood, yes. And the only one left." He sighed. "Your father was to be an adept, and to join me, to learn the deep magics, once his calling was over. Those assholes ruined a lot more than just your lives," he muttered.

"What about us?" Easton asked curiously as they followed him into the temple. "Can we join the priesthood when we retire? Is there some rule that says we can't have a female partner?"

"Of course you can. Nothing about this religion says you have to be chaste. Do as thou need, for thy own pleasure, and the pleasure of those you love," he said as they walked through a set of doors, then another, deeper into the temple. "I admit, I would enjoy the company."

"Not sure I'd enjoy being smacked upside the head twenty times a day," Leo muttered from the back.

"I doubt you would have allowed an insurrection to happen, Leo," Kildare said. "The priests, while they meant well trying to keep me shielded, did not do their duty to Him and there are repercussions."

"Ears like a bat!" Leo mouthed to Carter, who snorted, and Finn gave them a sharp look.

Another door was ahead of them and it opened as they approached, the room beyond massive and...adorned.

"I realize you have never been here, few have, but this is the room of names. The trees of all thirteen families, the purest of bloodlines in our order."

Around them were massive etched and stylized trees in the walls, thirteen of them. No names, only jewels inlaid in each trunk, one large diamond, obsidian, emerald, sapphire, ruby, opal, and more...a small podium in the center with what looked like a crystal bowl, small enough to fit in the palm of the hand, sitting there.

"Are we on these?" Leo forgot himself enough to ask.

"Yes," Kildare said, "a drop of blood in the bowl will show you which. All descents of the original thirteen will be tied to a tree. Blood remembers." He motioned to the bowl. "At your leisure."

Emerson looked to Finn. "Should we? Make sure it's safe?"

"I doubt the priests would lead us wrong, but certainly." Finn nodded for Emerson to step up to the bowl.

Pulling out his pocket knife, he looked to Kildare. "Just a drop?"

"Yes," he said and smiled.

Emerson stuck the point into his index finger and then helped the blood to well. Turning his finger, he let it drip into the crystal bowl and watched it disappear. A tingle ran through the room as the ground lit, and then the far wall, the tree in the center, with a large citrine stone, glowed.

"Your family," Kildare said as he pointed to the tree. Pinpoints of light glowed and were snuffed out 'til it was just one. "And that is you."

"I...wow," Emerson said. "Do we have a name, the family I mean?"

"Long ago, the trees were known as their species. Ash," he offered.

"That's so cool! Okay, do me!" Leo grabbed his own pocket knife and rushed toward the bowl, leaving the others laughing as he stabbed his finger and dripped it in.

Once again the blood disappeared, and a tree lit, pinpoints going out until there was two. Petra arched a brow.

"Rowan," Kildare said.

"Why are there two?" Leo asked, looking confused. "Did I have a twin?"

"No, but someone else shares your bloodline. A cousin. Younger. Or a sister." He smirked.

She looked to him. "All family ties still alive will be on each tree?" He nodded to her. "Didn't you say you guys remembered sisters?" she said to Finn.

"Yeah, but where?" Finn shrugged, looking as confused as the rest of them. "Most of the women's communes have gone dark apparently."

"She'd better not have been in the harem." Leo's face had gone hard as granite. "I'll dig those fuckers up and murder them all over again."

"There *are* six more houses," Emerson said. "We need to test everyone in the harem, too."

Kildare nodded." As soon as we are done with you all. Who is next?"

"We came in here to find Petra's family," Finn reminded them all. "Let her see. And then maybe Easton, if he wants to confirm what we found in the journals?"

"Yes, please," Easton said in a small voice, looking shaken.

"Will you come with me?" she asked Easton, her nerves getting to her. "I'll go...then I can be there with you?"

"Sure." He took her hand and squeezed it tight as they stepped up to the bowl.

"I need something..."

Rix was there in a moment, handing her his switchblade. "Here."

She smiled at him and pierced her fingertip, handing the knife back to Rix. Settling in, Easton crowded around her, and she steadied herself, liking the closeness of her snake. The drop hit the bowl and the ground lit up, then the trees around the walls, all of them. Lights blazed and went out, each on the wall until they were all dark.

She sighed, trying hard not to cry. None of the houses... None...

"My word!" Kildare said and bowed to her.

"What? What are you doing?" she asked as she looked around. "None of the trees are lit."

"Yes, they are," Rix said. "You're standing on it."

She looked down, and the three amethysts on the ground were lit, the roots around the floor glowing and pulsing.

"What...what does this mean?"

Kildare looked up to her. "You are Yarrow," he said and bowed again. "Bloodline of the first, of Gaia, well, her sister Estra." He chuckled. "Which makes sense..."

"Okay, that's going to need another history lesson," Finn said drily. "Assume we know none of this, Brother Kildare. What exactly does this mean?"

"When Gaia and He created their union, the thirteen came to them, to speak the gospel, and revel in worship. One was Estra, Gaia's sister. She became High Priestess of the movement, and Gaia's right hand. She was loved by both her sister and her mate, He Who Sleeps, and was doted on.

"Her bloodline was the one to consecrate this temple, this land, and keep it for him." He looked to her, still standing there, though now Easton was wrapped around her, which she was grateful for, not trusting her own knees to hold her up. "It is the most holy, and explains why you were gifted her. The Antrithos bloodline was the most accepting, the most magical because of purpose. He sent her to you because we needed a rebirth." He smiled.

"And my family?"

He shook his head. "There has never been a male Antrithos bloodline, because they have always mated outside of The Order." He looked to them all. "A failsafe in a way, to keep Gaia's bloodline in the world. Estra's last living descendant we knew of was almost one hundred years ago. The matrons said she passed without an heir." He smirked. "Even then they hid your line for Him."

"Why do I feel like everything we've ever known is a lie?" Leo said sourly. "I've never even heard of the Antrithos bloodline."

"Does this mean that her orphanage wasn't Order? Or that it's been a secret for a hundred years?" Carter asked, looking as confused as the others.

Kildare shook his head. "I don't know of any compounds in Ohio, so it is very possible they were an offshoot, and were hiding. Devotion, or rather, High Priestess, do you have any information of the women that raised you?"

She told him what she had told the guys, the matrons, the weird little things they did. Kildare nodded to all of it and when she finished he looked to Carter. "Definitely Order, but hidden. Considering the state of things since around your father's time I can see them taking matters into their own hands, or there was divine intervention. I think you need to see for yourself, though."

"We have plans to visit when we get back," Carter said with a nod. "I just hope they've kept good records. A lot can happen in a hundred years."

"Indeed. Are you okay, Priestess?"

"I...I'm not sure I like that name but...yes. Knowing you belong somewhere..." she trailed off and looked up to Easton.

"Well I guess we should get this over with," he said bravely, taking the knife and stabbing his finger, probably harder than he needed to. They all watched as the blood dripped into the bowl and the room lit up.

Bright, it bounced from tree to tree, and landed on a tree, the opal there pulsed and then burned strong.

"Cypress," Kildare said, pride in his voice. "You are an Ambrose, and the last of your family line." He looked at him, affection burning in his eyes. "My line."

"So it's true then? All of what was written in Emerson's dad's journal? The Elders had my mother killed and I was just thrown out like trash?"

"Honestly, I don't know. I know your grandfather was killed in their insurrection. Last I knew your mother, who would have been Glynnis, was pregnant but then she disappeared. We assumed she'd died in childbirth." He shook his head. "As far as I knew, you had died with her. Once the other Elders took over, The Order hid me, hid the other two priests that were of the old guard. We ran things from the shadows for the priests, which is why things didn't progress like they wanted. I didn't know you existed. I honestly didn't believe it was you after you were brought in. It wasn't like I could check, they didn't know I was here. If they did?" He shook his head. "Now I know." He walked forward and produced a knife as he did. "I cannot offer you regrets, but I can offer you my life, in penance for your own."

"Why should you pay for something you didn't know about?" Easton shook his head. "Your knowledge is more important to us right now than some silly honor killing. I've seen and dealt enough death in my life, Brother Kildare. Maybe you could help us make it be that no other child ever has to go through what I did. Consider that your penance."

He looked at Easton once more, then nodded. "We all have a second chance it seems, and you are a paragon to our blood, Easton." He bowed to him.

Easton nodded uncomfortably, clearly not happy about the way the priest was acting but unable to say anything about it.

"Well then." Finn rubbed his hands together. "Now that's all settled, perhaps we should get a move on with the more practical stuff?" He headed for the door. "Come, Brother Kildare! We have an Order to revamp!"

"Sometimes he's a really imperious asshat," Leo said to Carter, who snorted.

"Just be glad you aren't the one in charge," he reminded Leo. "Heavy is the head and all that."

Kildare shook his head. "Much like his father when he was young," he said softly. "Priestess, I think you should go back and see where we are with that thread of this tapestry." He looked to her.

She nodded. "There is much to do here..."

"And much of it you cannot do," he offered. "But you can do *this*."

She nodded again, looking to Easton and Carter. "I don't think I want to go alone."

"I'll come with you," Carter offered. "I have to speak to the priests still about options for therapy," Easton told her. "But depending how quickly that goes, I might be able to come with you, too."

"Okay...but if not, that's good. We can talk when we get back, yeah?"

Kildare looked to her. "If you find what I hope you are going to find, bring them back," he said softly to her. "We can't function as two separate entities, He and Gaia wouldn't have wanted that. And you, you have the bloodline to do it."

She nodded. "I...yes, I'll try."

He walked after the guys then, Easton following, leaving her and Carter in the room alone. Smiling to her lover, she took his hand. "Come on...let's go and solve this mystery."

Chapter 44

Turning onto the drive up to the place she spent her formative years, tension filled her being. The entire trip back over the ocean wasn't like this, it had been more relaxed, snuggling with Carter in the cabin of the plane, she had napped, and they had talked, though it wasn't anything super important. Brutus had stayed back at the compound in the Balkans, and Emerson had promised to keep him fed and safe 'til they returned.

When they had touched down in Ohio, they had climbed into the Range Rover that had been waiting for them, and driven the forty minutes to the little town she grew up in. Little, if anything had changed there, though she knew that she still got the alumni email from the high school there.

"Whatever we find here, I'm going to have to say something to my friends," she said softly as they winded through the trees toward the large house at least half a mile away still.

"I'm sure they'd understand," Carter said. "Finding that they belong to The Order might feel like belonging to a family after all this time."

"More like they are going to want their own Order boys," she said with a wry smile. "You think Easton is going to be okay?"

"He'll be fine. He's just really excited about being able to be physically intimate. It's softened the blow of the rest of it a little bit. Although I think if he could raise those fuckers from the dead and skin them all over again, he totally would."

If she was honest, she was extremely excited about any kind of connection with her Snake. "I would be right there with him," she said solemnly. They crested the hill and she saw the large house looming ahead of them. It had always looked to her like this large imposing façade, a place rife with secrets and history. Now she knew the secrets were real but they had nothing to do with the building. It had everything to do with the women therein.

"Still looks the same," she said as they parked on the far side of the circular drive. The building was black brick, with deep wood accents, two turrets reaching to the sky, the wraparound porch dusted with the snow that had only fell last night. "Though it's quieter than it used to be."

"Makes sense if the whole purpose of them being here was to hide your bloodline," Carter pointed out. "Now that you're out in the world they can age out the rest and close up if they want."

"Well, they need to answer for a lot of things," she said. "Come on."

They walked up the stairs and opened the door, stepping into the foyer of the large house. It was largely the same, right as well as a bunch of bouquets of flowers all over the place.

"Can I help you?" they heard from their left, and turned to see a woman she didn't know standing there. She was older, dressed in a green wrap dress, shoes with kitten heels, her salt and pepper hair in a bun, and she wore sparse makeup.

"Yes, hi, we'd like to speak to the matron or whoever is in charge," Carter said politely.

At the word matron she stiffened and then looked to Petra. "Ms. Franklin?" she said and smiled.

"I don't know you," Petra said.

"Oh no, I was brought on two years ago," she said. "I'm Matron Elise."

"What happened to Matron Verna?"

"I am sorry to say she passed away, a few months after I was brought in to succeed her."

"Perhaps we could talk somewhere more private?" Carter suggested. "We have questions that might be better suited to a less public discussion."

"No one is here. The matrons took what's left of our girls to the movies today," she said and motioned down the hall. "Coffee? Tea?" she asked as the followed her. "I didn't think you would be back here, Ms. Franklin, and in the company of an Order male," she offered as they made it into the kitchen she remembered so fondly. "So, you have probably come for answers then? Though I am intrigued... How did you find him...or did he find you, and are you safe?" She looked to Carter. "Is she safe?"

"She's safe. The previous regime has been eliminated and we're in charge now," Carter said. "We'd burn the world down to keep her safe."

The woman smiled at him. "That so? Well then..." She went and started making coffee. "So what are your questions, because if you are here, Mr..." She looked to Carter.

"Just call me Carter," he said respectfully. "And mostly we want to know about how this orphanage came to be and how Petra ended up here. If you know anything about the recent history of The Order, you'll know that our knowledge of the feminine side of it is sorely lacking."

"That's an understatement." She snorted. "Let me get her files," she said and walked out of the room. Petra's stomach was clenching. This entire thing was giving her severe anxiety. But the scents.... The scents of the house were a comfort. Camphor and sage, and rose and lavender...the happiest times of her childhood were spent in this room, with those scents.

"Here we are," Elise said as she walked back in with several files in her hand. She set them on the table.

"Have a look. I can tell you what I know, but..." Walking over to the coffee maker, she set another pod to brew.

"And what do you know?" Petra said as she opened the top file seeing her photo, a recent one.

"I know that you, like all the other girls that are here, were brought here after He contacted a matron and gave order to leave, to bring the girls here, away from the compounds and away from The Order."

"Wait, the God contacted a matron directly?" Carter stared at her. "Was this around the time several of the women's compounds went dark?"

"He contacts us all the time," Elise said.

"How?"

Through dreams, subconscious whispers." She smiled. "Unlike the masculine, the feminine of his Order has always been directly attached to him...well, some of us. Some can't hear him at all, though we had ideas about that as well."

Petra looked at the file, scanning over the information there. "I was originally in...Maine?" she said, looking up. "And she brought me here."

"On his orders." Elise said. "If you read her account, she says what he said."

Petra sifted through the pages and found one written by hand, and began to read. "On April seventeenth, He visited me. Told me I was to bring three of our girls west, to the black house in the woods, where they would be safe. He said they were special, and they would be needed, to ensure love ruled."

She looked to Carter. "This is dated four months before the compounds started to go dark. It also says the matron in Maine told her to go when she told her she had dreamed him. She brought me, Clary, and Muriel with her. Left the rest there." She looked up and then back down. "Muriel had a sister they left. Why would she do that?"

"Because He willed it," Elise said. "They knew what was coming. This house was a safehouse only few that were close to Him knew about."

"What about your other friends?" Carter asked. "Is there any mention of them in the file?"

"All their files are here," she said and started opening them. "Vic from San Fran, Carlee, Baton Rouge, and Fiona from Montana. All of us brought in the same week, along with several other girls of varying ages." She looked to Elise. "They did it to keep us safe?"

"On His orders. I was brought in once Verna started getting sick, from the Idaho compound. It's still there, hasn't been found by The Order. Or didn't get raided. I don't know why some did and some didn't. And I don't know what happened to the girls that were taken. They all weren't, some made their way to Idaho, and some south to Mexico and farther to Peru."

"Do you have contact details for them?" Carter asked. "Now that The Order is back on track with input from the Temple, we'd really like to put everything right...back the way it used to be."

"The way it used to be." She sighed and smiled. "Before those assholes started fucking with the natural order." She brought them both coffee. "You know not one of the matrons alive have been to our original temple because of those assholes? Our girls are largely out in the world, without their counterparts, without Him." She shook her head. "They don't know what it feels like to have the love of one such as He, to feel his influence." She looked to Petra. "But you do." She took her hand. "Touched, faintly, but it was enough to find him."

"Find *them*, my Seven."

"Seven?" she arched a brow. "Is she a devotion?"

Carter glanced at Petra and gave a small shrug, as though it were up to her whether she wanted to tell the matron if she were a devotion or a priestess.

"Apparently I'm more than that, but yes, I am a devotion," she said proudly. "For my Seven."

"There hasn't been a devotion in a long, long time. Doesn't surprise me you were tapped. Your bloodline...of course He would want you to help bring things back to normal."

"What do you know about it?"

She smiled. "All the girls here are special, though some more than others. Your bloodline, it runs in two others."

"Sisters?"

She shook her head. "In this case no. Estra had seven daughters, and those daughters had daughters. You all stem from the same bloodline, untainted by the masculine...or rather, kept safe for the right masculine." She looked to Carter. "You and your team."

"Are you saying there's males for all of us?"

Elise nodded softly. "Eventually, yes. Not all females will be devotions, some will end up wives, and partners."

"And the mothers of the boys? Like Carter and my other guys?"

"Special in that they and their families were Order, but they weren't of the Antrithos bloodline. The girls here?" She smiled. "Most if not all that have passed through these halls are of the blood."

She looked to Carter. They had their answer. Direct descendants to Estra, to Gaia. "Carter, could this be why they were collecting women?"

"I'm sorry. Collecting?"

Elise frowned as Petra told her what they had returned to the Balkans to find out. "And these girls, women...are they okay?" She nodded. "I would like to see them."

"I think they're planning to bring them back to the US, but Finn is a bit snowed under with all the practical arrangements right now," Carter said thoughtfully. "I had assumed that they'd been collecting women to try and fulfil the prophecy under their own control...same reason they tried to kill Easton and his mother. But it could be that they were somehow trying to find a true devotion they could use themselves."

"It wouldn't have worked, though," Petra said. "Kildare said only one of them were of the main blood, Stephan. It wouldn't have been enough."

Elise sighed. "I knew this was going to happen. Leave men to focus on governing something this important and ambition gets in the way. The feminine? We had no problem, aside from the men." She looked to them. "You found your Seven recently?"

She nodded. "It's been four devotions. Before that they were...sacrificing."

Elise blanched. "Idiots! Not you, Carter, the assholes that sent you to sacrifice."

"Kildare said that sacrifice is needed."

"It is, but for the veils to be that thin...there's a reason for us to worship during that time."

Petra's eyes went wide. "For Him to be close to Gaia."

Elise nodded. "There is no wonder He guided you to them, and no wonder you fell for them. They speak to you, yes...your blood?"

"They...they make me whole. Even that first time..." She smiled at Carter. "I didn't know who they were..." She proceeded to tell Elise the more pedestrian story of how they met. The matron seemed pleased.

"This all makes sense. He set it in motion."

"What is your understanding of the meaning of sacrifice?" Carter asked curiously. "We were pretty much raised in a death cult, told it was all about the killing. But lately, from what we've been reading, it seems any kind of blood in any amount is a sacrifice. We've clearly missed out on an education in the importance of blood."

"Sacrifice is something given freely," Elise said. "And The Order of He Who Sleeps was never meant to be something vicious and unyielding, bringing pain and misery to the world for His glory. He and Gaia had balance, and for a long, long time, there was a balance. Devotions would endure pain and pleasure to sacrifice for him, the embodiment of his love, Gaia.

"He Who Sleeps loved her, wanted to possess her, and He wasn't a...gentle lover. She endured His attentions with grace and caring, learning to love His own way of having her. She counselled in our most sacred texts, written by her, that sacrifice was the truest proof of love. What the masculine did perverted that, because I believe they didn't want women to have any power over anything. They wanted to control it all, but it was always a partnership, between Him and Gaia. Together great and terrible things were achieved."

"So the pain *is* a part of it...that's interesting." Carter looked at Petra and smiled. "The texts we have are mostly personal journals containing speculation and the priests aren't exactly forthcoming with information. One of my brothers, Emerson, is going to be rolling out an educational package for every member of The Order that will be mandatory to attend any future rituals. I think I speak for all of us when I say that we'd be extremely grateful if you and the other matrons would consider contributing to it."

"Of course. A return to an Order that is whole, both sides, is what we always wanted." She chuckled. "Verna would have loved this. She had hope, that our girls would find their counterparts. I'm so happy at least one of you did."

"Do you know," Petra asked, "what happened to the mothers of my guys? Their fathers had relationships, marriages...and sisters."

"All sisters are sent to Idaho," she said. "They are safe, especially those of the thirteen bloodline. The mothers, some were there...some didn't make it. It's the way of it. Their bonds with their men are different and largely they cannot live without them."

"Is there someone there we can speak to?" Carter asked. "The women from the Balkans might be more comfortable going directly to Idaho. Or perhaps we could send you to the Balkans to liaise with them, if you have nothing urgent to manage here?"

"Four girls just hitting their teens," Elise said. "And my sisters can manage them. I would love to see the mother temple, and bring the women taken to the secure compound. Some might wish to move on from there but..." She looked to him. "I think that can be managed."

"Well then," Carter rose to his feet. "I'll go and make some calls and leave you ladies to catch up."

She smiled at him. "Don't go too far, love. And take your coffee." She winked.

"Yes, ma'am!" With his own wink and a grin, he left them to it.

Chapter 45

"They just touched down," Emerson said to Easton and Finn as he walked into the study they were using as headquarters. "And they have a matron in tow."

"Of her own free will?" Jack asked from the far wall.

"Apparently, and they have news."

In the two days Petra and Carter had been away, they had been busy. They had met with the others that had been there and helped, brought them to the family tree room, and tested everyone, including the captive females. Three of the men there were from one of the thirteen families, and oddly one was Damon. Finn had offered each of them their own teams, as they had been learning more from Kildare, and the more worshipping on a larger scale, balanced, would bring more abundance from He Who Sleeps to all.

All three of the men had asked to create one team, and brought in two more men, so they were a five-person team. Emerson had worried it wouldn't be enough, but Kildare had told them that only *they* needed to be seven. Other teams, if any would be what worked for them. Kildare had also counseled each of the single practioners and duos to find their own devotions, or wives, in women that understood their...needs.

There was so much they didn't know. Single practioners were more plentiful, though only those that worshiped with a female of the blood were heard. Duos were even more plentiful, and Kildare had been suggesting they look toward the women that were left in the world that belonged to Him, so that they would bring more to the cause.

But the biggest thing, the fact that they were close to Armageddon. Why? Because what the council of

Elders had been doing was starving Him, and He was both agitated and angry. He was close to the point of surfacing, and it was only Petra's acceptance as a devotion that had staved that off. When Jack had asked why the council would do that, Kildare had said something very ominous.

"Because they wanted it to end. If they couldn't be all powerful, they would murder the world for their ambition, and clearly, He wouldn't be a pawn. She, your devotion, our new high priestess, was his ace in the hole. He would never want to ruin the world that gave him Gaia."

"Are they on the way in?"

Emerson nodded to Jack. "She's freshening up, and Carter is seeing Brutus."

"We should order her some tea," Easton said absently. "She usually has one around this time. It might help reset her body clock."

"That's really thoughtful of you, brother." Finn squeezed his shoulder, still hesitant at the previously unwelcome form of contact, but Easton leaned into it.

"I'll go," Leo said. He hadn't been doing anything important anyway.

Emerson nodded and dropped two books the Kildare had handed him. "Found the rule books. Kildare had them in his quarters holding up a table."

"Of course he did," Finn chuckled ruefully. "Did you get a chance to page through them or is that a now job?"

"I did." He smirked. "It's fucking nuts what we don't do. What rites we are missing, the ones that are dual rites."

"Well, I guess the good news is that the women seem to be on board with going back to the old ways," Finn said with a tired smile. He'd barely slept for days, but they were close to hammering it all out. They were all looking forward to going home and sleeping for a week.

"Carter said something about the main women's compounds being in Idaho," Easton said. "I think that confirms it's a good idea to move HQ to the US. We're there and the ladies are there. Makes sense to have the governing council there. Did you ask the priests about setting up a chapter house in the US?"

"Not yet." Finn rubbed his eyes. "I wanted to speak to this matron they've brought back first. There's no point organizing us and the priests if the women want to resettle here."

"This is the original temple," Jack said thoughtfully. "So they might. Either way I don't think Kildare is moving."

"Hey..." they heard as Petra walked into the room. "Miss me?"

"Like you wouldn't believe." Easton was the first one into her arms and the others all shared a soft smile. It was so good to see him breaking out of his shell.

"I made you tea," Leo announced, returning to the room with a large tray and dropping a kiss on her cheek as he passed. "We hoped it might help the jetlag."

"What's going to help the jetlag is a cuddle." She giggled and snuggled into Easton. He let her go, and Jack went to her, hugging her.

"Missed you, baby cakes." He winked.

Emerson watched her go to each of them, himself, which he kissed her and grabbed her ass, and then to Finn who she wrapped herself around.

"You look awful, my love," she said softly. "You and me, nap later?"

"There's so much to do," he sighed. "But sure. If we have time. I could do with some sleep."

"I'ma make sure you have time, love." She kissed his cheek. "You are no good to anyone dead on your feet."

"So what did you learn?" Jack said as she detangled from Finn and went to Easton and hugged him again. It was clear she missed him very much, and she was receptive to things progressing with him.

"Wait 'til Carter gets here...let's talk about what you guys learned?" she asked.

"Emerson was just telling us about the books he found about all the rites we should have been doing over the last several decades," Finn said. "We were musing over the possibility of whether it would be a good idea to move headquarters to the US since we're there. Where's the matron?"

"With Kildare seeing the women. I suspect she will be in shortly to meet you all. She was enraptured with Carter."

"Who wouldn't be?" Leo smirked. "Wait until she meets the rest of us."

"Before she gets here, maybe you could tell us your impression of her," Finn said. "Does she seem legit? Are they happy we ousted the old Elders?"

She nodded. "She seems happy. I mean she's resentful of what happened within the organization, especially the fact that they had to hide, but..." She shrugged. "She wants a return to both sides being together, and to bring the feminine together once more." She grinned. "And she told me something very special. Well, told us...me and Carter. And my friends are going to love it."

"Well? Tell us?" Emerson asked.

"Not 'til Carter is here." She shook her finger at him. It was clear she was enjoying this.

"Tease," Leo accused, but he was grinning. "Where is that fucker anyway? How long does it take to say hello to a dog?"

"Brutus missed his daddy," she said as Carter walked in with the aforementioned dog at his side. Smiling at the massive dog, she went to him and snuggled him. "Hello, Mr. Man," she said softly and then took Carter's hand. "They are pouting I wouldn't tell them stuff without you."

"You could have done," he said with a smile. "It's not like I haven't heard it already. The matron isn't here yet?"

"Apparently she's with Kildare," Finn told him, clapping him on the back. "It's good to see you, brother."

"Likewise." Carter settled into a chair. "You look like shit. Aren't they letting you get any sleep around here?"

"You two could give anyone a complex," Finn sighed, shaking his head. "Maybe if little miss secretive here would just tell us what she knows, I might actually get a chance to have some sleep today."

"Napping with me," she said proudly. "We haven't really done that, have we?" she said to Finn. "But I suppose I could tell you," she grinned. "Not only am I Order...I'm super special," she teased.

"Spill it, sexy," Emerson said. "Don't be stingy or someone is going to spank you."

"Really not a deterrent," she said. "So, I, along with the rest of the girls in my house, are direct descendants to Estra, Gaia's sister, which you know from the temple. But what you don't know, and get this, Estra's line was never intermingled with other Order families. The women were their own thing, because they only gave birth to women."

"And now?" Emerson asked. "If we were to knock you up...just girls?"

She shook her head. "Matron Elise told me that our line was meant to be pure, like a failsafe. If we have kids, they will be the reemergence." She giggled. "So if you guys knock me up, I can and will have boys, each the head of their own line of seven of the original thirteen."

"And what about the others?" Easton asked while everyone else was still mulling over the issue of kids. "Order brothers have been single for as long as I've been part of The Order. Are they open to the idea of wives and devotions?"

"Yes, actually. Elise came to my house after my matron, Verna, passed. But she's from Idaho, and that house has long been hoping for a return." She looked to them. "Also, Idaho is where the mothers went. And the sisters." She looked to Finn. "Your sister is there."

"I was going to visit anyway when we get back, but that's a nice bonus reason," he said with a grin. "Thanks for asking about her."

"Some of the mothers are there, too. Some didn't make it, but..." She looked to Leo. "Your mom is still there."

"What?" Leo had gone pale. "I thought they sacrificed them? They told me she was dead."

Crossing the room, she took his hands in hers. "I asked Elise about that. She said your father, and the other fathers... they sent them to Idaho, and that they perpetuated the lie that they were dead to protect them, and you. She's alive, and a matron in Idaho. Elise said she's always been sad she lost you but...now you can reconnect? Talk about your dad?" she said hopefully.

"Are any of the others there?" Easton asked curiously. "I know mine's dead, but it would be nice for the rest of you guys to have some family."

"Not that I know of personally. Elise mentioned some of them passed due to complications but we can find out. Only reason we knew about Leo was I mentioned his name and she said his mother had photos of 'her Leo' in her rooms."

"Well we should check it out when we go there," Jack said. "What else?"

At that Petra grinned. "My friends are of the same bloodline as me, so..."

"So they could be devotions?"

She looked over to Bradley, who had been sitting on the floor, among two stacks of books. "Hi," she said.

"Bradley," he said. "Are you saying your friends could be devotions, too?" She nodded. "Excuse me," he said ad walked out.

Jack laughed. "He's going to go tell Damon."

"So does that mean you're half-sisters? Cousins? Different branches?" Finn asked. "One of the things I've been curious about and Kildare couldn't answer is how we avoid inbreeding."

"Different branches of Gaia's line, through Estra," a woman said as she walked in. "Petra and the girls from the Ohio compound are all direct blood descendants to Estra. Estra, nor her line, ever mated with any from The Order, let alone any of the thirteen." She looked to them. "All of their blood, her blood, is pure and the children from these women will be completely new lines into The Order."

"Matron," Emerson said. "It's an honor."

"It's an honor to meet you all, paving the way for a better future. We are all in your debt, sons of the thirteen."

"Just trying to do what's right." Was Finn blushing? "We're very glad you're here to help us. How are the women holding up? Understandably, they've been reluctant to speak to us much."

425

"They are...traumatized to say the least. We talked, they would like to leave here, as I'm sure you can understand this is a place of pain for them. I would like to suggest we bring them back to Ohio, to where Petra was raised. There is room, and it is a safe place, for healing."

"Not to Idaho?" Carter was surprised by that but Finn nodded.

"If they need time and space away from the others to heal, that's fine," he said, grabbing his phone to make a note. "I'll get transport arranged."

"I can do that," Carter said. "Let me liaise with Matron Elise and organize the transfer. You have enough on your plate."

"Use the jet," Emerson said. "In fact, Carter...we should buy some new transport." Given the amount of money they now controlled from the dead Elders, they had much at their disposal. "Matron, how ready for a large amount of people is Ohio?"

"Well enough. We make do with what we have, same with the rest of the compounds," Elise said to him.

"Not anymore. Carter, can we make sure Elise and the other matrons have access to the accounts? I think also modernizing anything that needs it, and ensuring they are all more than comfortable is paramount."

"I'm meeting with the accountants tomorrow," Finn said. "I think, at least to start with, we need to have some kind of budgetary plan in place. It might be an obscene amount of money, but rebuilding and education and rehabilitation are going to be expensive. I'll make sure Matron Elise has access to an account with a generous allowance, but we aren't going to make the mistakes of the Elders we ousted. All that money is going to be accounted for and transparent. If you want a new jet, put in some paperwork explaining why it's necessary so that we have something on file."

Emerson laughed. "Okay, okay...but for now, Matron, my company jet is at your disposal."

"Generous of you. Thank you."

"Thank you nothing, you fit so many puzzle pieces together for us, it's the least we can do."

"I would love to sit and talk with you all soon, before I leave of course..."

"Dinner in the main hall will be for everyone in attendance tonight," Jack said.

"Wonderful. Thank you, gentlemen." She looked to Petra. "And thank you, Priestess."

She nodded.

Elise left moments later, leaving Petra with the seven of them. He looked her over, heart hurting, at how beautiful she was. And she was theirs.

"So...you going to tell your friends?" Rix asked.

She nodded. "Though it might be something I might have to do in person, they are going to call bullshit."

"I'm sure we can make that happen. Though something tells me Damon and the guys will want to meet them as well," Jack said.

"Yeah, the way that Bradley ran out of here was pretty telling," Leo laughed. "But you said they didn't freak out when you told them about us, so they might not be averse to an introduction to other groups."

"And now you can tell them the whole truth," Easton pointed out. "No more secrets between friends."

She nodded. "I think that's the best part of this. My friends, my family get to be part of this, too."

"Do you think they would want to be?" he asked her. " I mean I know they were interested but..."

"I think so. I mean it would be different for them than with us but that's not a bad thing. And we don't know they would end up involved, either."

"Still, it's family they didn't know they had before," Leo pointed out. "I mean you guys are the family I chose, but finding out my mom is alive means something completely different. I'm sure they'll be excited about all of it."

"Plus, it's pretty cool to find out that God is actually real," Carter said, amused. "I still remember the look on your face when you saw the power coming out of the well at Halloween."

"I wonder if that's how or why they ended up where they are," Finn said thoughtfully. "Didn't you say they were scientists or something? Perhaps He will work through them to make groundbreaking discoveries."

"That might be true, though how is it I went into art?"

"Safe to say it's how you connect with Easton," Rix said.

"And me," Finn reminded her. "We were all in your life in some way before we knew we were supposed to be. That had to be him making maneuvers."

"That is true," Emerson said. "Could it be that the devotion complements their group?"

"Who is to say they would be devotions? Fiona is not interested in a buncha dudes..."

"But the others?"

"Vic and Carlee are both interested in it, especially how I handle seven of you."

"That's easy...with two hands." Jack winked at her. "Well, most of us."

"In any event, it's not really important right now," Finn tried to herd them all back on topic. "You can run all the studies you want when this is settled, but for now we need to deal with more practical shi—uh, stuff."

He tried not to look at Matron Elise and it was adorable. Petra didn't think Elise would care about the odd swear word, but it was sweet that Finn was trying. "The meeting tomorrow with everyone that's on site...did you get the sound system sorted out?"

"Everything is handled," Rix offered. "Our girl is back, questions have been answered, So why don't we take a break, yeah?"

Petra went to Finn then and grabbed his hand. "Come, my Devil...we have a nap in our future, yes? You did promise and I could do with Finn cuddles."

Emerson laughed at her cuteness. Ther leader needed her almost as much as Easton did but he knew the other man had his own plans for their sweet victim. "Go, take him with you and make him sleep a few hours. We can reconvene at dinner."

"But I haven't spoken to—"

"Go, Finn!" Carter said in his commanding voice, the one that even Finn didn't dare counter.

"Fine," Finn sighed. "But if everything goes to pot, it's on you guys."

"You act like it's a hardship to get naked with that woman," Rix said offhandedly. "If that's the issue I'm sure one of us would gladly take your spot."

"Hey, no one mentioned naked..." Jack said with a pout.

"Oh, I thought it was implied?" Petra said with a giggle. "Skin on skin snuggling."

"Maybe one of the others should go with you then," Finn said. "I'm exhausted, my love. I don't have the energy to play. I thought you meant we were going to sleep."

"I did mean we were going to sleep," she said seriously. "I'm beat. But there is nothing to say when we wake up we don't have any clothes on." She winked at him. "Plus, I like being surrounded in your scent, Finn."

"How could I refuse a request like that?" He smiled. "Well then, I guess we should go."

Emerson watched them walk out, arms around each other's backs, Petra whispering to Finn as they went. He smiled to himself. If nothing else, their girl was good to keep them healthy and happy and that made all the difference. Before her, their bond was there, but nowhere near as strong. Now? They were able to do so much, and he knew it was her strength, her acceptance of them as they were, that brought them to this point.

Chapter 46

Easton walked into the room where Petra had been staying after a quiet knock on the door. She was awake but had her headphones in, which was probably why she hadn't reacted. He needed to be firmer next time, he told himself. Announce his presence instead of requesting entry. He wished the raw masculinity his brothers seemed to exude had been bred into him, too, but he'd been too broken as a child to become that kind of man. It didn't mean he couldn't, though. The God had blessed him with a gift beyond measure and today was the day he'd finally get to test it out.

"Hey, Petra," he tapped her on the shoulder and had to hide a smile at the way she almost jumped out of her skin.

"Saints running!" she said as she looked at him, eyes wide, and then giggled, pulling her headphones out. "Hi... I'm sorry I was miles away." She closed her notebook, and looked him over. "Everything okay?"

"I did knock," he said apologetically. "I had a free few hours, so I was hoping I could take you on a tour of the original compound. It was destroyed but parts of the old temple are still standing, and some of the ruins are quite beautiful."

"Easton, you never need a reason to come to me," she said softly. "I'm always here for you." Slipping off the bed, she grinned. "Kildare told me at dinner about the old temple, and there's some frescoes there? I would love to go with you."

"There are some beautiful frescoes," he agreed. "When I was younger, I used to practice photography on them, trying to capture the colors and the light." He wished he'd brought one of his cameras with him. It would have been amazing to take some photographs of Petra in the ruins.

She had a beauty about her that would have been stark against that destruction...a goddess amongst the stones. They'd have to come back one day when he was more prepared. Maybe he could do a whole series, some when she was round with child. He could see the artworks now—a maiden, mother, crone series...light in the dark...grayscale maybe, highlighted with silver leaf and sharp slashes of the colors of the frescoes in the background.

Realizing he'd spaced out, he blinked and took her hand. "Sorry, I was getting inspired. We should go. I borrowed a car so we don't have to walk over. It's cold out there."

"Oh..." she nodded. "I'm yours for the foreseeable future." Squeezing his hand back, she grabbed her sweater. "Let's go, yeah?"

"Maybe grab a coat, too," he advised. "December out here is not to be trifled with."

She nodded and grabbed the peacoat Carter had brought for her, as well as gloves. "All set."

"Then let's go." They headed down to one of the garages where Easton opened her car door like a gentleman and then drove them over some rocky terrain toward a massive ruined complex in the distance.

"This is where the women were held," he said, pointing out where some of the buildings were still standing, although they looked in poor condition and would no doubt fall derelict quickly now that they were no longer occupied. They continued on until the ruins became so dense that the car couldn't go any farther and then they got out to walk. A cold wind whistled through the tumbled down walls but he knew they would get warm soon.

"The temple is just up ahead," he reassured her, helping her over a pile of rocks.

"I'm used to the cold," she said. "Ohio is bitter as hell, but this isn't so bad. I mean it's better being with you. This place is amazing. How old is the complex? It's not normal to find temples and such in the Balkans, right? Most of that was saved for Turkey and Greece."

"We're not sure," he said. "The original parts of it are probably dated to around the same age as Gobekli Tepe, but it's been expanded and built on so many times over the years that it's hard to know what's still original. And now that we have the technology to date things more accurately, we can't get down into the lower levels where the original stuff is. The ruins are too unstable. The excavation would take years and the Elders would never have authorized it. Which is fair. We don't really want outsiders poking around in our history. It would be nice if we had some archaeologists in The Order, though."

"Never say never," she offered. "Though it stands to wonder why you don't. I mean Order is in like, tons of obscure jobs. Something like that would have been beneficial."

"Would it?" He didn't see it. Proving it was old meant nothing because it would never be open to outsiders. They'd never be able to publish papers about it or invite the scientific world in to study it. The Order had always been and would always be secretive and there was no monetary benefit to studying what was down there. It was simply knowledge for the sake of knowledge.

"If for nothing else than to know your history, your ancestors and such," she offered. "Given so much has been kept from all of us."

"We still have all our texts," he reminded her. "Those were rescued after the collapse. I don't know about artifacts, though. It's possible there's other stuff down there. We should ask the priests."

"And maybe figure out if any of The Order are accomplished spelunkers. Sounds like something Kendrix would do for laughs."

"If we didn't know for sure that there was something worth rescuing, I don't think Finn would allow anybody to go down there," Easton said. "This region is still tectonically active. There are dozens of quakes every year. Imagine if even a small one happened while a team were down there? We'd never get them out. It's best just to leave the secrets where they lie."

He led her into the old temple building which was sheltered from the wind since parts of all four walls were standing, and under the cracked dome. He'd swung by earlier to light a fire and drop off some blankets and cushions, and he'd also rigged up some floodlights to show the frescoes in all their glory.

It was dark in the cavernous space now and she stumbled slightly over some rubble on the tiled floor, but he really wanted to see the moment when he turned all the lights on and she saw the riot of colors exploding from the walls. "Come and sit here," he told her, moving her gently to a pile of cushions. "There's something I want you to see."

Her eyes were wide, taking everything in. "Easton, this is amazing..." she said as she took in what she could see. "And it's warm...did you set this up? Like a date?" She blushed.

"Maybe?" He gave her a shy smile. The truth was much deeper than that but he wasn't sure how much of it he was supposed to say. Ever since the gift, the God had been speaking to him from time to time, guiding his advice to Finn and encouraging the artistic way Easton viewed the world.

It was the God that had pushed him to come here today. Somehow it felt important to reconnect to their roots, to reaffirm their faith here, in the place where it had been born. They'd rooted out the darkness amidst their core, but it wasn't enough. He Who Sleeps needed a reconsecration. And what better people to do it than His most broken and blessed, and His high priestess? But those kinda of concepts were too huge to speak of and so instead he simply told her to watch as he plugged in the floodlights and the dome flared into glorious light.

"Holy..." She gasped as she looked. "Easton, this is..." she looked to him. "My god..."

"Gorgeous, right?" He looked around at the illuminated works, some of them still shining with gold leaf paint. "I don't know why they didn't replicate this when we moved. The current temple is boring in comparison."

"Because we didn't have artists," she said softly. "Elise said that a lot of the work in the original temple was done by the feminine, though there were two done by two of the men that worked with them." Her eyes were filled with awe as she swept them over the walls and up to the dome, or what was left of it. "Easton, I think you should paint something in the temple...bring back the tradition."

"I'd have to ask the priests," he said, but already he was wondering if that was where the images he'd seen earlier had come from...if his triptych idea for Petra had maybe been an inspiration from the God himself, asking him to bring creativity and color back into The Order. He didn't think the priests would say no. "I'd paint better with some visual inspiration," he said with a teasing glint. "You know, to see how the light falls on bare skin. Most of these frescoes are of rituals. If I'm going to paint, I'd like to paint our holiest of rituals."

Biting her bottom lip, she arched a brow. "Oh?" A blush crept up her face. "What's that?"

"The connection between male and female. Sacrifice. Creation." He wanted to paint all of it.

"That sounds...super involved..." Her eyes were heavy and color rolled to her cheeks as her breathing hitched. He could tell she was imagining it.

"I might need you to model for me several times until we get it right," he teased, loving the way her skin was flushing with heat. And then abruptly he felt scared. What if he let her down? What if this newfound confidence failed him and he bailed at the last minute? That would be so mortifying. She'd never seen him fully in the grip of a PTSD hallucination and he knew how ugly it was.

In one of his cruelest moments, Stephan had recorded Easton flipping out and then made him watch the video over and over in some misguided attempt to "fix his whiny ass issues." He couldn't do that in front of her. Not Petra. Out here, away from everyone, he could seriously hurt her if he lost it. And then gentleness descended on his heart like a heavy weight, the hand of God moving in His servant, dispelling the fear and summoning hope in its place. He could do this. The God was with him. He was no longer lost.

"I'm going to need you to get undressed," he said confidently, smiling inside at the way her eyes widened.

"I...okay," she said shyly. It occurred to him that what was between them had never been like this. Before it had been what she was bade to do, and while she might like it, and crave it even, this was different, because the situation wasn't set up with an end game in mind. She could be as nervous about this as him. Her bravado an act before.

She was soft and sweet, and as she slipped free of the clothing, taking her time in doing so, the nerves were there, floating to the surface every so often.

He wished she could feel what he felt...his certainty that this was right where they needed to be at this exact moment, doing this exact thing. He wondered why God spoke to him and not to her. Unless it was part of her sacrifice to consecrate the temple...maybe that was it. Maybe she had to come to him, willing in the face of her uncertainty, to make it a true devotion.

She had to want to be here with him, now, doing this. He shed his own clothes much less hesitantly than she had. She probably deserved a show, but he'd waited for this moment for too long to be fancy about it. He just wanted to know what it would be like to touch and be touched without descending into his own personal hell.

He stroked the skin of her thigh, awed at how soft it was, even rippled with goosebumps from the chill in the air. His hand travelled up over the curves of her belly and cupped a breast, and God...the exquisite softness of it made him want to weep at its beauty. Nothing could have prepared him for this. Nothing.

She was breathing more heavily now, clearly turned on, but he couldn't contain his wonder over the feel of her skin. He had a crazy urge to rub his face on it like he'd seen cats do on TV and then realized he could do that if he wanted to, so he did. He had no idea that a woman's warm skin would smell so good.

Some sort of fruity product but underneath it, something that was purely her. It was intoxicating.

Focus, Easton. He mentally slapped himself. He couldn't stay here all night rubbing his face all over her. They had a lifetime for that. Tonight, they had a sacred duty.

He took her hand and placed it on his chest, his throat aching with unshed tears over the wondrous joy of not being destroyed by that simple touch. He moved it around and she let him, allowing him to use her hand

437

to touch parts of his chest and throat and thighs before he was sure it was going to be okay. "I think I can let go," he said, choking up and trying to swallow down the tears. "Can you keep touching me?"

She nodded. Using both hands on him, softly, slowly, learning the feel of his body. Her eyes were on him, drinking him in as she did and she scooted closer, bringing his hand to her mouth. She kissed the inside of his wrist, then each of his fingers, the tips, and smiled at him. The color was in her cheeks but it wasn't embarrassment. No, lust colored her, made her lids heavy.

He leaned in and kissed her, and in every way that counted, this was his first kiss. He lost himself in the taste of her, the soft yield of her lips and the tantalizing texture of her tongue as it darted against his, challenging and then retreating. God...all these years he'd been missing out on this.

His heart felt like it might burst. He let instinct take over and his hand drifted down her body, seeking the cleft between her thighs. And that was a shock, too, the soft, silky wetness of it had a heat he hadn't expected at all.

"East..." she moaned and scooted closer, her legs now over his. "You like to tease..." She giggled and then kissed him again, then nuzzled his neck. "Gods, you smell so good."

He couldn't speak. He was too lost in the sensory overload of her hands and her lips and her wetness on his fingers. "I don't know what I'm doing," he blurted out and then cringed, waiting for her to laugh.

"Could have fooled me," she said softly and nipped him, just behind his ear. "You are making me feel so good, East..." A shudder ran through her. "Keep doing what you're doing..." She gasped as he pressed on her clit. "Oh gods...if it's wrong I'll tell you, but...I'm yours,

I'm your plaything, your girl. This is so new to me, too, with you, but it's so perfect. Make me yours, East...the way you want to..."

She didn't need to ask twice. He didn't know what he was doing consciously, but his body seemed to have some sort of primal muscle memory as to what had to be done as he moved over her and between her legs.

Arching, she wrapped a leg around his hip, her hand wrapping around his shaft for moments, and then she trailed her fingers down it. "East..." Her whisper was a whine of need.

"I'm right here." It took him a few moments to find the natural way to line up with her, almost losing his mind just at the feeling of his head sliding through her wetness until he felt the soft give that told him he was in the right place. And then he pushed. It felt like the world caved in on him.

The heat, the slide, the wetness...fuck, the heat. It was so good. Too good.

He jerked, unable to stop himself, one thrust, and everything came undone. He came helplessly, spurting into her after one thrust like a fucking teenager. He was mortified. God, he wanted to die. Why had God asked this of him? He could tell his face was scarlet as he started to withdraw, but then Petra stopped him.

"It's good...and it's okay," she said softly, peppering him with kisses and then grinned. "Really hot that I turn you on this much." She arched, slipping him slightly more inside, running her fingers down the nape of his neck and back. She whispered nonsense to him, her body stroking his.

"You aren't gonna laugh at me?" He was on the edge of tears, he was so mortified.

"Why would I laugh, my love?" she asked seriously. "The fact that I affect you so much, that you like me that much..." She smiled. "I'm not a little girl, I know some secrets, and something they don't know," she whispered. "I would never laugh at you, for anything...well, unless you're being silly then I'll laugh. This isn't that."

"I'm so embarrassed." He rested his face in the curve of her neck, too ashamed to look at her. "It's not like I've never seen you naked before. Or come in my own hand."

"And have you ever been snug inside me before? No, and that's why," she offered. "Nothing to be embarrassed about. Especially when you feel so good there, so fucking perfect..."

"I do?" He didn't think he was anything special. He'd seen most of the others naked at one time or another and he was definitely average in the bunch.

"Perfect," she said softly and arched again, slipping him another inch inside. "I knew you would. Sometimes it's a lot to take, too much with some...but with you?" She smiled and ran her fingers between his shoulder blades. "I know you are going to fit me perfectly. No pain, no discomfort, nothing weird, just you and a perfect fit..."

He could feel himself getting hard again, the way she was moving against him giving him a slick friction that was hard to ignore. "I guess we're going to need to practice this a lot," he said, trying to poke fun at his own distress. "I've gotta build up a tolerance to your perfection so I can thoroughly defile it."

"Practice makes perfect, and you will never hear me say I don't wanna...not when it's this fucking perfect. Can I tell you a secret? First time is always quick, regardless. But the second." She giggled. "Easton, I can feel you thickening...fuck, that feels good. This round is going to be long and you're going to love it almost as much as I am." She grinned.

"Remember, my love, I'm yours. I want you to take me how you want to."

He wanted to take her every way there was to take a woman. But for now, this was the only one that mattered...looking into her eyes and doing this with intent. It was a sacred thing, a holy thing, ordained by God. He could do it. Experimentally, he began moving his hips, trying to find an angle that felt good to him and also made her happy. He was starting to learn her body, the soft sounds she made and the way her breath caught when something gave her pleasure. It was beautiful to watch.

"That's perfect," she moaned and slung her leg over his hip, the other moving farther to the outside, opening herself to him more. "East, this is all I ever thought about before...you, me... Fuck, I wanted this so badly... So good..." Her little moans were gifts. "Mmmm...take long strokes...pull all the way out and push in slowly. Oh fuck... You feel that?"

"It's so tight," he choked out, almost losing his mind at the way she was clenching around him. "Fuck... Petra!"

The orgasm ripped through her, squeezing him, fluttering, pulsing around him. She shook softly, goosebumps raising on her skin as she arched, holding him close. "East..." she panted into his ear. "Fuck...good...do that again..."

"Yes, Priestess," he gasped, trying not to lose it over the sensations he was experiencing. He'd had no idea it would feel like this. So overwhelming. So intimate. He did as she suggested, feeling the unexpected trembling in muscles he hadn't used this way before.

"Turn..." She moaned and they rested on their side. She hitched her leg higher on his hip, pulling him closer. Looking into his eyes, she smiled. "Fuck... East," she said again. "So fucking good..."

Pride swelled through him, suffusing every fiber and cell in his body. He was doing this. He was making her writhe and moan and cry out his name. He felt like a god. He picked up the pace, wanting to drive her higher and wilder.

A gasp was wrenched from her as she surrendered to him, moaning, moving with him. "I'm so close... East...baby..." Shudders slipped through her. "East, can I ride you? I need you deeper..."

He didn't answer, rolling them instead so that she was on top. They'd moved off the blankets and his back was pressed into the cold tile floor, but he didn't care. There was such a fire between them that it was all he needed to keep him warm.

Rearing up, she rolled her hips and sighed. "So much deeper," her words a whisper as she watched him, her eyes on his, hands on his pecs, her movements a slink and roll of her hips and upper body. Hair clouded around her and she threw her head back, panting. "So fucking good..." and then she was kissing him, their tongues tangling. She melted into him as his armed wrapped around her, hips still moving. "East," she said and moved back, pulling them to sitting position, her thighs over his hips, her arms around his neck. She sobbed and bounced, eyes on him. "This feels right," she said of their position, and kissed him.

"Take what you need," he managed to say, even though at this angle he was so deeply inside her he didn't know where he stopped and she began. They were moving as one.

"I only need you, Easton. So fucking good..." She kissed him again, and he felt the telltale squeeze start inside her, knowing she was reaching that peak again, and only for him.

This time he was going to come with her. He could feel it spiraling and tightening in him, too...that explosive release of everything he was into, everything she was until they were free-falling together. He braced his feet against the floor, feeling sharp stones cutting into his feet, and yet the pain felt natural, too. The blood of their lovemaking was a worthy sacrifice of reconsecration.

"Easton!" she screamed as she shattered, the world around them ringing with her cries for him.

The strong grip of her body on his sent him soaring over the edge, too, mindlessly pumping into her, milking out the last of his cum and making her take it all. When it was over, he couldn't help but to laugh at the state of the pair of them. Covered in dust and gravel, mixed with their sweat and the bodily fluids dripping out from where they were joined, mingling with the smears of blood from his hands and feet and her knees. They were a worthy sacrifice. The God was pleased.

Chapter 47

Two days after she and Easton had connected in the original temple things felt...settled.

It had been two days of finalizing travel for the matron and the girls back to the States, Emerson and Carter working with Elise to ensure the work on the Ohio house was already in full swing once they got back, and of course, contacting and connecting with the other compounds.

Idaho, Peru, Mexico, Norway, Ontario and New Mexico were all still online and rejoicing at the turn of events. Several of them went dark, into hiding once they heard what happened in San Francisco, Manitoba and Maine, but now, they were blazing bright and back on the map, figuratively, and eager to make The Order whole once more.

And everyone had wanted to meet her, and learn about the hidden bloodline, and the others that were now out in the world. She was going to have to chat with her friends soon, explain to them everything, and hopefully bring them in.

Because the guys were all interested in meeting more women of the blood. The lot of them had resigned themselves to what they considered lesser women, but knowing the blood flowed in women of worth, they were all excited. Especially those that Finn had deemed groups and duos eligible for a devotion. Those not involved in the main rites would be allowed to find wives of their own choosing within the feminine order, consensual of course.

They were leaving in the morning, to get back to real life, with a grateful Order sending them back. The promises they made, the headway they forged...no one had thought it possible, but due to the efforts of her guys, Finn especially, they were well on their way to the purity that The Order originally had before men's ambition.

But tonight, they were alone together, in the suite of rooms that had been set up for the 'governing body and devotion,' their own sanctuary while there in the Balkans. The priests had chosen to remain there, and Elise had let them know that several of the matrons were going to travel there, to work with the priests, and help clear up a few muddled rules, rites and options.

So they were alone, the eight of them, for a meal and some connection time. The priests said there needed to be a commitment between them and her, or rather a recommitment. She and Easton had already done it, and afterwards the well had been active and the priests had suggested they all commit, in their own ways, to ensure the tether from her to them, and them as a group to Him was taut, tight and strong.

She walked into the great room of their suite to see her guys, for the most part, were already there. The low table was laden with food, drink and everyone looked comfortable, smiling at her.

"So I'm fashionably late?" she said as she pulled at the wide cotton pants she was wearing, as well as the open front cardigan, which was the uniform for the high priestess, apparently.

"Still waiting on our high priest," Jack said of Finn. It was largely in name, but they would be the one to run any group rites together, as well as Order rites, which they found out they had been neglected for longer than any of them would have liked. "Priestess garb is pretty sexy in a comfy way."

She nodded. "Flowy and comfy."

"And easy access," Emerson said with a wiggle of his eyebrows.

"That's probably the point," Easton said, shaking his head. "Nothing serves the God better than a man and a woman coming together as one."

"As he and Gaia did," she said and went to her sweet Easton and leaned down to kiss him. Things between them were amazing. After they had connected at the temple he had went to bed with her, held her through the night, then made love to her in the morning, waking her with a gasp. It was a honeymoon if ever there was one. She loved it. While her guys were all pretty severe when it came to sex, she and Easton were...pure. It was about them together, and the worship. She loved it as much as she did him. "Love you," she said softly.

"Love you right back," he said, still getting that dreamy look on his face every time he looked at her. It was actually staggering how much innocence there was in him after all he'd been through in his brutal life. He was so full of joy and unexpected sweetness.

Smiling down at him, she kissed him again, seriously not sure she would ever be able to get enough of him.

"East the only one getting sugar?" Jack said as he pulled her into his lap and kissed her as well. "You look beautiful, Priestess," he said with a grin. "And extremely fuckable."

With a giggle she nodded. "Same, baby." Things with Jack would always be easy. He was just easy, and with him, things would always be interesting, both in the bedroom and out. Hugging him, she got up from his lap and shed the cardigan style sweater, showing off the sleeveless V-neck shirt, made of the softest cotton. She was going to love being here, all comfortable when she was in the priestess element.

"Did they tell you any more about how this works or what's expected?" Leo asked, gesturing to her clothing. "I kinda liked your personal style back home. Especially those cute little skirts."

"Well when we are here, and I'm wearing the priestess hat, I'll be wearing this. When we have rites, I'll have something similar." She grinned. "But when I'm home, it's just me, and when we have rites...well, it's what my guys prefer most." She winked.

"So, naked and shaking," Rix said with a smirk.

"Who's naked and shaking?" Finn walked in, looking tired. They'd tried to make him wear robes, but he'd flapped around in them for about six hours and then lost his shit the umpteenth time he tripped over the hem and almost took himself out. He'd thrown them into the fire with savage glee and no one had dared challenge the look he gave them whenever anyone mentioned it.

"Who else?" Rix grinned at him. "You look more comfortable now." He motioned to his attire.

"Yeah. Fuck those robes," Finn said flatly, taking a seat. "Even the tripping constantly wouldn't have been so bad if it hadn't been so windy around my balls. I'm rewriting parts of The Order constitution just to make them optional." He shook his head. "I didn't even ask for this job. I just wanted to do the right thing and somehow found myself in charge."

"Maybe you should abdicate and nominate Carter in your place?" Leo suggested with a cheeky smile and Carter glowered at him. "No thanks."

"I tried to abdicate," Finn said. "The priests laughed at me and then carried right on with the meeting."

"Of course they aren't going to let it happen. You're the leader for a reason," she said. "And anyway, I was looking through the rites that need both of us. They are pretty fun..." Actually they were sexy as hell, and she knew her naughty Finn would enjoy showing the entire

Order that she was theirs, but she belonged to him utterly. "Lots of sexy with my favorite Devil."

"I don't know. It's one thing to be in multiples between us, but I'm not an exhibitionist in that way," he admitted. "I know I'll probably get used to it, but there's a big difference between three of these guys watching and a hundred or so strangers or people I've only met a few times."

"Maybe if we'd been raised this way, it might have made more sense," Carter said sympathetically. "If it were normal to do those kinds of thing in public, I mean. If we'd grown up seeing that, it might not be so weird to take over doing it."

"What's actually bothering you about it?" Leo asked a reasonable question for once instead of poking fun. "Is it the performance aspect? You think people are going to critique you?"

"It's not that." Finn gave her a small smile. "I know how to please my priestess. I'd never worry about that. I guess I'm mostly slightly icked out by working every day with people that have seen my dick. I don't have that European level of comfort with public nudity "

"Few do," Emerson offered. "I don't. I mean you guys aren't in that equation."

"Well there is the option of doing it behind a screen," she offered. "Not all of them, mind you, but the ones involving sex...like actual sex..."

"And the others?" Emerson asked.

"Some are actually not sex at all. Nudity, yes, but some are just touching, holding...hell, there's this weird one that is almost like Kama Sutra poses to act out a story between He and Gaia..."

"I'm sure you don't have to actually do them if you don't want to," Carter pointed out. "There's nothing stopping you from rewriting things in collaboration with the priests. If the idea is just to build the sacrifice and teach the young, you don't necessarily have to do it the old-fashioned way."

"You volunteering to overhaul hundreds of years' worth of rites?" Finn asked with a tired smile, but Carter shrugged.

"They must have been updated in the last few hundred years or they wouldn't be in an English we understand," he pointed out. "The priests must be used to this stuff."

"We'll think about it." Finn smiled at her. "We haven't really had a chance to talk about any of this since it happened. Just kind of caught it all on the fly and kept running."

She nodded. "You think I am excited about being this high priestess?" she offered. "Though the clothing is much more comfortable than yours." She winked.

"We should talk about that," Carter said seriously. "How are you feeling about it? I doubt you expected any of this when you decided on your little unmasking stunt."

She considered her scarred lover. "Honestly, I didn't think past wanting you seven. Is it a lot? Sure. Am I floored? Yes. But it also feels, I don't know, right? I mean I don't really have a problem with any of it, considering the past three years you guys have been, in a sense, preparing me for this."

"Then you're dealing with it a lot better than I am," Carter laughed easily. "I still catch myself looking around in total disbelief every now and then."

"I wish our parents were here to see this," Finn said. "I think they'd be proud."

"Well, by what Elise said some of the moms are still about. Leo, you planning to see your mother? Finn? Sister?" Jack said. She knew he had hope that his own mother was around somewhere.

"Of course!" Finn said, right as Leo blurted out, "Of fucking course I am! What sort of stupid question is that?"

Emerson laughed, mirth shining in his eyes. She shook her head. "I know all of them would be proud of the men you became. Hell, I'm excited to meet them, and tell them just how much you are all loved," she said. "Dirty fuckers that you are."

Rix smirked at her from across the table. "And it's exactly what you love."

"Yes, it is. I don't think you guys understand how important you all are to me, I mean with all of this, the only thing that really matters is I get to keep you, all of you, as mine." And it wasn't something she had thought would ever happen. Now part of The Order herself, she was seeing the dreams come true. "Still need to talk to the girls about it but..."

"Hopefully they'll see how happy you are and be curious about joining," Carter said.

"And I know a few guys who'd be happy to persuade them if they aren't sure," Leo laughed.

"It's all kinda crazy, right? I mean a direct bloodline to Gaia. And our lovely little victim is part of that bloodline," Rix said.

"Kildare said our children will be powerful in a way others in The Order haven't been. Blessed with his favor," she offered. "I mean if we have kids."

"We will," Easton said happily. "I've seen it."

"What do you mean?" she asked, curiosity consuming her.

"Since He healed me, He communicates with me sometimes. Mostly guidance or reassurance, but sometimes in images that I think I'm supposed to paint. I had one of those visions the night we were in the old temple. It was a painting of you as the triple goddess—the Maiden, the Mother and the Crone. I could see you heavy with child as clear as day." He shrugged, unselfconscious about the amazed and envious ways the others were staring at him. "Somehow I knew that I must paint it and that one day it would be true."

"I...really?" she whispered. "Babies?"

"At least one," Emerson said. "Do we know who?"

She looked to Easton. "Have you started painting already?" The idea of being a mother never interested her before, but now, the idea of having one, or all of these men's children...

"Not yet. I was going to ask you to model for me when we get home." He smiled. "I didn't think you'd mind."

Obliviously not. She loved that she was already his muse, the show that was going to go up soon after they got home. Lorne had been planning one hell of a party for it. She was excited that she would see something she was not only proud of him for making, but proud of herself for being part of, even if she didn't know originally that she was.

"Oh, I think you can entice me."

"As for who the father is, He didn't show me that," Easton said to Emerson. "I don't think it really matters. It or they will be raised by all of us."

"I would have all your children," she said with a smile.

"Probably what will happen. I mean, we are seven of the original thirteen, with the most holy of bloodlines." He grinned. "Who else is excited about knocking Petra up?"

"New kink unlocked," Leo said with a smirk, making them all laugh.

"So..." Emerson said with a chuckle, "why don't we get to why we are here. Commitment. I don't think we can all be as bad ass as Easton...I mean, original temple and everything..." he teased. "But..." he crooked a finger at her. Getting up, she went to him and settled into his lap. "I'm committed to this, to you, to all of us, sweet girl. Nothing is ever going to tear us up, and know without a doubt that anyone that tries to take you from us will be dealt with so severely the warnings will echo in eternity."

With his words finished he pulled something out of his pocket and slipped it onto her middle finger on her right hand. "I love you, Petra. Always and only you." He kissed her.

She looked down after his lips pulled away from hers to the pretty onyx ring, his own house's gem. "I found it in my father's vault."

"I love it...and I love you. Thank you."

"Show-off," Leo muttered.

"Is that what we're supposed to be doing?" Finn asked, looking at Easton. "Are words enough? What is He wanting here? Were we all supposed to bring gifts?"

"I don't think this came from Him. It was the priests." Easton shrugged helplessly.

Rix went to her and Emerson and picked her up, wrapping her legs around his waist, as he engaged her in one hell of a kiss. The passion, the want behind it...when he pulled away she was breathless, feeling overly warm and dopey. "Wow," she murmured.

"Always wow with you, my little victim." He leaned his head on hers. "No one else in the world I want to chase...or catch."

Her giggle bubbled up and she nodded to him. Lord. Her most volatile and unhinged of her lovers had his own way about things, and she adored it as much as she adored his brand of seductions. Kendrix was intense, but he knew without a doubt she belonged to him.

Setting her down, he lifted his shirt and winked at her. Her eyes lit on the carved P just to the side of his pant line. He bled for her. The highest form of praise from him.

"I love you," she said softly and he winked.

"Come here," Carter said and waited as she scampered across to him, enjoying this little ceremony immensely. "I don't have the words and a scar like his," he gestured to Kendrix, "would just be another scar in a sea of scars on me, but I can promise you a life of love and a legacy. Every animal we rescue together will be a testament to the kind of people we are and the love we have between us. I hope that's enough."

"Carter..." she said and kissed him senseless. They were evenly matched on so many things, but their love of animals was the one that brought them together. For them, it was a promise, past a commitment to each other because it went past them together. "I love you so much."

"Love you, too." He handed her off to Leo, who accepted her with a grin.

"Fuck the pretty words," he declared. "I'll get a new tat when we get home. I'd have done it here, but I don't trust anyone that isn't my guy. And you can choose where it goes. You'll be written in my skin for life. That enough commitment for you?"

"Anything?" she teased him.

"I didn't say anything. I said you could choose where it goes. And at this point, I'd remind you that getting something tattooed on my dick means you won't be riding it for a couple of weeks. Understood?"

"I would never do that, it's way too important." She giggled. "But I do like the idea of Property of Petra tattooed on your groin."

"Absolutely fucking not," he snorted. "I don't know whether to be amused at your attitude or horrified that you think I'm that trashy. Property of Petra..." He shook his head in disbelief. "What I was actually thinking was a rendering of your namesake place from the desert. Petra without words. Like the classy motherfucker that I am. Fucking 'Property of Petra.' Go to Finn. I don't want to look at you anymore," he said, eyes filled with mirth.

She giggled, leaning in and nipped his lip. Lord, she loved to teased Leo. She didn't even get a chance to say something snarky as Jack grabbed her.

"Sweetness, you know I'm committed to this, and to us."

"I know..."

"Good because I signed us up for a naughty Kama Sutra class." He grinned. "Take that, Skeezie Keezie."

With another laugh she kissed him and then was in Finn's arms.

"I don't have anything to offer you," he said. "I've been working so hard to build a better Order and a better life for us that I didn't even know what I was supposed to be doing here tonight. But I hope you know that everything I change and everything I build is for us...all eight of us. To keep us safe. To bring our kids into a safer, more loving world. To serve Him with humility and grace. I intend to keep working toward that for the rest of my life, and I hope that you'll all be with me on that journey."

"You have everything to offer me, Finn. Everything you are is everything I always wanted, my Devil." She said the last softly, just enough for him to hear. "I love you so much...love everything you are." She kissed him softly. Gods, the man was so good, so genuine.

"I love you, too."

"Well thank fuck that's over," Leo declared. "I'm fucking starving. Let's eat!"

She shook her head and settled next to Easton, snuggling close as she lay her head on his shoulder. He wrapped his arm around her waist, keeping her close as she listened to the guys fill plates and shit talk each other. Jack settled a plate in front of her, and she smiled at him, then looked to Easton.

"Home soon...you ready to see Niobe?"

"So fucking ready." He smiled dreamily at her again. "Looking forward to you meeting her, too."

"Me, too," she nodded. "Sleepover when we get back? I can sit for you..." she said hopefully. All she wanted was to cement their lives together, and she knew starting with Easton would make all the difference. "I'm going to have to go see the girls, but I honestly just want a few days hiding with you and the guys." She grinned.

"Of course! I'd like that a lot." His eyes were unfocused, like he was already picturing her naked in his studio.

"Do you want one of us to come with you to see your friends?" Carter asked, ever the gentleman.

"I'd like all of you to come and see my friends with me. I mean, they want to meet all of you."

"I'm sure we can swing that," Finn said with a smile. "Remind me again where they are tomorrow and I'll file a flight plan with the jet before we go home."

"You got it, baby. Now...who am I sleeping with tonight?" She grinned as the room erupted in arguments and Emerson grinned back at her, shaking his head.

Chapter 48

2 weeks later, New York City

"Okay, okay. We are all here, finally," Carlee said to her as Fiona pulled away from the hug she was giving her. "So, dish finally, because I have been chomping at the bit to find out what the ever loving fuck is going on!"

With a laugh, Petra shook her head. "Let's sit...yeah, you are going to wanna sit down for all this."

They sat around the living room of the brownstone she and the guys had rented in New York, all smiles because she was finally together with her best friends, her sisters in The Order. Well, they didn't know that yet. Finn had sent the jet to get them, and they had finally been able to meet all in the city for a girls' hangout. Or what they thought was a girls' hangout.

"Seriously, Petty...you need to say something, that smile is starting to look all black hole sun," Carlee quipped. "Come on, stop being a bitch and talk!"

"Okay, Okay," she sighed. "So...god, this is going to be harder than I thought."

"What, you're marrying someone?"

"Um...no... No, I don't think I can?" she said absently. "No... I... Okay... So, we, the four of us, as well as the girls that were with us in Ohio...we are part of a very special bloodline dedicated to He Who Sleeps." There. She knew she sounded crazy but it was out there now. She could work from there.

"I fucking knew it was a cult!" Fiona declared triumphantly. "I knew it!"

"What the fuck is a He Who Sleeps?" Victoria ignored Fiona, who was nudging her for support.

"Who," Petra said and proceeded to tell them the story Kildare told them about the God, His consort and the thirteen. They watched her, eyes wide, and when she was done she smiled. "And all of us belong to the most precious bloodline."

"How do you know?"

"One of the matrons told me. And I can prove it...we just kinda have to go to the Balkans to do the ritual."

"And that's my cue to call an ambulance." Fiona shook her head, reaching for her phone.

"An ambulance?" Victoria stared at her. "She sounds pretty coherent to me."

"What part of any of that didn't sound completely delusional to you?" Fiona gaped at her. "She thinks she's the high priestess of some cult and that magic is real."

"That's not quite what she said," Victoria started, but Fiona sighed.

"That's exactly what she said. She thinks she and these guys are somehow blessed by some god that lives in a well. She's clearly hallucinated magic sparkles. She's been completely brainwashed and the sooner we get her into psychiatric care, the easier this will go."

Petra shook her head. Fiona was going to be the hardest to convince she knew but... "Honestly, Fi, when have I ever believed in magic or anything supernatural? That's all Carlee."

"That's why I'm so worried," Fiona said bluntly. "I mean...you're talking about glowing stones. Maybe they drugged you."

"My guys do a lot, but they don't traffic in drugs of any kind," she said with a laugh, because whatever they put in the champagne to stop her remembering the route to the devotional mansion every year was for safety and protection. "Honestly, I didn't believe this either, 'til things started happening. I mean three years of being their devotion, and I only know everything because I wanted them, because I wanted to be with them."

"Yeah...explain that?" Carlee said. "Cuz I'm still spotty on that."

Petra told them how she met her guys, the real story, and watched as they were collectively horrified, and intrigued by the time she was done.

"So lemme get this straight. You saved a girl from getting murdered by seven dudes, took her place, and then they kept it going for three years, the last of which, last Halloween weekend, you had a plan to unmask them and did, and this is why we are here now?" She nodded to Carlee. "Hot. What kinda masks?"

Petra laughed. "A lady never tells," she said and Carlee frowned.

"Damn it, Petra...won't tell us who is the biggest, won't tell us about their masks..." she pouted. "You are mean as hell."

"Have you collectively lost your fucking minds?" Fiona was starting to look upset. "She hooked up with guys who openly claim to be serial killers and you're asking about dicks?! What the fuck is wrong with you all?"

"Maybe because you're looking at this wrong?" Carlee said to Fiona. "She figured out why we are orphans, Fi...she figured it out. This isn't her just pulling this shit outta her ass, this is her, after doing the work, giving us the truth. It's all fact-checkable, right?" Petra nodded. "See? That's why I'm not freaking out. Because it's fucking real, Fi, and we...we belong somewhere..."

"How do you look wrong at serial killers? How do you 'fact check' magic? What are you going to do if we fly halfway around the fucking world and it turns out it was just some mindfuck trip these people, who are clearly a cult, put her through? You're so blinded by your desire to belong to someone or something that you're glossing over how utterly fucking crazy this all sounds!"

"And you're so focused on what's acceptable that you can't fathom that this might be real. I mean what the fuck, Fi? The major religions aren't a cult? They aren't killing in the name of their own gods?" Carlee asked.

"We've never believed in them, either!" Fiona said hotly. "And there's a massive fucking difference between huge, global organized religions and some tiny cult that no one has ever heard of! It's not about what's acceptable! It's not acceptable that anyone kills in the name of religion. Not the big religions. Not these guys! Replace this Finn dude's name with Charles Manson and it's history repeating itself all over again!"

"Perhaps I may be of assistance here?" Easton had cracked open the door and drifted in unheard under the shouting. He was wearing a beatific look on his face that Petra had never seen before. "The God wants you to come home, Fiona. If you require a miracle to believe, then He loves you enough to give you one."

He held out his palm and a flame sprang up on it, burning so hotly that they could feel the heat on their faces, but Easton's hand was untouched. "Behold His power," he intoned. Walking across to the modern glass hearth, where a fire had been laid but not lit, he stood a couple of feet away and tossed the flame. The fire roared into life and the others gasped, but Fiona was pale.

"How do I know this isn't a trick?" she demanded. "This might just be parlor magic. Someone with a remote for the fire. Some kind of gel..."

"Fiona." Easton looked sad as he walked toward her and displayed both sides of his hands. "There is no trick. But if you still doubt, then He will tell you

Himself." He touched two gentle fingers to her forehead and Fiona went rigid, her eyes rolling back in her head like she was being electrocuted. When she came back to herself, twenty seconds or so later, she was weeping.

"I need a moment," she choked out and ran to the bathroom, locking herself in.

Petra looked to him. "Thank you, my love. That was getting hot. Fi is like a dog with a bone sometimes." She looked to her remaining friends. "This is Easton, my Snake," she said proudly. "Easton is a brilliant artist, and owns a piece of my heart. He's also kinda a conduit for He Who Sleeps. A reward for what he's endured."

Carlee looked him over and blinked. "And hot as fuck to boot." She grinned. "I'm Carlee, and it's nice to meet you, Easton. You treating our girl good?"

Petra looked to Victoria and smiled. "You okay? You have been quiet. And believe me, I know how this sounds..."

"Do you?" Victoria shook her head. "Fiona's objections weren't unreasonable and you guys are making out like she's the crazy one. A dog with a bone? You asked her to believe in magic, sight unseen. I'm with you guys. I believe what I just saw. But I don't blame her for being suspicious, and I think you need to go a little easier on her."

"She also didn't feel the calling that you did," Easton said gently to Petra. "He understands. That's why He sent me in. I'll go and see if she's okay." He went to the bathroom door and knocked, quietly murmuring something they couldn't hear. Then the door opened and he went in, closing it behind him again.

"He seems rather sweet for a multiple murderer," Victoria said drily. "Are you sure that bit was all true?"

She nodded. "Had Fiona not lost her shit, I would have told you guys what happened to me at Christmas." She sighed. "And this is going to make it all seem more crazy but...I was kidnapped while the guys were in the Balkans...and before you think it had to do with them, it didn't. The dude was apparently obsessed with me being a good girl and wanted to force me to marry him," she said bitterly. "I was stuck in south Philly for three fucking days, asshole snatched me from the shelter. My guys came to get me, strung him up and killed him," she said matter-of-factly. "They have the capacity to do it, but it's not who they are. Well, it's who Kendrix is..."

"I heard that," she heard from the other room and giggled.

"Seriously, it's not like they are just psychos from the cradle, they were taught this, all for the glory of someone that was not their God. They were lied to. We were lied to. Things are better now, and while He expects sacrifice, it's not like Fiona thinks. Everything has balance."

"So what does this mean for us?" Victoria asked. "Do we have to join? Like...is it mandatory? Are we expected to turn up and do stuff? This is so far out of my comfort zone, I think I'm going to need a little time to process it."

"Well, you don't have to do anything you don't want to do. Our bloodline is special, because, well, we are direct descendants to Gaia, via her sister Estra. Gaia and He never had children, but her sister kept our line from the thirteen, and kept it pure so to speak. We are, for all intents and purposes, royalty in their world. If you choose not to join, that's on you."

"And if we want to? Will we get seven horse hanging studs to service us?" Carlee asked with a grin. She heard someone snort from the other room. Clearly the guys were listening en masse, and probably worried since Easton hadn't made it out of the bathroom yet, with or without Fiona.

"The Order has males looking for their own devotions, as many do not wish to kill, and will take part in the balance through self-sacrifice and their own kinks," Petra said to Carlee.

"So we are called devotions?"

"Women that belong to a group, yes. If you end up with one or two men, they are just your men, and you are their woman. It's all very personal."

"Can we think about it?" Victoria asked. "It's a lot. I mean, I'd love to see where my people come from, and do some reading and get to know the family, but I can't just make a decision like this right now. I want to meet people and see places first."

"No one would ever make you," she said with a nod. "I'm hoping you guys will come to the Balkans with us, to meet the other matrons, and the priests..."

"And hot dudes?" Carlee asked.

"Yes and meet hot dudes. There's a spring festival that we are bringing back. A more elaborate version of the May Day celebration we used to have. You are of the blood, so you can be there and not participate, and I think you would all enjoy it. I'm looking forward to it. Wine and cakes and flower crowns and..." She blushed. The rites she found with the guys would be the highlight of the trip, though that wasn't for them to know.

"I could probably swing a trip in May," Victoria nodded, starting to catch up with their enthusiasm. "They don't know what happened to our mothers? Why we were at the orphanage at all, instead of with them?"

"Our mothers were matrons," she began and then stopped as Easton and Fiona walked out. "Hey," she said as Fi came into view and then looked to Easton. "Everything okay?"

"We're fine." Easton was still smiling. "She just needs some time to process this. It's a lot. Being touched by Him can be overwhelming."

Fiona was still pale, with red blotches on her cheeks, and she had the crease in her forehead that meant a migraine was brewing, but she nodded. "I maybe need to lie down for a bit," she said, her voice quiet and raspy from crying. "But Easton says the other guys are here, too, so it might be nice to meet them before I go and rest?"

She nodded. "That was what I was working up to."

"Wait, you were talking about our moms," Carlee said. "What happened?"

"Oh. Well, our moms were matrons in a sense, they didn't handle housing or taking care of the girls, but once they got pregnant they came to their respective compounds. I'm sorry to say they are all dead. Matron Elise, she's the one that took over in Ohio for Matron Verna, she gave me the files. Mine, Fi's and Carlee's died in childbirth, complications, and they chose for each of us to live. Vic, your mother passed when you were three, she had been traveling, looking for others of the blood, and contracted something in South America. She died at the compound in Peru. I'm sorry. But I do know where they are buried, and I want the four of us to visit each, together."

"Oh." Victoria's face crumpled for a moment before she managed to pull herself together. "I was hoping...but never mind. It's not like I knew her to lose her, I guess."

Fiona put an arm around her shoulders and squeezed her close. "It's still a loss," she said. "But now at least we know we're all actual family and not just heart-sisters. That's pretty cool."

"And the compounds aren't in hiding anymore," Easton said. "They're open to all the medical technology and care that the rest of us have. No more women will die in childbirth if modern medicine can save them. You don't have to worry about it happening to you."

"Exactly. My guys made sure we would all be safe. I think it's about time you meet them..." She grinned "I know you lunatics are listening...get in here."

She stood as they poured into the room, Jack and Leo falling over themselves, causing her to laugh. "Guys, these are my sisters, Fiona, Victoria and Carlee. Girls, these are the loves of my life, Leo, Jack, Emerson, Carter, Fin and Kendrix. You guys met East already."

"Oh, that's not fair," Carlee said. "You do not deserve seven gorgeous men!"

"Rude," Victoria said, elbowing her in the side. "Sometimes you should pause before you blurt out whatever is in your head."

"Why wouldn't she deserve us?" Leo asked. "She's awesome!"

"Yes, I am. Pay no mind to Carlee, she's just sour cuz she doesn't have seven men that love her."

"Yet." Carlee grinned. "And it's fabulous to meet you guys." She got up and went, hugging each.

Fiona was more reserved, still reeling, but she gave each of them a smile and hello. Victoria was hugging like Carlee, obviously overwhelmed with meeting something akin to family for the first time in her life.

"We were listening," Emerson said as they all settled down, Petra in Finn's lap. "And we understand your apprehension. Just know that we never meant to freak you guys out, and neither did Petra. She's been agonizing about this for days. Do you guys have any questions for us?"

"I guess what I've been wondering while all this is going on, is whether or not we'll be able to carry on with our own lives," Victoria said. "If I'm going to join, do I have to go and live in one of these compounds Petra told us about or can I carry on with my studies?"

"Not at all, your life won't change...well, unless you take on a devotion position, and even then it's nominal. It would depend on the group you connected with, and how they want to work...though I can tell you, many are interested in a devotion, and will move heaven and earth for her to commit to them." Emerson winked at her. "But you can still do everything you do, I mean does being Catholic mean you have to be a nun?"

"I guess we just don't know enough about it all yet," Victoria said thoughtfully. "It sounded like all the women live in compounds, but if that's not the case then I need to know more."

Emerson nodded. "Before we put a stop to it, they were in hiding, because of what the assholes that seized power did." He told them of what their fathers went through, and what happened, that they know of, to the different compounds, and Petra had interjected with how they, the four of them, got to Ohio. They listened, and were rightfully horrified with some of it.

Jack picked up the story with, "Originally, from what we saw, many grew up in the compounds but they went out into the world. Many went to boarding school like you guys did. Hell, we did."

"Well then, it would be an honor to be part of the rebuilding," Fiona said quietly. "We shall be the last out of hiding and the first of the new Order."

Petra smiled at her friend. Whatever Easton said to her had changed her mind quickly. She would have to ask him later.

Carlee nodded. "I'm not going to lie, this is trippy as hell, but...fuck it. We have always been searching for something...and it appears we were right."

"Do you finance student loans?" Victoria teased, not really expecting them to say yes, but Finn nodded.

"Part of what we're aiming to do is build the financial empire the way it was always supposed to be built," he said. "Part of that is making sure that every generation is well-educated to the best of their abilities. The God is generous with His gifts, but they're wasted on those that don't know how to use them. So no, we won't finance a loan. We'll pay off your tuition as an investment in your future as a productive member of The Order."

Petra grinned. "And housing, like ours, will be handled, too. As well as other things. The Order wasn't supposed to be for the few, but for all of us. Our people are good, well now they are and He? He's wonderfully generous, and happy...well, now He's happy." She looked to Easton.

"He's happier every day," Easton confirmed. "Even more so now that the children of Estra's line are rejoining the fold."

"So, what do you guys do?" Carlee asked. "I mean I know Easton is an artist..."

"I run a few businesses that keep money rolling in," Emerson said. "Jack owns a small holistic company, specializing in goods ethically made and subsidized in communities that need the income."

Jack nodded. "It's pretty awesome to be able to help."

"And you guys are okay with Petra still working?" Carlee asked.

"You ever tried to make her do something she didn't want to?" Leo laughed. "Ain't worth your life. If she wants to work, she works. If she wants to be a spoiled princess, that's cool with us, too."

"I couldn't not work," Petra said. "Carter and I are going to open a sanctuary at the new house." She beamed at him. "And Leo's pharma company is working on the depression issue with natural ingredients."

Carlee arched a brow. "So like... Okay and don't take this wrong, but you guys are straight up serial killers, but you...care about the world?"

"Most of us didn't kill for the fun of it," Finn pointed out. "We had been brought up to believe that it was necessary for the survival of the God and the Earth. We tried to take people who didn't deserve to live."

"I do..." Kendrix said with a shrug.

"And just what is it you do?" Carlee asked him.

"I'm a spinal surgeon for dogs and cats," he said with a grin. "Best in the world."

"So clearly it's all about balance," Carlee said with a smirk.

"We're not bad people," Finn said with a shrug.

"Speak for yourself," Leo sniggered. "Kendrix is bad to the bone."

Kendrix grinned. "No, I'm balanced." He winked at Petra. She shivered and Carlee grinned.

"Ooh, this is the one that chases you?! Okay, I can see the appeal. He wear that mask, too?"

Petra blushed and Carlee laughed, the sound hearty and light.

"We've all got our kinks," Leo said with an easy shrug. "It's the way we were raised. Don't be surprised if you find yourselves getting chased by guys with a few surprises up their sleeves."

"Do not threaten me with a good time, Leo."

Petra looked at Vic and Fiona, knowing that while she was quiet about it, Petra wasn't close to being the wildest of them.

"I don't know why you're looking at us," Victoria said. "Carlee's the hoe of this group that's up for anything. I doubt any of these guys would be into my kind of kinks. I doubt they're into being dominated."

Carter choked and covered it with a laugh. "Brad is going to love you," he said. "Not all of us are into topping. You kink how you kink. The God loves you anyway."

"On which note, it's been lovely to meet you all, but I need to go and take some meds and lie down in a quiet and dark room for a few hours," Fiona said regretfully. "But I'll see you all for dinner?"

Petra nodded. "Up the stairs, first door on the right is your room." She winked.

They watched Fiona leave and Carlee looked at Victoria. "I didn't know you topped."

"That's because any time anyone mentions anything vaguely sexual you jump right in about dick sizes and whether they have brothers or not," Victoria pointed out. "You're not exactly the most discreet of people, and the world I move in is all about discretion."

"Clearly," Carlee said. "Also, there is nothing wrong with being an out and proud sexually liberated woman. Cuts out the middle man when they know what you want."

"She has a point," Jack said.

Petra rolled her eyes. It was an old argument about Carlee's sexual liberation. "Remember when Carlee lost her virginity?" she asked Victoria. "We didn't hear the end of it for weeks."

"No one is saying there's anything wrong with it," Victoria said. "You can fuck who you want to fuck and I'm not judging. As long as you're safe. It's just not how the rest of us operate, and in my world it would be dangerous."

Emerson nodded to her. "You're in Chicago, right? Have you heard of Façade? It's a members-only club but it's super high-end clientele. I used to belong to it, well technically still do, legacy membership."

Petra arched a brow at her lover. "I didn't know you were into the scene..." Some of her guys were into some severe kinks but none mentioned the scene until now.

Emerson shrugged. "I explored. My kinks are tame compared..."

"Heard of it?" Victoria chuckled. "I'm on the VIP list. I'm not rich like most of the members, but I have an excellent reputation."

"Indeed. And here I was going to offer to sponsor you." He winked. "Family and all."

"Well, if you're ever out my way, hit me up and I'll get you VIP access," Victoria gave him a genuine smile. "I've never had family to spoil before. It would be an honor."

She listened to them talk, Leo engaged with Carlee about something having to do with her own schooling and she leaned into Finn and whispered, "This is going really well. I mean we had a hiccup with Fiona freaking out but Easton fixed that. He's getting all the cuddles later."

"One of them was always going to freak." He shrugged. "They love you. And serial killers are a lot to swallow. If I'm honest, I'm surprised Fiona was the only one that freaked."

"Carlee is too much of a free spirit to freak out. This is like everything she's ever wanted, you know? Vic, she's freaking, but she's more quiet about it. Fiona has always been the biggest passion of all four of us." She ran her hand over his stomach and sighed. "But I have hope we will be able to count them among The Order sooner than later. All of us wanted to belong growing up, and having just us... It feels good to know they have the opportunity to be cared for like you guys care for me."

"Oh, they'll be cared for, all right," Finn chuckled with a smirk. "Carlee is absolutely going to find herself with a group or two."

"She is eager." She chuckled. "Thank you for this, and for wanting to meet them. I know this was hard on them, and you guys." She nuzzled his throat. "But it seems to be working out."

"Hey, Pet, you didn't tell us that Easton's show is coming up and it's you!" Carlee said. "We are so coming down for it."

Petra laughed. "I mean, you kinda had to meet him first," she said and snuggled closer to Finn. "Everything else, okay?" she said softly, her conversation directed back at him. "I know you're taking on so much, but are you okay, my love?"

"I'm tired," he admitted. "But once the new council is elected and running and have approved all the suggestions the accountants have made, there'll be a lot less on my plate and I can start to relax." He sighed. "I feel jealous of the others sometimes," he told her. "Since everything went down, they've all been able to come home with you and have some quality time, while I've been running around like a headless chicken fielding calls and emails fourteen hours a day. I miss you."

"I miss you, too. Maybe we need some Finn and Petra time, just us."

"The results of the elections are coming in tomorrow," he told her. "After that, I'm giving them a week to get up to speed on the mandate and the education package, and then I'm backing off and they can deal with it on their own." He smiled tiredly. "And then you and I can leave our phones and go away somewhere for a week. Just us."

"That sounds like heaven, baby. Someplace warm maybe?" The idea of being naked with him with sun-warmed skin did something to her.

"How about a beach somewhere in South America?" he suggested. "Sun, sea, sand, cocktails on command...?"

She nodded, "Hell yes, and sexy little bikinis." She brightened. "Can we maybe see the compound in Peru? Kildare said there's a well there...we should go and pay our respects."

"Sure. There are nice beaches in Peru and I'm sure they'd appreciate a visit from the high priestess."

"I mean, yeah but...I more just want to pay our respects to him. Seeing as he's the reason why we are together." She nuzzled his throat. "You know...we have some time...before dinner I mean. Feel like a nap with me?"

"Always." His smile was love mixed with relief. He really was exhausted.

She kissed him softly on the cheek and then stood. "You guys enjoy, I'm taking Finn for a much needed nap for both of us." She looked to Vic and Carlee. "You guys going to be okay?" In answer, Carlee made finger guns at her.

"Yeah. I'm going to have tea and then I'll go check on Fi," said Victoria. "It looked like she was brewing a doozy."

She nodded. "Great. So? Dinner in a couple hours, yeah?"

They left the living room, Petra leading Finn up to her room, and smiled at him. "That went really well," she said softly. "And I know things are just going to get better from here, for us and for them."

"They will," he said firmly. "I know it."

They gained the room and she slipped out of her flats, padding into the bathroom. "Get settled, my love.

We have a couple blissful hours of sleep on the horizon," she offered and heard the door open. Looking out, she saw Kendrix walk in.

"This a private nap party or can anyone join in?"

"Bed is big enough for team napping," Finn said with a grin. "Just promise you won't snore."

"Jack snores," Kendrix said as he jumped on the bed. She loved that her largely serious and severe lover was relaxing more with her. "Get that sexy ass in here, Petty..." He grinned. "I'm sure Finn doesn't wanna cuddle with me."

Five minutes later she was out of the bathroom and settled between the two of them, Rix snuggled to her back while she was curled against Finn's chest. "Bliss..." she murmured as Rix splayed his hand on her belly.

"Agreed." Contented, Finn closed his eyes and sleep was quick to come.

"You think this would be where we ended up when you unmasked us?" Rix asked softly.

"No...but I hoped. This is more than I could dream of."

"Well dream, my sweet sexy victim. Because against all odds, you got what you wanted. And I think we did, too."

She smiled to herself and felt him relax into sleep behind her, following soon after, with visions of a life imagined revealing from the mists.

Epilogue

8 months later, 2 weeks to All Souls.

Petra walked through the bottom level of the massive house, Niobe on her shoulder, chattering on about weird parrot things. Since coming back to the States, she had been spending a lot of time with both Brutus and Niobe, and these days they were both like her shadows. Brutus would normally be at her side but he was with Carter as they were overseeing the final touches of the sanctuary they had set up on the east side of the property, Barks and Scales Sanctuary. They were holding the dedication ceremony in a few days and Carter was obsessed with making sure it was perfect.

He had kept his promise, and they were already housing thirty dogs from tense situations in the makeshift indoor kennels there, safe because of her love, and many more would be, too. Their sanctuary would be able to house over one hundred dogs, and there were houses being built for cats, and one for the more exotics like reptiles and birds.

Niobe cooed in her ear, rubbing her head against hers. She reached up and stroked her breast, smiling. She did that when she heard Easton's voice, and they were coming up to him and Emerson now.

"Ah, there she is. How's your list?" Emerson said as he went to her and kissed her. Niobe flew over to Easton and cooed at him.

"Kitchen is being unpacked, I think Leo and Jack are still up in their bedrooms unpacking, and my amazing suite is all in place." She grinned. Her bedroom was the largest, with the largest bed, of course, big enough to sleep at least five of them together. So much nicer than her apartment, which she had vacated, though Emerson had told her he purchased the building, so if she wanted to use the space she could.

Emerson picked her up and spun her around. "I love this house," she said with a bright smile. The place had been finished completely only five days before, everything to their specs thanks to Damon. "He did an amazing job."

"Didn't I?" Damon said as he walked into the room. "It does my heart good to know our priestess approves."

"Brown noser," Emerson said dryly. "Why are you here?"

"Giving the pool guy the plans for the pool, grotto and hot tub," he offered. "You guys still on for coming next week, right?"

She nodded. Damon and his crew had taken a shine to Fiona at Petra's birthday party. She of course had made them work for it, but it seemed they were working out. Halloween was coming up, which meant Petra wouldn't be the only one doing time as a devotion. Of course Damon and the guys were probably nothing like her seven, but she had no doubt Fi could handle it.

Next week was their 'coming out' party, so to speak, where Fiona would decide, in front of the whole Order, if she would commit to being a devotion. None of them were going to miss it.

Victoria and Carlee were both playing the field as well, though Carlee was close to accepting a devotion spot as well. Petra knew it was going to be an on the fly situation, considering the courtship with the guys she was with was a lot shorter than Fiona and Damon's crew.

"You'll have to come and see the studio now that it's mostly set up." Easton was going from strength to strength. He was almost unrecognizable as the man she'd first met—a distant, cold, untouchable killer. His art had changed, too. His pieces were still edgy and heart-rending, but there was a sacred element to them too now. They'd discussed it as a group once but none of them could quite put their finger on what was different. Just that the art seemed...holy somehow. They'd been going for four or five times the price of his earlier works and since he'd also massively increased his output, Lorne was talking about opening a new gallery just for him and artists he wanted to support.

Seeing his studio was one of the things she had been waiting for. Before they moved she had spent a lot of time at his loft, but knowing he could work from home, in a studio built to his specs...she couldn't wait.

"I can't wait," she told him. "I'm yours any time you want me. Emerson? Did Finn get back from seeing his sister yet?" She had been dying to meet Jessica, but was giving Finn his time to connect with her. It was the same with Leo and his mother, Cynthia, though Leo was already planning on having her come for the holidays.

"He's on his way," Easton said when Emerson shrugged. "He texted to say he was leaving about five minutes ago. It's in the family chat."

Well, that explained it. She had no idea where her phone was. "Ah. Well Niobe has hidden my phone once again, so maybe you could get her to show me where it is?"

Damon laughed, shaking his head. "Mischievous little thing."

"You ready for Fiona?"

"Born ready," he growled. "Though we do have you to thank for that vixen. Expect a fruit basket."

"Better than the sex toys Xander and Hollis sent me for introducing them to Carlee."

"You'd think they'd have twigged that sex toys are kind of obsolete when you have seven partners," Easton said, shaking his head with disbelief. "It's not like we ever leave you wanting for orgasms."

"They are both deviants, I'm sure it was the first thing that came to mind," Damon said. "I mean Xander owns a swingers club for fuck's sake."

And that was one of the reasons Carlee was right up their alley. She liked both Hollis and Xander and what was better was they were not against adding to their burgeoning group to lock Carlee down. "True. So you staying for dinner? Carter promised pizza and beers."

"Would that I could. I have a date with Fiona tonight." He grinned. "But you guys have fun. I'll be back next week, give you guys time to break this beast in."

She laughed. "Well then go." They said goodbye to Damon as Jack walked in carrying her phone. "Vic is on the line."

Where did you find it?" she asked with a grin.

"In my room," he said and kissed her, handing the phone off.

"Hey, Vic..." she said.

"Hey! I just wanted to check in and see how the grand move in is going?" She sounded cheerful and upbeat.

"Just about done," she said brightly. "You are coming to the devotional dedication for Fiona, right?"

"Wouldn't miss it for the world!" Victoria sighed happily. "I wish she'd tell us what the God said to her. She's really changed." Easton had refused to tell Petra, too, although in his case she thought it was maybe because he didn't know. All he'd said was that it was between Fiona and He Who Sleeps, and it was no one else's business what had passed between them.

478

"She might...one day," she said with a wistful smile. "And you? Make any decisions yet?" she asked as she walked away from the guys and out onto the back courtyard area. "I know Brad..."

"Brad is a very good boy," Victoria said affectionately and Petra heard something in the background that might have been 'thank you, Mistress' but she wasn't sure.

"I bet." She sighed. "You got a bet on Carls? I know Xander and Hollis are all up in her mac and cheese but there's also Leland, Reece and Ulmer..." She was expecting Carlee would keep them all, considering there was no rule stating she couldn't. It really was her dream come true.

"I think she'll just keep adding men until someone tells her to stop," Vic laughed.

"And if they're all cool with it, I don't suppose it matters."

"Yeah. My thesis got approved so I officially have my Master's now. I'm trying to decide if I should stop there or go for a doctorate," Vic replied. "You know how much I love studying, but I also kinda want to feel useful to the family somehow."

The family. God, she loved hearing that. "I mean, you could do both? Why not? Leo has been suggesting I get my art history doctorate...though it would just be for me, unless I wanted to focus on mythology." Which she actually could do, but...she sighed and looked down at her stomach. Putting her hand on it, she sighed again. She wanted to tell her guys, but they hadn't been all together since she found out. With Finn coming home, she could finally do it, and that would change all their lives once again. In the wake of that, would going back to school be worth it?

"Well that's the thing, isn't it?" Viv said thoughtfully. "Finding a doctorate in a field of study that would be related and useful. I'll think about it. Anyway, I have to go. I really just wanted to make sure you were okay and not stressing out too much."

"I'm okay. Finn should be home soon..." she said with a small smile. Vic, Fi and Carlee all knew, as they had been with her when she found out, but like the good sisters they were, they pretended like they didn't.

"Well give the guys my love and I'll speak to you soon," she said. They exchanged goodbyes and hung up, just in time for her to see Finn parking his car and walking across the driveway toward them.

"Speak of my Devil," she said as she rose and went to him. "How was it?"

"Wonderful. She's coming over for dinner next week to meet you guys. She wanted to come today, but we weren't sure the house and everything would be ready in time." He stretched, easing out the driving kinks in his muscles. "How is everything going here?"

"Good, I think everything is handled here, though I don't know if Carter is back from the sanctuary yet. I hope he is...it's been a while since we were all together. I have something to tell you guys."

Carter came jogging around the massive house, his cheeks ruddy from the fresh air and the way he was smiling. "I thought I heard your car," he said to Finn. "Welcome back, brother. I hope it went well."

"It did." Finn grinned, clapping Carter on the back. "You came just in time. Apparently, Petra has something to tell us."

She nodded to them. "Come on, let's go find the guys."

Ten minutes later they were all wrangled into the living room, and she was standing with her back to them, fidgeting with her hands.

"Baby girl, what's going on?" Jack asked.

"Yeah," Emerson said from his seat in the new wingback chair he had been going on and on about sitting in, with a pipe reading books about war in. "Don't get me wrong, I'm comfortable as fuck..."

"Well tell them then," Carter said. "Don't keep everyone in suspense."

"You act like you know," Rix said as he sat his tablet down.

Taking a deep breath, she bit her lip and then spoke. "We have been blessed."

"No shit," Jack said.

"Well I had guessed." Carter shrugged. "She hasn't had wine at dinner the last three nights running and she keeps touching her stomach. It was either digestive issues or a baby, and she keeps smiling, so of the two it wasn't hard to figure it out. What?" He threw up his hands when everyone turned to stare at him. "Not my fault you're a bunch of unobservant apes."

"Way to steal my thunder." She laughed and shook her head, turning around, her hand on her stomach.

"I didn't say anything!" he protested. "I let you tell them! That was what you meant by being blessed, yes?"

"I was working up to it," she said and shook her head again, mirth in her eyes. "Big old meanie. I thought East would be the one to know."

"Hold on...you're pregnant?" Emerson said, his eyes wide as he looked at her.

"I was starting to suspect, but I haven't seen you as much as Carter has," Easton laughed. "You're not very good at hiding it. But I'm happy. Really happy."

"Same!" Finn said, breaking out of his shocked stillness and grabbing her up in a hug. "This is awesome news!"

"When exactly did this happen?" Rix said as he kissed her on the head, his smile broad.

"I think Leo's birthday," she offered. That had been a wild weekend. Emerson had surprised them and took them all to Bali for four days, and it had gotten really naughty.

"Well, I guess we need to start booking appointments and classes and figuring out which of these empty rooms the nursery is going into," Carter said, ever practical, nudging Leo who was still sitting there with his jaw hanging.

"But we are close to All Souls…" Jack said. "This is great news but…can we…can you work as a devotion?"

She nodded to him. "It's only been about three months," she offered. "No problems playing with my boys in our new playground this year."

"Fuck yes," he said and pulled her into a hug, kissing her sweetly.

"He will protect her," Easton reassured them. "He is pleased. And I'm sure the rest of The Order will be, too, when we announce it."

"The first of a new generation." Emerson went to his knees and kissed her still mostly flat belly. "Hello, you special, perfect child," he whispered to it. "We all can't wait to meet you."

She sighed and ran her fingers through his hair and then looked up. "I didn't expect this to happen so quickly but…by His will…" The guys all nodded.

"We should celebrate," Rix said, the look in his eye pure possession. "We really do have much to be thankful for."

"I got first…since you know…it's my baby…" Jack said and they erupted into arguments on whose kid it was. She went to Leo, who was still clearly astonished and smiled at him. "This okay?" she asked softly.

"I'm gonna be a daddy," he whispered, tears in his eyes. "I can't believe it."

"You're going to be a daddy," she agreed. "And the best daddy." Her lips found his with a sweet kiss.

"I can't believe it," he said again, a tear seeping from the corner of his eye, but at least now she knew they were tears of joy.

She grinned. "The first of at least seven. I love you."

"God...pregnancy kink is really going to be a thing," Jack said. "The five of you are a mess right now."

She looked over from where she stood in Leo's arms to see the six of them standing there, desire and need in their eyes.

"How can a girl say no to a scene like that?" Standing, she slipped her flats off and grinned. "You want your devotion? Well, your Devotion wants you. Hope you got your masks handy..." She looked at each of them, as Emerson handed them their masks, seemingly from out of nowhere, feral grins gracing their faces. "Whoever catches me first wins..."

She whooped as the guys tore out of the living room after her as she raced through the massive house. She knew someone would catch her, and quickly, though it didn't matter who. They would all celebrate the gift He had given them, and much like she wanted when all this began, nothing would ever tear them apart.

Authors Note:

This book was a bear... and you will notice that there's a few scenes missing. That was deliberate. We have a tendncy to cut out scenes that don't move the story alone.

But ladies, do not fret! We have them! Our plan is to put them out in the winter, as a companion to the book... If your interested in them, we would love to hear from you!

So let us know you are dying t experience some of these scenes... and we will deliver!

Thank you so much for reading, and we hope you liked it!

Dags and Aurora